Damas

Final Track

"Final Track injects fresh blood into the Horror genre. It gave me chills!!!"
Liz Conville – Reader of an insane number of books (100+ per year)

"A twisted mind beautifully intertwined with 80s glam rock, but enough about the author… Final Track is an exciting psychological thriller that will transport you back to a time when big haired rock stars ruled the airwaves. Can't wait for Mahoney's next adventure!"
Rich Beasley – Convivial raconteur who never left the 80s

"If you knew a book may give you nightmares could you read it? Dark, engaging and twisted like a sister, Final Track could easily become a crime fans favourite fiction book of the year."
D. Sweet – True crime guru

"Final Track is a dark love letter to the 80s, a grisly glam-rock concept album that'll take you back, and give you chills."
Sarah L. Johnson – author of Infractus

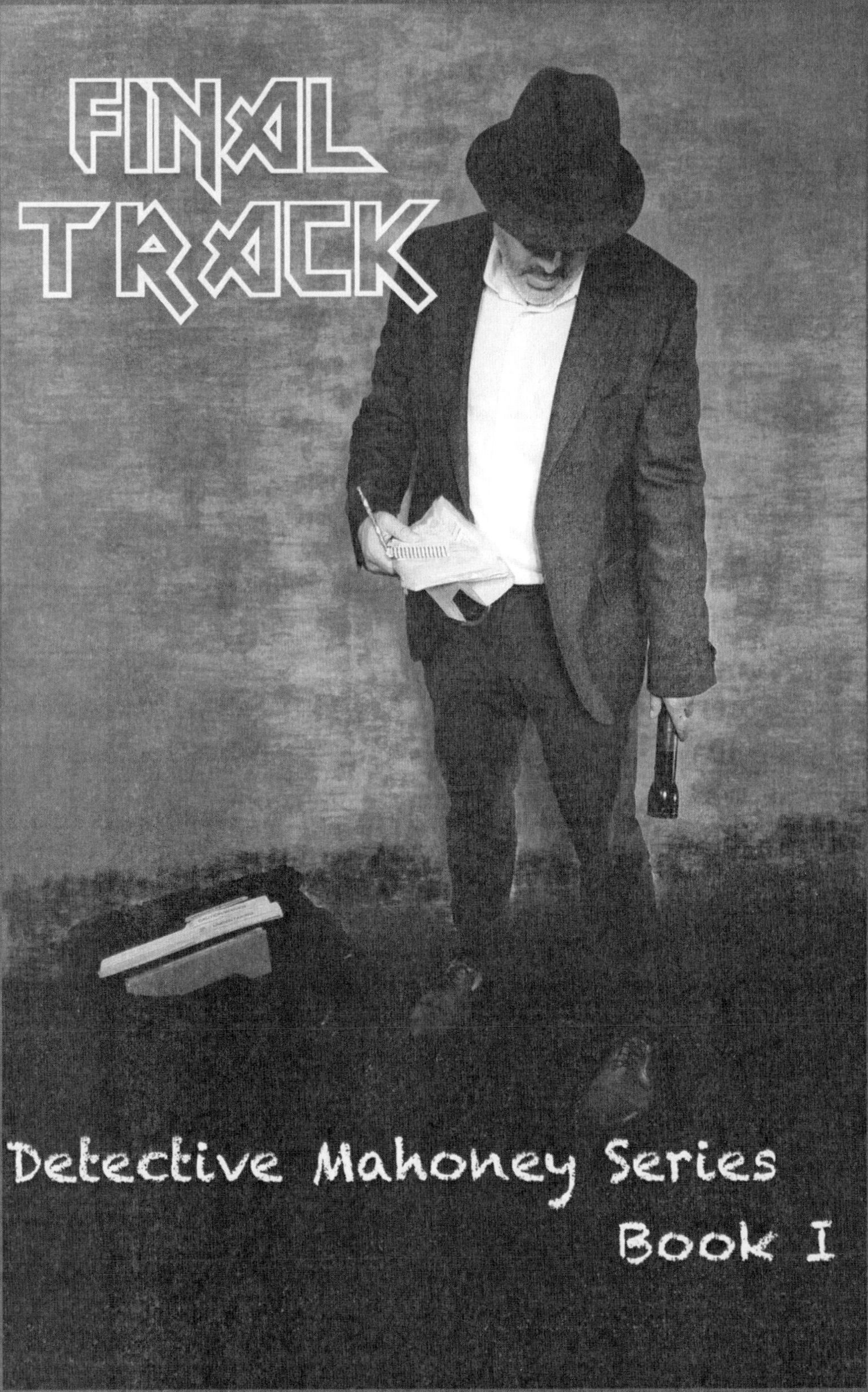
FINAL
TRACK
Detective Mahoney Series
Book I

Final Track © 2019 Julie Hiner

Printed in Canada
BlitzPrint
First Printing 2019

Publisher: Julie Hiner
KillersAndDemons.com
killersanddemons@gmail.com

Editing by: Taija Morgan
Cover Photo, Title Photo, Bio Photo by: Aune Photo
Cover Model: Sarah L. Johnson
Cover Design: Julie Hiner

ISBN: 978-0-9958243-4-8

First Edition

First and foremost, I dedicate this book to my husband. He continues to show me how to challenge myself, and he supports me every step of the way regardless of how strange and creepy my projects might be.

Secondly, I dedicate this book to every person out there who loves to get lost in a book. My blood, sweat and tears went into this story. It is my hope that you will be taken away to another world, even for a few hours.

NOT YOUR
FOOL

Paralyzed

A spine-prickling screech pierced through Seth's mind, slamming against his skull. His raw throat stung as he screamed again, but the only sounds escaping his mouth were mere raspy whispers. Digging deep, he frantically grasped at the scraps of energy he still possessed. He was desperate for someone to hear his cry for help. He longed for the sharp pain of tight binds slicing into the open slits in his wrists. At least then he could feel something. All feeling below his shoulders had disintegrated moments after the silver needle pierced his skin, connecting with his vein.

A fetid stench filled his nostrils. Fluorescent tubing glared down at him, electrifying his eyes. Exercising the little movement he could still control, he turned his head. The cold of his steel-slab bed chilled his cheek, relieving the heat flushing his face. Blinking hard, he tried to dissolve the multicoloured amoeba shapes floating across his sight. Shooting his gaze beyond the conical zone of light bathing him, he peered into black space. Squinting, he determined he was caged in by walls of concrete. A glimmer caught his eye. Little sparkling diamonds danced over the grey walls. His brain contorted, trying to make sense of the image his eyes were projecting to his mind.

Creaking footsteps on old wooden stairs jolted him. His predator approached, sliding his hands along the silk scarf that instilled terror within Seth upon appearance. Seth's body seized as the softness was wrapped around his skin. He could feel the noose tightening around his neck, constricting his airways and wrenching his throat. Several wispy breaths escaping his lips, he struggled to breathe. He gasped in agony. The room blurred around him.

Panic-infused thoughts thrust through his mind. *Is this it? Is this my death?* His drooping eyelids bolted open. The skin around his skull seized. *My life has been nothing more than a pathetic waste.* A chill tickled its way down his spine. His ears burned.

A flash of a man appeared in his mind. The man lifted his head, long dark hair slipping from his face. Seth stared into the man's eyes. His own eyes. The vision swelled within Seth's teetering consciousness. Blurriness dissolving, the image grew clear. Shapely lips lined in soft pink wove a dramatic dance. Eccentric wails vibrating from the imaginary man's mouth, his voice rang through Seth's mind. Entranced faces stared at the man, their eyes glazed, their bodies swaying from side to side like one giant being.

The world spinning around him, the fluorescent brightness fading, Seth began to move through the dark tunnel opening in his mind toward the brightening image. The man's voice vibrated through the air, deepening the trance of his audience. Soft pleather pulled against his legs, revealing his muscular contour. An unbuttoned, silky red blouse flowed over his bare chest. Gems glittered from the leather bands winding their way up his arms. High on his pedestal, his voice heightened, his message dominating. Looking through the man's eyes, out at the mass audience, he carefully scanned their faces, searching for the one. His gaze landing on the only pair of eyes that mattered. Her face. Her adoring eyes looking back at him. The way a mother's eyes should look at her only son.

A loud snap jolted Seth back into his horrific reality. His right cheek stung. Beads of sweat stuck to his forehead, growing in numbers until they slithered down his face. His mind raced with wild thoughts. *I'm going to die. I never made her proud. She never loved me.*

Another strike slapped his blazing cheek. The sadistic monster leaned over him, crazed eyes bulging from their sockets.

Memory Mug

etective Mahoney's mind was free from the ghost faces that usually cluttered it. At least for a few minutes.

He closed his eyes and breathed in deeply, allowing the aroma of rich dark roast to awaken his senses. He exhaled slowly, opened the cupboard, and looked at the three mugs perched on the otherwise bare shelf. He gently wrapped his fingers around a bright-blue handle and looked at the words "Best Dad" painted in summery yellow and pink. A little warmth swelled within as he held the delicate piece, his head swarming with a thousand memories. He could still feel her in his arms the day she was born. She'd been a New Year's Day baby, 1977. Had he really lost a decade? Where had it gone? *To hunting down evil. But at what cost?*

He reached for the coffee pot. As he poured, he watched the bright blue vanish beneath a jet-black pool. He leaned back against the counter, taking a long swig. Swirling the liquid around his tongue, he lingered over the smoky-sweet flavour. Rolling his head in slow circles, he released the tension in his neck. A crackle drew his attention to the eggs sizzling in the frying pan. He resisted taking them out, willing to wait until they were perfect. Longing to sink into the space of a day that wasn't filled with an unending list of tasks, he took a sip from the blue mug.

A sharp beep invaded his peaceful moment. His shoulders slumped as he reached for his cell phone perched on the kitchen table. *I hate this clunky thing.* Pushing the *on* button, he cleared his throat and attempted to sound alert. "Detective Mahoney."

"Bug," Peggy's voice sang back, "I know this was supposed to be your day off, but I've got one for you."

He leaned against the counter. "Where?" He looked regretfully at the sunny-side-ups in the pan, like two glowing suns. His heart sank as he wondered how many days of breakfast in a box he would have to endure.

"Frog Lake Park. A family outing was ruined by a dreadful discovery. A young child found a body. Poor thing, I simply can't imagine."

"Got it." He lingered a moment in the silence. "Hey, Pegs?"

"Yes?"

"This 'Bug' thing, it's really hanging on, isn't it?"

"Yeah." She giggled. "It's your track record. You always catch the killer, always lock him up. Squash him like a bug."

Mahoney's lips involuntarily curled into a smirk. "I guess I've started my fair share of nicknames around the team."

"Yes. And they mean it as an endearing term. You've built this team. They look up to you."

They look up to a washed-out man whose mind is clouded with corpses? "All right, Pegs. Gotta kick myself into gear."

"Take care of yourself out there."

"Will do."

Mahoney placed his memory mug gently on the counter and stared at it. Taking a step back, he shifted into gear. *Another day. Another body.*

Not Your Fool

Mahoney drummed his thumbs against the steering wheel, lulled by the dark inflections of the bluesy riff wafting from the CD player. It was difficult not to succumb to the beauty of his surroundings as the lines of houses dissolved into a lavish forest. An internal Zen washed over him despite the threat of a long, gruesome day lurking within the trees. A crackle echoed through the air as the tires of his burnt-orange '69 Pony rolled from the smooth pavement onto a makeshift road of soft wood chips. He was soon pulling into the parking lot that led to the lake entrance. A secluded area of immense wilderness, Frog Lake Park was a lovely spot for hiking, picnicking and family outings, right in the city's backyard.

He pulled into a stall of the nearly empty lot and gazed at the vast lake spread out far beyond where the eye could see. A million diamonds sparkled under powerful rays of sunshine bouncing off the clear blue water. Bountiful, lush green woods bordered each side. A handful of people were huddled on the otherwise barren brown beach, which formed a bridge between the water and the trees. He slid out of the driver's seat, stood up tall and adjusted his belt. Bending over, he reached back through the driver's door and stretched his arm across to the passenger side. Retrieving his well-worn charcoal derby, he settled it onto his crown. Shutting the door firmly, he took a few long strides toward the beach as he scanned the scene. A young, male officer crouched down, talking at eye level to a little girl. Her curly blonde hair fell softly around her shoulders. She held a long stick, and her pink rubber boots were covered in thick mud. An imaginary hand tugged at Mahoney's heart. He gave his head one quick shake and took in a short but deep breath.

He looked back over his shoulder and confirmed the occupants of the parking lot. He saw a single police cruiser, a black-and-brown Jeep Wrangler, and a shiny black Ford F150 tattooed in bright-white letters: *Crime Scene Unit.* He was about to turn his attention back to the interview in progress when a glossy-blue Chevy pickup pulled up. Blake Sutton and Jack Hayes, two long-time members of his team, were soon walking toward him. He smiled to himself, wondering if they purposely co-ordinated their attire. They almost looked like twins in their matching jeans and jean jackets. Sutton's brown curls and muscular arms stood out against Hayes' buzz cut and lean figure.

Sutton slapped Hayes on the shoulder. "Yeah right. Do I look like a newbie?"

Hayes put up his fists as if to retaliate. Noticing Mahoney, they both stood at attention.

"Morning, boss." Hayes grinned.

Mahoney cleared his throat. "Good morning, fellas. Guess our day off took a turn." He gave them a stern stare.

Sutton returned in a friendly tone, "This one's on me. I actually made solid *plans* for today. Rookie move."

His stance strong, Mahoney looked at them both squarely. "Appreciate the promptness. Gut tells me this is gonna be a long one."

Sutton scanned their surroundings and chipped in his confirmation, "Yeah. I agree with your gut."

The uniform left the family to process the cruel twist their picnic had taken and marched toward them. Once he was within earshot, Mahoney flashed a glance at the polished nametag on the stiffly pressed shirt. *Geez, he looks fresh out of training. Wonder if this is his first homicide.* Mahoney extended a firm hand and asserted a certain formality. "Officer Bennett, I'm Detective Mahoney. Homicide unit." He nodded sharply to his right. "These are my boys, Detectives Sutton and Hayes."

Officer Bennett returned Mahoney's welcome with an equally firm shake and nodded at Sutton and Hayes. "The family appears to be the only witnesses. It's early in the season, not many people venturing out to the lake quite yet. My partner is on his way to the gate to block off the entrance. Scene needs to be locked down. Medical Examiner went in to confirm the body. She called back, declared it as suspicious. I called it in. I suspect that's when you were contacted."

Mahoney tipped his head in acknowledgement. Movement across the beach distracted them as a tall, muscular woman emerged from the foliage. She wore matching army-green pants, covered in pockets of various sizes, and a long-sleeved shirt buttoned to the top. A mid-sized pack crammed with zippers and openings was hoisted on her back, and her feet were protected with solid hiking boots. She looked ready to take on the Bright Angel Trail at the Grand Canyon. A flicker of recognition fluttered through Mahoney's mind until his memory clicked. *Ah yes, Medical Examiner Blackwood, I think it is.* He had seen her in passing but had never worked a case with her. The word was she was new in town, experienced in the wilderness, and employed primarily to scenes bordering the city. He had also picked up morsels of talk that she had a real gruesome background, having worked on the most sadistic cases, the likes of Edmund Kemper. She gracefully conquered the thick sand.

Being wary of touchy feelings regarding whose scene this was, as if it *belonged* to one particular organization, Mahoney resisted taking the lead.

"Detective, I presume?" Wild Woman inquired his way.

"Detective Mahoney," he extended politely. "These are my guys, Detectives Sutton and Hayes."

"Your guys? You're the primary detective on this?"

Mahoney nodded his response.

"Good. Better to have everyone here and do this once. I'm Medical Examiner Terra Blackwood." She extended her hand, and he returned her impressive shake.

Medical Examiner Blackwood quickly got things moving, bringing the uniform back into the proceedings.

"Officer Bennett, I see you were filling in Detective Mahoney and his team," she said.

The officer straightened. "The family just got out here about a half hour before they called in. The little one was exploring the woods with Charlie." He indicated the golden retriever sitting obediently next to the pink-booted girl. "Charlie found the body. He stopped dead, just behind some sort of run-down shack, and started barking. Wouldn't budge. The girl tried to console him, then she saw what she describes as a *'really gross foot with big cuts and lots of blood, sticking out of the leaves.'"* He rushed to the point, saying, "She left the scene immediately, ran back to her parents. They confirmed the foot, came back to the beach and called."

Mahoney nodded to Officer Bennett, then addressed him directly, suggesting, "Probably a good idea to get them out of here soon. Make them comfortable, allow the initial shock to pass, and then it might be easier to dig into any details they can provide. Officer Bennett, I assume you can transition them."

The officer nodded and proceeded to head back toward the family.

Mahoney addressed Blackwood, asking, "What did you see out there?"

"Confirmed exactly what the girl said. The only body part visible is the foot. Everything else is covered. I can't do an examination without evidence removal. I left the crime scene techs to do a preliminary four-corners footage. Although atypical, another one will need to be done after the body is uncovered."

Mahoney and Blackwood locked eyes. He wondered what her take on this was. She decisively answered his inquiring gaze, "Scene is going to need some real processing. Eventually, we are all going to have to go in there. The best way to minimize corruption is for us to go in together. One path in, same path out. I'll lead so we can retrace my original steps. You'll have to be in tow with your team…if you can deal with that."

Mahoney stifled any hints of amusement. "Got it. We can handle that." He was relieved that she wasn't going to argue his team's involvement.

They proceeded to walk, lined up in a row like a mother and her ducklings, embarking on a slow trek as their shoes sunk into the soft sand. Mahoney talked over his shoulder to his guys, reinforcing the procedure to uncover whatever horrific scene they were about to deal with. "As usual, pen in one hand, notebook in the other." This had always been Mahoney's approach in directing his team so that the natural human instinct to touch things would be repressed. *Nobody* entered a scene without inadvertently taking or leaving evidence, or both.

They trudged along in silence. Reaching the trailhead, the dirt path was easier to navigate. They soon found the abandoned shack. Blackwood continued to lead the way as they left the dirt trail. She shouted back, "Use my footsteps. There are other tracks here that I purposely avoided." Mahoney immediately found himself altering his stride to shadow each of the prints where she had first trudged.

On the backside of the shack, they found themselves in a circular clearing. Mahoney stepped onto a soft bed of grass surrounded by a wall of tall trees, swaying slightly in the breeze. The sweet aroma of honeysuckle spattering the bushes was drowning in a stale smell of decay. Mahoney scanned the silent shelter, then stopped his gaze abruptly on the pasty flesh protruding from long, lush blades. He followed Blackwood as she made her way across the circle. He watched as she crouched down and took a closer look.

"The gross foot," she confirmed as she retrieved a pair of thin latex gloves from her pocket. She pulled the tight encasing over each hand. The ankle was encircled with scarlet lacerations, digging deeply into the ashen skin.

Here we go again. He had been down this path a million times before. Usually, it was a domestic situation or bad drug deal. Someone in a position that escalates out of control, leading to a surprise exit. *Not today.* He followed Blackwood as she stood up and made her way into the wall of trees. The exposed foot led to a bed of carefully stacked branches, thick with foliage. Two men— *CST* flashing iridescently on the backs of their jackets to clearly indicate their roles as Crime Scene Technicians—were removing the branches one by one with extreme care. Their hands were encased in a second skin, protecting every potential clue from being tarnished. They were bagging and tagging every single piece that belonged to the constructed cover.

One of them paused, looking their way. "This scene is more complex to process than the usual. We did a preliminary round of four corners before anything was touched. We'll do another set of photos after the foliage is cleared away."

Mahoney nodded. "Let's take our time, folks, and stay focused. Be thorough and precise. A clear path of evidence will ensure we catch this bad guy."

"Agreed," Blackwood said, her tone almost friendly, "first step is to allow these guys to reveal what's hidden." The group stood patiently, respecting the slow process. As the green blanket was disassembled, a lifeless form was exposed. When the task was complete, everyone silently took in the horrific details.

The vacant body was clothed in a long, jet-black cloak, flowing over the arms and down the legs. The arms were stretched out to each side, dark tassels streaming down, creating the illusion of eagle wings. A swarm of flies circled around the exposed flesh. Dark crimson slashes slit both wrists, from which thick black-red had oozed, now caked in place. The bloodless fingers were curled inwards, obsidian-painted nails shining in contrast. The cloak lay flat against the chest, slightly open in the front, exposing a long silver chain draped down to the navel. A large, oval pendant, the colour of an arctic ocean, lay strikingly against the pasty skin.

Mahoney stiffened slightly. *Haven't seen something like this in a long time.* His mind reached back, searching through images of bodies. He steadied his voice and prepared the team. "Looks like we may have a young one here."

Mahoney scanned down the corpse. The legs were encased in black leggings, the material cut in a pattern that reminded him of fishnet stockings. Openings in the skin-tight pleather flashed hints of savage dark-purple bruises. The team remained silent, taking in the gruesome intricacy unfolding before them.

Blackwood chimed in, breaking the eerie quiet, "This is a humdinger of a scene."

Mahoney scanned back up the body. Long, raven hair feathered its way onto the shoulders, covering most of the face. His gaze was drawn in an instant to the thin lips lined in rouge, dramatically posed as if the victim had been enunciating a critical word when her last breath of life was taken. *What would you tell us if you could talk?*

As soon as the techies had completed their second round of photos, Blackwood crouched down and leaned in. She pushed the dark strands aside with care, revealing an immaculately painted face. Mahoney crouched down beside the body, not able to resist taking a closer look himself. The eyes were painted with heavy smoky shadow, high cheekbones accentuated with strokes of pink. Her makeup appeared to be applied with painstaking effort and untouched by whatever horrifying events had led to her demise.

Mahoney rubbed the scruffy bristle on his chin, continuing to stare at the sophisticated scene. *This is not the work of a beginner.*

Blackwood continued to brush aside strands of hair, revealing a neck that was brutally branded with two burnt-umber bands, circling their way around like intersecting rings. Each was rimmed in crimson. The hairs on Mahoney's neck stood at attention. He had seen many ligature marks in his time, but not like this.

Blackwood gently pushed aside the cloak beside the oval pendant. A permanent emblem of sadistic extremes was sliced into her abdomen, leaving the words "I'm Not Your FOOL."

Mahoney's stomach released a slight pang. *Looks like our city just got a ramp-up in killer calibre.* He stood up tall. Clenching his jaw, he shrugged off the sense of dread that hadn't haunted him in a long time. Shoving the images of bodies of the past out of his mind, he pulled his shoulders back and pushed up his sleeves. "Let's get to work, boys. It's going to be a long night."

Masked Horror

I t was early Monday morning when Mahoney pushed open the heavy door and sauntered into the cold morgue. The bright lights forced his eyes to attention. The weekend backlog had produced a mound of bodies. Twenty-eight of them. He counted as he wove his way through the rows of corpses.

Not all of them were victims of the types of killers he hunted. Some of them were victims of choosing the wrong lover. So deeply bound by passion, stuck in a promise to be there forever and to live up to impossible expectations, time and time again. Until one day he put a violent end to it all.

Some of them were stupid shits thinking it would be different for them, that they would be the dope man. The king of the drug world. Somehow more invincible than all the other suckers that drove themselves down that path. Until POP. His head was blown off in one clean shot.

Or they were only taken by one of life's tragic moments. Unexplainable by any logic, indigestible for the human heart. Leaving loved ones to drink until their livers shrivelled up, or to sink into their grief until they turned on the world in an angry mess.

Dammit. The single word shot through Mahoney's mind, his eyes widening at the sight of a tiny hand. Little fingers curled stiffly into a small palm. He hated it when there was a baby. The others he could turn off. He could almost convince himself they made the choices that led them to their cold slabs. Almost. But a baby didn't choose.

His breakfast swam violently against the current of his stomach acid as he passed by a medical examiner piercing a large needle through the open skin of a dead man's stomach. Thick string followed the needle, pulling the two sides of the man together. Mahoney's eyes were glued to the man's internal organs, squishing together under a canopy of flesh, but his feet kept him moving forward. His stomach halted its churning when he saw Blackwood. He could have sworn the tiniest jolt of joy shot its way through his internals. Quickly sweeping it aside, he forced all thoughts onto the case he was here to deal with. All of the other bodies would have to wait their turn for space in his mind. He could see every corpse he had just walked by taking a ticket from a dispenser and finding their place in line. The queue length was getting way out of hand. But somehow the tiniest of those lifeless forms always found a way to jump to the front.

"Morning, Mahoney," Blackwood greeted him cheerily, her eyes glued to the body lying in front of her.

"Good morning, Blackwood," Mahoney quickly returned the welcome with a hint of warmth. *Is this really only the second time we've met?* The thought fluttered through his mind. *There's something so damn familiar about her.*

"This one's a humdinger." She put down a tiny pair of forceps, then turned toward him. "Clear your calendar and start looking this over. We'll need some time to go through everything." Her words were precise, her tone crisp.

Mahoney walked serenely up to the dead body lying flat on a shiny steel slab. The dramatic display at the murder scene had been decomposed. No cloak. No pose. No makeup mask. All of these had been removed, leaving behind an uninhabited ghost of a figure. *The getup in the woods, it was so…theatrical. It brought her to life somehow,* his mind concluded. The drama had been stripped away with the clothing, leaving a bare, blanched shell.

All crimson and scarlet had been washed away. Her hands lay softly at each side. Her fingers spread out, bright operating room overhead lighting glaring off her shiny obsidian nails. A strong sense of sterilization stung the air. The hints of dark-purple savagery that had peeked through fishnet holes now merged with black and blue densely covering the green-tinged flesh of each of her legs. His mind buzzed, moving into full gear. Another day, another puzzle. The pieces were falling around him as the layers of this mystery were peeled away from the physical remains.

This guy wasn't out to directly off her. He wanted her to hurt.

Blackwood's voice cut through Mahoney's thoughts. "You've *got* to see this." As she removed a small towel that had been carefully placed across the dead girl's privates, Mahoney froze. His eyes fixating on the corpse's crotch. A pair of gonads stared back at him. The last thing he had expected to see today was another man's jewels.

After what seemed like an eternity of silence, he found his voice and meekly uttered, "That's a real stunner."

"Got that right."

"What a twist. Hollywood has convinced us murder victims are pretty young girls. Thing is, Hollywood tends to be right." Mahoney's mind resisted the new path the case had taken. "This is a new one for this city." *For me,* his mind continued after his voice had halted.

Blackwood nodded, finding his eyes with hers. "Thought I'd seen it all. Guess not. Our victim is a 19-year-old white male. Clayton Jenkins. A missing persons report was filed by his mother."

Mahoney's eyes lingered on Blackwood's purple eyes for a moment longer, his mind searching his memory. *So familiar,* he thought. He shook his head and jotted in his notebook.

Blackwood covered up the precious jewels, then picked up a clipboard. Running her eyes down the small black print laid out neatly on the crisp white sheet, she followed along with a pointed gloved finger. "I've looked over the timeline you sent. The call came in at 3:13 p.m., Sunday. The responding officer logged that he arrived on scene at 3:34 p.m. The information from the family gives us a rough timeline for the discovery of the body. Parents estimated it was about a half hour between the girl finding the body, them verifying it, and getting back to the beach to call it in. That leaves us to infer that the body was discovered at approximately 2:43 p.m. Is this correct?"

Mahoney flipped through his notebook. "Correct."

"Time of death has been confirmed by the entomologist to be approximately sundown on Friday." Blackwood looked up from her clipboard.

"Fairly fresh, then," Mahoney responded.

"Yes. Based on historical data for similar cases and considering the location of the scene, the body was found fairly soon after the victim died," Blackwood confirmed. "Take a few minutes to look it over." She turned to busy herself with the time-consuming cleaning process. This gave Mahoney some space to finish scanning the motionless body and create his initial observations. He looked at the victim's face, manually wrenching his brain, trying to twist it around the new reality that had forcibly entered its way into this mystery.

The soft skin of the ghostlike face shimmered brightly under the heat of the powerful fluorescent tubes. The thick layers of makeup had been removed, revealing a spattering of sickly yellow bruises tinged with putrid purple. *You took a real beating.* Added to the collage of cruelty was a clutter of cuts. The mask of makeup had been a farce, painting away the ruthless battering that had tarnished the young, unblemished skin. Mahoney noted to himself that her, or rather *his,* mouth had been closed. The thin lips now natural, free of the imposing rouge. They pressed together, forever silencing the victim's anguish. *He almost looks peaceful,* Mahoney thought. A slight cringe crept over Mahoney's face as he observed a nasty-looking welt across one of the cheekbones.

"The face must have been painted up real good to cover up that damage," he observed.

Blackwood turned back toward him, readily available to fill him in. Shaking her head, she let out a quick sigh. "The makeup was *thick*. It was like a mask. It reminded me of the papier-mâché I used to make as a kid, how we applied it layer by layer. The outlandish thing is, the makeup was applied *after* the victim was killed."

Mahoney pondered the chilling tidbit. "He prettied up a *dead* face?" Mahoney parsed through the cases stored in his mind, snapshots of news articles he had read. He knew of cases where the killer had interacted with the dead bodies of his own victims.

"You got it. A breakdown of the chemical composition of the makeup, the foundation applied to the victim's face, indicates it has only been oxidized since early Sunday morning. Using the time of death as a reference point, it would seem that the makeup was applied at least twenty-four hours after the victim was deceased. I've tagged this as face-related fact number one."

"Face-related fact?" Mahoney raised an eyebrow with curiosity.

"There are a series of facts related to the face. Give me the floor for a moment." Her eyes pleaded for his patience as she launched forward. "The makeup was extracted from the face using a natural cucumber paste and steaming procedure. All toxic substances, including phthalates, quaternium 15, and zinc oxide, the main ingredients in foundation, were lifted from the face. The steaming concoction is entirely free of surfactants and emulsifiers, the typical elements of a makeup remover. Therefore, all of the natural oils of the skin are left unharmed. If any fingerprints had been left, they would have been intact. We didn't find any, and the victim's face was absent of any traces of blood. Face-related fact number two." She took a quick breath, her voice quickly re-launching. "There are cuts on his face. We can see these. Face-related fact number 3. Based on the level of healing, these cuts were likely made hours before the estimated time of death. Face-related fact number 4. Using the time of makeup application as our reference point, the cuts were made before the makeup was applied. Face-related fact number 5." Blackwood cited her string of logic as if giving a grade-school presentation on the stars in the universe and her whole year's grade depended upon it.

Mahoney pursed his lips. Ignoring his amusement at her imitation of a young professor, he focused on devouring the information she was pouring out. "There wasn't any blood from these cuts left on his face. Why not? The face was washed before it was prettied up for a night on the town?"

"That is what we can infer." Blackwood continued to pursue her line of fact spouting. "To further back this up, the location of the ligatures implies the windpipe was constricted, which would likely cause bleeding from the mouth and nose."

"That blood is also MIA. That's a lot of washing up. A lot of fuss. Must have had a big night out planned for his guest."

Mahoney's mind continued to take on a life of its own. *Why would the killer go to so much effort to polish up the face of a dead boy?* He stood silently, absorbing every detail, a chill running down his spine. His gut told him that he was in this deep. There was no going back once you were assigned a case like this. There was no saying how long it would take to catch the guy responsible. That is, *if* they could find him. A pink boot stepped into his mind. Pushing it away, he focused on the body in front of him. He couldn't afford to get distracted.

His gaze gravitated toward the raven hair. The bright overhead light shone off the dark strands. The mane had been positioned around the face, gracefully landing on the silver steel beneath. It looked like it was flowing. Racking his brain for any snapshots he had stored from the murder scene, he said, "The hair. It's shiny, clean. I could swear it looks the same as it did at the scene."

Blackwood provided a sharp response. "Yes. All of those points are accurate. Not a single tangle, clump of mud, spot of blood. Nothing. Based on the facts we already ran over, there should have been blood from the cuts on his face. This blood should have been caught in the hair."

Mahoney threw another layer onto the fire he was building. "There are many signs of a struggle. The hair should have been tangled."

Blackwood added in her own kindling as her voice took on a heightened intensity. "Let me throw you a few more facts. An analysis of the chemical composition of the hair cells showed strong traces of sodium laurel sulphate, a surfactant, and several co-surfactants including cocamidopropyl betaine. Shampoos are primarily composed of these two components. This is hair-related fact number 1. Based on the amount of time that these chemicals had been in contact with the hair cells when the analysis was performed, the hair was shampooed in the early hours of Sunday morning. Hair-related fact number 2."

"The victim was likely dead by sundown on Friday. The victim's hair was washed after the murder took place."

"Yes. There's more. The chemical composition also showed strong traces of both ammonium thioglycolate and hydrogen peroxide. The former is the primary ingredient in a perming solution, the latter in a neutralizer. These are used in conjunction during the process of administering a perm, essentially allowing the perm to take to the hair without permanently leaving it saturated. The ammonium thioglycolate, like the shampoo, has been in contact with the hair cells since the early hours of Sunday morning."

Mahoney's voice continued to follow his mind down the path it was taking. "So the shampoo and perm are both fresher than the time of death. That's one serious hairdo for a dead boy."

Blackwood pursed her lips. "Listen to this. It takes about three to four *hours* to complete the process of a perm. You have to wash the hair, partition it carefully into blocks, and roll it with rods, one little piece at a time. Then you apply the solution, wait, rinse, let the hair dry, apply the neutralizer, wait some more, rinse again, let the hair dry, and finally remove the rods." She picked up a rectangular box painted with the face of a gorgeous model, framed by perfect blonde curls. Blackwood lifted the box with one hand and pointed at it with the other. "It's all here."

"Jeepers. That's involved." Mahoney concluded, "All that hair grooming likely washed away any traces of the events leading up to death. All this information leads to many questions. Where did the murder take place? It was quite a trek we took across that beach and down the trail to reach the private enclosure where he placed the body. Did our guy carry the body all that way, or did he force him into the enclave before killing him? Was all the beautification done before or after the killer tucked the victim into his bed of leaves?"

Blackwood responded without hesitation, "My expertise is medical. My realm encompasses the facts about the physical body. I answer *what*. I make an attempt at *when*. I don't answer *who, where, or why*."

"Understood," Mahoney said. "Evidence is key. We're riding the same wave here. You provide me with the facts upon which I will create direction. We can't become stagnant." Mahoney paused, noting the look of discomfort that flashed across Blackwood's face.

Blackwood redirected the discussion. "Let's finish with the facts. I can give you one more piece of post mortem data. Using more chemical analysis, it was determined that the polish on the nails has also been exposed to the air since the wee hours of Sunday morning."

Mahoney shook his head, eyeballing the corpse's neck. The burnt-umber bands appeared immortally unchanged, winding their way entirely around the victim's pale nape. These sickly marks were branded on the corpse, into the afterlife as long as the body was intact. Mahoney thought to himself that even after the corpse began to decompose, they would remain imprinted in his memory. He wondered if they were also permanently painted within the mind of the killer.

"The neck ligatures. These aren't typical."

"According to an MRI scan of the brain, there's no sign of neuron damage. This leads to the conclusion that only hypoxic damage was done. That is, the brain was not completely deprived of oxygen. The victim didn't die of strangulation," Blackwood eerily declared. "The bruising around the neck also provides several pieces of information. The shape of the bruising indicates that the strangulation wasn't performed manually. It appears that some sort of tie was wrapped around the victim's neck with the two ends crossing at the front. You see where the ligature marks intersect here?" She paused, pointing in the vicinity of the corpse's Adam's apple. "This is likely where the pressure was applied. It is subtle, but if you look closely, you can see multiple sets of these ring-like ligatures and multiple crossing points, barely offset from each other. The inference is that the victim was strangled more than once." Her voice lost volume as she neared the end of her gruesome statement.

The hairs on the back of Mahoney's neck stood on end so stiffly that they threatened to pull themselves out by the roots. He could picture the hunter wrenching the life out of his prey, easing up, then squeezing again. *Strangling someone, especially from the front, that's personal. You're staring them right in the eye. And he wasn't doing this to murder. Was he getting off on the torture?* He had heard inklings of such things but had only been exposed once. A blonde curl swept through his thoughts. Forcing it out, he talked himself forward. *No time for this. Focus.*

Mahoney continued, "So he repeatedly strangled the victim, but not to kill him. Why?" Blackwood remained silent. He inquired further, "Were there any traces of material at all found in the ligatures?"

"None. Not a trace of blood, prints, or any material of any kind was found at all. At least not yet. I was about to proceed with a second scan of the body."

Mahoney clenched his jaw. "What about the cuts around the wrists and the ankles? Could they tell us anything about what kind of knife or tool was used?"

"Yes. It doesn't appear that the wrists or ankles were slit open with something sharp. You see how jagged and rough these lines are?" She pointed to the purple and yellow right wrist of the body. "And the bruising around them. It indicates that the blood flow was cut off. It is likely the victim was tied up, and the binds were tight. So tight, they eventually dug into the skin."

Mahoney swallowed. "Geez. This sicko tied the kid down. Made the torture easier."

Blackwood continued, "Let's move on to the note." She pointed to the creepy letters cut into the boy's abdomen. The sick message, left intentionally, for a purpose unknown, stared directly into Mahoney's eyes. *'I'm Not Your FOOL.'* He read them out loud. *Who was 'I'? Was the killer taunting him? Was 'I' the victim? The killer? Some third-party superimposed into the situation unknowingly?*

Blackwood said, "Look at the cuts. The incisions are thin, the edges are smooth. The cutting is precise. I sent some images over to the crime lab to do a matchup on the type of knife that was used to cut the message."

"Precise. Our guy must have some level of experience then. Getting an ID on that knife would help." A moment of silence passed, then Mahoney prodded her, "Have you ever seen anything like this?" He knew there was nothing like this in the ever-growing database of his own cases.

"Well, once… You never forget something like that. This guy, he cut the same message into each of his victims. Across their backs. Young girls in that case." Her mouth twisted up as she fell silent.

Mahoney stiffened, his hand finding its familiar place on the bristle covering his chin. "Was the killer caught?"

She froze. "No. Case went cold."

His eyes locked with hers. Time passed. "Worst kind of case." A pink boot trudged across his mind.

"Uh…yeah. I'll keep you notified on any further lab results. Come look at this." She headed toward the corner of the room.

On a separate table, the clothing was laid out in a display to mimic the image of the corpse as it had been positioned on its earthy bed. Like a jet-black raven with an eagle's wings, the cloak almost came to life as if it were soaring through the air, wings stretched out, long tassels dangling. The leggings were positioned below the cloak, the fishnet holes closing upon themselves, mimicking thin bird's legs. A small plastic box sat next to the mock raven-eagle. Multiple items had been carefully placed inside of it. The oval pendant that had rested on the body's navel now stared back at Mahoney, the ocean of colour beckoning him to determine what it all meant.

"Have these been processed by the crime lab yet? I'll need some of these items sent over to my department. The pendant. That'll be worth analyzing."

"Yes, everything in that box has been processed. It's all clean. This guy didn't leave a trace. Give me a list, I'll have them packaged."

His mind began to race. *These leggings, they're women's clothing. Was this guy a cross-dresser? And who wears a cloak like that?*

"I can give you a couple of facts. None of the clothing had any traces of blood. If the boy was wearing these clothes during the beating, or the murder"— she pointed at the eagle-raven spread out on the table—"then there would have been blood on the inside of both the leggings and the cloak. The likely inference is that the victim was re-dressed after he was killed."

Mahoney said, "There doesn't seem to be much dirt, mud, grass or other debris on the clothing. That would have been quite a trek to make, all the way across the beach and over the trail, if he was carrying the victim the whole way. It seems like the body was dressed after it was in its final resting place."

Mahoney's phone blipped. *I miss my beeper. They could find me, but I had a buffer of time to respond.* Unholstering it from his belt, he gruffly greeted the caller. "Detective Mahoney." Taking in the message being delivered, he grunted a reply. "Give me 15. I'm just finishing up with the medical examiner." Turning back to

Blackwood, he directed his body scanning to a close. "What else can you give me? I've got to get back to homicide, brief my guys. We need to get this moving."

"There isn't much more I can tell you right now. With the preliminary scan, I tackled the things that really stood out. Moving on to the secondary scan, I'll dig deeper for more details. There is one more perplexing thing though. I noticed small needle marks in the arm. A toxicology report is in progress. It's taking a while. It seems there were substances in the bloodstream that are turning out to be rather difficult to identify."

Ripping a page from his notebook, he handed her the list he had scribbled, indicating the items he wanted to examine further. He turned to leave. Pausing, he met her eyes with his own. "Hey, have you heard of cases where the killer interacts with the body post mortem?"

"Yes. I processed the bodies of a killer who claimed that the only way he could have them was to kill them. He referred to them as his ghost wives. He consummated each of those relationships, after he killed them."

An icy cold cut through his insides. "Was there any indication of that here?"

"No. I ran a standard kit. Nothing."

He nodded. "Thanks, Blackwood. Stand-up job here. Real thorough." He promptly turned and exited the dreary space. He was eager to escape from any response to the appreciation that seemed to flow from his mouth involuntarily.

He slid back through the morgue door, kicking the pink boot, the blonde curl and the purple eyes out of his mind.

War Room

Mahoney stepped through the door into the small, square room. Squinting into the bright lighting, he scanned the team. The windowless walls closing them in, the air was sticky with sweat and body heat. He wondered how many days they would spend crammed together in these tight quarters.

"Boys." He nodded to Sutton and Hayes. "Sutton, you pump some iron this morning?"

Sutton replied. "Got a quick session in. Just installed a power lifting cage in my basement."

"Good. Hayes, you snuck in a run?"

"Yeah. Just a five K. It'll do."

Walking over to the small round table in the corner of the room, he reached for the pot of coffee. Smiling at the petite woman perched next to the table, he continued his greetings. "Dara. Glad you're my analyst on this one. We're gonna need some real tight work."

As always, she was dressed in a pristine navy-blue suit and her long, grey hair was tied in a tight bun at the nape of her neck. The crime analyst was the one who held the golden key to the mound of information that pounded the homicide unit during a case. Usually in astonishing amounts and at an astronomical pace. Dara was one of the most organized and well-reputed analysts of the local homicide organization. In the entire province, in fact.

"Good to see you too, Bug," she returned warmly.

Filling his cup from the communal pot, Mahoney longed for a rich, dark roast. *Guess this generic stuff will have to do,* he told himself. *Perks of the job.*

Taking a sip from the chipped mug plastered in a fading red-and-green Christmas scene, his gaze landed on the clock mounted on the wall at the front of the room. The white face stared him down, the second hand ticking away. Sweat glistening on his forehead, his shoulders tensed. Shaking off the threatening pressure, he cleared his throat.

"OK guys," Mahoney ordered, nodding at Dara, "and gal." Observing her slight snicker, he launched into the day's work. "Let's get started. Sergeant told me to proceed. As usual, I'll keep him informed."

Mahoney made his way to the front wall. Turning to face his audience, he commanded their attention. "I trust you're all caught up on what we have so far." He waved his hand across the series of crime scene photos tacked to the cream-coloured wall to his right. "As you can see, we don't have much in the way of physical evidence. Truth is, there's no real trail here. All processing that has been done so far has turned up nothing. This guy didn't leave us any trace of himself." Mahoney paused, scanning his audience to scope out their reactions. "And as I'm sure Sutton and Hayes can attest to, this scene was, well, rather atypical of what we see around here. Quite elaborate."

Sutton spoke up, "Never seen anything like it. It was complex, dramatic…strange."

Hayes nodded. "Yeah. It really creeped me out. This guy must be some sort of nut job."

Dara's dainty fingers plucked the dark-framed glasses hanging from her neck by a string of glass beads, slipping them onto the tip of her nose. Lifting her pen, she proceeded to scribe away furiously in her comfortable spot tucked away in the corner.

Mahoney said, "We've got a real doozy of a situation here. I just came from the morgue."

Walking over to the cream-coloured wall, he stared at the photo collage. *Jeez. Sutton wants to make prime investigator someday. He handles this case well, that'll get him on track.*

Scanning his audience, he cleared his throat. "The victim is a young male."

Sutton's eyes widened as he took a sip of his Big Gulp.

"The killer, he washed and permed the kid's hair, after he killed him. Cool fact, a perm takes several hours."

Hayes shifted in his seat.

"This guy also washed the kid's face and applied all that makeup after the kid was dead."

Sutton, shaking his head, interjected, "This is messed up."

"The clothing the victim was found in, it's almost clean. No blood. A little dirt and grass, but not enough to insinuate he was dragged across that beach. It seems as though the kid was re-dressed after all the beating, struggling, and killing."

Hayes, resting his elbows on his knees, held his face in his palms. "This is crazy."

Sutton inquired, "You're saying the killer spent time with the victim after he had already killed him? I've seen this, on an episode of Unsolved Mysteries. It's messed up."

"Yeah," Hayes said. "What's the point of the hairdo and makeup? The kid was dead. And left to rot."

"Your guess is as good as mine. But it may be our only lead at this point. This guy didn't leave us much to go on." Snapping a file folder onto the long table running down the centre of the room, Mahoney said, "We need to go through every piece of information we have. Let's build a detailed timeline of torture, death, washing, and grooming. We need to start determining when, and where, each step was done. Nail down where the body was during each of these stages. Pinpoint when the victim was taken. This was a lengthy process with many steps. This guy must have left us something along the way." Mahoney sifted through the papers in the file folder, shifting his brain around the mound of details. *It's like shaking flour through a finely grained sifter, looking for a single, distinctive granule.* Looking up, he took a sip from his mug. "You all know how careful we need to be. We can't afford mistakes."

Placing the chipped, faded Christmas scene down, Mahoney walked up to the oversized printed calendar tacked to the front wall. Each day for April was displayed in neat little rows, one for each week. "Good prep, Dara."

Clicking open a pen, he jotted down notable events in the appropriate boxes, including *death, shampoo, perm, face wash,* and *makeup.*

Clicking the pen closed, he addressed his team, "We need to determine when the body was moved to Frog Lake. None of the forensics gives us any indication, yet. What do we have on the scene?"

Hayes moved the investigation down its first possible path. "Picture of the mud prints has been submitted. In processing now. The prints looked large. There was an odd ridge on the bridge of the foot."

"Good. See what you can do to get that moving along."

"Got it, boss." Hayes scribbled in his notebook.

"OK boys, what's striking about this scene?"

"Well, boss, the strangulation marks. When I re-examined the photos, well, it seemed like the victim may have been strangled more than once, or at least something was tied around the neck multiple times." Sutton took a sip of his Big Gulp.

"You're dead on. Blackwood confirmed that the victim was indeed strangled multiple times. And it wasn't the cause of death."

Sutton's eyes widened as his Adam's apple bobbed.

"Sutton, you take the lead on this. Re-examine those photos. The strangulation wasn't done manually, by hand. Looks like some sort of rope or tie was used, and it was done from the front. Let's get some ideas as to what was used. What kind of tie or rope."

Sutton nodded. "So, this guy was strangling his victim, for what then? For kicks?"

"Could be. Maybe our guy tried to strangle the victim to death, and he failed several times, so he moved on to something else. Maybe he was doing it for some sort of sick enjoyment but had something else in mind to kill the boy. Let's figure out what could have been used. What else?"

Hayes joined in. "The message. It was cut right into the body."

Mahoney shook his head. "Yeah. This kind of thing doesn't happen around here. What do you make of it?"

Hayes continued, "The words. The sentence was rather, well, it seemed angry."

"I agree. Dara. Dig deep. Try and find a source. You still coping with that old clunker of a computer?"

A smirk crept across her face. "Yes. Still waiting for that funding approval."

Shaking his head, Mahoney was tempted to interfere. If anyone understood the difference a new computer could make, it was him. He also realized that if anyone could secure funding, it was Dara. She had decades of experience putting just the right amount of pressure on without destroying her ability to get things done.

Mahoney drove forward. "Let's look at the clothes."

"I wonder what kind of thing this kid was into. I mean, look at those leggings. Do you think he was a cross-dresser?" Sutton sat back in the cheap plastic chair.

"Yeah. And that cloak. Those are some serious tassels," Hayes observed.

"The clothes are weird, I'll give you that. But, the lack of mud and grime and blood on them insinuates that he was re-dressed post mortem."

Hayes nodded. "Right. An attack and a drag across the beach would have messed them up."

"We might be able to show these pictures to people who knew him, depending on their reaction to all this. We need to confirm how the victim dressed. Dara, we need some direction on where someone might buy these types of clothes."

Without looking up, scribing uninterrupted, Dara nodded from the back of the room.

Mahoney kept the ball rolling. "Let's get a handle on the victim's history. We have an ID. We need to get to know him. Who were the people in his life? Where did he spend his time? What activities did he take part in? And, of course, who was the last person to see him?"

Sutton added, "We ran his name, as soon as we got that file you sent over for us." He paused; his voice grew quiet. "His mom and dad live here, in the city. Seems he just moved out."

"Of course, we'll start with them," Mahoney confirmed. "We'll do that one together. Who else is in his friend circle?"

Sutton opened his notebook, summarizing the information as he scanned a page. "Like I said, he just moved out at the beginning of the semester. He's taking, or was taking, chemical engineering." He whistled. "Smart kid. He had an apartment over in Rutland Park, near the college. He had a roommate. He worked at Hot Wax. A music shop over in Kensington."

Mahoney divvied up the work. "After we meet the parents, Sutton, you take the roommate. You also get the sweet task of ruffling through his garbage and anything else that catches your eye over there. While you're over there, poke around the college. Get a class schedule. See who you can talk to." Moving his gaze to Hayes, he continued laying out the plan of attack. "Hayes, you take the music shop. See what else you can do while you're in the area. Where did he take breaks? Grab a bite? Hang out?"

Mahoney turned to Dara. "I'm relying on you for the usual. Bank records. Phone records. Whatever you can dig up."

"On it, Bug."

Mahoney took another swig of cheap coffee, then flipped through his notebook. "There's a box of items on their way over from the morgue. I would've brought them myself, but you know the handling protocol. There was a pendant on the victim. In the shape of an elongated oval. The colour was striking. Kind of an icy blue, but with a tinge of white. Reminded me of an iceberg." Setting the mug down and flipping through a folder, he retrieved a photo. "Dara. I need one of your magical searches on this. Something strikes me about it."

Slipping her glasses off the tip of her nose, they hung by their beaded line. She stood, taking the photo from Mahoney. "I'm on it, Bug."

Rolling up his sleeves, Mahoney grabbed the folder again. "OK, boys. We've got a few paths here, let's follow them. You know the drill. Create trails, validate which to follow through a process of elimination. And, as always, find the truth through the pursuit of evidence. Let's get going. Meet back here tonight."

He watched the team shuffle out of the room. Walking up to the crime scene wall, he rescanned the photos. His mouth turned into a stern frown. A slight pang shot through his gut. *Haven't seen a scene this dark in a long time. And never here, not in this city. Dark vortex is pulling us in. This is only the beginning.*

Crushing News

Mahoney knocked firmly on the blue door. Footsteps tapped their way toward him. The door creaked open to reveal a small woman in a baggy, tattered sweater. Her hair was tangled, wild and sun bleached.

A hoarse cough hijacked her, her shoulders shaking in convulsions, her hand clenched against her mouth. "Sorry. Can I help you?"

Mahoney peeked at his notebook. Greta was her name, according to the profile of the victim. "Greta Jenkins?"

"Yeah. Who's asking?" Her tanned skin wrinkled around the corners of her mouth.

"I'm Detective Mahoney. This is Detective Hayes, and this is Detective Sutton. Ma'am, may we come in for a moment?"

Her face turned white in an instant. "Oh fuck. This about Clayton?"

"I'm afraid it is."

Motioning for them to enter, she opened the door wider.

Mahoney, removing his shoes, motioned to Sutton and Hayes with a silent nod to follow suit. Their socked feet sunk into the luxurious shag carpet as they followed Greta into a small sitting area.

"Sit down." Greta pointed her shaking hand toward a faded pleather couch-and-chair set. Stuffing poked through the plethora of tears scattered across the cushions.

Mahoney took the chair. Sutton and Hayes got cozy on the couch.

"Ma'am, you may want to have a seat." Mahoney cleared his throat.

"Sure." Greta found her way to a rocking chair directly across from Mahoney. A cherry coffee table sat in the centre of the circle of furniture, chips of missing paint exposing the white fleshy wood beneath.

"Ma'am, I'm really sorry to have to give you this news. Your son, Clayton, his body was discovered in Frog Lake Park on Sunday afternoon." Mahoney's forehead wrenched, hiding wrinkles of concern. *This poor woman. I hate this part. The world of an innocent person turned upside down in an instant.*

Greta stared at him.

"Ma'am, he was found dead." Mahoney looked straight into Greta's eyes.

Tears sprung from her eyes. The remnants of colour in her face vanished in a flash.

Sutton, springing into action, grabbed a box of Kleenex from the centre of the cherry coffee table. Extending the box toward Greta, concern hijacked his face. "Ma'am, we're so sorry for your loss."

"What the hell? I…I…I can't believe it." She barely got the words out between deep sobs. "I was worried. But…dead?" She let out a raspy wail. A stream of tears washed down her pale cheeks. She swiped the tears away aggressively with her hands.

Sutton returned to his position, tucked in close to Hayes. They all waited in silence, displaying patience and respect. After a few moments, Mahoney tested the waters. "Ma'am, could I get you a glass of water?"

"No. I'm fine." Blowing her nose and wiping her face, Greta attempted to get herself together. Crumpling the balls of Kleenex in her hands, she continued with a shaky voice, "What kind of fucking mess is this. I was worried. But dead? No." She snatched up a pack of cigarettes sitting on the cherry table. Pulling one from the pack and settling it between her lips, she dug into the pocket of her jeans. Her hands trembling, she snapped the lighter several times before it lit. Inhaling deeply, she closed her eyes. Smoky-mint infused the stuffy room.

Mahoney's eyes stung. Greta's palm turned toward her face as she nestled the cigarette between her pointer and middle fingers. A small, tarnished golden band circled her ring finger. "Your husband, is he home?" He noticed Sutton flipping open his notebook, indicating he would act as the scribe.

"Yeah. George. We've been in this house since Clayton was a toddler. Moved here when he was four."

"Is George home?"

"He went on a beer run. Won't be long. This is gonna blow his mind. Told me I was a nutcase, the way I worried about Clayton. Clayton just moved out. He's enrolled in a program over at the college. Wanted to live closer to campus. I'm proud of him. Got further than I ever could in school. But I was real unsettled since he moved."

"Was there a particular reason for you to worry, ma'am?"

"Like I said, George told me I was nutty. But, fuck, look at this. Should've stepped in sooner. He was my only baby, you know. After he moved out, well, he started hanging out at bars on the weekends. I know, all the college kids do it, it's normal for his age. Hell, I've seen my share of party nights. The 70s. You know? But, Clayton, he likes his rock music. And it ain't like the 70s. The scene is aggressive. No free love. Wild, angry tone to it all. And the drugs, they aren't the same either. There's some stiff stuff on the streets now. Clayton was a bit sheltered, being an only child. I was afraid he'd be in with the wrong crowd."

"That's understandable, ma'am." A little ghost hand gave a slight squeeze to Mahoney's heart. "Did Clayton visit you often?"

"Huh. Yeah. He did." A slight smile showed itself on Greta's face. "He would come for dinner, every Sunday."

Sutton and Hayes exchanged a look. Their eyes found Mahoney's. Sutton proceeded to ask what they were all wondering, "Ma'am. When was the last time Clayton came over?"

The tinge of pink that had started to return to Greta's cheeks drained away. "Well, yesterday, he didn't show up. It was so unlike him. I called him several times. But then George told me to stop obsessing. That a boy his age needed some space. Clayton was probably out with friends and lost track of time. I didn't buy it. Not like him. Even at his age. That's when I filed the missing persons report." The tears sprung to life again, trickling down both of her cheeks.

Mahoney said, "Ma'am, this is not your fault." He paused, hoping she would believe him. "Do you remember the last time you did see Clayton?"

"Well, he's missed two Sunday dinners now. Yesterday, of course. And he missed last Sunday as well. He called me the day before and told me he had a big test on Monday and needed to stay home and study. He assured me he would be here the next Sunday."

"Do you know what time that was when you talked to him?"

"Just after eight. We had just finished breakfast."

"Ma'am, do you happen to know the names of any of the bars that Clayton went to?"

She shook her head. "I'm out of the know on the cool joints nowadays. He did talk a lot about this one, but I don't know the name. Think I'd be more helpful." Hands shaking, she took a heavy drag of the disintegrating cigarette. "So what happened to my Clayton? It was those fucking college kids, wasn't it? They pressured him into a party by the lake, didn't they? Was it drugs? Alcohol? Fuck. Did he fall in the lake?"

"No, ma'am." Mahoney cleared his throat. "We suspect homicide."

"What? Murder? Who the fuck would want to kill my Clayton? He shouldn't have been hanging around those seedy joints." She took an aggressive drag. "You got photos?"

Mahoney jolted. "Photos?"

"Yeah. I wanna see what he looked like, when you found him."

"Ma'am, the photos of the scene, we don't usually share these with the family members."

"Yeah, yeah. I get it. Whatever procedure you have. Blah blah." She glared at him. "Listen, I want to see what my son looked like when you found him." She stood up, pacing back and forth beside the rocking chair. She spun and stared straight at Mahoney. "I demand to see. Now."

Mahoney sighed. His shoulders sunk. "OK. Please, sit down."

He nodded at Hayes. Hayes flipped through a folder, retrieving a photo of the cleaned-up version of the boy. He laid the picture on the cherry coffee table, in front of Greta.

Greta's eyes widened, then quickly retreated to their normal size. "His hair. He'd been growing it out, but not like that. It wasn't curly."

"Yes, ma'am. From our examination, it appears to be, uh, a new hairdo."

"Now show me a photo of how he was *found*."

A pain gave one short throb in Mahoney's gut.

He locked eyes with Sutton, then Hayes. Hayes shot him a curt nod.

Hayes slid a photo of Clayton, as he was found at Frog Lake, on a bed of leaves.

Greta looked at the photo. Her face turned ashen. Her hands flew over her mouth. "Fuck me. Who would do this?" She grabbed for her cigarette pack. Lighting up again, she looked at Mahoney. "I want to help. Look at this. It's disgusting." She looked at the photo again, smoke swirling around her face. "Where would he even get an outfit like that?"

"You've never seen him wearing this?"

"Of all the flower power, gypsy living, weirdo clans I've hung out in, this is new to me. I've never seen Clayton wear anything like this. When he came to dinner, he wore jeans and a button-up shirt."

"Have you ever seen that pendant around his neck?"

Her eyes scanned down the photo. She swallowed hard. "Nah. He didn't wear jewellery."

"Is there anything else that strikes you?"

She shook her head. "The makeup. He never wore it around me." Her small body slumped back against the rocking chair. Her cigarette clung to her limp fingers.

She's putting up a good front. This is a lot to take. "You said your husband is on his way home?"

She nodded, staring vacantly across the room.

"We'll wait here till he gets home. We'll, uh, need one of you to provide a final ID on Clayton's body. Your husband can do it."

"Oh, I'm doing it. I need to see him. One last time."

Mahoney took a card from his coat pocket and placed it on the cherry table. "In case you think of anything, or have any questions at all, please, call me."

Still slumped in the rocker, she looked at the card. "Detective. You *need* to find the sick fucker who did this."

Mahoney leaned his elbows on his knees and looked at her hard. "I assure you. That's what I intend to do."

Rose Quartz

Descending the creaky wooden stairs with care, Mahoney held his derby in place as he looked down, focusing on his footing. The stairwell was dark, and the stairs were old. Reaching the bottom of the staircase, he pushed open the midnight-blue door. The world that unfolded upon him was mind-boggling. Rows upon rows of rocks, stones, and gems, carefully organized, took up every possible inch of the space. He couldn't believe so many rocks were for sale. Some of them were polished smooth and shiny. Others sparkled under the bright lights, shooting off glints in all directions. Mahoney ambled down the main aisle in the centre of the enormous store, scanning the treasures.

Making his way to the counter at the back of the room, it appeared as though he was alone. A small silver bell was perched on the glass countertop, with a sign that said "kindly ring for friendly service." Crystals hanging from long golden chains lay in display underneath the glass. Mahoney hesitantly rang the bell. He waited. After a few moments, he rang the bell again, with more determination. The ding of the bell vibrated through the room. A pair of eyes peeked through a doorway leading into a back room.

A woman, cloaked in long, flowing, emerald-green fabrics and scarves of blue glided across the room to the counter. Her voice was like a rippling stream, her demeanour a ray of sunshine. "Good morning. How are you on this lovely day?"

"Good morning," Mahoney responded gruffly, shifting from one foot to the other.

"What fine treasure are you seeking to bring into your life today?"

"Ma'am. I'm Detective Mahoney. I'm from the local homicide department."

The woman's forehead wrinkled. "Oh my. That might explain the dark vibe that is following you."

"Ma'am, do you sell this stone here?" Mahoney slid a picture of the arctic-ocean pendant across the glass countertop.

"Oh. Now that is an extraordinary gem. Very special indeed." The woman stared at the photo, captivated into a trance.

"Ma'am. Do you sell that stone here?"

"Oh, well, that's topaz. It comes from rhyolite. We don't usually have that gem in stock."

"But you do sell it?"

"Well, now, I can get that stone, yes. But it would have to be special ordered."

"Ma'am, have you ever ordered that stone for a customer?"

The woman paused, still entranced by the photo. Lifting her head slowly, she stared at Mahoney. "Hmmm. I do believe I did order one of those. Yes."

Mahoney stood patiently, waiting for the woman to take some sort of action. *What is she doing? Just standing there, like that. It's like she's under some kind of spell.* "Ma'am. Would you have a record of the sale?"

The woman snapped to attention. "The topaz. Yes, of course." She turned to face an old wooden cabinet against the wall behind the counter. Pulling open one of the cabinet doors, she exposed a set of shelves built into the back, barely hanging on for dear life. Running her finger along the books housed on the middle shelf, she halted at a large, golden, bound book. Sliding the book from the shelf, she used both hands to support its weight. Plunking the book down onto the glass countertop, she opened it down the middle. "Now let's see here. What is the date today?"

"April 14, ma'am."

"Oh yes. Thank you." Looking back down at the book, she flipped through the ragged-edged pages.

Mahoney shifted on his feet. His to-do list ran through his mind.

"Now, when would that have been?" The woman pinched her chin, looking up at the ceiling.

Mahoney's to-do list amplified itself as items continued to attach themselves to the end.

"Oh yes." The woman looked back at the book, flipping to a specific page. "Here it is." She turned the book toward Mahoney, pointing at an entry.

Mahoney moved close to the yellowing pages of the book, squinting at the calligraphic-style penmanship. *Geez, this place is living in the past. Handwritten records.* He found her finger with his eyes, reading the black-inked entry.

Customer Name: Tom Keifer
Customer Contact: 867-5309
Item: 1 Topaz Gem, Arctic Colour
Date: March 21, 1987
Pick Up: April 4, 1987
Notes:
Called customer, could not reach.
Called customer again, still could not reach.
Called customer a third time, still no answer.
Customer came in, picked up stone.

Flipping open his notebook, Mahoney found a fresh page and jotted down every piece of information regarding the arctic topaz order. "The pick up date, is that when the customer came in?"

"Yes. I only enter that date when the person picks up the item. You know, I have an old photocopier in the back. I could copy this page for you."

"That would be very helpful. Thank you."

Heaving the old book into her arms, she turned toward the door that she had first appeared from. Looking back at Mahoney, her voice cheerily rang out. "It doesn't always work. But usually, a good kick gets it going." She disappeared through the doorway.

Mahoney leaned against the glass countertop. Looking at his watch, he wondered when he would be able to get to that next item on his list. *Chill out, Bug. Do this right.* Scanning the rows of gems, he decided to try and occupy himself. He walked along an aisle, stopping at a pile of shiny, polished, pink stones. The handmade label, taped to the back of the plastic box, indicated rose quartz. He picked up one of the shiny gems, running his fingers over its smooth contour. His gaze fixating on the soft pink, his heart swelled.

"Oh. I see the rose quartz pulled at your aura." The flowing-robed woman slid up beside him.

Mahoney jumped at the sound of her voice. Spinning on his heel, he met her gaze. She held out a piece of paper toward him. Taking it, he looked down at the photocopy of the record book entry.

"Thank you, ma'am."

"That stone, the one that called to you, it's good for self-care, you know. It's like a warm hug."

Mahoney stared back at the woman. "Well, thank you for your time, ma'am."

"Sometimes a gem finds us. Rose quartz sends a calming, soothing vibe. It opens the heart to all types of love, including self-love and romantic love. It eases any guilt you are carrying."

A blonde curl floated through Mahoney's mind. "I see. Again, thank you." As he turned to leave, the woman placed a hand on his shoulder. He turned back to face her. Her cheery voice rippled toward him. "That stone you are looking for, the arctic topaz, that's an exceptional gem, you know. It invokes a sense of peace and spiritual connection. It's a natural magnifier of psychic abilities. The shape of that pendant, the long oval, it's the symbol of rebirth. A compelling combination."

Mahoney's mind buzzed. *Psychic abilities and rebirth?* "How does that work, exactly?"

"Carrying the gem with you, holding it close to your being, will invoke the abilities it has within it."

His brain whirled with electric energy. Picking up a small, heart-shaped stone from the box of shiny pink polished quartz, she handed it to Mahoney. "Please. I insist. This gem is calling to you."

His heart swelling, Mahoney stretched a hesitant hand toward the flowing robe. "Thank you, ma'am." He spun on one heel and made his escape up the creaky old stairs.

Late-Night War Room

Mahoney pulled his Pony car into the dark, quiet parking lot. Sliding into a slot under a tall streetlamp, he grabbed his derby and slipped out of the driver's seat. The creaking of the old orange door pierced the quiet, empty lot. He strode to the main doors of the homicide headquarters in less than a dozen steps. *Good old HQ, my old friend. You always lure me back before bedtime.*

He went directly to the little war room. *We need to make this brief. Keep pushing.*

The bright lights burned his eyes as he stepped into the room. The stuffy, hot air closing in on him, his body temperature jumped up several degrees. He hung his grey herringbone-tweed coat over the back of one of the cheap plastic chairs and placed his derby on the table. The door swung open, followed by the entry of Sutton, Hayes, and Dara in tow.

"OK, team, let's get this going. We still have a few hours to follow up on leads." Mahoney strode up to the front of the room while the others settled into their positions.

"Who is our victim? Did we get anything from his circle of friends?"

Sutton got the ball rolling. "Lots of interviews. But nothing came of it. The roommate, he was home, and very co-operative. Seems that our victim was rather boring. Stayed home and studied most of the time, unless he was working. Guess he was serious about paying his own way. He didn't want to dig into Mom and Dad's happy retirement. The only fun he had was when he went out to rock joints. Guess he went on the weekends if he hadn't picked up a shift."

"And the school? Anything there?"

"Got his class schedule here." Sutton placed a piece of paper onto the long table in the middle of the room. "I caught all of his professors. They all said the same thing. Apparently, this kid was a straight-A student, and he never missed a class. Until last Monday. Seems he wasn't in any classes the whole week."

"The kid wasn't seen in a class all week? And no one said anything?" Mahoney raised an eyebrow.

Sutton said, "Yeah. I guess it happens. More than you would think. Kids take off on road trips. The freedom away from Mom and Dad makes them feel adventurous. Or they get real homesick. Sometimes they just drop out without telling anyone. The pressure gets to them. Even straight-A students."

"Why didn't the roommate notice anything?"

"He was away for the week. A little early spring vacation, apparently. I checked with the airline and the hotel. Story checks out."

"His trash?"

"Runner's diet. He ate a lot of yogurt." Sutton smirked at Hayes.

Mahoney sighed. "So, nothing. Hayes?"

"Same story. The boss at the record shop said the kid was a stand-up employee, could always be counted on. He often took shifts for other workers too. Last time the boss saw him was a week ago Saturday. The kid had given up a few shifts this past week, said he had a bunch of tests to study for. Boss was impressed. The kid did all the offloading of his shifts himself. Cashed in favours from the other workers which he had often covered for. The boss said most of the time these kids just tell him at the last minute that they won't be in. Anyways, the kid had a shift last Saturday night. Didn't show up. The boss said he called him several times, but there was no answer."

"Anything else from the boss? Where did this kid hang out?"

"I guess he worked through all his breaks. So the boss only saw him come and go to start and end his time at the store. The only thing he did mention was that the kid was super excited about a live rock show he was going to, a week ago Saturday, after the last shift he put in at the store." Hayes retrieved a folded neon-yellow piece of paper from a file folder. Unfolding it, he placed it on the centre table and attempted to smooth out the wrinkles.

Mahoney, taking the sunny-coloured flyer, pinned it to the growing collage on the crime scene wall.

Hot Rod
Saturday, April 4
LiveWire
9:00 p.m. Doors
Tickets $10

Flipping open his notebook, Mahoney scanned through a few pages. "The mom mentioned the kid liked live shows. The boss said he was excited about this show. I'll stop by this LiveWire tonight. Let's move back to the scene. What about those mud prints?"

Hayes took the lead. "Like I mentioned, the bridge of the footprint had a distinctive ridge." Pulling out a piece of paper with a photocopied boot print on it, and another displaying a shiny black boot, Hayes stood and pinned them next to the yellow flyer. "Seems like whoever left the prints wore Doc Martins. A heavy boot, with this wide, jagged bridge. There was a lot of mud. Enough for him to really sink his feet into. Enough for us to get an accurate print. Size twelve."

"Good work, Hayes. That's a lot of prints you went through quickly. Next step is to find out where these are sold." Mahoney scanned the boot print.

Hayes jumped on the answer. "Everywhere."

"OK, so this might help, but we need at least one suspect first. At this point, it seems this was the work of one guy. One set of prints. And the detail committed to the body…it seems personal." Mahoney turned to Sutton. "What about the neck ligatures?"

"Still working on that. But, it seems like we can rule out the usual suspects. Likely wasn't rope. The marks are smooth, lacking any distinct pattern. Ropes are strung according to specific patterns. The pattern tends to transfer onto the neck. The marks don't go deep enough to be something heavy, like chains. The list goes on. Point is, all the usual items have been ruled out. We'll need to expand our list, examine other items."

"Good. Stay on that. Dara, anything on the message left on the victim?"

"Bug, sorry to disappoint you, but so far I've come up empty-handed. I'll start doing more complex searches."

"Thank you, Dara. I got to all the gem shops. Seems like our guy may have had this pendant made. There was an order put in at one of the shops for this gem." Mahoney flipped through his notebook. "Got customer info. We'll need to run it, see what comes up."

Mahoney, examining his notebook, proceeded over to the map on the wall adjacent from the crime scene collage. A black pin pierced the location for Frog Lake Park. Picking up an orange pin, he marked the gem shop.

"OK, boys, push on with your follow-ups on those searches. Stop by the scene again at first light. Another scan with fresh eyes might help. We'll regroup in the morning as per our usual routine. We need to scour whatever we have. We need to close in on this guy. The clock is ticking."

Name Search

A proaching Dara's desk, Mahoney noticed her pink peony-and-bird painted tea set laid out precisely. "Dara."

Turning in her chair, she held a delicate teacup daintily with her pointer and thumb. "Bug. What can I help you with?" Gently placing the cup onto its matching saucer, she turned her attention to her computer.

"Oh, you think all I need you for is your genius computer skills?"

"Of course not, Bug." Smiling, she perched her fingers over the keyboard, ready for action.

"OK, you got me. Right now, yes, I do need your computer magic. I want to run the info from the gem shop."

"Shoot."

He slid his notebook onto Dara's desk. Her eyes scanning the page, her fingers sprung into action. In a split second, the computer was churning away.

"Damn, you're fast."

"Eh. I grew up with a typewriter. It's just practised hand-eye co-ordination. Your coffee must be getting cold by now. I know how much you hate that."

"Nah. I'm getting used to it."

Turning her attention back to the small black screen perched on her immaculately organized desk, she watched the strings of bright-green letters shooting down the screen.

"When are they going to get you a better system?" *Wish this slow chugging machine could keep up with her typing. I want answers.*

"Bug, you know how it is. Pressure will halt. Patience will win."

"Yeah. But just think how fast we could get results if your computer had more power. What's that computer you were talking about? The one you really wanted approval for?"

"Oh, the IBM PS 2. It has the new Intel 80386." Her eyes sparkled with delight. Catching his gaze, her cheeks flushed. "Uh, basically a lot more processing power than I'm working with now."

"Just think of what you could do with that baby."

The bright letters on the black screen halted. Mahoney stared at the search results, trying to decipher the cryptic lines. Dara interrupted the long sip of tea she was taking, placing the fragile cup down. Sliding her thick, black glasses onto her nose, she leaned into the screen.

"That name you got appears to be a dud."

"What?"

"There is no person by that name. The phone number also came up as invalid."

"You searched the whole city?"

"Yes. I could put in a wider search including the surrounding areas."

"Yeah, do it."

"It'll take a while."

"I'll check back later. But don't stay here too late. We've got some long days ahead of us."

She rolled her eyes. "Yeah, yeah. I'll need to explore every path I can think of before I'll be able to sleep. Something isn't right here. A name that doesn't have a person."

"Yeah. It reminds me...well, everything about this case reminds me..." He looked at his hands.

"I know. Not many homicide units have seen anything like that. But you and I have. We have to remember what we learned from it and apply it here."

"Yeah. You know, I still see the faces of those little girls. In my mind. They stare at me. I swear, they even talk to me. Geez, I sound friggin' nuts."

"No. You don't. Something like that, it's impossible to erase from your memory. I have dreams. Well, more like nightmares."

He shook his head. "You're right. We have to remember what went wrong. And not do it here." He pulled on his coat and reached for the chipped mug he had rested on her desk.

Dara interrupted his intentions. "You leave that mug with me, I'll get it back home."

"Dara, you don't have to clean up after us. You do enough."

"Well, I heard you've got a dive bar to check out on the way home. So you just skedaddle."

He knew better than to argue with her. "OK. Thanks, Dara." He met her eyes with his own, silently signalling to her the mounds of gratitude he felt.

Dive Joint

M ahoney pulled his orange '69 Pony into the parking lot. Sliding his feet onto the pavement, he scanned the scene. A fluorescent blue sign pulsated *LiveWire* through the darkness. Underneath the sign, a solid black door appeared to be the main entrance.

A few strides later, Mahoney arrived at the knob-less, black door. *How the hell do you get into this joint?* A circular wire hung as a makeshift doorknob. Mahoney pulled the wire and the door creaked open. Stepping through the door, he scanned the dive. To his left was a wide-open space, stretching along a stage and quarantined off from the rest of the joint by a rusty black railing. A ledge launched upwards to his right, perching a clutter of rusty tables and chairs above the open area. Mahoney guessed the open space was a dance floor, or whatever the young kids did nowadays when they watched a live music show. Straight ahead was the bar, partitioned off by a black countertop. Mahoney walked toward the bar.

As he approached, a young woman greeted him. "Hey there, honey. What can I get 'cha?" Wiping furiously away at the sticky countertop, she remained focused on her cleaning duties. Her long, blonde hair fell in big curls around her shoulders. Her body was hoisted up in a tight, shiny black corset, her ample breasts jiggling in motion as her hand circled over the bar.

Mahoney lifted himself up onto one of the high-top chairs directly in front of the friendly server. "Ginger-ale, please." Wildly dressed, long-haired rock stars jaunted across television screens lining the top of the bar.

Tossing the wet rag aside, the server looked up. Snatching up a tall glass, she dug it deep into a bin full of ice, then launched it underneath a tap. Snapping the faucet forward, she scanned Mahoney up and down. "Haven't seen you in here before, honey. You don't exactly look the type to be hanging around this place." Her candy-floss lips moved rapidly.

Scanning the space, Mahoney counted three patrons. One was off in the corner nursing a beer, the other two were back across the room, smoking cigarettes, deep in conversation. "First time here. I'm looking for someone." Retrieving the victim's photo from his coat pocket, he slid it across the glossy black counter.

Sliding a glass of bubbles toward him, the server looked at the photo. Hands on her hips, she looked Mahoney straight in the eye. "Look, honey, I don't know who you are, but it isn't my job to keep tabs on people around here." She turned back to the wet rag, scrubbing the countertop with vigour.

"I didn't properly introduce myself. I'm Detective Mahoney."

Stopping mid-swipe, the server looked up from the rag. "Detective?" Taking a couple of aggressive chomps on her bubble gum, she narrowed her eyes.

"I'm with the homicide department. I don't mean to cause you any inconvenience. I'm just looking to determine if this kid was in here. He may have been at a show here, a week ago Saturday." Sliding the photo toward her again, he retrieved the yellow concert flyer from his coat pocket. Unfolding it, he placed it next to the picture.

The server stared at the photo and the flyer.

"Were you working here the night of this show?"

Chomping on her gum, she lifted her gaze to meet his. "Yeah."

"Do you recall seeing this boy?" He pointed at the photo.

Biting her lower lip, she narrowed her eyes again. "Look, mister, I don't mean to be difficult, but, my customers, they just come here for a good time. To blow off a little steam."

"I understand. This kid, he isn't in any sort of trouble. In fact, I'm trying to find out what happened to him."

"Something bad happened to him?" Her eyes widening, she stood up a little taller.

"Yes. We found his body. He's dead."

"Dead?" Her hand slapped over her mouth. Her eyes glazed with moisture.

"Miss. I'm sorry if this is upsetting. But, I'm trying to find out anything I can about what exactly happened to him. He may have come to this show. Can you remember if you saw him here that night? It would be helpful if you can try and remember. Anything you can tell me might help. I would appreciate it. His family would appreciate it."

Her hand shaking, she moved it away from her mouth, resting it on the black countertop. "Well, it gets crazy crowded in here on a night like that. You know, tightly packed. I'm always running my feet off."

"Take your time. Think about that night." Mahoney pushed the photo back toward her.

Taking a deep breath, exhaling loudly, she steadied herself and took another look at the picture. Wiping a tear from the corner of her eye, she suddenly snapped her gaze straight at Mahoney. "I did see him. He's been in here before." Her pink-painted nail tapped at the photo as a look of contemplation washed over her face. "I don't think he's ever come in during the day. Those ones I really remember, 'cause there's hardly anyone in here during sunlight. But, this guy, I think I've seen him a few times at the live shows. It's his eyes." She picked up the photo again. "They're so blue. And, I remember, 'cause he always tipped well, but he only ordered cola. I don't think I ever saw him drink." Smiling, she leaned against the back of the bar, her shoulders relaxing.

"No drinking?"

"Nuh-uh. He only drank pop when I served him."

"You say he tipped well? How well are we talking here?"

"Well, I ain't gettin' rich off it, but he always threw in a few dollars. That's a lot for a college kid."

"Did he ever seem like he was high or on drugs?"

She narrowed her eyes. "You sure ask a lot of questions."

He smiled. "It's my job. Listen, miss, anything you can tell me might help me figure out what happened to him."

"Alright. I can buy that." She leaned in closer. "No. He never seemed drunk, on drugs, on anything like that. He seemed real straight. I honestly think he just liked the music."

"Thank you. That's a real help, miss. One more thing. Did he ever hang around with anyone in particular?"

"He was a real loner. Always came to the shows alone and left alone, as far as I remember. He often hung around a bit after the shows, chilling by the bar. He kept to himself."

"Hmmm. Did you ever see him approached by anyone?"

She pursed her lips. "I don't think so. Look, mister, is something going on around here?" Her lips smacked as she continued to chomp on her wad of gum.

"Don't worry, miss. There's no reason to be alarmed. This boy was found far from here. We don't know that his disappearance had anything to do with him coming here. I'm just checking out the places he hung out at."

"Look, mister, is there anything else you need to know? You know, that might help you?" Leaning both elbows on the freshly wiped bar, her shoulders relaxed and her breasts pressed hard against the top of her corset. A sweet cloud of perfume drifted across the bar.

Taking a sip of sweet ginger, Mahoney contemplated her offer. "It seems pretty quiet in here." He scanned the room again, eyeballing the three patrons. "You said it gets quite busy during a show?"

"Yeah. It's quiet during the day. And Monday nights are always slow. The busiest times are the weekends. And it's really packed if there's a live show going on."

"How often is there a live show here?"

"Every Saturday night. It's great. We're the only place in town that offers a live show every weekend. So we get a big crowd."

"What kind of music do these bands play?"

Leaning closer to him, her blonde curls fell over the front of her shoulders. "Oh, management is trying to bring in a variety. But, we mostly have rock bands. They're talking about diversity in the musical acts, you know, to support live music, but, really, we're a rock bar." Picking up a blonde strand, she fiddled with the long curl. Pursing her candy-floss lips, she stretched her wad of gum into a big bubble. A snap hit the quiet of the room and she slipped the deflated gooey mess back into her mouth.

Watching the bubble-blowing routine, Mahoney took it as a sign that she had begun to relax around him. He drove his line of questioning deeper. "Miss…"

"Sasha." Interrupting him, she met his gaze. "You can call me Sasha."

"Sasha. What kind of people come to the live shows?"

"Oh, a lot of college kids. A few older dudes. The old guys usually hang out in the back areas, at the tables."

"How do these kids dress? Do they dress a little different than normal when attending a live show?"

"Oh, yeah. The kids that come in here, they glam it up. You know, fit into the rock scene."

"Do the young men dress more feminine?"

"Oh, you mean the leggings and jewellery. Oh yeah. Have you seen the latest rock videos? The rock stars, they wear whatever they want."

He pointed to the photo again. "Do you recall how he dressed, when he came to the shows?"

"Yeah. Real straight. Jeans. Button up shirt. He stood out 'cause he dressed so normal."

Sipping the last bit of sweet ginger, Mahoney slid the tall glass across the black countertop. Hanging his tweed coat over his arm, he retrieved a small card from the pocket. "Listen, miss…"

"Sasha. I told you, call me Sasha." Stretching her lips over her bright-white teeth, she shot him a broad smile.

"Sasha, thank you. You have been a real help. If you think of anything else that you saw that night, please give me a call." Sliding the card across the black counter, he pulled his tattered wallet from his coat pocket.

"This your cell number?"

"Yes. My work phone. You can always reach me there."

He opened his wallet. A picture of his daughter stared back at him. Her bright, blue eyes pleading with him to come home. Her face blurred. A ghost face replaced it. Blood red lips asked him, *"Us or her, Bug? Us or you?"*. He yanked a bill out and snapped the wallet shut. Handing the bill to the waitress, he stood up to leave.

She slid the bill back toward him. "It's on the house. The drink."

"No. That's not necessary."

"Oh no, I mean, pop is always on the house. You know, management's way of encouraging the kids from getting out of hand."

"Oh. Fine then." Mahoney eyeballed the bill. "Consider it a gratuity. Thanks again." Tipping his derby, he turned and strode toward the black door.

Nightcap

Mahoney took a left turn down the familiar street lined with trees and flowerpots. Turning the steering wheel toward the quaint little shopping area, he attempted to maneuver his mind away from the invasion of pink boots and blonde curls. Unable to shake the image of that young girl, stick in hand, innocence in her eyes, his only success in steering was with his car. As the engine drawled to a halt, he made a swift exit from the driver's seat. Charcoal derby in one hand, grey tweed coat in the other, his long strides delivered him with speed across the parking lot. Slipping through the door, the warmth of the cozy pub wrapped around him.

"Hey, boss! My man!" Simon jovially welcomed him as soon as he had one foot in the door.

Nodding his head, Mahoney launched himself up into one of the high-legged chairs at the bar. His back pressing hard against the chair, his shoulders relaxed.

"The usual?" Simon inquired.

Looking at his watch, Mahoney took a mental inventory of the near-empty shelves in his fridge. He was sure he had a full bottle of ketchup, but doubted there was anything to put it on.

"Yes. I'll be dining with you tonight, Simon."

"Got it, boss!"

Dreaming of collapsing into his bed, Mahoney perked up a little as Simon's enthusiasm rung through the air.

"Rough day?" Simon asked with a concerned tone. He slid a frosty glass across the slick countertop.

Looking into the tall glass filled to the brim with ginger bubbles and loads of ice, Mahoney couldn't help the slight smile that spread across his face. It really was the simple things in life. When the days were long, he could always count on this place. He could haul in his weary body and sink into a chair. He barely had to utter a word before his order would be up.

"Yeah." Mahoney expanded his brief reply, just a little. "Tough one."

"New case?"

Mahoney nodded his response, taking the first sip of his ginger-ale. The cold liquid refreshed his parched mouth as the bubbles tickled their way down his throat.

"Yup, a new one. Might be on this one a while." Mahoney figured the least he could do was chat it up a little. He knew it was the bartender's job to feign interest in the life of every single customer. To join them in their despair as they purged their deepest secrets and he poured their next glass of relief. Despite this traditional cliché, Mahoney actually believed that Simon really did care. The high chairs and countertop at the front of the Stepping Stone Pub had been Mahoney's dinner table for over a decade. Simon, just a young one, had been working here for almost four years. Long enough for Mahoney's instincts to know that Simon wasn't a fake friend for the sake of a bartending reputation at a run-down neighbourhood pub.

"By the looks of you, this case had a taxing start," Simon noted, shining a wine glass with a white towel.

"Let's put it this way. It's a new one for this city."

"Ah. Brand-new case. Fresh today." Stroking his chin with his thumb and forefinger, Simon cited like a university professor, "So, you are in the initial phase of your investigation. The body is in processing. Your team will soon be scouring the history of the victim, attempting to generate leads. Within a fortnight you will be leaning into the research phase, interviewing persons of interest and canvassing areas both at the scene and related to the life of the victim."

Mahoney let out a full-on chuckle. His mind scanned through the series of nightcaps where he had divulged the principles of homicide investigations to Simon. So eager to learn, the bartender had provided a great practice audience for the course that Mahoney had been roped into teaching to the new recruits throughout the winter. Of all the times he had given that presentation, Simon may have been his single best student.

"Yes. You're on track."

"So, any good leads?"

Mahoney hesitated. Avoiding the question, he took another long swig of soothing ginger. He wanted to satisfy Simon's interest, but he knew that prying ears were impossible to identify. Especially in a pub with a plethora of loners dotting the bar stools, nursing their fifth drink. "It's a little early for anything concrete." Mahoney turned his attention toward the television over the bar.

Simon held another wine glass up toward the glint of the overhead pot lighting. Chuckling, he said, "Top secret detective stuff. I get it. Change of subject required. How's your love life?"

The tightness in Mahoney's back pulling at his shoulders, he took another gulp of his drink. Grimacing, he looked back at Simon. "Could be better."

"What happened to…what was her name, the runner? Susan?" Simon asked.

"Sherry," Mahoney said. His brows furrowed as he looked at Simon.

"Oh right, Sherry. Yeah. The way you talked about her, she seemed nice. Smart too."

"Yeah, she was. It, uh, it didn't work out," Mahoney said, looking directly into the dissipating fizz in his glass.

"Oh. I'm sorry," Simon replied, resting his hands against the bar and looking straight at Mahoney. "There're other fish out there. Isn't that what your friendly neighbourhood bartender is supposed to say?"

A laugh rumbling in Mahoney's throat, he just couldn't resist Simon's charm.

"Yeah. Other fish. An ocean of them." *But she was a catch. Intelligent. And a beauty too. But I pulled my trick again. Pulled away as soon as she started getting close.*

"OK. I'm two strikes in. One more and *you* can kick *me* out of my own bar." Simon threw his hands up, animatedly indicating his surrender. "So, rough day on the job on a super-secret case, and a pretty girl that's gone from the picture. What else is there to talk about?" Simon continued, stroking his chin in a contemplative fashion. "Got it!" he declared, stretching his pointer straight up and cocking his brow. "How 'bout them Jays? Did you catch any of the game last night?"

Mahoney smiled. He had to give Simon credit for his effort in getting him to chat, even when he wanted to be a hermit in his empty apartment. "Caught a few highlights of the last inning." He pictured his little old black-and-white TV, perched on the unpacked cardboard box. A mess of wires connecting it to the wall and the VCR on the floor.

"Oh, baby! You saw that? Man, that was some sort of cra-zay! I don't know how he caught that fly ball. Some sort of magic, that was."

Mahoney listened to Simon banter on about the game for a few minutes, the exhaustion slowly taking over him.

Sliding a piping hot pizza toward him, Simon eyeballed the critically low level of the bubbly refreshment. "Another?" Simon nodded to the glass.

"Sure." Mahoney's stomach grumbled at the sight of gooey cheese and greasy pepperoni, reminding him that he hadn't eaten all day.

Devouring the pizza with zest, Mahoney's mind continued to be soothed by Simon's upbeat babbling. Wiping the grease from his hands with a thin paper napkin, Mahoney paved the way for his departure. "That's the end of the road for me tonight." Fishing his beat-up wallet out of his pocket, Mahoney slapped a few bills onto the counter. He stood up wearily, perching his derby on his crown, and tipping his head to Simon as he turned to leave.

Looking down at the bills, Simon declared his resistance, "boss, that's too much."

Mahoney had already reached the door. Back turned to the bar, he dismissed Simon's concern with a wave of his hand.

LIKE A FAIRY

Oasis Invasion

Seth's heavy limbs sunk into his bed. Like air bubbles floating to a watery surface, tiny beads of tension released themselves from his body, escaping through his pores. Here in his oasis, he was able to find a small bit of peace despite the chaos that shook through the rest of the house. He reached for his headphones perched on the nightstand, right where he had left them. He pushed play on his Walkman and was instantly swept away to another world. Listening to Steven Tyler *ca-ca-ca-ca-ceow*ing away, his mind was soothed. Shifting his weight and relaxing his shoulders, he sank deeper into the soft mattress. Closing his eyes, he began his escape into the world of his rock idols.

BANG! BANG! His eyes popped open as he was jolted into reality. His heart pounding hard against the wall of his chest, he frantically scanned the room. *What the fuck was that?* His mind raced, grasping to make sense of the interruption. The doorknob shook violently. "Let me in!" Doris screamed at him. Doris, the woman whom he had stopped calling Mom a long time ago.

BANG. BANG. He could hear her fist pounding against the door as she demanded his attention. As usual, it was all about what *she* wanted. Releasing a loud sigh, Seth removed his earphones and dragged himself to his feet. He shuffled his way over to the door, hesitating briefly, then reaching for the latch. A slow click was immediately followed by a loud swoosh as Doris forced open the door and burst into his room. The yelling started before she had taken a single step onto the plush, red carpet.

"How *dare* you lock me out of a room in my *own* house. What are you doing in here?" she barked at him. She glanced around, her eyes quickly landing on the Walkman lying in the middle of the crumpled blankets on his bed. "Are you filling your head with that trash again? Those fairy boys with long hair, dressed in girl clothes? Why do you encourage yourself like that? How many times have I told you to stop listening to that garbage. You're girly enough. You're such a fairy."

As she continued on, belting out verbal darts, Seth's face reddened, and his forehead glistened with sweat. He dug his hands into his pockets, rocking back and forth from one foot to the other. He was lightheaded, struggling to breathe. His mind drifted off in an attempt to block out the invasion until her voice violently made a way in again.

"I *should* have left you locked up in that institution. You belong with those freaks."

After what seemed like an eternity, Doris finally backed out of the bedroom doorway and thumped her way down the stairs. Her voice continued to fill the house, never ceasing. Seth's head was spinning. His arms and legs were tingling. He had to get out of here. He could not bear to be near her any longer.

Snatching up his backpack, he tiptoed down the stairs. He sneaked silently through the front door, delicately latching it behind him. The cold air hit him like a slap across his cheek. He could still hear Doris yelling even though a house separated them. He wasn't sure if she was actually hollering or if he imagined it. His legs took on a life of their own and started running. The chill of the night pierced his lungs. Gasping a few times, he found a rhythm. Taking a long, deep breath, he allowed the fresh, crisp oxygen to infuse him with new life. He lost all track of time as he sprinted to nowhere. Eventually, he started to slow down, coming to a stop. He glanced at his watch and was surprised to realize he had left the house nearly a half hour ago.

He closed his eyes and tipped his head back, turning his face toward the brightly twinkling stars embedded in the darkness. Just as his shoulders started to relax and his heartbeat began to steady, he heard her voice again. She wasn't even here, yet she could still control his thoughts. Her voice began to increase its volume, turning into a scream, stabbing at his brain. The shrieking invaded every corner of his mind, migrating through his body, spreading into every molecule and infecting each tiny ion. His arms and legs were heavy, immobilizing him. Hot tears rolled down his cheeks as he tried to swallow, but the lump in his throat would not dissolve. All he could do was feel the puncture of each stab. *"Fairy. You and your long hair and girl clothes. I should have left you locked away with the freaks."*

His mind continued to spin faster, increasing in speed at an astounding rate. The world blurred around him. His knees buckling, he crouched down, touching the ground to steady himself. His heart was beating so hard, threatening to break through his chest. He hit the ball of his palm against his forehead repeatedly, willing Doris to shut up. He could hear himself yelling inside his head, *Just Stop,* until his voice was breaking through the dense, imaginary wall that seemed to have erected between his mind and the outside world. He screamed at the top of his lungs until his fury dissolved into weak desperation and his voice was barely a whisper.

Seth rested his forehead on his knees and curled tighter into a ball, wrapping his arms around himself. Looking up, he teetered back and forth on his heels, gazing blankly into the distance. Sliding off his backpack, he removed a carefully folded item at the top. Slipping the silky material of the sleeves over his arms, the robe flowed around him, calming his mind. He stroked his arms, enjoying the beauty of the soft shade of red. Toppling onto his side, the cold grass soothed his cheek. He rolled onto his back and spread his arms and legs out wide, letting the sweet, earthy aroma fill his nostrils. Closing his eyes, he surrendered to the darkness that laid its cloak around him. He found stillness for a few moments, his thoughts starting to clear and a path forward opening in front of him. *I wish I could just disappear from this world,* he thought to himself solemnly. *If only someone would just come along in this dark, lonely place and kill me. Free me.*

Like A Fairy

Mahoney was jolted by the beep of his cell phone. His brain swelled, and heavy lids drooped over his bloodshot eyes. He had been dreaming of collapsing into his well-worn couch. He could almost hear the tinkling of an ice cube against crystal as he longed for the soothing of bourbon and the numbness that followed. He reached his limp hand toward the passenger seat, pushing the 'on' button and holding the heavy phone against his ear. Clearing his throat, he attempted to sound commanding as he said, "Detective Mahoney."

"Bug." Peggy's voice filled his ears.

Dammit. "Pegs. You know I love talking to you. But…"

"I know. A call from me means there's another one."

"Get me on my way."

"Eagle Woods. There's an officer on scene with the witness. The medical examiner is already in full swing. She specifically asked for you, something to do with your current case." She was quick with her delivery of the crucial information.

"I'm a few clicks away." As if placing a pebble directly in a critical cog of interlocking gears, he consciously halted his mind from bolting into action. Attempting to savour the few moments he had before the pebble would be crushed to dust, and his mind would be clouded with more dark images, he slid into easy pleasantries. "Pegs, help me kill the rest of the drive. How's Tommy?"

"Good, Bug. Thanks for asking." He could hear the smile in her voice.

"Is he still watching those detective shows?"

"More seriously than ever. He declared the ones that all the other kids watch, oh, how did he put it, too cheesy and unrealistic." She let out a soft laugh. "Have you ever heard of Philip Marlowe? I had to get HBO. Not an easy feat up here in the north. And don't even get me started on the search I have underway for the books that inspired the show. He insists on reading them. Some author that none of the bookstores in this town have heard of." Her voice was full of warmth. He could picture her glowing, as she did when she talked about Tommy.

"Ha. Your kid's smarter than I am." He listened to her chatter, images of her softly lined, full red lips drifting through his mind.

She continued on with content, saying, "I shouldn't complain. I can't really say no when he spends all his time reading and writing. And at *his* age."

"Impressive for a teenager," Mahoney supported her conclusion. "Pegs, I'm pulling into the park now."

"Bug, stay safe."

"Will do."

Pushing his phone into the holster on his belt, he made a swift entry into the park entrance. The last morsels of sunset had made their exit. A uniformed officer was talking to a young woman decked out in smooth lycra running shorts and matching sports top. Her socks were pulled up to her knees. His attention was caught by the brilliant neon-green stripes on her trail shoes flashing through the descending darkness. Grabbing his worn charcoal derby before closing the creaky door of his trusted Pony, he made strong, long strides toward them. Turning to him, the officer jumped the gun on the introductions.

"Detective Mahoney?" the uniform politely questioned. "I'm Officer Davis."

Mahoney nodded his head, solidly reaching for the officer's extended hand.

Officer Davis continued without pausing, "Medical Examiner Blackwood requested you. She wasn't in there long before coming out." The officer nodded his head toward the abundant forest. "She said something about a strong similarity to a case you are currently on. She's back in there now with the crime scene techs."

A slight tingling crept up Mahoney's spine as he clung to the word *similarity*.

"The trailhead is at the edge of the trees over there." The officer stretched out his arm, pointing toward what appeared to be the end of the dense woods. "Once you get onto the trail, walk about a half a kilometre. They're off the path, on the right, in the brush. The witness is a hardcore runner. Seems she explores the less-used trails inside the woods. Only reason she found the body. Unless you need anything else, I'll finish up with the witness."

Mahoney nodded. "I'll head on in."

As they parted ways, Mahoney made his way toward the forest, the tall cedars looming down at him. Finding the trailhead, he embarked on his journey into the isolated wilderness, the darkness cloaking around him. The woods continued to run along the right side of the dirt path. The path opened up on Mahoney's left, revealing a sinister scene. Threadlike strips of cotton clouds stretched across a voluminous moon. The celestial sphere glowed, creating porcelain shimmers on the ripples of the indigo lake. Unclipping the flashlight from his belt and slowing his pace, he methodically traversed the trail. Stopping often to pull aside branches, his eyes were fixed on the foliage. There was a quiet peace about the secluded space, but his suspicions were telling him a bone-chilling scene was lurking just behind the pines.

The haunting wail of a loon pierced the silence, causing Mahoney to jump as a shock bolted through him. Snickering, he muttered to himself, "Geez. This is like a scene out of American Werewolf in London."

He had barely continued forward when his eye caught some movement from an opening into the abundant thicket. He stopped and began to dig his way through the roughness of the brush. About a dozen steps in he found Blackwood, standing still, one hand on her hip and the other holding what appeared to be the most powerful flashlight he had ever seen. Her focused gaze stared down at a lifeless form, bathed in thousands of lumen.

In response to the rustle of his entry, she twisted in his direction with a jerk. Blinded by the light, he raised his hands in defence. As recognition struck her, she removed the powerful rays from their piercing position.

"Wow. That's quite a light," Mahoney threw out.

"Yeah. It's a Sunfire 6. It's as bright as a 4 D Cell Maglite despite its compact aluminum casing." She looked as delighted as a child taking inventory of her loot on Halloween night. Stifling a snicker, Mahoney's gaze found hers. Her expression turned sheepish. "Ah, it does the trick. Detective Mahoney, nice to see you again." A hint of warmth flickered on her face before making a quick escape. *Is she happy to see me?*

"Blackwood. You interrupted my date with a nightcap and a soft bed," Mahoney said. He could have sworn she almost chuckled.

Her stance stiffened, and her tone changed abruptly. "The crime scene techs just finished uncovering the body. They did a scan of the immediate area, then proceeded to determine how wide the circumference of the crime scene should be. Take a look. I think you'll see some familiar things." Her eyes took a stance looking directly at the pale white corpse contrasting sharply against the midnight background. Leaving him to a private viewing, she wandered over toward the brush, in search of the techies who were foraging for evidence.

He sighed, and thought to himself, *So much for that drink or a good night's sleep. Better get this scavenger hunt started.*

Moving closer to the body, a whiff of spoiled eggs infused his nostrils. Coughing, he exhaled deeply. *How long has it been hiding in here?* He scanned the mystery form up and down. The body was veiled in a red, sheer robe, barely covering the most private areas. Darkened purple bruises were battered into the green-tinged skin, densely covering both exposed legs. Ruby gashes coiled around the delicate wrists and ankles, rooting their way to the bone. Wild, tangled hair covered most of the face and ran its way past the shoulders. The head was tilted to the right, exposing one side of the neck, and a hint of more viciousness.

Shaking his head, he allowed a slight wince to surface. *I miss the more merciful murders of the old days when this city was a mere town,* he thought forlornly to himself.

Donning the familiar second skin on each hand, he walked in closer. Crouching down, he gingerly moved the hair away from the face as he peered at the grisly remnants of gruesome events. Sickly caramel-coloured demarcations were permanently encircled around the neck, the ghastly remnants of breath-stifling suppression. Hardened globs of scarlet encrusted the earlobes and the corners of the mouth. A jewelled earring dangling from the ear gave off a glimmer.

"Fuck." The word escaped his mouth before his mind knew it was happening. An ice wave cut through his gut. Realization washed over him, his mind connecting the distinct ligature mark to that of the victim they had found only the day before. He wondered how his unit would handle this. Serial wasn't a word that he had dealt with in a long time. His guys had never experienced it.

Taking a deep breath, he redirected his mind back to the body. The victim's glassy eyes stared back at him, inquiring, *Why, Bug?* Her lids were lined in black. Her lashes were thick with mascara, clumps of dark oil clinging on for life. Black water stains streaked her cheeks. He could picture the tears escaping from the corners of her emerald eyes, streaming their way down her porcelain skin. Despite all his years of witnessing the aftermath of murders, his spine was tingling as the corpse continued to send him a chilling stare.

He rescanned the body with deliberation. He noticed the legs were sheer and smooth. A glint drew his gaze toward a set of rhinestone bracelets, weaving their way up an arm covered with callous contusions. *How did I miss that?* He refocused, homing in on the details. The chest was flat. His surroundings faded from his consciousness as he became lost in his quest to discover every tiny aspect revealed by the spiritless figure.

He was snapped back to reality by a blip. He raised himself to stand, unholstering his hefty cell phone. "Detective Mahoney here," he barked hoarsely. "Yeah, keep going. Once you reach the trailhead, about half a click in. I'm, or rather we're, in the woods to the right." He clicked his phone off with impatience, crouching to continue his assessment. What was it that had drawn him in? He had to find out.

Blackwood now rejoined him. "Take a look at this," she directed with some tension in her voice. She shone her flashlight on the corpse as her sheathed hand pulled the satin frock. Mahoney took a long, hard look at the victim's bare body. His hand returning to its familiar place on his day-old bristle, he quizzically peered down. "Oh what fresh hell is this?" he muttered. A set of family jewels stared back at them. The link to the existing case strengthened its bond.

This is dark. Reminds me of all those little girl corpses. The way they were painted up. A black cloud suffocated that town. Now my cozy little city's being pulled down the same dark vortex.

He shook the thoughts from his mind and focused on the corpse. Pulling out his notebook, he rescanned the form, starting with the face. *Gonna be a long night.*

Bloody Note

Pulling open the heavy door, Mahoney motioned Blackwood forward. Watching her roll the gurney into the dark morgue, the cold air hit his lungs. They moved into the silent space. It was just them and a dead body. Blackwood snapped on a switch. Hot light flowed from the fluorescent tubes, bringing a small patch of the room to life. Pushing the table toward the brightness, she settled it, clamping the wheels to a stop.

"Are you sure you want to stay?" Blackwood challenged Mahoney with her tone.

The golden badge that he would be receiving in a matter of months presented itself within his mind. *20 years. That's a long time. If you fuck up this case, they won't be calling you Bug anymore. All you'll leave behind is a stack of corpses.* Rushing his affirmation to hide his hesitation, his words contradicted the doubts floating through his thoughts. "I need preliminary trails. Now."

Blackwood moved into her process, her own script, executing the steps that she seemed so well versed in. She walked over to a set of immaculate shelves housing a plethora of items placed in perfect rows. Scanning the available inventory, she stretched the ever-familiar sheathings over her hands. She perched a small tape recorder on a square table next to the body. Making one more round, she returned with a steel box. Placing it on the table next to the recorder, she snapped open the silver clamp closing in the contents. Walking up close to the body, she looked at Mahoney. "Ready?"

A pink boot kicked his mind into gear. "Yeah."

Pressing a button on the small recorder, the wheels started spinning inside the clear plastic casing. Turning to her toolbox, she retrieved a large, transparent bag. Zipping open the top, like a mom eager to fill it with lunchtime contents, she laid it beside the body's head.

Pausing to record her steps, she stared at the body. "Tuesday, April 14 4:30 a.m. Autopsy for case number 87000150. Initiating preparation of body with the removal of clothing. The first item is a red robe."

Positioning a gloved hand behind the head, she lifted it away from the steel slab, pulling the dead body up in a semi-sitting position. As she slid the red robe away from the body, a flash of white caught both their eyes. They watched it flutter to the ground. Blackwood released the head back against the steel slab with care.

"Halting removal of red robe to retrieve an item that fell from the robe onto the ground." She clicked the recorder to a stop. Putting the robe gently aside, she bent over and picked up the mysterious white item.

"Paper," she declared, opening the folded pieces of a single sheet. "It's a note." She placed the paper on the steel slab. Mahoney's eyes widening, they both stared at the chilling message. Blackwood snapped the recorder back into motion. "The item that fell from the red robe is a single sheet of thick, yellowing paper. It appears to be approximately 6x9 in size. A note is written in red lettering. The written phrase is 'Dude Look Like a Fairy.'"

Mahoney said, "The letters are written in red. Look at the consistency. Is it blood?"

Shooting him a glare, Blackwood took control of her process. "Packaging the note for crime lab processing."

Retrieving another transparent bag, she gently placed the note inside. She clicked the recorder off and turned to Mahoney. "It could be blood, yes. The crime lab can process the substance to determine what it is."

She labelled the clue with a dark, permanent marker. Bending down, she pulled a steel box from underneath a table adjacent to the slab housing the body. Snapping several clasps open, she lifted the lid, revealing layers of built-in shelving. She placed the packaged note onto one of the shelves.

Returning to her interrupted process, Blackwood clicked the recorder back into action. Picking up the red robe, she laid it out with slow, cautious movements on the steel table, next to the evidence box. "Proceeding to scan the red robe and package it for crime lab processing."

Scanning the robe, Mahoney pointed out his own observations. "Look at that. Could be mud or dirt. And that…"—he stepped closer—"could be blood."

Blackwood clicked the pause button with a loud snap. She whipped her gaze to Mahoney, narrowing her eyes. Her face was inches from his. "The purpose of the scan prior to the packaging for the crime lab is to identify any substances and remove them for processing."

Raising an eyebrow, Mahoney turned silent.

Blackwood turned to her toolbox. Retrieving a small silver cylindrical tool with an adjustable clamp on the end, she clicked the recorder on. "Proceeding to remove identified substances from the red robe, each for processing." Retrieving several samples from the red cloth, she sunk into a deep focus. Adding several plastic bags to the steel box of clues, she recorded her progress. "Three evidence bags added for processing. All samples retrieved from the red robe. Bag one contains a crusted red substance. Bag two contains a dark black substance reminiscent of mud. Bag three contains a green item, appearing to be a blade of grass."

Folding the robe, she placed it in its own plastic home. Repeating the same meticulous process multiple times, she stripped the body of all glimmer and glam. A series of plastic bags stacked upon the shelves, filling the evidence box to the brim. Each transparent bag had a corresponding verbal record of its retrieval. Shutting the lid over the precisely placed plastic bags, Blackwood made a quick call, summoning the next purveyor to move the items along the assembly line of processing. Retrieving a fresh evidence box, she turned to continue with her process.

Mahoney leaned back against an empty steel table. His mind wandered. *I'm not sure I'm gonna get anything by sitting here. A jewel. A red robe. The bread crumbs are so obscure. I need something concrete. This guy is a freakin' ghost.*

The fluorescent light glinted off the long jewelled earring in Blackwood's hand. Mahoney, jotting in his notebook, wondered if this spectacular piece of jewellery could provide him a lead. Interrupting her path once again, Mahoney prodded her, asking, "How long will it take to get answers from all this?"

She snapped the recorder to a halt. Narrowing her eyes, she shot him a glare and a harsh tone. "Look, I know you wanted to sit in to get anything preliminary. I know you're eager for leads. But I need to focus here. This process is careful, meticulous work. If you rush it, something could get overlooked or mis-processed. I know time is of the essence. I *get* it. You and your guys have this tiny window of time to create some sort of trail. But your path will only lead to a dead end if the trailhead is based on incorrect data."

"OK." Giving her a moment to digest his agreement, he continued his challenge, "You agreed. I'm here to create preliminary paths."

"You can create all the possible paths you want. But do it in silence. Or you will have to leave."

Her ultimatum stinging his ears, he clenched his jaw. The pink boot stepped a little further down its path in his mind. He could risk losing early leads, or he could suppress the urgency building within him.

Raising his hands, he stepped back, finding a stool to perch on. "All right."

Giving her shoulders a quick roll, she stepped back into her script. Walking over to a large, rectangular stainless-steel tub, she grabbed a spray bottle.

Proceeding to sterilize an already sterile surface, she sprayed and wiped down the four sides of the sink. Filling up the sink with water infused with some substance Mahoney's squinting eyes couldn't identify, she walked back over to the body. Performing a careful cleaning process, she moved over the bloodied body, starting with the legs. As the blood was washed away, the bruising was amplified. Purple, black, yellow mixed together in a cruel collage.

Mahoney sat slouched on his stool, remaining on good behaviour as he created a pathway in silence. He had seen beaten bodies before, many a time. Yet the level of brutality unfolding before him was shocking. Reviewing the facts extracted from the remnants of the first victim, and the slew of information that he was still digesting, he searched for similarities. Opening his tattered briefcase, he retrieved files from the first body. In a flash, he had re-created the first scene on a steel slab parallel to the one that held the current victim. He scanned the legs and the arms of the body they had retrieved from Frog Lake Park. *The shape, the colour, these bruises match up. What kind of sick tool did this guy choose? How long did he torture them for?* Mahoney whipped out his notebook and jotted down a reminder to get the pictures of the bruising from both bodies to the lab. He wanted a formal comparison.

Returning his attention to the ongoing cleaning process, he observed how different the body looked. Most of the bloody gore was gone. Blackish red turning to blue and purple. One form of violence replaced by another. *How much did this kid have to endure?*

Now working on the face, Blackwood dabbed at the crusts of dried blood with delicacy. A series of small transparent bags were placed above the boy's head. One of them held a hardened glob of blood. Another housed a white swab smeared in black. Clicking the recorder to off, and looking up from her work, she dared to take a break.

"I think a round of chemical analysis similar to what was done on the makeup removed from the first victim's face can provide us with some hard evidence. We may also get something from analysis of the blood that was left. This body was much less clean than the first one."

Would she be his key to hard evidence? The root to a tight case? "Good."

She continued taking him down a potential path. "This body, it's past the bloat stage. It's well into putrefaction. Bloat occurs two to four days after death, lasting for several days."

Mahoney dared a guess. "So, the kid's been dead for about a week?"

"We'll need to wait on the entomologist for a time of death. But, likely it's been at least five days. Look at this bruising. It's severe. The colouration indicates several different stages. It appears the victim may have been beaten over the course of multiple days. I will do a more thorough analysis and provide a full report."

The brief break over, she turned back to the body. Mahoney watched as the crusts of blood were removed, bit by bit, from the pallid face. The victim seemed like a doll. Once dressed up and played with, now stripped down and cleaned. All dirt and grime from the afternoon's playdate removed. All costume discarded, ready to go back in the toybox until tomorrow.

Turning back to her toolbox, Blackwood's plastic-covered finger slid over a series of sharp, shiny tools, landing on the perfect one for the job.

"Now comes the real part." Shooting him a warning glance, she clicked the recorder back into action. "Level of bruising appears to vary from 3 to 5. Suspect possible internal bleeding. Proceeding with main incision and lifting of the rib cage. Intention to begin internal organ examination with the lungs."

Her hands hovering just above the centre of the body's chest, she lowered the pointy end of the shiny tool, piercing the skin at the top of the shoulder. Sliding the tool across the breast, she halted at the abdomen. Eyes glued to the incision process, a tingling took over the back of Mahoney's neck, crawling down his spine. He watched Blackwood slice a matching incision from the right shoulder, meeting it with the end of the first one to form a V. Mahoney shifted on the stool, attempting to wet his parched throat with a swallow. The cutting process complete, a large Y covered the entire upper body of the boy.

Pulling the V section of the skin upwards, Blackwood peered inside. Mahoney stayed perched on the stool. Retrieving another item from the toolbox, a whirring sound rang through the air as Blackwood clicked a small, circular contraption into motion. Crunching filled his ears. His shoulders tensed as he watched the saw cut along one side of the rib cage, then the other. Blackwood lifted the entire section of bone away from the dead boy. The inside of the boy was utterly exposed. His mouth opening slightly, Mahoney stared as Blackwood lifted a roughly oval-shaped organ out of the body.

Blackwood inspected the organ in her hand with interest as she recorded her progress. "Removal of right lung complete. Proceeding with an incision." Placing the organ on a silver dish, she slit it open slightly. A burst of burgundy oozed from the slimy oval. She clicked the recorder to stop. "Never seen this before. There's actually blood in the lungs. Usually internal bleeding causes the victim to die of asphyxiation." She clicked the recorder back on. "Significant amount of blood appears to have flooded the right lung." She paused the recorder, turning toward Mahoney. "I need to make some final confirmations. But it appears that the cause of death was internal bleeding. The level of bruising indicates severe beating. And as I mentioned, the lung was actually flooded." She paused, swallowing hard. "It looks as though the victim drowned in his own blood."

Mahoney's eyes widened, then retreated to their normal size. "OK. We'll go on this, with the clause that we receive your updates as they come in." Settling back onto his stool, a tingling grew within his arms, migrating to his heart, reaching for his legs. *Drowning to death. In his own blood.* Scanning through the images of past cases, he struggled to find one that matched the level of brutality the current victim was slowly revealing. He settled in, watching Blackwood sink back into her process. Waiting for another cruel clue to appear, hoping a door would open, his mind wandered. *The linkage is real. The brutality is real. This case is only just beginning.*

Double Body Recap

Mahoney burst through the war room door. "Mornin', boys. Hope you got a little shut-eye."

Sutton and Hayes looked up from their breakfast sandwiches, eating them straight out of to-go boxes.

"A few hours. It'll do," Sutton confirmed.

Hayes swallowed a bite. "Hey, boss, did you know they have veggie breakfast sandwiches at Timmy's now?"

Sutton scowled. "Ha. That's not food. A man needs meat."

Mahoney shook his head. Dara perched in her corner, a fresh page in her typewriter. *Geez, does she sleep in that suit?* Mahoney was always astounded at her impeccable appearance and puzzled by how she made it to the war room before anyone else, no matter what time she was called. "Good morning."

"Good morning, Bug."

The aroma of coffee filled the room, luring Mahoney to the little round table beside Dara. Pouring himself a cup, he admitted his disappointment. "Should have stopped for a dark roast. Damn this generic shit."

Sutton threw a jab, lightening the mood. "You're a simple man, Bug. Nothing fancy, except your coffee and your bourbon."

Dara giggled. Mahoney threw his boys a smirk, then shot a glance at the two series of photos now plastering the cream-coloured wall across the room. It was hard to believe, two bodies in just forty-eight hours. *This dark vortex has its claws in us now.*

"Nice job on the setup. Appreciate the prompt work, team. Let's get rollin'.'"

Wolfing down the remnants of egg, cheese, and English muffin, Sutton and Hayes were at full attention.

Mahoney said, "OK. Two bodies, in less than two days. Turns out the second body we found has been dead longer."

Walking over to the life-sized calendar on the front wall, he snapped open an orange marker. Notes marked in blue indicated times and information on the Frog Lake boy. Mahoney added orange markings for the Eagle Woods kid. Two bodies, two colours. *How many colours will there be a week from now? Two weeks from now?*

"I was with Blackwood for a bit this morning," Mahoney said. "I have some preliminary results."

Wiping his greasy hands with a thin paper napkin, Sutton abandoned his breakfast box, finding a chair up at the front. Hayes, already sitting up at the front, flipped through his notebook, searching for a fresh page.

Dara glanced up from her intense typing. Mahoney continued charging forward. "We'll use these preliminary results to create our paths. But, as always, we will validate and adjust as more evidence is processed." Pulling a folder from his tattered brown briefcase, he snapped it onto the table running down the centre of the small room. Looking at Sutton and Hayes, he purged the immature information. "We have another young male, and a slew of similarities linking this one to our Frog Lake boy."

Sutton took a long sip from his Big Gulp, swallowing hard. Hayes shifted in his seat, lowering his notebook.

Mahoney said, "Looks like this body was much less clean than the first one. The hair was a mess. The face was bloody. Seems like our guy painted up a dead body, again. But, I wonder why there was less cleanup done before the body was prettied up."

Sutton provided a potential path. "Maybe our guy had less time for some reason. Had to rush."

"Yeah. Or maybe he was interrupted," Hayes said.

Mahoney questioned, "There was only one witness at Eagle Woods. The runner. It was late, I don't think she was brought in for further questioning."

Hayes flipped through a file on the long table. "No. She wasn't. We should pay her a visit."

"You boys go together. She's had a chance to process, to calm down. Maybe she can remember something. Hayes, chat her up with running lingo. Make her comfortable." Mahoney took a swig of coffee, pausing to consider the sunny-yellow mug spattered with dots of white where the paint had chipped away. *This department needs new mugs.*

Hayes continued, still perusing the files as he said, "Seems similar to the first kid. Parents in town. Enrolled in school. Had a job on the side."

"The first thing we'll do is pay a visit to this new kid's family. We'll do that one together. Sutton, you take the school. Hayes, you take the workplace."

Sutton nodded, lips wrapped around a long red straw. Hayes jotted in his notebook.

Mahoney closed the loop on the interview plan. "We need to create a circle of relationships here. Find out more about this kid. Try and find out who he knew. Let's hope we get more on this one than the Frog Lake kid."

Moving closer to the cream-coloured crime scene wall, Mahoney rubbed the bristle on his chin. Examining the photos from Eagle Woods, he said, "Again, this second kid was less made-up. Our guy could have been in a rush or abandoned his plans. After you boys conduct a second line of questioning on the runner, scan the area. This park, it's right on the edge of the city, but it's in a neighbourhood."

"Yeah. It's surrounded by houses. Easy access. You'd think maybe someone saw something," Sutton said.

"You boys scope it out. See if you can't dig us up some more witnesses."

Hayes nodded, continuing to jot down notes.

"OK. Let's talk clothes. The cloak, the leggings, now this red robe. You can't tell me this boy was just struttin' around in barely anything? Where did the rest of his clothes go?"

Hayes added to the growing list of tasks. "Sutton and I can scan the area, maybe widen the perimeter."

"Dara, did you find anything on that cloak yet?"

Slipping her dark glasses down her nose, she looked up from scribing. "Yes, Bug. I just got some results early this morning. I have a list of specialty clothing boutiques for you boys to check out. There aren't many places in the city that sell the kinds of clothing our Frog Lake body was found in."

"Great work, Dara. I can take a stab at that list. Sutton and Hayes, you focus on the Eagle Woods scene. I stopped by that dive bar last night. I got lucky. The server on duty was accommodating."

Sutton popped in a jab. "Of course she was. You have a way of charming them, don't you?"

Mahoney brushed off the comment. "Yeah, yeah. I think she works a lot. She was at the live show from the flyer. She even remembered seeing the Frog Lake victim that night. His good-kid reputation is intact. He wasn't a drinker. But he was a good tipper. Guess he really just likes the music. Appears the clientele dress with flair. Seems to be a rock scene thing."

"My daughter has a poster of this rock dude on her wall. He does dress, well, kinda similar to the Frog Lake kid. No cloak. But tight pants and makeup." Sutton cocked his brow, pondering the connection.

Turning back to the front of the room, the white-faced clock stared at Mahoney. "Let's wrap this up." Spinning to face his sparse audience, he kicked them into gear. "A handwritten note was found in the red robe of our Eagle

Woods boy. 'Dude Look Like a Fairy.' Those were the words. They *may* have been written in blood. Two bodies, two messages."

A quizzical look washing over his face, Hayes inquired, "What the hell does that mean?"

"I have no idea. Dara, can you layer this onto the searches for the first message."

Dara nodded, scribing away.

"And, there was an earring on our Eagle Woods boy. Long and shiny. I need to add this to your list, Dara."

"Got it, Bug."

"One more thing. We got a likely COD on the second body. Blackwood found blood in the boy's lungs. Looks like he may have had severe internal bleeding, from the beating. He probably drowned in his own blood." A chill surged up his back as the words left his mouth.

Sutton stopped mid-sip from his Big Gulp, staring back at him. Hayes leaned back in his chair, halting his unstoppable note-taking.

"We'll get a confirm on that. And the COD of the first body is still in question. This is a gruesome case, boys. I know you're aching to stop this guy. But we need to make sure we are thorough." Giving them a moment to process, he stared at his notebook. Straightening his stance, he forced confidence into his voice. "There are a bunch of things still in processing. I'll follow up with Blackwood. Let's get a move on. We have enough trails to pursue today. We'll reconvene at seventeen hundred, as usual."

Maple Syrup

Mahoney stepped through the doors of Donny's Diner. The all-day breakfast spot was almost empty. Mid-afternoon on a weekday would see most people caught in the hustle of the nine to five schedule. The sound of bacon sizzling met his ears. The aroma of grease and dark roast wafted into his nose. A cheerful vibe rippled through the room, bouncing off the sunny-yellow walls. Waving from a booth, Blackwood motioned him over.

As he slid in across from her, she looked up from the plastic menu in her hand. "I'm famished!"

He smirked to himself. *She just finished cutting up a body, and now she's ready to wolf down breakfast.* His stomach grumbled, reminding him it had been a while since he last ate.

"Hey, T," a waitress greeted them in a cheery tone. Looking at Blackwood, she said, "Man, you look like you've had a long night. Can I start you off with some coffee?"

Eyeballing the menu with wide eyes, Blackwood jumped at the offer. "That would be fabulous. I'll also have Donny's Big Breakfast. Please, and thank you." She smiled at the waitress, slipping the menu back into the holder against the window.

His stomach continuing to grumble, Mahoney decided to address it. "Make it the Light and Easy for me. And a coffee sounds swell."

As the waitress slipped away from the table, Mahoney and Blackwood were faced with each other. Never having been in a situation to talk about anything other than dead bodies, Mahoney shifted on the soft bench. "T? Hmmm. I take it you've stopped by here a couple of times."

"Yeah. This place is great after a long shift. It's cheerful. I like to feel a little uplifted after spending a long night with a cold, silent friend."

"Got it."

They paused as the waitress poured their coffee. "Fresh pot for ya. Your breakfast will be right up."

Mahoney lifted the cup toward his nose, breathing in the aroma. His brain tingling to life, he perked up a little. "Anything new for me?"

"It seems the Eagle Woods victim died around sunrise on Wednesday, April 8. Chemical analysis confirmed that the makeup was applied post mortem. The hair, though, doesn't appear to have been groomed up the same way as the first victim. It's almost like this was a practice run or something. Similar, but not as involved."

Mahoney nodded. "Did you notice how smooth the legs on this one were? The victim was a male. Wouldn't his legs be hairy? Was he into some strange grooming? Or was this more of the beautification process of the killer?"

"The legs were smooth, yes. As if they were shaved. We can't confirm if or when."

"Geez. It bugs me that the hair was such a mess. I mean, he took time on the body, but paid little attention to the hair? Hopefully, my boys can dig something up from the scene. I think maybe our guy was interrupted."

Blackwood nodded, nose deep into a white porcelain mug.

Mahoney said, "And the clothing. The outfits of each of the victims are quite different from each other. Yet, I can't help but notice a similar flair."

"Now that is one thing I can't help you with. All I can do here is try to confirm whether or not this new body was dressed before or after finding the final resting spot."

"Here you go," the waitress chirped cheerily, placing two large plates in front of them.

"Thank you." Mahoney noticed Blackwood's eyes sparkling with delight as she launched for the fork beside her plate.

Mid-chomp, Blackwood looked up from her vigorous dining. "Just before you called me, I got some results on the toxicology report on the first body."

"And?"

"It appears there were chemical compounds in the victim's bloodstream. Traces of strata-octin were found." She paused.

"Get on with it," Mahoney prodded.

She put her fork down on the table, meeting his gaze. "This is an extremely rare substance. It's a mutation of a neurotoxin. It inhibits the firing of action potentials in neurons."

"OK. So why do I care about this?"

"When administered to a human, the person becomes unable to move. Yet, they remain completely aware of their surroundings. This mutation is different than a neurotoxin. It's weaker. It has fewer side effects. Multiple doses are possible. It's a cleaner way to get someone to stop moving."

"So, the victim couldn't move, but he was aware of the torturous routine he was undergoing?"

"Possibly. Equally outrageous is the source of strata-octin. Pufferfish, porcupine fish, ocean sunfish, rough-skinned newts, moon snails, and even the venom of the blue-ringed octopus."

Mahoney shook his head. "What? Where the hell would someone have access to marine animals, here in the prairies?"

"I don't know. You should get your computer wiz on this. I'm running a toxicology report on the Eagle Woods boy."

"If we're lucky, Dara can carve out a couple of paths with this. Can you push more on the toxicology report for the Eagle Woods boy? We need that nailed down."

Her sigh reached across the table, seeping into his ears. "I'll try. I've pushed them hard already. The process is a lot different here than back home."

"OK. I get it. Got to be careful with pressure. Too much can create a lack of co-operation."

"Yeah. And, Mahoney, COD on the Frog Lake boy matches the COD on our Eagle Woods boy. Both drowned in their own blood from severe internal bleeding."

"So he used the toxin to immobilize the Frog Lake boy, not to kill him."

"Yes. It appears there were several injections over time." Her voice lost momentum. Shaking her head, she picked up her fork and continued devouring her colossal breakfast.

Mahoney wondered if this was creeping her out. *Geez. This guy is insane.* Placing his mug on the table, he looked directly at her. "There are two things concerning me."

Blackwood, digging with relish into a large pile of hash browns, paused at his serious tone. "What, Mahoney?"

"First off, the level of battery and torture is severe. The bruising, the internal bleeding drowning the kid's lungs, and the poisonous injections." He paused, taking a swig of coffee. "Second thing is the level of similarity. Two bodies, two notes. Post mortem grooming. Weird outfits. Identical neck ligatures. The lacerations around the ankles and wrists. It all points to one killer. This is beyond what we are used to dealing with in this city." Looking down at his barely touched breakfast, Mahoney felt his gut surge. *I can't hold back here. We need to work together.* "Look, I know you've worked some pretty big cases."

Swallowing a considerable bite of maple-syrup-drenched pancake, she put her fork down. "Yes, Mahoney, I have. I did work on some cases that, well, were deemed to be the responsibility of some really disturbed individuals. The guys that led to the creation of the term serial killer. These guys left quite a body count in their wake."

Mahoney thought about the thick stack of articles he had taken home with him last night. He had stayed up into the wee hours, absorbing anything he could find that at all resembled what he had seen at Frog Lake Park. The pink boot in his mind once again kicked him into gear. "What do you know about criminal profiling?"

"I'm not qualified to provide direction in that area. The cases that I dealt with involved the victims of killers that executed their murders just at the brink of the behavioural science stream that became criminal profiling. These guys were the ones that became subjects to the research performed. The research that fuelled the creation of the behavioural analysis unit of the FBI." Hunger continued driving Blackwood as she shoved another chunk of gooey pancake into her mouth.

"We don't have any criminal profiling up here."

"It's still a really new field. It hasn't reached very far."

"Given our two scenes here…we don't see stuff like this. Not here. I wonder if we need input from people who have."

Abandoning her fork and pancakes, her face flushed with seriousness. She looked him dead in the eye. "Mahoney. I can hook you up with a contact. He runs the criminal profiling unit of the FBI. They are still in their infancy, but…they do have something established there."

His hand rested on his bristly chin. *What am I getting myself into?* "Have you been on a case where there was resistance to profiling?"

Digging through her backpack, Blackwood produced a thick book. Flipping it open, she drew her finger down a page. "Ah, here it is. Yeah. I have. Seen lots of resistance."

Plunging her arm back into her pack, Blackwood retrieved a small coiled notebook. Ripping a page free, she jotted down the information. Sliding the paper across the table, her voice affirmed, "You can trust these people. They are professional. They've dealt with all sorts of disbelief in their methods. They can help you introduce this to your team." Leaning her pack against the window, she interlocked her fingers and rested her hands on the table. "I've seen some brutal cases. This one is up there."

Leaning back against the soft booth, Mahoney raised an eyebrow. Extending his hand toward the paper, he said, "Blackwood. We need to keep this between us. For now."

"Got it." A ray of sun spread into a multitude of directions through the diner window, catching a streak of silver in Blackwood's jet-black hair. She threw him a smile.

Shimmering Cloak

Mahoney approached the red door. Plucking his notebook from his tweed pocket, he flipped it open to the page listing the clothing boutiques. His eyes checked off each store until they landed on the last one. *I've been at this all afternoon. This one had better turn up something.* Checking the name printed in gold lettering across the sign hanging from an intricately woven wrought-iron perch, Mahoney verified the match. *Gold 'n' Glimmer.*

Turning the black knob, he swung open the door and entered the store. He was instantly bombarded with a plethora of fancy items. *Geez. What is this place?* His eyes jolted around, taking in the overwhelming amount of glitter and glam. Landing on the wall to his right, his gaze scanned a series of pleather pants. Shiny black, bright red, and even glimmering gold hung neatly in a long row. Wildly patterned choices topped off the collection. *Guess golden pants aren't crazy enough for some folks.* Mahoney released a slight chuckle. *Good thing I know how to amuse myself.* The amount of time he spent alone seemed to be increasing at an unreasonable pace.

Standing up tall, Mahoney moved away from the red door, venturing forth into the unknown land of flashy clothing. *Now, if I was a shiny black cloak with tassels, where would I be?* Looking to his left, he saw a meticulously organized display of boots. Some were clad with silver buckles, others were adorned with sparkling rhinestones, and the remaining ones were patterned to match some of the leggings he had perused. Scanning the belly of the store, between the boot- and pleather-plastered walls, his eyes wandered over silky blouses and flowing scarves in soft reds, pinks, and blues.

Approaching the front counter, a glint of sunlight catching a rhinestone-studded belt caught his eye. Both sides of the counter offered carousels of perfectly positioned accessories for the finishing touches on any outfit. *This place is something else,* Mahoney concluded to himself. He'd been to several stores already, but this one was beyond anything he had seen. *What were these kids into?* Mahoney scanned his mind for the image of the Frog Lake boy dolled up in such elaborate attire. *Where would they wear stuff like this? Was it really just blending into the so-called rock scene?* Mahoney turned his attention to a shuffling sound coming from an open door in the corner of the room behind the counter.

A tall, lean man appeared from the back room. Mahoney wasn't prepared for the display moving toward him. The man's tight black pants clung to every contour all the way up his legs and over his loins. A white blouse gathered in ruffles down his chest and around his wrists. Long black hair framed the man's pale face, jet-black strands secured by a shiny black police-like cap adorned with red stripes.

"Oh, I do apologize. I didn't hear anybody come in. Can I help you find something?" the man inquired in a deep, smooth voice. Sliding up to the counter, he rested an elbow on the glass, his chin on his hand.

Mahoney stared at the man's porcelain face. Two eyes, lined in black, touched with shimmer, pierced through him. Mahoney froze, his gaze fixated on a small, dark heart painted just beneath the man's left eye. Clearing his throat, Mahoney pushed his mind away from the makeup. "I'm Detective Mahoney. I'm investigating a case, and I'm wondering if you could help me find a rather unique item of clothing?" Retrieving a photo of the dark tasseled cloak from the Frog Lake boy, he slid it across the countertop. "Would you carry this cloak?"

The man picked up the photo, his shiny red fingernails catching Mahoney's eye. "You are looking for a rather, as you said, unique item. You have

come to the right place. This was one of my creations. I may have one left."
Looking up from the photo, the man scanned Mahoney from top to bottom. "Is
the cloak for yourself, sir?"

"No. Not my style. I'm investigating a situation. Would you have a record
of the purchases?"

"Yes. My boutique, as you can see, is small and specialized. I design most
of the clothing myself. I run a tight ship here. What kind of situation would have
you looking for this cloak?"

"I'm investigating a homicide. Would you recognize this man?" Sliding a
photo of the Frog Lake victim over the counter, Mahoney met the darkly lined
eyes with his own. "I'm trying to figure out what happened to this young man.
He was wearing this cloak when he was found."

A red-tipped finger pulling the photo across the counter, the man looked
at it intensely. After a few moments of silence, he looked back at Mahoney. "No,
I do not believe I have seen this man before. I get a lot of repeat customers. But,
I'm sure I haven't seen him."

"Thank you. Is your clientele primarily male or female?"

"Both men and women shop here. Probably more men. My store is a
boutique, I offer specialty items that can't be found anywhere else. There is a
certain culture growing in this city. Some have a more eclectic taste."

"Does your clientele—well, where would they wear the type of clothing
they buy here?"

"I don't think the way a man dresses necessarily indicates anything about
his orientations and his activities. If that's what you're getting at." Crossing his
arms, the man drummed his red-tipped fingers across his arm. "Some people
simply have a more cultured taste for fashion."

"No, of course not. I didn't mean to imply anything. Like I said, this boy,
I'm trying to figure out what happened to him. He was found in the cloak I'm

looking for. Anything you can tell me about why he would be wearing this cloak might help me to find out where he spent his time and even who he knew."

"I see. Well, I do often get customers in here from the local live music scene. Members of bands or people going to the shows. I'm not much for their type of music, but they like my clothing. It's hard to find the kinds of items I sell."

"Thank you for your candour. These band members that come in here, do you get repeat customers?"

"Yes. Actually, the local scene is quite small. Taste of Evil, Raging Fire, Queen's Face and a few others, they come in regularly. Sometimes a couple band members from out of town will drop in for last-minute items if they're doing a show in town."

"What about those going to the shows? Do the same people come in?"

"Yes, I do have a few regulars."

"You said you sold a few of those cloaks? Would you be able to check on the sales records?"

"Of course." Turning to the small computer perched at the end of the glass countertop, the man clicked a switch. The computer churned, slowly coming to life. "It will just take a moment. I don't have the most up-to-date computer here, but at least I have one. I like to keep track of everything. It helps me to determine what designs are more popular."

"Thanks." Leaning an elbow against the glass countertop, Mahoney scanned the eclectic collection. *Specialized boutique, you got that right.* The pink-bubble-gum-chewing dive-joint bartender told him that her clientele dressed to fit into the rock crowd. Now this boutique-owner man was dressed like one of Mahoney's dead boys. And he was also spouting that his customers were dressing with a flair for the purpose of a live rock show. Could it really be that was all this glimmer and glam was about? Was it nothing more? *Geez. I am not with the times.*

Chugging to life, bright green flashed across the small, black computer screen. The boutique owner leaned toward the screen, typing proficiently over the keyboard. "Ah, here it is. Yes, I sold three of the cloaks. I thought so."

"Do you have a record of who bought them?"

"Yes. I do." Turning the screen around to face Mahoney, the man pointed a red-tipped finger at the screen.

Mahoney jotted down the three names in his notebook. *None of these names match my dead boy.* Staring at the screen, he read each name again, hoping he had merely mistaken the missing name that he was sure would be on here.

"Do you recall where you were last Friday Evening? April 10."

"On Fridays I'm here until nine 0'clock. It's a good time to be open for last minute shoppers before weekend shows. Then I go to Coconut Joes."

"Would anyone have seen you there?"

"Yes. It's my usual stop. They know me. I meet some people there."

"And these people could also verify you were there."

"Yeah." The man leaned over the counter. The painted heart loomed toward Mahoney.

"What about last Wednesday morning? April 8."

The heart moved as the man spoke. "I go to the gym at six o'clock every morning. They know me there too. Jim's on fifth."

"Thank you." Mahoney snapped his notebook shut and turned to leave.

"I do have one of those cloaks left if you're interested," the boutique owner's rich voice crooned.

Mahoney's mind clicked. *Now, that might not be a bad idea.* "Sure, why not."

The boutique owner slipped into the back, returning moments later with the black cloak.

Mahoney fished his tattered wallet from his pocket, sliding his credit card across the glass counter.

"Thank you." The boutique owner rang up the charge in a flash. He handed a bright-red bag with golden letters over the counter. "Enjoy your purchase." His pink lips smiled slyly at Mahoney.

"Oh, I'm sure it will come in handy." *It will be the perfect way to determine if the cloak on my dead boy has been tarnished in any way. Maybe this guy left us something we missed.* Taking the bag, Mahoney slid a card toward the boutique owner. "Thank you for your time. If you think of anything else at all, please, give me a call." He turned toward the red door, silently bidding the eclectic boutique a farewell.

1700 War Room

Mahoney took a long swig of his dark roast. *Ugh. Cold.* He longed for a leisurely breakfast and his own mug. Thinking of his tiny apartment kitchen, he wondered how long it had been since his day off had been interrupted. *Wasn't that only a few days ago? Feels like a lifetime.*

He entered the tiny war room. He was expecting it to be hot and stuffy, and to smell like Sutton and Hayes. He was pleasantly surprised at the burst of fresh mountain air hitting his nostrils. His eye caught Dara at the front of the room, spraying a mist of fake freshness.

Mahoney smiled. "Nice touch. On top of your genius, you definitely add something unique and refreshing to a case."

Pausing, can of fake fresh air in one hand, a soft white rag in the other, she turned and smiled back. "Just trying to keep things pleasant."

"Well, it's much appreciated. There's nothing pleasant about this one. Takes me back in time. It's too bad our cozy little town had to grow so fast. Now we're facing this gruesome big city type of crime. Too bad my boys have to take on a case like this. It changes a man, you know?"

"I do. Sutton and Hayes are tough. They can handle it. And they have you to guide them with that trusty gut of yours. Not to mention your experience with this type of case." Their eyes met, speaking silently of cases of the past.

Sutton and Hayes burst into the room. Sutton carrying a Big Gulp and a paper bag drenched in grease. Hayes carried an oversized Styrofoam cup.

"Speak of the hooligans themselves," Mahoney said, throwing the jab their way, and a smirk to follow. "No grease for you, Hayes?"

"Protein shake. Champ's dinner."

"Wow. It smells nice in here," Sutton said.

"Yeah, like we're outside in the mountains," Hayes said.

"Compliments of your friendly neighbourhood crime analyst," Mahoney said, nodding at Dara.

"Thanks, Dara," Sutton said.

"Yeah, thanks!"

"My pleasure, boys."

Mahoney took his position at the front of the room in a flash. "Let's get rolling. Two bodies in less than forty-eight hours. It's a doozy, boys. It's been a long day, but we can still squeeze out a few more hours."

"Got it, boss," Hayes said, settling himself at the back of the room, sipping his shake. Sutton plunked himself down in a cheap plastic chair up at the front, chomping on his burger. Dara poised herself, ready to scribe.

"OK. Anything further from the scene at Eagle Woods, boys? Any new witnesses?"

Sutton replied, "Yeah. We interviewed around the neighbourhood. There's a little shopping area quite close to the park entrance. And actually, there are homes on the perimeter of the park. Gave us quite a pool to work with."

Hayes piped in. "Yeah. We scoured, went door to door, dug up a couple of good leads."

"There's one lady," Sutton said, "she lives up the hill from the pond at the south end of the park. Runs the trails daily, after work. She takes her dog with her. Anyways, she was running through the north end, where the body was found, last Friday. Said her dog freaked out in the bush. Seems like it may have been right where the body was. Says it's unusual for him, even though there's lots of wildlife around. But she just pegged it as being a rabbit or something. Weird thing is, she found this later, caught in his collar." Sutton placed a sealed plastic bag on the long centre table. Inside the bag was a small, torn sliver of red silk. "She didn't think anything of it at the time. Says that kids often play, or party, in some of the enclaves later at night. She just figured it was carnage from a late-night gathering. She had tossed it in the garbage. But when we talked to her, it struck her."

"Great work. Friday, you say? What timeframe are we talking here?"

Sutton flipped open his notepad. "Aaaah…here it is. She said she gets home from work at 5:30. She's on the trail by 5:45. She runs for a solid hour. Half an hour out, half an hour back. Since this would have occurred close to her turnaround point, it would have been about 6:15 p.m. Seems her routine is the same every day."

"Good. We can start a solid timeline on Eagle Woods." Mahoney walked over to the wall at the front of the room. Next to the map of the city marked with different coloured tacks was an oversized calendar. Two timelines were in the process of being created. One for each of the bodies. Mahoney picked up an orange marker for body number two at Eagle Woods, and added a note on the square representing Friday, April 10.

Time: 6:15 p.m.

Event: Witness' dog enters bush in vicinity of body

Evidence: Torn red silk fabric, found in dog's collar at witness' residence

Putting the marker down, Mahoney turned and said, "You boys got the standard photos when you retrieved the evidence from the witness?"

"Yeah, boss." Hayes retrieved a series of photos from a file folder. He stood up and pinned them along the cream-coloured wall, adding to the growing collage of the Eagle Woods scene.

"Nice work, boys. Let's get that piece to the crime lab. If we can match it to the robe, we've just added a strong piece to our timeline."

"There's something else," Hayes said. "We found a couple of teenagers who had apparently been conducting one of the late-night parties, as the runner described. Seems they usually go into the enclave where the body was found. It's close to the park entrance, so they're not deep into the woods. Less chance of a wildlife encounter. But it's also closed off, nice and private for their little parties. They were on their way in there last Saturday night, but they were scared off. Someone was already there."

"Did they give you a description?"

"Yeah. A bit." Flipping through his notebook, Hayes said, "They said a man, average height. Nothing really that distinctive about him, except he had long, dark hair, tied back in a ponytail. When they got to the entrance of their hideaway, it looked like he was bent over something. They said it was dark so they couldn't see what he was doing. He yelled at them. Spewed some weird shit. They thought he was high or something. So they got out of there, quick."

"Do they remember what he said?"

"Something about them intruding, trying to steal his doll. He seemed upset, so they couldn't totally make sense of what he said. It also spooked them good. They figured they shouldn't stick around."

"OK. Anything more on the description?"

"No. It was dark."

"Timeline?"

"They said it was about 9:10 p.m. They remembered because they had just finished watching a show at the one boy's house. Said it only takes about 10 minutes to walk over there."

"Great work, boys. Wouldn't hurt to do a second round tomorrow. If you dug up two witnesses today, you might dig up something else tomorrow." Mahoney walked up to the enlarged calendar and added more with the orange marker in the square for Saturday, April 11.

Time: 9:10 p.m.

Event: Witnesses, teenage boys, entering vicinity of body

Evidence: Potential sighting, average-height male, long dark ponytail

Stepping back, Mahoney eyeballed the calendar. "So, if the runner's dog did encounter the body, and the party kids did see our guy…" Pausing, he rubbed the back of his neck.

Sutton finished it off, saying, "Then our guy was visiting a dead body?"

Mahoney turned to face Sutton. "Yeah. What about the interviews with the people who knew our Eagle Woods boy?"

Hayes took the floor. "Nothing. Same as the first victim. Seems that he was a good kid. A good student. A reliable employee. Visited Mom and Dad regularly. But no one knew anything about his social life. Couldn't dig up any friends, girlfriends—nothing." Hayes scanned the open page of his notebook. "Wait. So far, he was last seen on Saturday, March 21."

"Two victims seem quite alike. But that doesn't help us." Mahoney turned, staring up at the large calendar. Rubbing the bristle on his chin, he shared his thoughts, "Or does it?" Stepping up to the calendar, he added more orange notations. "Boys, it seems both our victims went missing on a Saturday, two weeks apart. Our Frog Lake boy was last seen at a rock show. I wonder if our dive bar had a show going on the night of the disappearance of our Eagle Woods boy."

"We need to follow up." Sutton sipped his Big Gulp.

"I'll take that. I've already established rapport with the bartender."

"Yeah, you have." Hayes snickered.

Sutton elbowed Hayes. "What about you, boss? You were following up on the cloak. Anything?"

"I got through the list of clothing stores. Or, boutiques, rather. Got lucky on the last one. It's quite the place. I had a nice long chat with the owner. He was quite helpful." Mahoney flipped open his notebook to check his facts.

Sutton teased, "Oh, so you're good at charming the men too, hey? You're just too smooth."

Hayes chuckled loudly from his front seat. Dara giggled from the back of the room.

"OK, boys. Yeah, yeah. You know, getting people to talk is a skill. Dara knows, patience not pressure." Mahoney's voice returning to a stern tone, he scanned the open page of his notebook. "OK. Like I said, I got lucky on the last boutique. The owner said he carried the cloak, and he had sold three of them."

"There were three of those cloaks bought?" Sutton's eyebrow raised in surprise.

"In the last few months."

"Who wears these things?" Hayes inquired.

"Good question. The boutique owner was also dressed, well…his getup was just plain weird. He said he was a clothing designer. Guess that explains it."

"Weird? How, boss?"

"He had on tight black pants, like our Frog Lake boy. His shirt, well, it was more like a blouse. White. And ruffled. His cap, well, I don't know, it looked like a flashy police cap. His face was made-up. Kind of like both our dead boys. Except…well, he had a dark heart painted underneath one eye."

Sutton, meeting Mahoney's eyes with his own, took a sip from his Big Gulp.

Hayes shifted in his seat. "Strange. What was he doing the night of the Frog Lake murder?"

Mahoney responded. "His shop was open until nine o'clock. Then he went to his usual joint. I stopped by there. Seems to check out."

"What about the morning of the Eagle Woods murder?" Sutton asked.

"At the gym. Same routine every morning. He's there for two hours. Checked out."

"So the victims and the boutique dude all dress, or dressed, well, kind of like women?" Hayes concluded.

"Yeah. I asked about his clientele. Seems that the local live music scene digs the stuff he sells. Band members and kids going to the live shows come into his shop. Between this guy and our dive bar waitress, seems like the clothing may simply be an indication that they hung out in the rock scene."

"Maybe we should check out other joints in town. Any of you been to a rock concert lately?" Hayes laughed. "We can rule you out, Bug. Don't think those places play the ancient blues."

Mahoney shook his head. "Yeah, yeah. I get it. I'm an old man. And no, I have not been to a rock concert anytime lately."

Dara giggled from the back corner. Flashing back to serious mode, she drove them forward. "Bug, I can do a thorough search of the city for rock joints. With live shows."

"Get on that. And I'll follow up with the joint from the flyer. If the Frog Lake victim was seen there the night he disappeared, maybe the Eagle Woods boy was also seen." Mahoney backtracked the discussion. "Strange thing is, the boutique owner didn't recognize our dead boy, even though the kid was found in the cloak. But, he did have a record of sales. Dara, were you able to get anything on the names I gave you?"

"Yes. Same thing that happened with the name from the gem shop happened with one of the names you gave me."

"You mean a dud?"

"Yeah. Two of the names checked out just fine. The third name doesn't belong to anybody living in this city. I extended the search area, and nothing. I did the same for the dud name from the gem shop as well, but it came up empty. I'll extend the search even wider."

"Do what you can. He could be using fake names." He said, "Boys, follow up on the two names that came up." Reaching into his brown briefcase, he pulled out a bag. "There was one cloak left at the shop." Pulling the shiny black cloak from the bag, he held it up in a glorious display. "It's a stretch, but maybe a comparison with the one on our Frog Lake boy will turn something up."

Sutton raised an eyebrow. "When this is over, you could finally upgrade your tweed."

Mahoney shot him a glare. He probed his brain for the next direction. "Dara, anything on those messages yet? Did the second one lend any insight?"

"Without any context for the messages, no. Bug, the messages seem so abstract. I'll keep at it."

"Alright. Let's review our timeline." Mahoney moved over to the dates and notes scribbled across the whiteboard. "Saturday, March 21, Eagle Woods boy last seen. Saturday, April 4, Frog Lake boy last seen. Eagle Woods boy dies around sunrise on Wednesday, April 8. Frog Lake boy dies around sun down on Friday, April 10. Dark pony tail man seen at Eagle Woods scene at 9:10 pm on Saturday, April 11."

"So, he had them both locked away at the same time? Double torture." Sutton said.

"Eagle Woods boy dies Wednesday morning. Then this guy with the ponytail is seen on Saturday night at the scene. But the runner's dog caught the red fibre in his collar on Friday." Hayes said.

"Seems he dumped the body, then went back to visit." Mahoney shook his head.

Sutton continued. "Then Frog Lake boy dies Friday night. He's dumping two bodies in a matter of days. Busy guy."

"They were both last seen at Saturday night rock shows. That could be a pattern. Take a new victim every two weeks. But, there's no clear pattern for the times of death." Hayes said.

"So he could be taking a fresh victim this Saturday." Mahoney rubbed the bristle on his chin. "And, he ordered the gem the same night he took the Eagle Woods boy. But, the gem was found on the Frog Lake victim."

Sutton whistled. "A lot of planning."

"OK, boys. Let's recap, then let's move. We may be able to squeeze in a few more tasks before getting a bit of rest." He stood tall, looking each at each of them in turn. "Look, team. I think we can all agree that this one isn't like the others. This is messed up. It's a different kind of crazy than we're used to seeing. We're gonna need all the puzzle piece collection skills we've got."

"Yeah, boss. Agreed." Sutton sipped his sweet pop.

"We may also need other types of manpower. We need to consider additional approaches here. This is unchartered territory for our unit. For our city."

"What're you getting at, boss?"

"I'm going to do some…additional research, let's say. A little side trip. I need you guys to be on top of things for the next 24 hours. You can always reach me." He pointed to his cell phone. "You know the drill. Follow our usual routine."

Sutton looked at him uncomfortably. Hayes shifted in his seat. They both looked Mahoney square in the eye. Sutton took a sip of Big Gulp.

"Boys, you got this. Focus on the investigation. Continue to scour Eagle Woods. Check out the names from the clothing boutique. Follow up on anything Dara comes up with. I'm gonna be on you as always. Trust me. I know I'm reaching a bit here, but the calendar indicates this guy could be in a pattern of taking a victim every two weeks. If that's the case, we have a bit of a time buffer here. If it's not, well, it's a risk I need to take to ramp up our investigation."

Sutton leaned forward in his chair, matching Hayes' stance.

"We are grasping for real results here, boys. We are driving out as many paths as we can, but nothing concrete is materializing. My research will be a boost. Help us on our hunt."

Sutton sat back in his chair. Hayes nodded. Dara looked up from her scribe duties. Slipping her glasses down her nose, she released them to hang from their sparkly string of beads. Looking Bug in the eye, she gave him a firm nod.

"OK, boss," Sutton confirmed. Hayes nodded his agreement.

Sutton and Hayes swiftly made their exit. Dara hung at the back of the room, gathering her things.

Mahoney approached the crime wall again. *A case like this, we need help. This killer, he's different. Either we get some expertise in here or we're gonna spiral down that dark vortex. I won't go down that path again.*

Marine Life

Mahoney leaned in over Dara, peering at her computer screen.

"OK, Bug, give me a moment here." Dara pressed her petite fingers along her black glasses, securing them against the bridge of her nose.

Her fingers typing at an incredible speed, a line of cryptic code words appeared on the screen. She hit the enter button. Sitting back in her chair, she plucked up her cup of tea.

Mahoney eyeballed her tea set perched on the corner of her desk. *She never did like the crusty chipped mugs around here.*

The search halting on her computer screen, Dara placed her teacup back onto the floral saucer. "We've got something, Bug."

Looking at the screen, Mahoney narrowed his eyes. Trying to make sense of the gibberish, he shook his head.

Dara smiled. "Bug, don't worry yourself. The language for conducting searches is very primitive. It's not intuitive at all. The poison that was in the victim's bloodstream was primarily composed of strata-octin. As Blackwood indicated, this substance comes from a variety of marine animals. You know what else was found in the bloodstream? Taurine. When I add this into the search, the source of our poison is narrowed down to the blue-ringed octopus."

"OK, but where the hell does one find a blue-ringed octopus in this city?"

"Well, my search actually turned something up. Turns out there are a handful of aquarium shops that carry specialty marine life. One of them carries our octopus."

"That's surprising. But are we saying our guy bought an octopus and extracted the poison himself?"

"The venom is excreted through the salivary glands. It would be a difficult process to manually extract."

"Jeez. So, dead end?"

"No. There's more, Bug. I also ran an additional search to focus on applications of this toxic combo. Turns out our octopus can help with migraines, other types of severe pain, and drug withdrawal."

"Can we determine where these treatments are available?" Looking back at the screen, he strained his brain to figure out how she got so much from the mess of bright-green lines streaming their way down the black background.

"I was able to retrieve a list of medical facilities that treat migraines. I was also able to determine where the drug addiction facilities are in the city. But it's unclear as to whether any of these facilities use our substance."

"How many of these places are there?"

"I was able to find about two dozen. I'll call them. Find out if this special little octopus is being put to use." She picked up her flowered teacup, sipping delicately from the brim.

"Thanks, Dara."

"Hey, Bug. You know, the blue-ringed octopus is a resilient creature. But even this exotic life form requires a healthy dose of crab and shrimp to live."

"And?"

"Just like detectives, the blue-ringed octopus needs sustenance and rest. When's the last time you ate?"

"Breakfast to go, this morning."

"Pegs was kind enough to order you a sandwich. Please grab it from her on the way out."

His shoulders relaxed. "Thanks, Dara."

"You're welcome."

Mahoney grabbed his tweed coat from the back of his chair and strode down the hallway.

Eat and Run

Mahoney walked through the door of the Stepping Stone Pub. A shiver ran through him as the warm air met his cold body.

"Hey, boss! Good to see ya." Simon called from across the room, his face consumed by a wide smile.

Mahoney's shoulders dropped a couple of notches as the tension holding them up disintegrated. The bright, cheerful, crowded space was exactly what he needed to distract his thoughts. He also knew there wasn't a single item worth considering in his fridge. He needed some sort of fuel before heading into the next leg of his journey. Glancing at his watch, he only had a few hours. Walking up to the bar, he stood by his usual spot.

Simon provided a much welcome pre-emption to him having to think or take any sort of action. "The usual? Will you dine with us tonight?"

"I will."

Removing his tweed coat and derby, he placed them on the bar and sat down.

Simon slid a bubbly beverage his way. *Man, a bourbon would taste really good right about now.* He sighed, accepting his reality. *You can't always get what you want.* He smirked to himself, then took a sip. *You need to keep a clear head, Bug.*

The room was buzzing with energy, filled with chattering voices, and hot with body heat. Mahoney relished in the noise, the commotion, being able to hide in his spot, unnoticed. He loved the energy, the feeling of being around people who were going about their normal lives.

Simon returned behind the counter. "Geez, boss. It's busy in here tonight. Man, you look whipped. That case beating you up?"

"This is a tough one."

"Really? I would have thought you've seen everything by now. What, with your twenty-year mark just around the corner."

Mahoney looked at Simon, smiling at him. "Well, truth is, I've only seen something like this once. And it wasn't here."

Simon whistled. "Wow. Must be a real whopper of a case then. No clues?"

Mahoney paused, his mind scanning the press release from earlier that day. "We just a got a second body. Looks like the same guy."

"Really?" Simon's eyes grew wide. "You mean a *serial* killer, right here, in our city? No way."

"Well, it *could* be. But a murder case isn't declared serial until there are three victims."

Simon turned, responding to a call from the kitchen. He returned a moment later with Mahoney's dinner.

"I'll leave you to eat. You need to look after yourself." Simon smiled, then turned to tend to the restless crowd lined along the bar.

Mahoney stared at bubbling cheese-covered pizza. *I need to eat this, then get out of here.* He knew he needed to kick himself into gear before he relaxed too much and the exhaustion took over. The greasy dough hit his stomach like a welcome hug. His mind cleared as he lost himself in soothing replenishment. The noise of the chattering crowd drowning away to a soft hum, he emptied his glass.

"Another one?" Simon appeared out of nowhere, his voice piercing through the invisible bubble that Mahoney had erected over his mind.

"No. I have to run. Thank you, Simon."

"Eat and run? You're still on the clock, then. No rest for you tonight?"

"No."

"I guess I'll be seeing you again tomorrow night, then."

"Not likely. I'm taking a quick trip. Research, for the case."

"Really?" Simon leaned against the back of the bar, his eyebrow cocking. "In the middle of this case?"

"It'll beef up our techniques."

"Oh man. You're adding new investigative strategies? You'll need to give me a lesson."

Mahoney reached for his wallet. "Sure, Simon. When things settle down." He quickly paid the bill, tipped his hat, and made a swift exit.

FLYING MISSION

Glam Demon

The screeching vocals of a rising rock god exploded through the small room. Seth violently banged his head to the beat, long hair flailing wildly, fist pumping through the air. As the singer's voice dramatically drew back, slowly losing volume, a deep riff reverberated through the jammed space. The guitarist—clad in tight leather, sinewy bracelets weaving their way up both his arms, grey metal skull rings covering his fingers—scanned the mob with savage eyes. Adrenaline shot through every vein in Seth's body. His mind buzzed with the electric energy engulfing the entire room. Small venue. Standing room only. Cheap cover charges. Local talent, on the rise, in the hopes of becoming the next glam demons. This was a rare era where even his second-rate hometown was swamped with a slew of high-calibre shows.

Seth closed his eyes. His nerves twitching in anticipation. His senses yearning to be filled. The live event was better than any other form of consumption to feed his addiction. Vicariously living through his idols as they transformed into their ultimate selves in front of thousands of people. The one place where he didn't have to suppress who he truly was in order to survive.

The leader of the pack dropped to his knees, back arched, as he moaned into the microphone. The overhead lights glimmered off his sequinned belt. Glossy black leather plastered to his muscular legs revealing every curve, heightening his masculinity. Silver bangles slid up and down his arm, mimicking his manic movements.

Seth fixated on the lavish lord. His mind began erasing the manic mass packed in tightly around him. One by one, the crazy fans vanished as his mind projected his alternate reality, the space opening up around him as he became the sole audience member.

Dramatically rotating his arm in full circles, the guitarist strummed the electrified strings with aggression. His legs rooted into the stage in a half squat, his fingers ground the final repetition of the guttural riff. The lead singer slithered his sinewy body toward the front of the stage, seething with sexuality. Gyrating against the tall metal rod, he took it in one last embrace. His final wails filled the room to the point of bursting, his mouth stretching so wide it threatened to devour the metal bulb. The insanity of the crowd grew, the energy in the room building toward a climax.

Seth joined right in, screaming his heart out, pushing the limits of his lungs. The voice of the rock god simmered through Seth's veins, euphoria shooting through every inch of his body. His eyes turned glassy, his senses mesmerized by the scene emanating from the stage.

The room began to quiet. The barbaric vibe clung silently to the hot, muggy air, mixing itself with the stench of sweat and booze. Seth made his way over to the bar. One last libation for the road. Approaching the sticky countertop, he secured eye contact with his favourite server. She had his poison poured before he could speak. She was a spicy little thing. Short, voluptuous, and not afraid of using what she was gifted with to increase her revenue. Hoisted up in a leather corset, tightened to the pre-suffocation point, she made her way over to Seth in a flash.

"Here you go, sweetie," she crooned, sliding the shooter his way.

Passing her a bill much too large for the cost of the potent liquid in the tiny glass, he turned before she could protest.

He emptied the drink in one quick shot, soothing the fire raging in his throat from screaming it raw. Glancing at the restless crowd, he knew it was time for his departure. He sprinted to the black door in the back corner and slipped into the cold night.

Tainted Badge

D *ammit. I need this to move. Now.* Mahoney could see a vision, crystal clear, of what he knew deep down in his gut would happen. He'd seen it before. Pink boots and blonde curls swirled through his head. White ghost faces staring him down, their bodies stacking themselves, reaching higher and higher. He trusted the old-school methods that he had committed 19 years of his life to. They worked. But not for a case like this. The hunter he was chasing down had changed all the rules. His victims weren't someone he had known for years. Someone who had driven him crazy with a mile-high stack of expectations that wouldn't stop growing. Someone who had chipped away at him, piece by piece, until he was driven into an emotional space. One who took him outside of reality and morphed his being into a one-time killing machine. A new persona that he would snap out of the instant his fresh kill stopped breathing.

No. This hunter was a new breed. *My sweet little hometown has never seen something like this. I need to save them from the darkness, the gore, the grief of a bunch of dead bodies. I need to spare them from being afraid to walk down the quiet streets they grew up on. I owe this town that much.* Beads of sweat sprung across his forehead. Pulling his navy-blue handkerchief from his shirt pocket, he swiped it across the moisture. The one time he had seen a case like this, he had stuck to the old-school methods he was trained on. He resisted going against the grain. He did as he was expected to do. That time the killer ran free. The case was as cold as ice.

A glimmer of gold flashing through his mind, he pictured the badge that would be pinned to his lapel a few short months from today. His mind charged ahead in time, down two simultaneous paths. One lead to a mound of brutally beaten bodies left for dead by an unidentified hunter hiding in the shadows. The other led to families untouched by grief and a man behind bars. Staring far down each of the two roads, his brain refused to budge from the path it wanted to take. His gut was telling him what to do.

I need to turn these tidbits into a real trail. Something concrete. A timeline, but only a dud name, and two others with strong alibis. Mahoney pictured Sutton and Hayes digging for clues and Dara typing away furiously on her keyboard. If there was anything to turn up, he knew they would find it. *And we have a time window here. If I'm gonna do this, it has to be now.*

He grabbed his black duffel from the bottom of his disastrous bedroom closet. Tossing a single change of clothes into the bag, he zipped it shut. Slinging the strap over his shoulder, he sauntered to the main room. He poured himself a shot of bourbon. No ice. Shooting it back, he enjoyed the sting in his throat and the slight numbing that followed. He took one look around his empty, lonely apartment, then slipped through the door, shutting it hard behind him.

Cherry Bomb

"**D**etective Mahoney?" a crisp, clear voice welcomed him, its home a tall man in a suit pressed to perfection. Nodding his acknowledgement, Mahoney stood up from the plush leather of the couch in the waiting area.

"I'm Agent Williams, department head. We spoke on the phone." His smile was sincere, matching the professionalism of both his voice and his attire.

Grabbing his beat-up brown briefcase, Mahoney extended his arm in return. "A pleasure, Agent Williams. Thank you for meeting with me on such short notice."

"I assure you, the pleasure is all mine. You're on the type of investigation that my team is well versed in. I believe this will quickly become apparent. Please, join me in my office." Agent Williams turned a shiny polished black shoe toward a brightly lit hallway.

Mahoney fell in step directly behind. Noting what a tremendous amount of natural light made its way into the office space, he mentally compared it to the dimly lit hallways of the homicide quarters back home.

Agent Williams broke Mahoney's thoughts. "I hope you don't mind, I took the liberty of inviting one of my agents to join us. This agent is, well, a bit of a…firecracker. She does tend to rattle others sometimes. But she has a solid background in the FBI, and a doctorate in psychology. She was a critical piece in creating our department, and fundamental to the development of criminal profiling. Our methodologies are strongly based on extensive research that she has conducted, some of it single-handedly. Her style can make some people, um, rather uncomfortable. But I assure you, her presence will elevate the value of your visit."

He had been shocked to have secured a last-minute meeting with Agent Williams thanks to Blackwood. The faces of some of the worst serial killers known flashed through his mind, remnants of files he had read on the interviews that had been conducted with them. *I wonder what it would be like to stare one these hunters down, look him in the eye? Face to face?* Mahoney's mind wandered down an inquiring path.

Agent Williams slowed, opening a door into an office bursting with sunshine and offering an incredible view of the city. Mahoney almost chuckled as he thought of how impossible it would be for his own minuscule homicide unit to even dream of these digs.

"Please, make yourself comfortable." Agent Williams motioned toward a set of plush leather chairs circling a glass coffee table. Before they could settle themselves, a woman, petite in both height and breadth, slid through the doorway. Her black pantsuit was skin tight, her fire hair slicked back in a low ponytail. The white ruffles of her blouse escaped through the ends of each black sleeve, framing her small hands. Rhinestones sparkled off her arm, catching the sunlight pouring in from the window.

"Detective Mahoney," her red lips stated. "I'm Agent Quesnel." Pumping out a powerful shake, her tiny hand was lost in his.

Agent Williams said, "I've ordered some coffee service. I'm sure you need something after your travels. Am I correct that you are heading back later today?"

Mahoney shifted in his seat, eager to get on with the proceedings. "Yes. I'm taking a late flight back. With our current case, it was barely possible for me to be away for twenty-four hours."

Placing three crystal glasses on the coffee table with a clink, Agent Quesnel poured each of them a shot of bourbon. Shooting a sharp glance at Agent Williams, she slid a crystal glass toward Mahoney.

"I can't express my gratitude enough. To both of you," Mahoney reinforced.

Agent Williams responded, "Well, as I expressed earlier, the gratitude is mutual. We don't get many law enforcement agencies seeking us out. Criminal profiling is, well, a fresh take on things. Adoption of new methods by organizations that have been executing the same processes for decades does not come easy. Methods based on analyzing behaviour are often viewed as nothing more than, well, hocus pocus."

"I understand," Mahoney promptly supported. "I've been questioning my own mental state. But, the case we're on, well…it reminds me of a case I helped out with years ago. I think it needs a different approach."

"What can you tell us?" Agent Quesnel said.

"Two bodies were found in a matter of forty-eight hours. They have extreme similarities. The crime scenes weren't typical. The level of brutality is…incomprehensible."

"Did you bring files?" Agent Quesnel, taking a sip of bourbon, met Mahoney's gaze.

Grabbing his tattered briefcase, Mahoney produced two folders. Pulling out several photos, he laid them in a series on the table, attempting to recreate the crime scenes.

Agent Quesnel scanned the photos eagerly. Showing no hesitation, she was forthright with her analysis. "These two scenes are definitely linked. The neck ligatures are a dead giveaway. It's his signature. Was the strangulation the COD?"

"No. The medical examination revealed that both victims were strangled repeatedly. But it didn't cause death in either case."

Agent Williams shook his head. Without flinching, Agent Quesnel continued her unfiltered analysis. "Hedonistic sexual offenders have on average 4.8 paraphilias. Erotic asphyxiation is quite common. He's probably getting off on it."

A shudder rippled through Mahoney's internals. "The autopsies pointed to internal bleeding as COD for both victims. There were traces of substances in both bloodstreams. The killer immobilized them while leaving them aware of the torture they were being put through."

Agent Quesnel stared at a photo in her hand. "He was serious enough to cut his message into the second victim. What he's saying is really important to him. It's symbolic. It might be part of his fantasy. There wasn't any message left on the Eagle Woods body?" she inquired, flipping through the photos.

"He wrote it on paper. With the victim's blood." Flipping through a folder, Mahoney handed over an additional photo.

Reading the message aloud, she drew out each word, "Dude Look Like a Fairy." Leaning back into the black leather, she pondered the message. "Do you have any leads on the meaning of these messages? Or links between them?"

"Not yet. It's a tricky piece."

The door opened a crack, and a face peered in. Agent Williams responded, "We won't be needing the coffee after all. Sorry." The face disappeared and the door shut.

Assaulting him with her next question, Agent Quesnel looked straight into Mahony's eyes. "You've been on the second body for nearly two days now?"

Not backing down, he returned her stare. "Bingo."

Keeping her glare for a moment longer, the room was silent. Looking back at the photos, she released him from her interrogation. "Using the victim's blood keeps it personal. Cutting it into the body elevates the closeness with his victim even more."

Shaking off the tension, Mahoney refocused his mind on the details of the case. He provided more fuel for the analysis unfolding before him. "There's more. A lot more. The hair of the Frog Lake victim was washed and permed, after the murder."

Agent Quesnel launched another wave of analysis. "Post mortem ritual. That belongs to the big guns. The second body found was actually the first victim?"

Mahoney nodded.

"Looks like your killer is progressing. Fast. He likely has a lot more practice than we know about."

Mahoney's neck tingled. He didn't even want to think about unfound victims. The road ahead would be hard enough to stay on top of new ones, never mind processing the ones already stacking up. Rubbing the bristle on his chin, his forehead furrowed.

Agent Williams joined the conversation again, attempting to ease the wave of worry that washed over Mahoney's face. "We understand the stresses of dealing with heavy caseloads. You and your team must already have a lot to process. But, as Agent Quesnel is pointing out here, these kinds of cases tend to see many victims before the killer is found."

Mahoney cleared his throat, forcing the worry from his face. "I'd like to increase our chances of stopping this guy before it gets out of hand."

Agent Quesnel piped in eagerly, "Green River, committed for forty-nine accounts of murder. Bundy, suspected of at least thirty accounts. The Hitchhiker Killer, he was suspected for ninety accounts. These guys rack up a good body count fine-tuning their modus operandi. They practice their preparation, evolve their method of execution, they hone their post mortem ritual."

Forcing his mind to remain clear, Mahoney absorbed the disturbing numbers. Comforted by the fact that the shock value alone of these real-life cases could perhaps be enough to sway his audience back home, he avoided letting the gruesome facts get to him. "You think the post mortem activities are part of some sort of ritual?"

"Your guy may be really hung up on a script. He may be extremely compelled to follow it strictly, especially during the murder, and for the activities that he performs on the dead bodies. Did you check for any signs of rape or penetration?"

"It seemed unnecessary as both victims were male. But, Blackwood ran standard kits." Shifting in his seat, sweat escaped from the pores of his forehead.

"Look, if you want to catch your killer, you can't be hung up on *old-school* ideals. The killer may or may not be male. Either way, sexual acts may have been performed. Penetration may have occurred. Objects may have been used. The type of fantasy that drives someone like this may be sexually driven. The point is, a closed mind will not lend itself to the opportunity of finding a path to the answers." She glared directly into his eyes.

"Blackwood told me I could trust you. I came to you for advice, not for an attack on my department." Mahoney's face flushed with red. He'd been pushed to his limit.

Agent Williams took charge, his voice growing stern for the first time during the meeting. "Agent Quesnel, why don't you take a moment here?" Looking her in the eyes, he forced her to step back. "We are all here for the same good intentions. We need to work together if this meeting is to be productive. We all have strong convictions. Sometimes those convictions fire us up a little. But we can use this to motivate us in the right direction here."

Agent Quesnel shot back the bourbon in her glass. She walked over to the liquor tray, exhaling loudly. After pouring a slosh of bourbon, she spun one shiny black heel to face Mahoney. Sliding back into the leather chair, her gaze dropped.

The tension in her voice had vanished. "I've been face to face with these killers. This guy won't stop. He can't."

As she raised her gaze again, Mahoney's stare met hers. "That's exactly what my gut has been telling me. That's why I'm here."

Agent Williams said, "Detective Mahoney. If it would serve your team, I could lend you Agent Quesnel here. I am sure she would be delighted to join in your investigation, as per your guidance."

Agent Quesnel shot back the remaining bourbon in the crystal glass perched in her hand. Placing the glass on the table with a click, she met Mahoney's gaze. "Yes. I would be. Absolutely delighted." Her voice was tinged with sarcasm. But as she glanced back across the photos on the glass table, Mahoney caught a glimpse of sincere interest in her eyes.

Mahoney stood. "Agent Williams, thank you. Agent Quesnel, it's been a pleasure. Please make the necessary arrangement. Time is ticking away."

I Love My MTV

Seth plunked himself down at the bar, directly in line with one of the TVs. Sasha slid her way over to him. *A sign of a good bartender,* he observed.

"Hey, sweetie. What can I getcha?"

Not letting his gaze wander, he looked her right in the eye. "Good ol' Night Train. Plus one of my usual stress relievers." He loved her no hassle, no invasion of privacy service. She always got his order served up quick. She wasn't just eye candy.

Sliding a tall glass and a shot across the black counter, she leaned toward him. "You want it switched to your MTV?" She rolled her eyes up at the boob tube.

"Thanks, Sasha."

Taking a long swig of sweet liquid, he gazed up as the channel switched. Not having a television in his room at home, he was a regular at *LiveWire*, even when there wasn't a show going on. Not many people in here in the middle of the day, he appreciated the quiet, and constant streaming of videos. Taking in his rock gods visually was definitely better than just listening. He could absorb the more visual aspects of their art, their personalities. The flowing attire, extreme makeup, and glittery jewellery captivated him. MTV had opened up a whole new world for Seth. It was a portal into the minds of the musicians he idolized. It enabled him to see the artist's interpretation of their own lyrics, to absorb the message intended by those who had created it. Here, in this rocker bar where he could escape everything in his life that caged and wounded him, he felt safe. It was the closest thing to a home that he could identify with.

Looking up at the screen above him, he watched a wild man with a tiger's mane crawling on his knees across a stage. Back arched, barbaric chest exposed, the wild man screeched into the microphone, asking Seth if he knew where he was.

Chugging back the Night Train, he nodded at Sasha for another round. *I wonder where my friend is?* Scanning the bar, he looked for the familiar face. The guy wasn't actually his friend, but Seth had seen him several times, chilling out alone. He hadn't mustered enough courage to talk to the guy, but he thought he looked like someone that maybe he could get along with. The guy reminded him of himself a little. He didn't often like to talk to people, but right now he felt like he might actually be able to battle his nerves and chat.

He grasped the shot glass she had delivered to him between his thumb and pointer finger. Shooting the clear liquid to the back of his throat, he relished in the slight burning sensation. Experiencing a slight numbing, he smiled to himself. Taking a long swig of the potent white wine that had also appeared, he settled himself against the back of the chair. Looking back up at the boob tube, he watched the crazed rock star stare him down, sliding toward him, threatening to come out of the screen and watch him bleed.

Systematic

All heads turned. All eyes stared. Dressed sleekly in black, Agent Quesnel stepped a shiny platinum boot through the door. Stealthily sliding into the stifling hot room, her fire hair caught a glint off the fluorescent lights.

Detective Mahoney cleared his throat loudly. "Everyone, meet Agent Quesnel. She is joining us from FBI headquarters in Quantico. Agent Quesnel is part of the criminal profiling unit." Mahoney paused, providing some space for the new direction he was forcing the case into. No one moved. Mahoney eyeballed Sutton and Hayes. They promptly stood from their plastic chairs.

"Agent Quesnel. Pleased to meet you. I'm Detective Sutton, this is my partner Detective Hayes."

"Nice to meet you, agent." Dara stood from her corner perch, the sweetness in her voice dissolving some of the stiffness in the air. The two petite women locked eyes as they exchanged a firm shake.

The war room was always stuffy, but it suddenly felt like a small sauna in overdrive. Mahoney sliced through the silence, leading his pack forward. "For the benefit of Agent Quesnel, let's run through this from the beginning. Don't think I am unaware of the thoughts on criminal profiling around here. It's fresh out of the gate. It's not tried and tested like our old methods." His tone was strict. He made eye contact with each of them in turn. "The fact is, this case is unlike any this city has ever seen. We haven't dealt with *serial* murder before. We would be completely ignorant to believe that the methods for catching the typical killer are the only ones to consider here. Any questions?"

Agent Quesnel coolly slid onto the seat of the plastic chair next to Hayes. Crossing her legs, the fluorescent lighting gleamed off her shiny platinum boot.

Mahoney cleared his throat, grabbing his Styrofoam cup. After a quick refresh of his parched throat, he walked over to the evidence from the first scene. "First crime scene. The physical evidence includes clothing and jewellery. Chemical analysis on the hair revealed that the killer washed and administered a perm. He also washed the face and applied a substantial amount of makeup. This was all done post mortem." Moving along the table to the collection of items from Eagle Woods, he continued, "Second crime scene. The physical evidence is very similar to that of the first scene. Clothing and jewellery. Totally different outfit. The hair was not washed or groomed in any way. There was makeup applied, but the face was not washed. Both hair and face were riddled with mud and blood. Time of death was prior to that of the first victim," Mahoney concluded his first two efficient summaries. Taking a swig of coffee, he charged on. "Both victims were injected with toxic substances, one of which caused immobility, but did not cause death. Both victims died from internal bleeding. They were beat to death."

Agent Quesnel shifted toward the edge of the seat, expression intently focused on Mahoney. Sutton took a sip of his Big Gulp. Hayes leaned back in his chair.

Agent Quesnel showed no hesitation in adding her own layer to the story. "Makeup post mortem in both cases. Washing and hair styling comes into play in the second victim. Sounds like we have a strong element of ritualism here."

"Ritualism?" Hayes piped in keenly.

"Yes. It is common for a serial killer to follow a ritual. Essentially, a script. He likely has a deep need to stick strictly to each step, without deviation, to feel the satisfaction he craves from the act of murder." Oblivious to any discomfort caused by the dark layer she settled onto the investigation, she delved forth. "There's also a clear element of progression here. The first victim wasn't washed, and his hair wasn't styled. The second victim had both his hair and his face washed, as well as a full perm. That's a lot of attention to pay to a corpse. The killer clearly progressed the extent of his post mortem ritual, significantly and quickly."

She reminded Mahoney of Blackwood. Technical. Concise. Instead of medical facts about dead bodies, her expertise was the behaviour of the evilest men walking the earth.

Mahoney scanned Sutton and Hayes. Both sitting back in their chairs, Sutton staring at the red straw lingering near his lips, Hayes focused on his notebook. *What are they thinking? Are they closing their minds to this?* He wished he could look right into each of their brains to uncover their thoughts. *We can't afford to waste time here. We all need to get onboard with each other. Fast.* He wiped his forehead with his kerchief, then placed it back into its corduroy-pocket home.

Sutton broke the silence. "Progression? It seemed our guy was rushed, maybe interrupted."

Agent Quesnel responded, "That could be. But to pull off the complexity involved in these scenes, without leaving a physical trace, takes a lot of organization. It is possible the first victim was simply a practice round." Standing up, she walked over to the cream-coloured crime scene wall, driving them further into her world with her detailed analysis. "As I described, this killer is likely following a script. He is executing a set of steps that he must stick to when executing his murders."

"Why?" Sutton said. "To cover up evidence?"

"Partially, yes. But not completely. The main purpose of a script is to achieve the maximum amount of satisfaction possible."

Sutton shook his head. "What? That is messed up. So, you're saying he's getting pleasure out of this? Like, getting off on it?"

"Yes. I am. The more he perfects his execution, the more he *gets off* on the act. So to speak." Her lips contorted into a slick smile.

Sutton and Hayes stared blankly. Dara looked intrigued. It was pretty much what he had expected. The first time someone is exposed to this, it's shocking. No matter how many years they've been on the force, and no matter what role they have played.

Mahoney nodded at Agent Quesnel, motioning her to continue.

"Guys like this, they have such strong and uncomfortable feelings that only dissolve when they kill. They have such an innate desire to execute these acts that they simply *have* to do it. They must act on their compulsions to find relief."

"What?" Sutton sat up in his chair, staring her down. "You're saying he *has* to kill. Nobody *has* to kill. It's a choice to take another person's life." Face flushing with heat, Sutton paused.

Hayes said, "I agree. What you're saying is screwed up. It's like justification for what this guy has done. Just look at those photos. What he did to these victims, it's sick. It's wrong."

"But we can't deny that acts of this calibre are driven by something much more intense, much more complex, than your typical murder."

Sutton stared Mahoney down. "Look, boss, we're on a ticking clock here. We don't have time to consider this guy's *feelings*. Don't we need to focus on the facts and get moving?"

Mahoney stared back at Sutton. *He's worried about his perfect record as a detective. He wants to be leading his own cases in a few years. But I've seen this type of killer. He hasn't.*

Agent Quesnel crossed her arms. Shaking her head, she took a seat, glaring at Mahoney.

Hayes dug the knife deeper. "I'll be honest. I don't give a flying fuck how our guy feels. He deserves to rot in hell. I just want to find the bastard."

Mahoney looked at Hayes. *Best partner a detective could ask for. Always backing Sutton up.*

Agent Quesnel stood up and walked over to Mahoney. Standing on her tiptoes, she glared into his eyes, her face a mere inch from his. "Listen, Mahoney, you're wasting my time here. I thought you wanted my help. Your guys don't get it. This is useless."

She's a fireball. But she's right. Mahoney spun on his heel and took his place at the head of the room. "OK. Everyone, pipe down. Sutton, back off. Hayes, put a lid on it. Agent Quesnel, please take a seat. All of you, hear me out."

Finding Dara's gaze, he willed the tension to dissolve from his body. "We are all on the same team here. We are all on a tight timeline. We all want the same thing out of this. I get it, the purpose of bringing you all together doesn't simply spell itself out on the wall." He scanned the room, making a moment of eye contact with each of his team members, new and old. "You all know me. Agent Quesnel, we don't know each other yet, but I believe I expressed my intentions quite clearly by flying halfway across the continent to meet with you in the middle of this ridiculous case. Now, work with me."

Sutton's face relaxed. He eased his back against the cheap plastic of his chair and nodded his head. Hayes took a breath deep enough to resonate through the room. He shot Mahoney a look of acknowledgement. Agent Quesnel uncrossed her arms and settled herself back into the chair next to Hayes.

"Sutton, Hayes. I understand what you're saying. We do have to get moving. We also have to make a sincere and educated attempt at moving down the right path. If we charge forth on a dead end, we will only end up wasting more time, and risk never finding this guy. You may or may not be aware of the case I worked on in '73 out in Toronto. We don't have time to get into the details. A lot of little girls are dead, and we never solved the case. In my entire 19 years, it is the closest thing I've seen to what we're dealing with now. You can't deny this situation is messed up." A pink boot treading through his mind, a blonde curl floating along with it, he shot his gaze to the back of the room. Dara returned his stare, smiling softly, encouraging him along.

Sutton and Hayes nodded in unison. Sutton spoke for both of them, "Got it, boss."

"Agent Quesnel, please proceed." Mahoney motioned for her to take his place at the head of the room. Stepping aside, he leaned against the wall across from the crime scene collage.

Without a second of hesitation, she picked up right where she had left off. "Let me introduce you to the concept of *fantasy*. We all have fantasies, of some shape and form. Things we dream of. Things we deeply desire. This dream, this fantasy, it is very personal, individual, unique. What I fantasize about is unlikely to be the same thing that you fantasize about." She landed her gaze on Hayes. "Would you agree?"

Hayes smiled sheepishly. "Well, yeah, I do think that what I fantasize about is not what you fantasize about." His eyes bolted to the ground.

Agent Quesnel removed her focus from Hayes. "The difference between the fantasies that most people have and the fantasy that our killer has is that he has one fantasy that is so intense it takes over his life. His actions become more and more focused on playing out this fantasy, over and over, until it is perfect. Everything he does becomes part of living it out. It will impact his ability to be a normal, functioning part of society."

Sitting up in his seat, Hayes looked her in the eyes. "That's fucked up."

"Yes, it is."

"So, you're saying that this guy, our killer, his whole life becomes a series of murders." Hayes narrowed his eyes.

"Yes, I am."

Sutton's shoulders relaxing, his face took on a quizzical look. "Huh. That actually makes sense. I mean, look at how much effort our guy put into each of his victims."

Nodding, Agent Quesnel latched on to the comment. "So, his whole life becomes about living out this fantasy. Looking at the crime scenes here, we can't deny that this guy has some strange, complex vision that he is trying to create. The steps he goes through—his script—are quickly evolving. For example, with the first body, he didn't wash the hair or the face. He simply dove into making up his victim. The hair and face of the second body were washed first, then the makeup and hairdo were done. He was perfecting his routine. Coming closer to making his victim look the way he needed him to." She crossed her arms, scanning her small audience.

Mahoney stepped away from the side wall, approaching Sutton and Hayes. "Fantasy. This is a much different motive than our usual guys have. What do we normally do? We look at the evidence and create paths. Thing is, this guy, he didn't leave us any real evidence. Our paths have been leading to nowhere. We keep our methods. But we create parallel paths."

Agent Quesnel took Mahoney's pause as a cue. She walked up to the crime scene wall, creating a hook into the state of their investigation. "I see you've been looking at some of the key pieces left at these scenes. The cloak, the pendant, the earring, the robe, among others. You may already be considering behaviour and profiling without realizing it."

"I don't follow," Sutton said.

"Script, progression, compulsion, fantasy. I've gone into all of these. One more important thing is symbolism. All of these things come together with the application of things, objects that resonate with this guy. They are symbols of his message, and his message is a critical window into what his fantasy is. Might I recommend that we review what you've found on each of these and see if we can't find a concrete way forward?"

Sutton nodded, taking a big sip from his Big Gulp. He glanced at Hayes. Hayes flipped open his notebook.

Tension dissolving, the air cleared like blue sky cutting through dark clouds. The rusting tarnish invading the golden badge flashing through

Mahoney's mind halted. He walked over to the side wall again, nodding at Agent Quesnel to continue.

She jumped right in. "Mahoney. You guys create potential paths and find suspects by looking at the evidence."

"Yeah."

"In this case, the killer has left absolutely no trace of hard evidence. At least that hasn't been found so far. This cock blocks you."

"Say what?" Mahoney's brow wrinkled.

Sutton and Hayes, giggling like schoolgirls, exchanged a glance.

"You know, when you're trying to get a girl's attention, and her friend won't leave. She blocks you from accessing the girl."

"Aaaah." Mahoney shifted from one foot to the other, crossing his arms.

"Well, the lack of evidence here is blocking you from finding the killer. From even coming up with a list of suspects."

"Right." Sutton slid the red straw into his mouth.

"So, boys…what do you do when you need another way in?" Agent Quesnel looked at Sutton and Hayes.

Sutton, still smirking, took a stab. "Uh, find another girl."

"Exactly. In this case, we find another way. Take a break from looking at the non-existent evidence. Take a stab at one of the profiling elements. We have a lot to go on in the fantasy department."

Mahoney said, "So you just give up on the girl?"

"No. You leave her for now. But if she warms up to you later, you go back. We keep our eye on her, just like we keep our eye on the evidence. Keep looking, and if something pops up, we have a winner. But in the meantime, don't go cold on trails or suspects. We can use another doorway in. The fantasy that he is trying to live out."

Sutton nodded. "Yeah. I like it. We can't sit here going stale."

"Let's review this fantasy again. We can infer from the scenes and the timelines for each body that the clothing, the jewellery, the hair, the makeup, all of it, is a big window into what turns him on. What he is trying to live out. His fantasy."

Mahoney jumped onboard. "This is good." Popping open a pen, he walked over to a clean spot on the whiteboard. "What do we have that could be part of his fantasy. Cloak. Leggings. Red Robe."

Sutton helped out. "The jewellery. The pendant and the earring. Oh, and the rhinestone bracelets."

Mahoney turned, pen in hand. "The pendant led us to the gem shop. But the earing and the bracelets – just costume jewelry. Can be bought anywhere."

Hayes said, "The hair. Long. Curly."

Mahoney scribbled all the items down. "The victims. They are similar. Both good kids, top students, reliable employees, and good to Mom and Dad."

"Yes. This may be an indication of the killer's victim type. You can use what the victims have in common to home in on his behaviour." Agent Quesnel plunked herself down in a plastic chair.

"Where he might hunt," Mahoney concluded.

Sutton said, "The dive bar, where they went for rock shows."

"Yeah. Both victims were seen at the dive joint at Saturday night shows." Mahoney concluded.

Agent Quesnel shifted forward in the plastic chair. "At the boutique, where the cloak was purchased, Mahoney, didn't you say that the clientele there tends to be band members or college kids that go to live shows?"

"When I scoped out the rocker bar, I was looking for people who knew the victims. Maybe we should look for people who know the type of guy that might be our killer."

Agent Quesnel finished it off for him, "Or even look for the killer himself."

Sutton questioned, "How do you look for a guy when you don't know what he looks like?"

"You look for someone who behaves how our guy would. Likely he will display odd behaviours. If he is looking for a victim, he could be paying extra attention to the other people in the bar. If his fantasy involves rock music, he may be unnaturally fixated on the band. He would likely be alone. He may be uncomfortable talking to others or being approached in any way."

Mahoney snapped the cap on the pen. "We go back to the dive bar."

Agent Quesnel finalized their plan, saying, "You and me. We go together. When is the next show?"

"The server, she told me there was a show every weekend."

"It's a date then. We'll observe our potential killers in their environment. Maybe our guy will be there, dreaming up how he will execute his next attempt at his fantasy."

"His next attempt at murder," Sutton finished off.

Hayes looked up from his notepad.

Mahoney said, "Or where he is hunting his next kill."

Sutton plunked his Big Gulp onto the long centre table. Hayes sat back in his chair. Mahoney leaned back against the side wall, tension dripping from his shoulders. The slight pang in his side swelled into a piercing pain.

Rocker in Disguise

Mahoney unfurled from his orange Pony car. Several layers of old school encased him. His worn derby perched in its familiar place on his crown, his grey tweed coat covering the corduroy jacket beneath. He had barely taken a step when she closed in on him, out of nowhere. Tight black leather stretched over her legs, disappearing into tall, dark boots wrapped in metal buckles. Gold glam clung to her breasts, and rhinestones circled her waist. *What is this?* he pondered. Finding her face, realization washed over him as her greeting reached his ears.

"Mahoney. You plan on going in like that? They'll peg you before you step foot in the door. You gotta lose the old school, embrace the style of the rock scene." She slung a duffel bag his way, along with her words.

"What's this?"

Shooting a glance at the bag, her only response was a quick nod.

Pulling open the zipper, he rifled through the duffel's interior. Fetching a long-sleeved, sleek black top, he held back in disapproval. Going in for another dip, he retrieved a pair of black jeans. F*rick, I'm too old for this shit.* He shook his head. *When's the last time I wore denim?* he questioned his blank mind.

"C'mon, you trying to turn me into one of those rocker freaks?" he said.

"That's the idea. Where we're going, corduroy isn't going to cut it."

Yeah, yeah. I get it. You walk in the door looking like Sherlock Holmes, and you'll have eyes on you in a flash. If our guy is around, he could bolt. I guess I need to lose the corduroy.

He strode toward the HQ main doors. After a quick transformation, he emerged back to the dark parking lot. He carried the duffel bag in one hand, and a red bag with gold lettering in the other.

She slowly eyeballed him from head to toe, one eyebrow raised with skepticism. "It'll do, corduroy boy," she said with a click of her tongue. Turning on her heal, she briskly walked back toward the parking lot. "Let's get a move on." Verbally pushing them into action, she opened the door to her sleek, shiny black Camaro. "I'll drive."

Following her lead, he sunk into the plush passenger seat. As she turned the key, a rough riff blasted from the cassette player. Quickly grasping the nob, she lowered the volume. The screeching voice questioning Mahoney, 'Do you know where you are?' quickly dissipated. Peeling across the pavement, she swung the Camaro into action.

In a flash, they were pulling up to the dive joint. Gliding the Corvette into a spot in the corner, her hand paused on the keys. Turning her head, her eyes bore into his.

"OK, we need to agree on our strategy." Her lips shone with candy-apple gloss.

"My main focus when I scoped this place out was to determine if either of our victims hung out here."

"Our focus now has changed."

He nodded. "We're looking for our suspect. If both victims hung out here, our hunter might be finding his prey here."

"Dead on. In addition to that, if his fantasy is rooted in rock music, he may himself be coming to these live shows. If he is attempting to recreate some sort of experience that he has, or had at some point, related to a particular show, song, or band, then he may be getting his inspiration here."

"We should go in together."

"I agree. We'll need to make it look like we're, you know, together."

Mahoney shot her a look. Raising his eyebrow, he smirked slightly. "I knew you were warming up to me."

"Oh don't get too excited. I don't go for men who dress in corduroy."

"OK, we'll look a little friendly. Then we'll spread out. Be able to scope out a wider zone."

"Yes, good idea. We need to be watching for anything strange, out of the ordinary. If a live rock show has anything to do with his fantasy, then he'll be getting off on this. We need to be alert for anyone enjoying it a little too much, or any peculiar behaviour."

"Geez, it's like this is his form of a peep show."

"Could be. His brain is wired differently."

"OK, you ready? Let's get this over with." Mahoney looked down at his black clothing, too tight for his liking. He opened the red bag.

"What you got there?"

He pulled out the shimmering cloak he had bought at the clothing boutique. To his disappointment, it hadn't shed any light on the cloak found on the Frog Lake boy. *If this doesn't make me fit in, nothing will.*

"Wow. I'm impressed." She smiled.

He stepped onto the pavement and put on the cloak. As he raised his arms, the tassels flowed from each sleeve. *I feel ridiculous.*

Agent Quesnel slipped out of the black Camaro, boot buckles clinking as her feet hit the pavement. "Mahoney. Look like you own that cloak."

"Yeah, yeah." He followed her across the parking lot.

Approaching the black door lit up by the pulsing of the neon blue *LiveWire* sign, they strode through the dimly lit parking lot. Opening the door, they were greeted by a large, muscular man. Making a quick scan of both of them, he said, "Twenty- dollar cover. Per person."

Fishing bills out of his torn wallet, Mahoney thrust the money at the bulk of a man before Agent Quesnel even had a chance.

Scowling his way, she walked toward the bar. "Let's get a drink. We need to blend in."

Mahoney nodded, following her to the familiar bar in the middle of the room. Looking to his left, he saw the open space filling up with young people, eager for the show to start. The stage was decked up with a shiny drum kit, multiple guitars lined up in the corner, and a microphone with a scarf tied at the base of the metal bulb, flowing its way down the long silver stand.

"What's your poison, Mahoney?"

"Ginger-ale."

She snorted and turned toward the bar. He continued scanning the room.

Hoisting him a tall glass fizzing with ginger bubbles, she smirked at him, wrapping her candy lips around a long straw. The straw pierced its way into a tall glass filled with dark liquid. A red cherry pressed up against the side of the glass. "According to that flyer, the show's supposed to start in a few minutes."

"Let's wander over there." He nodded toward the back of the room. A small section dotted with high chairs and small round tables was raised up a few steps. "Could provide us a good view of the place."

"Good thinking." Clinking her tall glass against his, she spun on her black heel.

The back area was sparsely populated. They raised themselves up onto a couple of chairs, scoping out the span of the room. Mahoney's eye caught a lanky man with a long, dark ponytail. The man was pressing himself against the front of the stage, staring up at the set for the show. Every few seconds, he twisted his neck, darting his gaze around the quickly mounting crowd on the open area in front of the stage.

"Hey, check out that guy near the front of the stage." Mahoney's eyes fixated on the man. "The one with the dark ponytail. Looks anxious."

"Yeah, I see him. He keeps scanning the crowd. He does look nervous." She took a sip of her makeshift cherry coke.

The lights in the entire place dimmed to a low glow. The crowd erupted, whistles and shouts echoed through the small space. Four shadows crept their way onto the stage. The eruption heightened with restless energy. Mahoney checked in on Ponytail Man frequently, scanning the rest of the crowd in between glances. Electric sounds vibrated from the room as a guitarist approached the edge of the stage, strumming the first few notes of the show.

Mahoney scanned the entire room. His eyes making their way through the dense crowd packing themselves in tight, his gaze halted on a man at the back. Wearing a silky blouse, his long sandy-blond hair flowing, he stood a little ways back from the pack. He didn't have a drink like every other patron in the joint. He stood back, staring intently at the stage, rubbing his hands together. Mahoney looked back at Ponytail Man, confirming he was still in place. Ponytail Man's arms were raised, his head was banging the air in rhythm to the riff that was now vibrating loudly through the entire space.

Agent Quesnel nudged his elbow. "Hey. Take a look at the guy in the corner, to our left."

Mahoney discreetly shot his eyes over to the back corner, then quickly back at Agent Quesnel. The man in the corner was sitting alone, his eyes slowly traversing each patron in the bar. He didn't appear to be watching the show. His hair was shoulder length, orange-red, and black leathery bracelets wove up his arm. His black-nailed fingers wrapped around a short glass with clear liquid.

"I see him," Mahoney confirmed. "Check out the guy a little ways from the back of the crowd. Red blouse. Long, blondish hair."

Wrapping her candy-apple lips around her straw, she casually browsed the stage area. "Oh yeah. I got him. Wow. He's just standing there, rubbing his hands together. Hard to tell if he's fixated on the band or the crowd. Or both."

"Looks like we got us a pool of at least three."

"You stay here, keep your eye on Corner Creep and Back Crowd Lounger. I think I should wade through that crowd. I might be able to scope out anything else we can't see from up here. And I might be able to talk to that ponytail guy."

Mahoney glared at her. "You sure this is a good idea?"

"Look, corduroy boy, with all your years of experience, you must have been in the field. I'm sure you've come up close to some real creeps."

"Sure."

"I've been inches from the worst criminal minds known. I've picked up a few conversational skills. Don't worry. I can blend right in." Shedding her leather jacket, she hung it from the back of the high chair. Snatching her drink from the tabletop, she swiftly made her way down to the stage.

Mahoney glanced over at Corner Creep. He hadn't moved. He looked at the back of the crowd. Crowd Lounger was still there. No changes in either of them. Same poses, same stares.

Agent Quesnel slipped her way through the crowd. Her body slithering to the music, hands raised in the air, her cherry coke moving over the crowd. Her gold shirt glowed under the overhead pot lights bathing the stage area in a purple-blue haze, rhinestone-studded belt shooting off the occasional glimmer in response to the bright flashes of light from the stage. Her petite stature was of no intrusion to members of the pack. She was a glammed-up chameleon in a jacked-up crowd.

Mahoney took another inventory. Corner Creep hadn't moved an inch, continuing to pluck off each and every one of the patrons in the bar with his eyes. He sipped his clear drink obsessively, every few seconds. Crowd Lounger was still hanging at the back of the pack, rubbing his palms together. He spent most of his time staring at the stage. Occasionally, he scanned the crowd, then looked back at the stage again. Scanning the crowd, Mahoney's eyes followed a glint of light, landing back on a rhinestone. Agent Quesnel continued to sneak her way through the crowd. Looking as if she was totally lost in the music, like the rest of the pack. Every few moments she scanned her surroundings like she was looking for a lost friend. Strategically she made her way through the tightly packed mass, toward the front of the stage.

Ponytail Man slid off the elastic holding the black strands in place. Banging his head hard, his black waves jumped around wildly. He moved so aggressively with the music, he almost looked as if he was convulsing. Agent Quesnel slid right up next to him. Mahoney's throat caught mid-swallow, ginger bubbles tickling the back of his mouth. *Easy, Quesnel.* Swallowing the sweet soda, he placed the tall glass back on the table. Retrieving his kerchief from its foreign home in the back pocket of the black jeans, he wiped the bits of sweat trickling down his forehead. The crowd had thickened. Heat rising from bodies sticky with sweat wafted from the stage area up into Mahoney's backroom perch.

Mahoney looked at the stage. The act was now several tracks in. *Not bad talent,* he mused. *You take some raw blues, add in a sixth chord, and bam, you got yourself some good ol' rock 'n' roll.* Shaking his brain back into motion, he took tabs on Corner Creep and Crowd Lounger again. The obsessive consistency of their behaviour gave him goosebumps. *Are they here for the show? Is the guy in the corner looking for a victim? Is the guy hovering over the crowd fantasizing about the band members? They're not doing anything other than, well, looking creepy.* Agent Quesnel had settled into her front-row spot. The last chord of the current track rang out. She turned her head toward Ponytail Man and said something to him. He glanced at her briefly, then snapped his head back, looking down at his drink. He took a sip, then tentatively turned his head and returned the chatter. *Wow. She's in.* Each time she spoke to the man, he pulled back, as if tentative. Then he would take a gulp of his drink and move toward her, responding to whatever she had said to him. A guitar chord electrified the room. The conversation was over. For now. Ponytail Man returned to his intense fixation on the wild rock show.

Mahoney continued taking his inventory with no changes. He added to his routine a regular scan of the entire room. The show continued, the crowd growing restless as the band belted out their wild music. An hour or so into the show, the inventory was getting tiring. Looking toward the stage, Mahoney noticed Agent Quesnel making her way back toward him.

Plunking her glass onto the table, she met his gaze. "Show's almost over. Did either of your guys doing anything?"

"No. Stayed exactly the same the whole time. What about Ponytail Boy down there? Looks like you got nice and chummy."

"Yeah. I didn't see anything else notable, so I focused on him. I was able to get him talking a little. He said some weird shit. We should see if we can figure out who he is."

"What did he say?"

"Something about needing to tend to his dolls tonight."

"What? The dark pony tail guy at the Eagle Woods scene said something about the kids stealing his doll. We should get an ID on all three of our guys here. Don't think there's very many staff here."

Agent Quesnel scanned the room. "I think our best bet is the girl at the bar."

An electric riff vibrated through the air, building in volume. The crowd responded with shouts. The lead singer, wild orange mane piercing the air, approached the microphone one last time, stroking the scarf. Black pleather stretched over his muscular legs as he arched his back, kneeling on the ground. Wailing his last cries to his mesmerized audience, the singer gripped the long silver stand in one last embrace. The shout of the crowd climaxed. The lights snapped on, and the band vanished. The room buzzing with electric energy, the pack made its way to the bar. The only server on duty flew from one end of the bar to the other, serving up one more for the road.

"Let's hang back."

Mahoney squinted. "She's the same server I talked to before."

"Then we definitely need to talk to her. If she does a lot of shifts here, she might know who these guys are."

"I'm with you." Tilting his glass back against his mouth, Mahoney forced the last bit of ginger liquid from the bottom of his glass, ice landing against his lips.

Agent Quesnel plucked the cherry from the bottom of her glass by the stem. Slipping the bright-red fruit into her mouth, she pursed her lips. Pulling the stem free, she tossed it into the empty glass. Sucking on the fruit, she continued to scan the room. "Supposedly cocktail cherries cause cancer. I wonder how many you would have to eat?"

"A lot."

"I'll probably die from overwork, or one of my beloved killers will turn on me."

"Perks of the job."

Cold air wafted through the room as the black door on the far wall opened and closed continuously, the pack thinning out as its members made their exit.

"Looks like our cue." Mahoney slid from the high chair.

Making his way toward the bar, Agent Quesnel in tow, he confirmed the single server was the only one to battle out the duties of last call.

Approaching the black counter, sticky from the barrage of glasses and concoctions of the evening, Mahoney greeted the familiar face. "Excuse me, miss."

Long, blonde hair flying, the server spun around. Face glistening with droplets of sweat, wet rag in hand, she shot him a smile. "What can I getcha?"

"I would just like to ask you a couple of questions, miss."

She stopped, looking at his face more carefully. "Hey, I know you." Leaning against the bar, she abandoned the rag. "Yeah, you were in here last week. In the middle of the day. Yeah, I remember you, detective." She looked him up and down. "Nice getup. No suit today?" A sly smile crept across her face.

Chuckling, he leaned toward the bar. "My colleague and I, we just want to know if you recognize a few guys in here." He shot a look at the front of the stage. Ponytail Man had vanished. *What? He was just there. Dammit.* He looked at Agent Quesnel. "He's gone."

Agent Quesnel shot her eyes toward the stage. "He was just there."

Mahoney frantically scanned the room, back and forth. Nothing. He couldn't find the black hair. The guy had vanished into thin air. Scanning the room, he confirmed that Corner Creep and Crowd Lounger were still around.

"Who're you looking for?" the silky voice of the server found his ears.

"Sorry. The one guy seems to be gone. He was up at the front by the stage. He had long dark hair, tied back on a pony tail."

"There's lots of guys with long hair around here. I wouldn't have noticed the stage during the show. It gets crazy at the bar."

Mahoney shook his head. "OK. Do you recognize the guy up in the corner over there?" He pointed up to the perch. "Or the guy in the corner over there?" He pointed to the opposite corner.

The server took a good look in both directions. "Yeah. They're both regulars. They come to every show, and they always do exactly the same thing. The guy on the perch, that's Roy. The guy over in the other corner, that's Tom."

"Do you know their full names?"

"Yeah. They both start a tab early in the evening before it gets busy in here. That way they can hide in their corners and still get service." She opened the register, flipping through a stack of papers. "Ah, here. I've got the tabs." She displayed them for Mahoney as he jotted in his notebook.

"So, Roy sits up in the same corner every time?" Agent Quesnel pursued.

"Yes. The whole night."

"And Tom?" candy-apple lips continued.

"Tom secures his seat up in his corner. Right before the show starts, he makes his way onto the stage area. He hangs back, at the back of the crowd. Then he hangs around after, up in his corner."

"There're a lot of people in here during a show. How you do keep track?" Agent Quesnel questioned.

"Oh, of course, I don't remember everybody. But these two, they come in early, stay after, and sometimes come in during the week when it isn't busy."

"So, you work here a lot?" Agent Quesnel said.

"Yeah. We're a little short staffed. Had a string of servers start and quit. I like it here. Pay is decent. Boss is easy to deal with. I've had, well, worse situations. This gig's OK."

Mahoney drove the questioning to a conclusion, saying, "Miss, one more question, if you don't mind."

"Sasha. You can call me Sasha." She flashed him a full smile and a single bat of her lashes.

"OK. Sasha. Are there any other guys that you remember who have a solid routine like these two? Or that act strange in any way?"

"Hmmm. That's a tough one. I mean, lots of regulars come here. There just aren't that many places to see live shows. And, strange…well, depends on what you think is strange. I mean, people who come here, they're young, they want a wild night out, blow off some steam."

"OK. Well, if you think of anything else, anyone who strikes you as different, please give me a call." Mahoney slid a card over the sticky black counter.

"Oh, you gave me your card last time. I still have it." She leaned back against the back of the bar, giving a tiny bite to her bottom lip.

"Thank you, miss."

"Anytime. And it's Sasha."

Placing the card back into his wallet, Mahoney turned toward the black door.

"Isn't that cute," Agent Quesnel mused.

"What?"

"Oh, c'mon, you didn't notice?" She nudged his arm with her elbow. "She was flirting with you, detective."

"You're crazy."

BLEEDING JUNGLE

Straitjacket

April, 1977

The door slammed shut, leaving Seth engulfed in complete darkness. Stomach seizing, his heart hiccupped a mess of palpitations. He squeezed his eyelids together tightly, threatening to squish the white matter of his eyeballs into mush. Brain swelling, his head spun.

Wrapping his arms around himself in a suffocating hug, his hands plastered against his back. Rubbing raw against the rough material encasing them, his palms were on fire. Drenched with sweat, his thin t-shirt clung to him beneath the heat of the heavy jacket holding him captive. The long casings binding his arms wound their way around his upper body. The weight of heavy buckles lay heavy against his chest. The binds were tight, sucking the life out of his extremities. Tiny convulsions rippled through his arms and legs as he glared into the darkness. The heat in the bottom of his belly pulsated, growing with each throb until a fire raged within him. Flames of fury forced their way up his throat, clawing at his mouth, and prying his lips open.

"Fuck. You. Doris."

His words vibrated violently through the air, shaking the tiny closet that held him prisoner. Atoms of anger dissipated through his body, declaring mass destruction on any ounce of terror grasping for existence. Screaming with force, stretching his lungs to their limits, he repeated his demonic cry until his voice grew hoarse. "I hate you, Doris. I want you to die, Doris. Let me out, Doris." Collapsing, his back hit the cold floor hard.

His eyes adjusting, he could make out a thin line of light framing the door. Kicking the door hard, he pounded his boots against the wood until his legs fell to the ground in a limp mess. Numbness seized his arms, a million pins prickling their way from his shoulders down to his wrists.

I can't frickin' feel my arms. How long can they stay this way? His thoughts raced, imploring his mind for an answer. He lay still for a while. His mind grew hazy as he lost track of time, space, and reality. His will to fight disintegrated into the tight, dark space surrounding him.

I'm fucking finished. His inner voice vibrated through his mind. *Is this what you want, Doris? Is this how you win?*

He kicked feebly at the door one more time, knowing it was futile. Tears escaped from the corners of his eyes, trickling down his dust-covered cheeks in a hot, sludgy mess. The jacket wrapping his body into submission mimicked the isolation depriving him of control over his destiny. He knew this path. All he could do was wait until *she* decided to release him. *If* she released him. She was always threatening to lock him up in her own makeshift institution for good, saying she should have left him in the mental hospital with all the freaks.

Frick. She wouldn't really leave me here for good...or...would she? Fuck.

Bolting up to a sitting position, the sudden movement brought his tight jacket cage to life again. The buckles growing heavier against his chest, the walls creeping closer to him, the darkness suffocating him, everything turned in on him. A sudden pressure threatening to rip his bladder open, his ass cheeks clenched. The thin rectangle of light glowing around the doorframe tilted to the side, toppling over, then spinning round and round. Spinning faster until it became a blurry, bright oval. A wave of half-digested food rose, crashing against the walls of his stomach. A slight gag gurgled in his throat. Swallowing hard, he willed the revolt back down to where it came from. Leaning back against the wall, he slammed his eyes shut. A wave of realization washed over him as he acknowledged to himself that there wasn't anybody to hear him. At least nobody who cared. There wasn't a single soul in this world to help him.

A crevice opening in his mind, a plethora of images rushed at him. A steel slab cold against his cheek, concrete walls caging him in, fluorescent lights stinging his eyes. The terrifying images closed in on him. His head spinning faster, blackness took over his mind. A sudden glimmer of sparkly diamonds dancing on the walls shook him as his mind moved toward a new vision. Silky scarves, flowing robes, long shiny hair, glittering gems, and glossy pleather all swirled around in his head. His mind removed itself from his body, separating his mental being from his physical surroundings. He broke through into another realm. An alternate reality. The sweetness of his hallucinations took over him, transporting him away from the terror, the pain, the reality in which he lived.

Bleeding Jungle

P ink boots and blonde curls floating in his head, Mahoney struggled to focus on the road. The rain pelted hard against the windshield of his trusted Pony car. His head spinning, the images in his mind were taking on lives of their own. Pink boots and blonde curls swirled around, weaving themselves into ghostly, white faces with lavender eyes staring him down. Blood-red lips shooting their words at him.

"Bug, you failed us."

"Bug, there is no hope for us."

"Bug, we are gone."

Giving his head a hard shake, trying to fling the voices out of his mind, he stared intensely at the watery road ahead. The voices fought back.

"Bug, the boys, they will be lost too."

The wind and the rain bared down against him. Pelting hard against the windshield, watery bullets threatened to shatter the glass. The flash downpour increased its magnitude, the intensity driving into overload. A strong pang sliced through his gut. Beads of sweat sprouted from his forehead, drizzling their way down his face. The wiper blades swooshed frantically back and forth, rivers of water pouring over them. He madly blinked his eyes, trying to see through the wet blur.

The side of his stomach throbbed, pain threatening to slice through him again. The dull pang had been increasing exponentially over the last two days. Like an octopus, reaching its tentacles from his gut, slithering through his insides, wrenching each of his internal organs. He clenched his jaw, tightening his already deadly grip on the steering wheel, turning his knuckles white. He reached for the round silver button on the dashboard and cranked it up. The wailing desperation of Robert Plant filled his car, warning that the levee would break any second.

A gust of wind threatened to sweep his car away as he swerved violently toward the side of the road. Jolting the steering wheel sharply, he guided himself back to safety. He blinked his eyes dramatically, slapping himself across his unshaven cheek.

"Focus, Bug. Get it together." he barked at himself. Grinding his teeth, he stared intently at the road ahead of him. Sweeping through the corners of his mind, he pushed the little ghost faces into a back room and slammed the door shut. The pounding rain came to a sudden halt. The black clouds hovering over the city drifted apart. The sun made a brilliant appearance, tearing through the cotton darkness, yellow rays of warmth plunging through. Mahoney pulled off the fast-moving freeway. His car drifted down a quiet street. Perfect rows of flowers in full bloom lined meticulously manicured lawns, bordered by white picket fences. Radiant reds, lush purples, pretty pinks, and bright yellows popped against the dark-green grass. A chorus of chatter rang out as a group of small children circled the end of the street on shiny bicycles, ringing their bells and laughing gaily. Mahoney's heart pulsed with warmth. *Geez,* his mind muttered. *Those kids need to get out of here.*

The street was cluttered with police vehicles. Pulling up to an opening against the curb, he emerged from his car. Clenching his jaw again, he erased every ghostly face from his mind. He forced himself to abandon all feelings of slicing pain. Clearing his throat and standing up tall, he perched his derby where it belonged. Taking long, steady strides, he moved swiftly toward a group of uniformed officers, huddling, plotting their next play. Among them he noted Sutton and Hayes, hanging at the back of the huddle. *Glad my boys are here.* His shoulders and jaw relaxing, his gaze snapped away from the huddle, landing on an approaching silhouette.

"Mahoney." Blackwood curtly nodded, a little breathless.

"Blackwood," he returned politely.

"Given the tidbits I've overheard, this one may confirm everything your gut has been telling you." Intensity filled her almond eyes. Her face was grim with seriousness.

Relief washed over him as he knew he had the right person on his side, at a critical moment. "We should get on it, then," he said, turning back toward the huddle.

Blackwood's hand touched his arm, halting his mission. "You look pale, Mahoney. You OK?" Concern rippled through her voice.

"Fine. Let's go," Mahoney persisted.

Blackwood closed her eyes, her fingers gently maintaining contact with his arm. She foraged forth with a risky statement composed of a single word: "Bug." Her voice was soft, but it amplified as it rang through the air, sharply searing Mahoney's ears. Silence clung to every air molecule between the two of them as his eyes locked on hers.

Blackwood had embarked on a passage for which she had given herself permission. She had uttered the very name, exploding with significance, that only those in Mahoney's immediate circle had earned the right to use. Mahoney held his stern gaze, remaining silent. He had to let it go. They had work to do.

He cleared his throat. "I'm fine. We need to get this show on the road."

She hesitated, her eyes clinging to his. They were suspended in time, alone amongst the playing children and the officers dotting the picket fences. Suddenly snapping back to reality, she blinked rapidly and moved forward. The air was thick with the unresolved tension between them. Passing Mahoney, she risked one more short glance his way. Their eyes met again, but only for a split second. Whatever needed to be said would have to wait.

As they reached the huddle, Mahoney didn't waste any time. "Officers," he curtly addressed them, then threw his first dart. "Those kids over there…" He nodded at the children on bicycles, giggling as they circled the end of the street. "They shouldn't be there. This scene needs to be secured, pronto." All officers nodded their agreement vigorously. Two of them took off immediately to remedy the situation.

"What's been done?" Mahoney said.

One of the officers brought them quickly up to speed. "Two of our officers are down in the ravine, behind the houses. They are interviewing the witnesses. Two teenagers, apparently having a private party at the bottom by the stream, found the body. One of them ran up to the house at the end of the street here, borrowed their phone to call it in."

Mahoney thanked the officer with a warm nod. He turned to Sutton and Hayes. "Hayes, make sure the scene up here is secured properly. Then make sure statements have been taken from the residents of the home the call was made from."

"Got it, boss." Hayes turned toward his mission.

Brushing past formalities, Mahoney gathered the team. "Blackwood, push those techs to get a move on." He waved toward the shiny black truck rolling up against the curb a half block away. "Sutton, stay with me. We need to get down there. Now."

"Sure thing, boss."

Blackwood was already off on her mission. Sutton and Mahoney moved toward the last house on the street, finding the pathway entrance. Mahoney halted, scanning the street. Blackwood was walking briskly toward them, techies in tow. The pathway was lined on both sides with white-barked trees abundant with fresh leaves. The treetops met and joined, forming a canopy of luscious green over their heads. The fences on either side of the path were overgrown with round, dense bushes. The sweet aroma of honeysuckle, dripping from little white flowers, mixed with the earthy aroma seeping from the foliage.

The makeshift tunnel of leaves enclosed around Mahoney as he led the group down the path. He soon came to an opening perched at the top of a steep, grassy hill. The hill stretched out on either side of them, plunging into a ravine below. Multiple dirt paths, formed by thousands of exploring feet, snaked their way through the grass, down the steep incline. The trickling of a clear stream meandering its way through the ravine floor rose up, singing in Mahoney's ears. Two uniformed officers were perched on the rocks at the bottom of the embankment, talking to the lone pair of witnesses.

Blackwood grabbed Mahoney by the elbow and pulled him aside. Pointing discreetly with her eyes she spoke softly, "That must be where they found it."

Mahoney's gaze followed hers. A circular opening in a stone wall lead into a dark tunnel. A slight shiver wove through him.

Blackwood turned to look back behind them. "We are literally in someone's *backyard*." Her voice was low, revealing a tinge of shakiness.

Mahoney said, "Let's interrupt the interview and get the run-down. We need to get moving before we lose our sunlight." He addressed Sutton briefly, saying, "Let's get the run-down. No time to waste."

Sutton pushed something furry and green into his jeans pocket. "Got it."

"What's that?"

"Uh, nothing, boss."

"Sutton."

"My good luck charm. A rabbit foot. Green."

"Oh." Mahoney pictured the smooth, pink rock nestled in his pocket. "Well, let's hope it brings us the luck we need."

Sutton nodded then stepped inline.

As they cautiously shuffled their way down the steep hill, slick with rain, Mahoney had some time to give the young witnesses a once-over. Scanning them from top to bottom, he noted their ripped jeans hanging low, barely clinging to the edge of their asses. Their feet were donned in Converse. Two longboards leaned against a large boulder, carefully perched until getaway time. *Skaters,* he thought to himself. His eye caught a glimpse of several empty Club cans tossed amongst the rocks, not far from the boards. *They must be 16, 17 tops. Not quite legal.* He looked back at the boys. The one had long hair, falling past his shoulders, head donned with a baseball cap fittingly placed backward. The other had greasy-looking dreadlocks descending from his wool toque, poking wildly around his neck. Cautiously reaching the bottom of the steep descent, Mahoney took charge.

"Officers, boys." Mahoney nodded politely at the uniforms and the teenagers. "I'm Detective Mahoney, from homicide. Since it's getting dark fast here, I'd appreciate it if you could bring me and my team up to speed on what you've found." Mahoney focused his gaze warmly on the two young boys.

One of the officers prodded the young witnesses. "Jeb, can you walk us through the events again, for the benefit Detective Mahoney and his team here?"

The boy wearing the wool toque hesitantly spoke, his voice shaky as he said, "We were hangin' out down here. We come here a lot. It's quiet. No one bothers us. We don't bother nobody either. My dog, Chomps, was roamin'. We were just chillin' when I heard him freakin' out. Barkin' was coming from the tunnel." He pointed to the same dark opening that Blackwood had observed on their way down. "I went in to get 'im. I was sure he was jacked up over a small animal or somethin'. But when I found him…" His lip trembled. He lowered his gaze to the ground.

"Hey," Mahoney said, "this stuff isn't easy for the mind to process. It's not cool when it's not in the movies." *Geez, this kid is too young to be involved in this.*

Jeb raised his head and looked right at Mahoney. Continuing, his voice steadied a little, "I could hear Chomps barkin' from inside the tunnel, so I went in. Real dark in there. I found him, just sittin' there. Barkin' his head off. There was this girl. She was kinda sittin' against the wall, crouched over like she was upset or somethin'. I grabbed Chomps, got him calm. I couldn't really see her face 'cause it was all covered with tangled hair. I asked her if she was OK. She didn't say nothin'. Just sat there." Jeb stopped. His head drooped. He stared at the ground, hugging himself as his fingers clawed at his shoulders. Taking a deep breath, he continued, rushing to get it over with, "I went right up to her, shook her shoulder a little. I talked louder. Asked her again if she was OK. Nothin'. I got a little closer, looked at her face. I could see one of her eyes through her messy hair. It was just staring back at me, all glassy like. Then I realized, shit, she ain't movin'. She looked dead. I grabbed Chomps, and we ran back here." Jeb's voice halted as his body swayed. His friend grabbed his arm and guided him to sit on a large rock.

His friend said, "We just come down here to chill, man, we don't want no trouble. But, man, when Jeb came out of that hole, I knew something ain't right. When he said he friggin' found a dead body, I was like, shit, this ain't our business, man. Jeb was shaking. He could barely stand. So I sprinted up that hill and knocked on the first door I found. When I told them there was a dead body down here, man, they were like 'we'll call the police.' I said thank you, man, and got back down here to Jeb."

"Thank you, boys. Officer Peterson, here, will continue to talk with you. I appreciate your help. It's not easy for anyone to see what you found, Jeb." Mahoney put his hand on the shaken boy's shoulder. Turning back to his team, he moved things along. "OK, let's get moving."

Mahoney led the small group across the wet grass toward the tunnel. Crouching over, Mahoney stepped into the darkness, a wave of cold chilling him. Snapping his flashlight from his belt, he flicked it on. A tingling crept up his arms, then down his legs. *Where the hell does this go?* He plunged his gaze as far as he could into the darkness, his flashlight only scratching the surface of what lay ahead. His heart pounding, his forehead grew moist. *What the hell did this guy leave for us this time?* His mind raced through the dramatic images plastering the cream-coloured crime scene wall back at HQ.

Coming to the other end of the cylindrical passageway, he stretched himself back up to full height. "Watch your heads here," he crisply instructed the rest of the team in tow. Imprisoned in a small, spherical cave, he scanned his surroundings. As Blackwood stepped through the opening, the powerful lumens of her Sunfire 6 brought the scene to life. His eyes followed the bright beacon as she moved the light slowly along the wall of the dark dungeon. The light halted, illuminating a gory discovery. A body perched against the wall directly across from them, crouching in an eternal pose, knees bent. The head was positioned forward, straight toward them.

In stark contrast against the darkness, a savage tiger mane voluminously sprung from the body's head. Wild, stray pieces of orange-red pierced the blackness. Tangled, thick strands snaked their way down an ashen face. A single glassy eyeball glared at them, its vacant stare piercing through the mess of hair.

Mahoney was jolted by a vicious vibration weaving its way through his body. *Geez,* his mind took the lead, *this scene belongs in a nightmare, a horror film. Not here.* Here in the backyard of a row of quiet homes lined with picket fences.

The upper body was clothed in a jacket of rugged yellowing textile. Full-length sleeves encased the arms, wrapping their way around the torso in a desperate hug, pulling the hands behind the back. Blackwood's flashlight threw a glint off a shiny silver buckle. Blackwood and Mahoney walked closer to the figure, side by side, the powerful light guiding them. Arm's length from the body, a spattering of buckles became visible. The fasteners were strategically placed along straps, enabling a suffocating grasp on the caged body.

A chilling realization washed over Mahoney. "Holy shit." He led them in the first conclusion, echoing the thoughts of all minds present. "It's a straitjacket."

Blackwood directed the bright lumens down the body, completing the initial scan. Jet-black, skin-tight pleather encased each leg, stretched to the limits by the bent knees. The carcass beneath threatening to burst free. White, bare feet smudged in oily mud sprouted from the openings in each black-pleather leg. Dark-red lacerations ripped apart the flesh of each ankle, scarlet globs clinging to the cuts.

Blackwood leaned in, as close as she dared, pushing aside the solid mass of tangled orange. All eyes fixated on the ghost face staring back at them. Caked in a thick white mask, like a sculpted bust carefully built with layers of plaster, the face continued to stare back at them vacantly. Thin black lines emphasized each of the glassy eyes, lids shimmering with silver dust. The thin slightly parted lips, painted a soft peach, tightly drew back in a mild scowl.

Mahoney lifted his tingling hand toward its usual resting place, stroking the rough bristle.

Blackwood broke the silence. "Looks like a similar paint job to the other two."

"That's some hairdo."

Blackwood's plastic-wrapped hand slid slowly downward, moving the stiff mess of orange mane away from the neck. Spherical contours stigmatized the bloodless neck, weaving their way around like a deadly snake viciously restricting its prey of life-giving breath. The soft, white skin turned putrid. The ligatures were the colour of the wet, rotten leaves covering the cave floor.

Mahoney shook his head. "This is the work of our guy."

Blackwood's hand released the wild tangle, reaching toward the orange-red strands plastered to the forehead. As she moved away from the sticky mess, a new world of horror was revealed. A series of letters immortally carved into the skin formed the assertion, "*I'm Gonna Watch D Bleed.*" The slices putridly plunged into the flesh. Once oozing with vital liquid, now caked with desiccated crimson clinging to the edges of each symbol.

A flush of adrenaline coursed through Mahoney's veins. Pins pricked at the nape of his neck, migrating down his arms, the hairs responding by standing at full attention. A trio of linkage stared him down, confirming the path that his gut had told him he was on as soon as he saw those pink, muddy boots. The black vortex closed in on him, pulling him down a swirling path to its dark centre.

Stolen Vessel

Seth's feet glued themselves to the concrete, halting his body. Police cruisers dotted the white picket fences, their blue lights piercing through the darkness. Voices strained to reach over the constant hum of the scene, attempting to convey critical orders. The peace of the quiet street hid beneath a cloak of chaos. Scanning the scene spread out in a massive display before his eyes, Seth strained to comprehend the change that had forced itself upon his plan. *What is this?* his mind implored with an aggressive tone. *Why are they here?*

He loved the forested ravine tucked behind the peaceful little neighbourhood. It was the perfect place to hide away with his music. It was close to home so Doris wouldn't be suspicious of where he had snuck off to. He could hide from her. With so many hidden spaces in the trees and rocks, he could relish in the privacy. There was one little cave that he was particularly fond of, and where he loved to hide his most treasured items.

Footsteps clicking on the pavement snapped his attention. A uniformed officer making his way with haste across the street was coming straight for him. Butterflies fluttered in his stomach as bile rose up his throat. The gap between him and the officer closing fast, he turned sharply, only to find himself caged in by thick foliage. Nowhere to go, sweat trickled down his neck. Seth forced his way through a wall of shrubs, scraping his skin on a branch of sharp thistles. Blood trickling down his arm, his heart thumped against his chest. The clicking faded as the footsteps continued past the bush. Seth wiped the moisture from his forehead with the bottom of his t-shirt.

Phew. He didn't see me.

Falling to his knees, his backpack slid off his arm, landing on the grass with a thud. Its unsettled contents gave off a rattle. Seth affixed his gaze on the pack. Ripping the zipper open, he plunged his arm into the bag. Retrieving a dark-purple vial, he rested it in the palm of his hand. Stroking the smooth, unbroken glass, a seedy smile spread across his face.

Distant chatter snapped him from his reverie. Dropping the vial into the bag, he closed the pack with a forceful zip. He crouched behind the thick bush he had pushed his way through. A commotion across the street grabbed his attention. Several uniformed medical personnel gingerly guided a long stretcher from a pathway onto the road. Rolling the bed with caution, their hands held a covered human form in place.

What? Seth explored his mind. *What is this? What have they found?*

Crumpling to the soft bed of grass, Seth grasped his hair with both hands. He pulled the strands hard as the spinning in his mind gained momentum. This couldn't be happening. If they had discovered his secret cave, where would he go to hide? To hide from Doris. To conceal his precious items so she couldn't find them. The last few ounces of control he had seeped from his pores, spiralling down an imaginary drain, washing away. *What am I gonna do?*

The medical van doors slammed shut. Popping his head over the thick, round bush like a marmot, Seth could see more uniformed personnel appearing from the pathway entrance. An iridescent flash of letters grabbed his eye as a couple of men turned their backs. A man emerged from the tree-roof-topped path. A pang of familiarity sliced through Seth as his eyes fixed on the beat-up grey hat on the man's head. Confusion riddled his mind as he shuffled through his memories, trying to place the distinctive-looking accessory. Pulling his pack snuggly onto his back, he cautiously rose from his hiding spot and slipped into the night.

Exploding Ulcer

Mahoney bent over, grasping at the side of his '69 Pony. His charcoal derby tumbled to the ground. Clutching his side, he squeezed his eyes shut tightly. *C'mon, Bug,* he berated himself. *Get a grip.* Fishing in his trench coat pocket for his keys, he heard a voice behind him.

"Hey, boss, you OK?"

Mahoney spun to identify the familiar voice. A fresh wave of pain sliced through his side. He fell back against his car. Blinking hard he strained to see the swirling face. *Where am I? Did I stop at the pub? Is that Simon?* His thoughts whirling through his mind, he leaned back heavily against his car.

"Let me help you." Simon reached out, steadying Mahoney by the elbow and helping him over to a patch of grass.

Sitting down hard on the sponge lawn of soft blades, Mahoney took several deep breaths. The world steadying around him, his thoughts began to settle.

"Simon. Aren't you a welcome sight. What are you doing here?"

"I live a few blocks away. I just finished a shift. I like to walk home. Helps me clear my head after a busy night." He smiled warmly. "Listen, are you OK? Looks like a crazy scene going on here. I could go get some help."

Mahoney considered Simon's offer. "No, no. It's nothing. Just a pain that's been nudging at me. I just walked up the hill from the ravine there." He pointed past the flashing lights of the cruisers still lining the street. "I just need a minute, it was…" He stopped at the interruption of tires crunching over gravel as the medical van peeled away. "Uh, it was steep. Just winded me a little."

Simon's face was washed with concern. "I dunno. Doesn't feel right leaving you like this."

Mahoney grunted as he pushed himself into a crouched position. He closed his eyes, relaxing the muscles in his face. Looking at Simon, he raised himself to stand. "You see, all good."

"I'm not leaving you like this. Looks like you've got a whole team out here. I'll just go get you some help." Simon turned toward the line of police cruisers along the white picket fence at the pathway opening.

Willing his dwindling energy into action, Mahoney called out, "Wait. Simon."

Simon turned. "Yeah?"

"Can you get Blackwood? She's tall. Dressed like she's ready to take on a safari."

Simon raised an eyebrow. "Yeah. Whatever you say."

Mahoney leaned against his car. Taking a few long breaths, he settled his racing heart. *Geez, Bug. Are you getting too old for this?* He silently threw jabs at himself, knowing they were lies to cover up whatever that stabbing pain in his side was. Wiping the sweat from his brow with his handkerchief, he folded it back into his tweed pocket. The world coming back into focus, the fresh night air washed over him. *You're just fine, old man. Suck it up.* Settling himself onto the hood of his car, he berated himself for agreeing to Simon's quest for help. Movement caught his attention. Her long strides carrying her across the street promptly, Blackwood looked at him.

Concern hijacked her expression. "Mahoney. You OK?"

"Just a little dizziness. No worry. Guess I need to get to the gym more. That steep hill took the wind out of me. That's all. Simon, thank you for the help. We'll be just fine now. You should really get yourself home, away from all this."

"All right. Looks like you're in good hands here." Smiling warmly at Blackwood, Simon turned and made his exit.

"Mahoney. Seriously. That kid, he said you were nearly passing out over here."

"Does anyone else know?"

"No. He gave me the details discreetly, once we were out of earshot."

"Good."

"I won't say a word. But you've got to be honest with me. Are you OK?"

"Yeah. Really. I feel better."

"You looked pale when we arrived. Is there something going on that you're not admitting?"

Mahoney sat silently.

"Look, trust me, I understand, when you get on a case you put everything else aside. Your own well-being included. I've done the same thing. We need you on this case. *I* need you on this case. We need to nip whatever is going on for you in the bud, so we don't lose your manpower here." Her eyes bored into him, pleading with him to co-operate.

Hesitating, he couldn't argue with her logic. "OK. I've had a little pain in my side for a few days. That's all."

"Listen. I'll make you a deal. You get that checked out, tonight, and I won't say a word."

Nodding his head, he bent over and picked his derby off the pavement. Placing it back onto his crown, he looked her in the eyes. "You've got yourself a deal."

"OK. Tonight, Mahoney. Tonight."

"I'll head back to HQ right now. I can swing by the nurse's station before the war room run-down."

"You better. I've got tabs on you. You're lucky your friend was around. Nice kid. What's he doing around here?"

"He lives nearby. He works at the pub I stop in at a lot, after work. I don't, uh, keep much food around my apartment. They serve up a mean pizza."

She smiled, her purple almond eyes looking into him. "OK. Get yourself to that nurse's station. I've got to catch up with that medical van." She turned, walking back to the scene.

He opened the creaky old door of his car and sat down in the passenger seat. Images surged through this mind. White ghost faces of the little girls he couldn't save. A tarnished badge of failure looming over him. A cloak with eagle's wings flapping at him, taunting him. And a dark ponytail running away from him, into the darkness.

Bleeding War Room

Mahoney swung the door open. The thick, hot air suffocating him, he stepped into the small, dark room. He flicked on a switch. The fluorescent lighting instantly came to life. His droopy eyelids snapped open, a burning sensation flooding his eyeballs. The smell of body sweat infusing his nostrils, he forced himself to step into the room. *Suck it up.* He snapped a file folder onto the centre table. Scanning the cream-coloured crime scene wall, three grisly stories dramatically came to life. *Good work, Dara.* Tied up with his boys at the scene into the wee hours of the morning, he knew he could count on Dara to get them set up back at HQ. A brief flash of his comfy bed in his cozy little apartment flickered in his mind. He sighed. *Who knows when you'll see your bed again, Bug.*

He opened the folder and scanned the bleak status of the slew of unsolved clues. *No clear match on the knife used to cut the messages. No suspects to check for size 12 Doc Martens. Any blood left behind belongs to the victims. Shiny earing turned out to be nothing but costume jewelry. Dammit.*

The door swung open. Hayes appeared.

"Hey, boss."

"Hayes." Mahoney nodded.

"Look, I, uh…"

"What?"

"Well. Should we really be focusing so much on this behavior crap?"

Mahoney's face flushed with heat. "I know you're by the book. I know this may seem strange to you."

Hayes nodded. "Yeah. It seems like we're wasting time."

Mahoney pursed his lips. "I also know I already explained this to you. What part of a bunch of dead girls and a killer gone free don't you understand?"

Hayes swallowed hard.

"I'm not straying us from the evidence. You should know better than that. If we don't expand our methods, we lose opportunities here. Opportunities to stop this madness." He stared at Hayes.

The door swung open, breaking his thoughts. Sutton, Dara and Agent Quesnel shuffled in.

Mahoney looked at Hayes. "We OK?"

"Yeah, boss." Hayes moved toward the coffee pot.

Mahoney plucked his Styrofoam coffee cup from the little round table. "Dara. Stand-up job on the crime scene wall." With a slight nod, he turned toward the collage of bodies.

Dara raised her eyes away from her thick black glasses perched on the end of her nose, sending him a silent acknowledgement.

"Let's get this show on the road. Blackwood is processing the body now. We'll need to go on what we all collectively found at the scene. I'll pay her a visit when we convene."

All eyes focusing on Mahoney, their heads nodded in unison.

"The conclusion we were already leaning toward with the Eagle Woods boy can no longer be avoided. These bodies are linked. Three bodies. Three sets of distinctive ligature marks, and three messages. Two cut directly into the bodies. Processing of evidence pending, of course. But we have to consider this path as our main trail. We can't afford not to."

Little pins prickled up his spine. He took a swig of dark roast, refusing to let the pink boot kicking at his brain into his thoughts.

"Let's talk about the hair." Walking to the front of the room, he pointed at a photo clearly displaying the wild orange mane. "The Frog Lake boy had permed hair. An extensive process. The hair on our new victim here, well, look at how stiff it is. It sticks straight out in all directions."

"You know what?" Sutton lowered his Big Gulp onto the centre table. "It kind of looks like what my daughter does to her hair, but a lot more wild. Backcombing, she calls it. She says it's 'in.' She goes through cans of hairspray like they're cartons of milk. Kids these days." Shaking his head, he retrieved his Big Gulp, finding the red straw with his mouth.

"Confirms our guy's habit of giving his boys extensive hairdos. We'll see what Blackwood finds. On to the face. Makeup appears thick again."

Mahoney took a long swig of cold coffee. Swallowing hard, he forced the swirling in his stomach to halt. "The jacket. A straitjacket. We all saw it. We need to find out where you would get a jacket like this. It can't be possible to walk into your friendly neighbourhood clothing store and buy something intended to restrain seriously ill and disturbed people. Let's get some direction on this."

Slipping her black glasses down her nose, Dara looked up from scribing. "I can do a search, Bug."

"Thanks, Dara. It's not something the boy was likely just strutting around town in. It's got to lead us somewhere." *Yeah, it has to. Right, Bug?* Mahoney wondered who he was trying to convince.

Dara, sliding her glasses back into place, proceeded with her notetaking.

Mahoney turned to face the front wall of the room. Scanning the map of the city plastered to the chipping paint, he took note of the two black pins. One at Frog Lake, the other at Eagle Woods. Sifting through a box of pins on the table against the wall, he picked up a third black one, careful not to prick himself. Placing it at Clear Creek Ravine, he turned to face his audience.

"Three bodies now. The first two were in opposite quadrants of the city. Didn't tell us much. Any thoughts?"

Sutton scratched the back of his neck. "The first two scenes, they were on the outskirts of the city. Both in large parks, way out in the wilderness. Quite secluded."

Hayes said, "Yeah. It's like this third one is more *in* the city. Right in the backyard of the houses on that street."

Mahoney rubbed the bristle on his chin, staring at the map. "Why?"

Sutton took a stab. "I wonder if it's, well, easier? I mean, easier for our guy to access? It would have been a lot of work to get the body all the way across the beach at Frog Lake, down the trail, and into the woods."

Hayes said, "Yeah. And the one at Eagle Woods, he would have had to get that body along the trail and into the secluded area. But this last one, getting it down the steep incline would have been challenging, but the trek into the cave was much shorter."

Sutton nodded vigorously. "Yeah. Less of a trek to get there, too, being right in the city."

"He could be keeping the bodies closer to him to make it easier to visit them," Agent Quesnel smoothly interjected from the back of the room, reminding them she was now an integral part of their investigative process.

"Visit? You mean even after he was done beautifying them?" Sutton raised an eyebrow.

"Yes. Spending time with them."

"What the hell for?" Widening his eyes, Hayes turned to face Agent Quesnel.

"Drawing out the fantasy he's created for as long as possible."

"Creepy. What would he, uh, *do* with a dead body?" Sutton turned to the back of the room.

Agent Quesnel slyly walked toward the front of the room, the fluorescent lighting throwing a glimmer off her black platinum boots. "He could simply enjoy being near the bodies. He went to a lot of effort to create the scene;

he might be relishing in the craftsmanship of his work. Everything he does to the victims, it's personal. These bodies, these boys, they could also be sexually stimulating him. In some of the cases I've worked on, there have been instances of the killer having sexual interaction with the corpse."

"What? That's messed up." Hayes leaned forward in his chair, resting his elbows on his knees. "Why in the hell would any human being have sex with a dead person?" Hayes shook his head.

"Necrophilia. Sexual stimulation induced by a corpse. It's a paraphilia, a sexual fixation. Serial killers have stacked paraphilias. That is, multiple fixations layered together. On average, from our studies thus far, 4 or 5."

Sutton and Hayes stared at Agent Quesnel, grasping her every word.

Sutton plunked his Big Gulp onto the table. "What?"

Agent Quesnel responded, "Example time. Brudos. He conducted necrophilia. He kept feet as trophies. Masochism pumped through his veins. And transvestism was in his core. So, he hung and tortured women, cut off their feet and kept them in his freezer, conducted sexual acts with the corpses, and even as a teenager he cross dressed."

"Jeez." Sutton sat back in his chair.

"Blackwood ran the standard process on the first two victims. Didn't find any indication of this, well, interaction. I'll follow up with her on the latest victim." Mahoney said.

Agent Quesnel said, "Even without any indication that he had sexual interaction with the bodies, his visits with them could still be sexually stimulating him. He could be pleasuring himself."

Sutton shook his head.

Quesnel continued. "Like I said, everything we see here indicates that the whole process is very personal to the killer. The grooming remains a fundamental part of his script, and it's evolving. Just take a look at the hair. When have you seen anyone walking around town with such a vibrant shade of orange-red? It could have been dyed. Dying hair is a very intimate process, similar to perming. The killer would have had his hands directly on that mane for a lengthy amount of time. As you pointed out, Sutton, a lot of product goes into stiffening a style like that. Backcombing is very involved. A small number of strands are partitioned, to which a comb is applied in the opposite direction of natural flow, toward the scalp. It takes a significant number of partitions to get through a head of hair like this victim has. It seems our killer is developing an increasingly intimate hair-grooming process with his victims."

Sutton whistled. "That's gross. You're saying our guy wants to touch these boys after they're dead. And he's paying them visits, even after the killing and grooming, uh, activities, are over."

"Likely," Agent Quesnel confirmed with confidence. "The same concepts can be applied to the clothing found on these victims. It is quite likely the killer himself is putting these outfits together."

"You're suggesting we assume the clothing didn't belong to the victims?" Hayes inquired.

"Yes. You're already going down that road. You've had reactions from some of the family members of these young boys that indicates this clothing wasn't typical of what they would be seen in."

Mahoney said, "It's possible these young boys developed different dressing habits than they had previously displayed. Especially after spreading their wings living away from Mom and Dad and hanging out at college parties."

"Of course. But, top off the family reactions with the fact that body number two was found in nothing but a sheer robe and body number three was found wearing a straitjacket, well, as you've observed, this isn't attire that anyone strolls down the street in."

"Good point."

"OK. So, let's say the killer did create these, uh, outfits. Why are all three so different?" Sutton questioned.

"His fantasy. Whatever fantasy he is trying to play out, these outfits are tied to it. You're already onto some strong paths based on the evidence, like the clothing boutique where the cloak was purchased. This latest item, the straitjacket, it's a very unusual piece of clothing. It could be a big lead. Assuming the cloak was an indication of the killer's behaviour led us to scope out the rocker bar for suspects, not just for victims. The jacket might tell us something about the killer himself. His behaviour. Or his past."

Sutton, sipping his Big Gulp, nodded. "What does this jacket tell us about behaviour?"

Agent Quesnel said, "This jacket, it's likely connected to some sort of institution. The serial killers my team has studied, they tend to have a track record either in penitentiaries or mental institutions. Their records often go far back, even into their teen years."

Mahoney said, "Agent Quesnel, you and I can work with Dara to find sources of this jacket. Sutton, Hayes, give Clear Creek Ravine another combing over. Given it's smack in the middle of a residential area, someone could have seen something. Especially if our guy is spending more and more time with his victims."

"Got it, boss." Hayes jotted in his notebook.

"When you conduct the interviews on the circle of friends, see what you can find out about his dressing habits," Mahoney said. "Be sensitive. Approach it as an inquiry into his style. Include his hairdo as well."

"You got it, boss." Sutton nodded, adding his own notes to the plan for the day.

Agent Quesnel said, "Dara, you've already started combining the first two sets of clothing and notes?"

Dara, looking up from scribing, nodded.

"Now we have a third layer we can add on. What if we combine the outfits with the messages? Assume they're related."

Dara confirmed the path, nodding at Agent Quesnel.

"He is putting more and more effort into his complex murder scenes, trying to recreate his fantasy to perfection." Agent Quesnel said, adding fuel to the triage of investigation. "Each time he fails, he could be growing frustrated and desperate to get it right. The more flustered he gets, the more he panics. His meticulous script begins to break down. He may soon make the mistake we need to solve this, if he hasn't already."

"Boys, really comb Clear Creek. Widen the perimeter. If our guy left us anything, we don't want to miss it."

"Got it, boss. We'll be thorough," Sutton confirmed.

Mahoney said, "Before we convene, let's review the timelines. Seems Clear Creek boy died last Friday night."

"Exactly one week after the Frog Lake boy?" Agent Quesnel inquired.

"Yeah."

Agent Quesnel said, "The killer may be solidifying his pattern. Saturday night rock show and kidnapping. Torture. Then kill, in time for the next live show."

"We got an ID on our victim already, thanks to a missing person's report. Sutton, can you check that file?" Mahoney moved over to the calendar displaying blue-coded and orange-coded timelines of the Frog Lake and Eagle Woods boys. Picking up a green marker, he added in the time of death of the Clear Creek Ravine victim.

Sutton said, "Eagle Woods boy disappeared March 21. Frog Lake boy disappeared on April 4. Clear Creek Ravine boy disappeared April 11. Does that mean another kid could have already been taken, last Saturday?"

Agent Quesnel said, "He's tightening up the timelines between abductions and between kills."

Mahoney stared at the black hands ticking loudly over the white clock face. A few droplets of sweat popped over his forehead. "We were at the dive joint, last Saturday. That guy with the ponytail, he was acting strange. Then he vanished. The other two creepy guys checked out." He paused. *Dammit.* "I'll have to go back. Find out if Clear Creek boy was seen. Sutton, Hayes, when you interview the circle of friends of our Clear Creek boy, be sure to ask about his presence at this joint, and any shows he may have attended or been planning on attending."

"Got it, boss." Hayes noted down the tasks. Smirking, Hayes added, "Should be easier to inquire about than his dressing habits."

Agent Quesnel walked up to the whiteboard. "These kills are insanely brutal. The killer appears to be hedonistic. Emotional. Yet, there is an aspect of organization here that seems superimposed. It's like the killer is trying to create a schedule. But, abducting the victims from the same joint seems impulsive. Or, driven by ego. Like he can't be caught."

Mahoney snapped the cap on the marker. "We'll stop in at the dive joint. Let's confirm what we can, fill in the behavioral aspect. Boys, you have a hefty day ahead of you. Scene scouring and interviewing. That's a big load added your already long list of items you are still following up on."

"No problem, boss. We got it." Sutton sipped the last drops of his Big Gulp, air-sucking noises from the empty cup echoing through the room.

"I don't know how you drink so much of that battery acid," Hayes said.

"I got a stomach full of greasy burgers to pad it." Sutton laughed.

"OK, boys, glad you haven't lost your sense of humour." Mahoney looked toward the back of the room. "Dara, you've got quite the growing list of searches."

"It's fine. Let's get you some mental institutions to scour. Then I'll keep digging into the messages. And, I've still got nothing on where the toxic cocktail came from." She slipped her black glasses down her nose, letting them hang from their sparkly beaded necklace.

"Agent Quesnel, you up to joining me for a tour of the city's finest places? We'll start with a skid-rock bar, then move on to a series of mental institutions."

"Yeah. Just the kind of crazy I'm into."

Sutton and Hayes shuffled toward the door. Mahoney slid up behind them and grabbed Sutton by the elbow. "Sutton, stay a minute."

"Sure, boss."

Dara and Agent Quesnel moved past them. Mahoney looked Sutton in the eye. "Listen, that rabbit foot…"

"Oh, I'm sorry, boss, it's stupid."

"No. It means you have instinct. You know how to listen to your gut. You want to become a prime investigator in a few years, don't you?"

"Yeah"

"Then you listen to that gut of yours. Now. On this case. And, push Hayes along a little. We need his by the book attitude, but we have to open our minds a little too."

"Got it, boss."

Stack of Bodies

Mahoney swung open the main door to the homicide headquarters. *See ya soon, HQ.* He tried to sift through the mound of data bombarding his brain. These war room meetings were piling on potential paths. They were supposed to be eliminating paths, not adding more. His mind swirling, his heart pattered at the thought of his first stop to visit Blackwood in her dark, cold morgue. Pushing the key into the driver's side of his car, he creaked the door open.

Pulling onto the main road, Mahoney tried to open his mind to the sultry riff wafting from the CD player. Popping open the pill bottle the nurse had given him, he tilted it against his lips, dropping a pill onto his tongue. Homicide was situated right next to the main police building serving as headquarters for the whole city, conveniently providing him access to things such as a quick checkup. Sam, the nurse, was always sweet. Her strawberry lips flashed through his mind. Clicking the top back on the pill bottle, he grabbed for the Styrofoam cup perched in the holder. He sipped the cold water that had replaced his coffee. *Dammit.* Washing down the pill, he shook his head. *Trust a damn ulcer to invade my gut in the middle of all this.* He focused back on the road.

Interruptions kept invading his mind, a little white ghost face circling around, pulling him away from the soothing blues. A silver, oval frame wove around the little white face. The ghost face turning the colour of arctic ice, the oval-framed lavender eyes and blood-red lips hung from a long silver chain. The chain weaving its way up a pale torso, circling around a branded neck. The frame swinging freely, the arctic-ice ghost face moving back and forth, hypnotizing him. Shimmering black, eagle-raven wings flowing from outstretched arms.

The arctic-ice ghost face pursing her lips, glared at Bug. The outline of more little ghost faces stretched against the pale corpse skin, trying to push their way to the surface. The little faces tore through the flesh, ripping a gorge all the way up the torso, weaving around the branded neck. Their little hands digging through the bloody flesh, trying to pull themselves free. Their cries rang through Bug's head, invading his thoughts, haunting him. Beneath the little ghost faces and hands were more little ghost bodies. Stacking atop each other, body after body, they were buried deep into the wet core of the rotting corpse. The ones on top continuing to claw with their little hands in desperation, ripping the flesh, forcing their way to the surface.

Now the eagle-raven body was covered as a fresh, red-robed corpse fell from above, stacking itself on top. The tiny ghost voices were stifled as the little bodies suffocated under the weight. Another corpse fell from the sky, an orange-maned maniac landing atop the red robe. The stack grew, body upon body upon body. Bug's mind spinning, his vision blurring, he grasped at the steering wheel.

Shaking his head harshly, he forced his eyes to focus on the road. Grabbing for his Styrofoam cup, taking a long swig, he swallowed the cold, soothing water. Wiping his brow with his kerchief, he steadied himself back into the soft driver's seat. *Geez, Bug, get a hold of yourself. Don't fall apart.* He blinked his eyes hard, taking several deep breaths.

Three bodies, one killer. As long as he'd been on the homicide department, nothing like this had happened in his hometown. Only the rare case of a true serial killer had been known across the country. But not in his city. Things tended to stay quiet up north. The only exposure he had to this type of murder was on the other side of the country. Any other cases he had read about had occurred south of the border.

Shake it off, Bug. This isn't the time to fall apart. Get things under control.

The last war room pow wow had left him grasping to keep a straight line forward. With the bodies stacking up in such a short period, the number of possible paths was increasing exponentially. They had no solid leads on the first two bodies. It was as if these boys had some separate, secret life that no one knew about. Or, they were merely in the wrong place at the wrong time. Either way, despite the deep-digging efforts of his team, they couldn't seem to turn up anything substantial.

Taking another swig of clear liquid, he focused on the road. Pulling at the collar of his tweed coat, he opened up some space around his neck. Removing his derby, he settled it across from him on the passenger side. He needed to get a move on. He had to catch up with Blackwood, then meet up with Agent Quesnel. Sutton and Hayes had jumped into their next lines of investigation. He imagined Dara typing away like a machine over at her computer. He pictured Agent Quesnel under the neon sign outside the black door, tapping her platinum-booted foot on the pavement. He couldn't be the bottleneck here. *Focus, Bug. One step at a time. Don't mess up. Starting with Blackwood will be good. Maybe she found something I can use for some solid direction on this last victim.* Picturing her purple almond eyes, his shoulders relaxed into the plush seat. *And maybe she can serve me up with a dose of her wilderness calm.*

My Only Friend

"**H**ey." Seth steadied his nerves as he ventured down a rare path of initiating a conversation. From his favourite seat up at the bar, he eyeballed the guy two chairs down. The chair between them was vacant. The bar was nearly empty. He'd seen this guy before. It was easy to remember the other patrons, given how empty this place was in the middle of the day. Plus, the guy had long, dark hair, like his.

The mystery guy smiled back at him warmly as he turned in his seat to face Seth. "Hi. I've seen you around here before, haven't I?"

"Yeah. Uh, I don't really get much MTV at home. Here, it's always on, if I ask. And, it's, uh, well, it's quiet," Seth responded, then quickly turned his attention to his tall glass. His cheeks grew warm as a flush washed over his face.

"I'm Simon." The familiar stranger extended his hand.

Seth twisted in his chair. Offering a meek shake in return, he spun back to his drink. *Geez, c'mon, Seth,* he scolded himself. *Don't be so frickin' weird.*

Simon took a long swig from the pint glass perched on the bar in front of him. "I think I've seen you at some of the live shows here as well?"

Seth sat up straight, turning toward Simon. "Yeah. I, uh, I love live music."

"Me too. Beating a live show is hard. This place may be small, but the acoustics are outstanding. They seem to be quite proficient at bringing in quality talent."

Seth took a long swig of potent liquid. Clearing his throat, he mentally smoothed his nerves and attempted to steady his voice. "Yeah. You're dead on. I don't usually like being so, um, packed in, you know, with so many strangers. But, well, I kind of lose myself in the music during a knockout show."

Simon smiled, nodding his agreement. "I hear you. Holding a job and studying at school leads to a lot of quiet nights at home for me. Sometimes it's nice to get out and be a little crazy."

Seth's shoulders relaxed a little. His stomach stopped fluttering. *I like this guy. He's nice. You can do this, Seth.*

Both taking long swigs of their drinks, their attention was drawn up to the multiple screens perched above the bar. Images juxtaposed themselves over the dramatic opening bars of a rock ballad. Two ponytailed women clicked their heals over the pavement as they sprung from a black polka-dotted red beetle-like car. Their mini-skirts hoisted out like tutus, their long legs slid through the night. Flashing to another scene, a shiny black limousine rolled to a halt, long-haired men slipping from the doors. Their leader, taking his place onstage, posed his pink lips dramatically, enunciating each word as he crooned to his followers.

Simon shook his head. "The whole video concept has really changed the game for musicians. It might eliminate the pure vocal artist. These music videos have turned songs into mini-movies. The concept is interesting, and I do appreciate how the platform has opened up entirely new ways for musicians to express themselves. However, I can't help wondering if this eliminates some excellent raw talent from the scene. I wonder if we, as the consumers, will have limited, or even complete lack of access to pure artists."

Seth was intrigued. His mind raced with a million responses. His palms were sweating, and his upper lip was moist. *Just keep talking to him,* he goaded himself. "Dang. You're the first dude I met who talks this way…I don't know anyone interested in this stuff." He stared at his drink, pondering what to say next.

Simon solved the problem for him. "You said you came here often, for the MTV. Sounds like you enjoy the video platform. What do you think the impact will be on consumers, like yourself?"

A smile took over Seth's entire face. "Yeah, I…I love videos. The music, like, comes alive. It's, uh, well, it's like I get a glimpse into the mind of the singer. Like I can see his message played out."

Simon raised an eyebrow. "Hmmm. I never really thought of it like that." He sat back in his chair, examining the screen again. "You have a point. I need to consider a wider range of videos. When I made my argument, I was thinking of the videos that have enabled the one-hit wonders of the world to become famous overnight, solely based on visual aspects. I was assuming that the consumer would become driven by the glamour of the movie format and forget about the real music behind it. I believe what you are pointing out, my friend, are the ones that elevate the message to a new level by leveraging the visual aspect, but still stay committed to the musical elements. This one is a great example." Simon raised his pint glass toward the screen centred above and between them.

The pink-lipped leader waved his arms dramatically through the air, the long, shiny black sleeves of his cloak spreading like wings around him. His golden-haired right-hand man shot his guitar into the air, catching it with one hand, sliding his other hand over its electric strings. An emotional riff rang through the bar.

Seth looked back at Simon. "Yeah, this band has flair. But they stay true to the message of the music. Most of this video is them onstage."

"I see. If my argument is to stand solidly on two feet, I must consider a wider range of repertoire," Simon agreed.

Seth snickered. "Yeah, man. Gotcha there." He motioned to Sasha. He only came in when she was on shift. It was easier to deal with her than someone who didn't know his order, or who didn't change the channel for him. "Sasha, can I please get another round, for me and my, uh, my new friend here."

"You OK, sweetie?" Concern washed over Sasha's pretty face as her eyes darted along the bar.

"Yeah. I'm great. Just want to buy a round here for my new friend." Seth nodded toward Simon. "Don't worry, I'm good for the tab, you know that."

"Uh, OK. Right on it." Sasha's voice riddled with hesitation, she spun around to take care of Seth's order.

"Thanks, man. That's nice of you."

"Sure. No problem." Seth leaned back, enjoying the images flashing on the screen even more than ever. It was nice to finally have some real company.

Coming to Life

Sitting in silence, perched on a high stool, Mahoney watched Blackwood. Her latex-covered hand running over the silver buckles, she stared down at the caged corpse. "Proceeding with the removal of the jacket." Recording her steps, she spoke into the small recorder perched on a shiny silver table.

Unlatching the top buckle, she pulled at the tight bind. A chill ran up Mahoney's spine. Working at it until it loosened, she moved her hand down to the next buckle. Mahoney imagined the constricting binds twisting his own arms around his back, caging in his body. Reaching the last buckle, Blackwood loosened the final bind. Heaving the body to a sitting position by the shoulders, she leaned the body's chest against her left arm. She pulled each side of the open jacket away from the body, as far as it would give. Lowering the body back down onto the steel slab, she stretched out each of the arms, laying them on either side of the torso. Tugging at the end of the long sleeve closest to her, the body's arm slid from its bind. After a pause, she repeated the hefty effort to break the other arm free. Peeling the top of the jacket away from the body, her back stiffened to a halt. Staring at the barbaric white chest, her plastic-gloved hand shot toward her mouth, a tiny gasp escaping from her lips.

Mahoney plunked himself off the stool and walked over to the body. The entire front of the body from chest to abdomen was collaged in red letters, cut into the skin. The killer had sliced a series of sadistic sentences, forming an entire bloody note, right into his victim. He had immortally tattooed his prey. *My God. Was the poor kid alive while the killer slowly worked his penmanship into his skin?*

Looking over the careful work, Mahoney imagined the small letters being carefully cut, one at a time, forming full sentences across the body. *These cuts are meticulous. How long would this take?*

Blackwood snapped the recorder off. Mahoney stared at the body. He read each carved message from the top of the body down to the waistline

"D Brought me to My Knees"

"I Wanna Hear D SCREAM"

"D Gonna DIE"

"I'm Gonna Bring D DOWN"

Mahoney's mind spinning, a chill trickled over him. Tiny motions pulled his eyes away from the letters of blood, landing on a small gathering of maggots feasting on a buffet of flesh.

Blackwood stumbled away from the corpse erratically. She struggled to lift the straitjacket as she placed it down. One of her purple eyes shedding a single tear, she turned and leaned against the cold steel of a large sink. Finding her temples with her pointer and forefingers, she pressed tiny circles into her head.

A little girl's face flashed through Mahoney's mind. His breakfast swelled in his stomach, menacing its way up his throat. He swallowed hard against the bile in his throat.

"Are you ok?" He asked.

Taking a deep breath, she opened her eyes, narrowing her almond lids. Spinning on her heel, she took several quick strides back to the dead body. "Yeah. Fine."

Returning to the jacket, she stretched it out on display, laying it against the silver examination table. Exploring every minuscule fragment of the yellowing material, she searched for even the tiniest scrap of a clue. Her unsatisfying search coming to a close, she bagged and tagged the item.

Returning to the body, she scanned the pale arms. Black-leather bracelets snaked their way up the pallid flesh, dark-red welts weaving alongside, marking the territory of the bindings. Similar, more massive welts thrashed across the pale torso, emblems of torture. She picked up a small camera and proceeded to capture a thorough collage of the bloody note and the red welts.

Picking a tweezer-like tool from her silver toolbox, she plucked a maggot from the festering red gash where it was dining. Giving it a new home in a plastic vial, she watched it crawl up the side.

Mahoney sat back down on the stool, observing in silence.

Screwing the lid onto the vial of vermin, her shoulders relaxed.

She broke the silence. "That's a lot of messages. And a lot of marks. The jacket must have been tied tight."

"This guy liked to suck the life out of his prey, in more ways than one. The toxins, the strangulation, and literally draining the crazy right out of this latest victim."

"I wonder why he used a straitjacket, and where would you even get something like that?" she said.

"Actually, we ran a search. Turns out that you can only get one at a mental institution. You would have to work there, or be a patient," Mahoney said.

"Good lead."

"There are only three in this city. I'll be checking them out today, with Agent Quesnel. Once we're done her. I'm trying to keep quiet." He smiled.

Welcoming the break, Blackwood smiled in return. "I can give you a couple of things. Preliminary, but they can be used for consideration until confirmed." Picking up the small plastic vial, she held it out for Mahoney to view.

Mahoney shrugged, watching the maggot crawling across the bottom. "So, the body's been sitting there a while then?"

"Not necessarily. These little critters can appear within twenty-four hours."

"Really? Fast little suckers."

"I'll send him off to the entomologist. He estimated the time of death to be after dark, the night of April 17."

"Yeah. We think he has a pattern. We're stopping by the rocker bar again today. Anything more specific about the time of death?"

"Mahoney, you know the most accurate I can give you is after dark." Her lips spread into a slight smile. "Although our creepy critter here just might facilitate a smaller time window. Maybe. And only if he co-operates with our entomologist." She peered into the vial as she talked as if her comments were intended for the critter. Placing the capsuled maggot onto a shelf of a fresh evidence box, she turned back to Mahoney. "Let's take one more look at the body." Tugging his sleeve, she guided him closer to the corpse. Her eyes rescanning the barbaric white chest, rereading the series of sick messages.

Mahoney's eyes widening, his hand shot to his bristly chin. Rubbing the stubble, he cocked an eyebrow. "Geez. That's one hell of an angry tone. Whoever 'D' is, they have it coming. Must have really ticked off this guy."

"Yeah. It's not the type of note that leaves a warm and fuzzy feeling."

Mahoney continued analyzing the notes. "That's a lot of work to leave all those messages. A lot of cuts. Letters are small. It would take some careful craftsmanship."

"Yeah. The letters are small and concise. That would take meticulous slicing skills. The cuts from our Frog Lake boy didn't lead to any conclusive match on a knife. There's more here. It might give us something. I just wonder if the victim was alive when the messages were cut. If he was aware, cognizant enough to feel the pain."

Mahoney's mind wandering, images of the body lying before him appeared. He saw the boy writhing in pain, screaming for help, a sick and twisted monster looming over him. The monster slicing the flesh open, oblivious of the pain being caused, or shivering in delight.

He snapped his thoughts back to the examination. "More messages. A chance to narrow down his selection of tools."

"It's possible. I'll take some photos and send them off with the evidence box."

"There're a lot of marks too. I guess that jacket must have been tied tight. I wonder how long he was wearing it. Is there any way you can tell?"

"I can analyze the marks. Try and determine by the depth of blood blockage and also the stage of bruising when the impressions were first made."

"That would be swell."

"I'm not very far into the examination. I don't think I can be of any more help yet."

"Do what you need to. I'll check in later."

"I'll get the photos of the cuts and our little crawling critter off right away. Then I'll do my usual initial scan. Likely we'll be able to get more chemical analysis on the hair and makeup, like with the other ones. Once that's going, I'll move into the more time-consuming analysis. I'll start with the marks and bruising."

"Sounds like a solid plan. Hey, what's that?" Mahoney pointed at a tiny piece of red embedded in one of the ligatures around the pale neck.

"Woah. Let's find out." Scanning her toolbox, she settled on a small pair of tweezers with little, pointed ends. Her gloved hand hovering over the neck, she plucked the red mystery fragment from the flesh. As she pulled, the fragment grew into a tiny piece of red fibre. Laying it carefully on a plastic square, she leaned in to inspect it. "Mahoney. It looks like a fibre, a piece of material. Could be from whatever was used to strangle the boy."

Mahoney's mind buzzing with excitement, he dared to dream. "Wonder if our guy slipped up. He's left us plenty of bizarre clues. But he's never left a piece of himself."

"I'll get it processed. Right away." Her gloved hands worked quickly, placing the fibre in a plastic bag. "I'm sorry I don't have more for you. There's a lot to process here. I feel like I'm crawling along." She shook her head.

"Take your time. Do it right. That's what I keep telling myself." He smiled. "Look, I've gotta get going. Quesnel will be waiting, and my boys need a check in. Keep me posted."

"You know I will."

Mahoney turned toward the morgue door. His heart fluttered a couple of times. *Bug, get yourself together. You have a killer to hunt.*

Stakeout Scarf

Mahoney stared at the green rabbit foot hanging from the rear-view mirror. Sutton took a huge bite of his greasy burger. Chomping away, devouring the chunk of meat, grease slid down his chin.

"Pig!" Hayes jabbed.

"Ya, you're one to talk. Look at that mess of yours." Sutton waved his enormous burger at the pile of crumpled wrappers crowding the floor beneath the passenger seat.

"It's not my fault. We've been cooped up in here for hours. What's a guy supposed to do?"

"Yeah. I know." Wiping his chin with a thin paper napkin, Sutton pushed a fist into Hayes' shoulder.

Hayes twisted his neck to the back seat. "Hey, boss, thanks for making the food run."

"Sure." Mahoney shifted uncomfortably. "It's tight back here."

"Sorry, boss. Truck is nice to look at, but not a lot room in the back." Sutton took another gigantic bite of meat and cheese. 'This is a bust so far."

"Well, you boys are gonna have to hang out a while longer. There were some suspicious looking guys during that rock show I went to with Agent Quesnel," Mahoney responded. "We need to keep an eye on this joint. I can't stay long. Gotta catch up with her."

Hayes picked up a pair of binoculars, scanning the parking lot behind the dive bar. "Nothing. No action."

"Yeah, and we're just jackasses sitting here. This job ain't glamourous."

"You thought it would be?" Mahoney asked.

"No. Well, maybe. At least some of the time. We finally get a huge case, and, well, it's just gruesome. And I miss my bed."

"Yeah." Hayes looked at the pile of crumpled garbage at his feet.

"Well, get used to it, boys."

Sutton mumbled with a full mouth. "Hey. Did you see that?"

Hayes whipped the binoculars in front of his eyes. "Yeah. There's something."

Mahoney leaned in between the two front seats and peered out the windshield.

"That car, it just tore around from the front of the lot, straight around the back there." Throwing his burger into a paper bag, Sutton wiped his greasy hands on his jeans.

Hayes peered into the binoculars.

"See anything?" Sutton poked.

"Yeah. I see the car. A guy is getting out. His hair, it's black, long, in a ponytail. He's got a garbage bag. He's approaching a big bin. He's looking around. Don't move."

"Did he see us?"

"Nope. We're clear. He's opening the bin. He's throwing away the garbage bag. I think he's gonna take off."

The car peeled out of the lot, disappearing down the street.

"Get the licence plate," Mahoney barked.

"There isn't one. The car, it's a Skylark. Rusty. Brown. Tailpipe looks like it's loose."

Sutton scribbled into his notebook.

"He's gone. Let's go see what he threw out."

Sutton started the engine and rolled the truck into the parking lot. Disembarking, they approached the garbage bin. They hoisted up the top, Sutton on one side, Hayes on the other.

"Phew. That is rank. We need Dara and her fresh mountain air spray." Sutton fanned his nose with his hand.

"Ha ha," Hayes laughed sarcastically. "You get the bag."

"What? No way. You get it."

"You boys figure this out. I'm calling that car in to Dara." Mahoney pulled his cell phone from his belt. Sutton and Hayes chattered in the background as he punched in the numbers.

"Rock, paper, scissors?"

"Fine."

Pressing the phone to his ear, he watched Sutton and Hayes. They curled their right hands into fists and pumped their arms in unison three times. Hayes held a fist out toward Sutton. Sutton held his hand flat.

"Paper covers rock! You go in that bin!" Sutton danced around, letting out a full laugh.

"Fine." Hayes glared at Sutton. Pulling a pair of latex gloves from his back jeans pocket, he snapped them over his hands.

Mahoney turned and walked a few steps across the pavement. "Dara. It's Mahoney. Can you search for a brown Skylark."

"No license plate?"

"No. It didn't have one."

"Year?"

"Not sure. It was rusty. So not new. I know it's not much to go on."

"I'll see what I can do."

"Thanks." He pressed the *off* button and re-holstered the phone.

He turned back to the bin. Hayes, on the tips of his toes, was staring into it.

"Frick. This guy threw the bag in. Looks like it's full of clothes. They're spilling out." Hayes stretched an arm into the bin, retrieving the garbage bag. Dropping it onto the pavement, a silk scarf slipped from the opening.

"Will you look at that?" Sutton bent over, peering at the scarf. The silky material was a striking shade of red.

Sutton and Hayes looked at each other. Hayes picked up the scarf. Sliding it through his hands, he halted suddenly. There was a tiny piece of material missing, from one the corners. The material was frayed as if it had been ripped.

"It has a tear. Looks like the same colour as the fibre lodged in the Clear Creek boy's neck."

"Bag it. And, boys, you're on search duty. I want anything you can find in the bin."

Sutton's eyebrow raised. "Yeah, got it." He looked at Hayes. "No more rock, paper, scissors for us. We're both going in that bin."

They both looked into the bin, the aroma of days of rotting garbage filling their noses.

"Keep me posted, boys." Mahoney turned to walk to his car.

Sutton's voice followed him. "Suck it up, princess. As the boss says: perks of the job, kid."

Mental Institution

Following the white-clad attendant, Mahoney squinted into the blast of bright light glowing from the long fluorescent tubes lining the white ceilings. The long hallway, decorated with a monochrome palette of white, seemed to be a desperate attempt to cover up a dark situation. Despite the brightness of the lights and the heavy, hot air, a chill slithered down Mahoney's spine. *Geez, how long does this hallway go on? It's like we're in a short repeating movie strip.*

Every few feet they passed a door. Each one painted white with a small steel-barred window at the top. *I wonder what it's like inside one of those rooms.* Passing the same door for what felt like the hundredth time, Mahoney looked back at two eyes peeking through a mess of wild, grey hair. Tears streaking the wrinkled face, a shrivelled hand pounded silently against the glass.

"Tony, assistance in room 42A please," the attendant, Marie, pleasantly spoke into a radio.

"10-4," a deep voice crackled through the radio.

Mahoney shot a glance at Agent Quesnel. Her shiny platinum boots striking against the glowing white floor, her heels clicked an echo through the long, silent hallway. Her eyes coolly scanned their surroundings, her poise calm and collected. *It's like she's window shopping in the mall on a Saturday afternoon,* he thought. *She meant it. The crazy in here, it's her gig.* It made him wonder how many of these places she'd been in. He had read about her research. He knew she'd been locked in four walls of steel bars, sitting face to face with complete psychopaths, sociopaths, and narcissistic personalities. He was curious—hadn't the balls to inquire. Or had the wisdom not to, until it became necessary.

"This way, sir, miss." The angelic attendant smiled wide, her bright-white teeth matching the walls. She spun her white-shoed foot, her stiff white slacks following mechanically like she was a doll playing out the movements forced upon her by her master. Following Marie down a smaller hallway toward a large, silver door, they paused at the entrance way. Marie scanned her access card against a grey box with a red light. The light turning green, she shot them another broad smile. A click followed by a buzzing noise rang through the silence as the large door opened slowly.

"All exits are on an electronic system, for safety reasons," Marie informed, maintaining her wide smile.

Entering the doorway, their surroundings instantly took on another tone. Soft light bathed ocean-blue walls. Offices lined a hallway adorned with green plants. The aroma of fresh leaves and earth drifted through the air. Marie led them into a small office. A window at the back of the office provided a view of a beautifully manicured green park. Benches lined a pond, the water glimmering in the sunshine.

"These are staff quarters. The park takes up about half of the back of the property. It's an oasis for patients. At least for the ones who get to go out there."

"Get to?" Agent Quesnel sharply inquired.

"Yes. A patient must be deemed at no risk to harm themselves, or others, to have park privileges. I must go check on the situation I called in. Please, have a seat. Dr. Crighton will be with you shortly."

The attendant disappeared in a flash of white. Agent Quesnel sank into a plush chair. Running her hands along the black-leather arms, she whistled. "Nice office. Wonder how much a psychiatrist rakes in up here."

Mahoney smirked. "I would have thought with your schooling, not to mention your wit, you'd be up to speed on that."

Agent Quesnel clicked her tongue at him, caressing the leather with her palms.

"My apologies for keeping you waiting." A tall man in a tailored suit slid through the doorway. "I'm Dr. Crighton. You must be Detective Mahoney and Agent Quesnel. Please, don't get up. Make yourselves comfortable."

The doctor slid into a chair behind a dark cherry-wood desk. Agent Quesnel resettled herself in the comfort of the leather.

Mahoney followed suit, plunking down in an adjacent, matching chair. "We are investigating a homicide. Well, a series of them, actually. Our last victim was found wearing this." Sliding a photo of the straitjacket across the cherry desktop toward the doctor, Mahoney said, "Our searches have indicated that the only place to obtain such a jacket would be at a registered institution. There are only three such facilities in the city, as far as we are aware. We're hoping you can help us determine where this particular jacket might have been obtained from."

Placing a pair of silver-wired glasses on the bridge of his nose, Dr. Crighton scrutinized the photo. "Yes, I see. This jacket appears to be standard issue. The cut and the trim seem legitimate. The buckles appear inline with what would be used. Did it have a tag sewn into the inside on the back? It would have had a series of digits inside, like a serial number." The doctor placed the photo on the desk. Removing his glasses, he poked a wired end in the corner of his mouth.

Mahoney retrieved a folder from his worn briefcase. Flipping through the folder, he slid a series of photos onto the cherry wood. "This is what I have. The jacket is in processing."

Returning the wired rims toward his eyes, the doctor sifted through the photos. "Ah. Looks like a serial in this one." Pulling the photo close to his face, he stared hard. "I can't make out the numbering."

Mahoney slid his phone out of his holster, his fingers speeding over the buttons. "Blackwood. It's Mahoney. Look, I know you're up to your eyeballs in corpses, but do you still have that straitjacket in your examination room?" His heart fluttered. What a break this could be. "Is there a tag inside on the back?" He paused. "Yeah. There should be a number on it." Clicking a pen open, he scribbled into his notepad. "Thanks. Hey, could you get some close-up photos of the tag?" Pressing his phone off, he passed his notepad to Dr. Crighton.

Dr. Crighton turned to the keyboard to his left, typing in credentials with proficiency. The computer screen sprung to life. "We are fortunate to have a newly installed database program. It lends us quick access to our facility's inventory. It goes back ten years. If this jacket was in our facility when this electronic inventory was created, then we will have a record of it here." Pausing, he looked at Mahoney. "I assume that you did bring a search warrant for the institution's records?"

Mahoney rifled through his briefcase, retrieving a thin paper and sliding it across the desk.

Dr. Crighton eyeballed the warrant, then turned back to the serial number. His fingers tapped away at the keyboard.

Agent Quesnel shifted in her plush chair, crossing a sleek black leg over the other. "What if this jacket isn't in your system? It still could have belonged to your facility? Or one of your partner facilities?"

Looking up from the computer screen, Dr. Crighton filled in the path of investigation for the jacket. "Yes, you are correct. If the serial number does not show up in my search, then we would have to go through the written records preceding our electronic inventory. Those go back twenty years, I believe."

"And the other facilities? Do we need to go to those locations?" Agent Quesnel continued pushing.

"I can be of some help. I can contact each. I am unable to cross-search those facilities. Our databases haven't been linked yet. However, they also have ten years of electronic inventory."

Mahoney swallowed, a few beads of sweat breaking through the pores on his forehead. "So we need to hope this jacket was in one of these facilities within the last ten years."

"Yes. Or a lot of manual record searching will be required."

"Doctor, how does someone get one of these jackets outside an institution?" Agent Quesnel asked.

"Not by permission. The use of these jackets is only permissible under the guidance of professional care."

Mahoney probed, "So, someone would have to steal it?"

"Yes. If it was taken in the last ten years. Before then, they were issued for outside use, in certain cases."

"Who would have access to these?" Agent Quesnel said.

"Currently, only registered personnel. The medical staff and the attendants. No one else in this building. The access cards are coded according to security access as granted to each individual employee."

The computer dinged. "Ah. The search results." Dr. Crighton slipped his spectacles on and scrolled through the lines of data on his screen.

Mahoney's heart pulsed. Tiny pink boots walked across his mind.

"I'm sorry. The serial number is not in our database. I can call the two other facilities immediately. A search of the entire set of records could take a little while. I'll also have my assistant, Ingrid, take you to the records room, if you would like to start looking through the manual records?" The man paused, his eyes inquiring as to the next step.

Mahoney thrust the decision forward without hesitation. "We need to get on this, now."

Dr. Crighton picked up his phone, pressing a single button. "Ingrid, dear, will you please come into my office? I need you to take some folks down to the paper records room."

Ingrid arrived in a split second. Dr. Crighton made the necessary introductions with haste. "I'll make those calls to the other institutions right away. If I can get a hold of someone now, they could possibly perform those searches immediately."

"Thank you, Doctor Crighton." Agent Quesnel shook his hand firmly. "Your help has been tremendous."

Mahoney followed Agent Quesnel's lead, saying his own farewell to the doctor.

"Please, come this way." Ingrid smiled warmly at them. Leading them down a hallway, they loaded onto a small elevator. The elevator doors creaked shut and the shaft shook its way down the extension cable from which it hung. *Geez, I hope this thing stays intact,* Mahoney thought briefly, his mind quickly moving back to the matter at hand. *I wonder how many files are down there. Manual inspection for a single number could burn a lot of hours. Hours we don't have.*

"Most of the office space here has been rebuilt. But some parts of this building are rather run-down. This elevator wasn't on the priority list for an upgrade. It isn't used very much. The paper records aren't usually required unless something from many years back has to be found." Ingrid continued smiling warmly at them.

Jeepers, these people seem so happy around here. Wouldn't guess they were working with such dreary cases. The elevator doors slid open. Ingrid led them down another hallway to a black door. Pulling out a large ring of keys, she sifted through them. Finding the correct one, the key scraped against the keyhole as she shimmied it in. "Most of the building is all scanning access now. But, again, the less-used spaces have yet to be upgraded." Opening the door, she flicked on a light switch. Dim lights buzzed, weakly coming to life.

Mahoney scanned the room. Concrete walls enclosed them. Long, tall shelving units filled with cardboard boxes lined the room. *Geez, that's a lot of files.*

"I believe you are looking for an item that will be in the medical supplies section. Rather hard to classify, but I'm fairly sure that's where we'll find the files." She walked past several tall shelves, turning down an aisle, and continuing about halfway down. "OK. So you will need…"—pausing, she looked at the notebook she had in her hand—"boxes 52A through 90Z." Looking up, she pointed to a high shelf. "52A starts up there. I'll get the ladder." She vanished behind the end of the aisle.

"Jeepers. That's a lot of files."

"Got that right." Agent Quesnel smirked. "Assuming there are boxes 52A through 52Z, that's 26 boxes per number. She said 52 through 90. That's nearly 40 boxes. Estimating, say 40 at 26, that's over 1000 boxes. And we don't know what these files look like. It's hard to say how long it will take to even make a single match on the number, let alone sift through an entire box."

"We need manpower."

Wheels squeaking, a tall ladder appeared from the end of the aisle. "I got it." Agent Quesnel sprinted toward the ladder, heels clicking on the cement floor.

Mahoney pressed the buttons on his phone. "Sutton. You and Hayes still following leads?" He rubbed the bristle on his chin. His stomach grumbled. *Beat it, appetite. No time for you right now.* "Can you round up Hayes then, and Dara. We're over at the main mental institution, on Centre Street. Bring us some coffee. Some *strong* coffee. We need to beef up our manual filing system over here. Might be a big break." Pressing the off button on his phone, he re-holstered it into his belt and turned back to the long aisle. Agent Quesnel was climbing up the tall ladder. The shiny black heels of her boots clicking against each step, she was nearly at the top in no time. Pulling out a box, she slid it onto a stair. With surprising agility, she alternated lowering herself and the box.

Next thing he knew, she was thrusting the dusty box at him. "Mahoney. You get first dibs." He had no chance to respond before she was climbing the ladder again.

"There's a table over here against the wall. You can set the boxes there. Might be easier to open them." Ingrid's cheery voice rang through the stiff quiet of the room. "I need to return to my duties. But if there is anything you need at all, please do not hesitate to let me know. Just take the elevator back to the fifth floor."

"Thank you, ma'am. A few of my colleagues will be joining us shortly. Would you make sure they find us?"

"Of course. I'll notify the front desk." Ingrid turned, walking back through the black door, a slight skip in her step.

Agent Quesnel set another dusty box down on the table with a thud. "Holy shit. This is crazy. But something tells me this is important."

Mahoney smiled in delight. "Hope you're up for a long night."

"Honey, you have no idea the long nights I've been through. Sponging up decades of data from psychiatric wards, prisons, and homicide precincts, and trying to turn it into something meaningful to the average mind, that results in a slew of all-nighters. Let's dig in."

A light buzzed from the ceiling before blinking off. The room grew a bit darker. Mahoney wished he had Blackwood's Sunfire 6.

Computers and Videos

Mahoney strode down the long hallway toward the tightly packed cubicles. Dara was perched at her desk, looking fresh as usual in her crisp navy suit, her long shiny grey strands tied in a perfect bun at the nape of her neck. In drastic contrast, Agent Quesnel perched on a chair she had pulled up next to Dara, her sleek black pants shimmering under the overhead lights, a platinum boot resting on her knee. The ruffles of her white blouse ran down her chest, and a hint of sparkle escaped from the rhinestones circling her wrist. Agent Quesnel leaned in over Dara's shoulder, both women lost in the world of the intricate online search they were concocting.

"Hello, ladies." Mahoney slid up behind them.

Eyes remaining glued to the small computer screen, Dara acknowledged him. "Bug. We're going to make you happy."

"What genius search are you inventing today? Taking over the computer world?"

"No, Bug. But we are making serious strides on these creepy messages."

Agent Quesnel took a sip from a coffee mug with the homicide department logo tattooed on the side. The first *i* was missing and half of the *m* had chipped away leaving *Hon cide*. Broken and worn, the mug reflected the feel of the department itself at times. *Or maybe it's just me that's broken and worn.* The sad thought floated through Mahoney's mind. Looking at the small computer screen, he squinted his eyes, trying to decipher the complicated string of symbols growing longer as Dara typed away.

Dara sat up straight, looking intently at the black screen, scrutinizing each bright-green symbol. "That should do it!" She hit the enter button. Neon lines blasted across the screen.

Sitting back in her chair, Dara plucked the dainty teacup she had set on her desk between her pointer and thumb. Her eyes brimmed with excitement. "Bug. Your agent here, she got us access to ARPANET *and* SMART! We are *on fire* in packet switching secret access network land. And Salton was nothing less than magic in creating his automatic text retriever. We're using a beta version."

Mahoney looked back at her with a blank stare.

Her cheeks flushing, Dara put her teacup down delicately. "Basically, we now have access to a computer network built by the U. S. Department of Defense. The architecture of this network changes the way that data is exchanged between computers. The databases connected to this network allow us to access more sources of data. And the test version of the text retriever is enabling us to search for information differently. More effectively. We've essentially got ourselves connected to a new-age computer network here, Bug." Her eyes lit up again as the computer-speak flew from her thin lips.

"With her computer skills, she's devouring the information available out there." Agent Quesnel sat back in her chair, a satisfied grin crawling across her face.

Mahoney joined in. "So, faster searches and more data."

Dara responded excitedly, "Yeah. And more effective searching. The way we find things based on our clues just got a serious makeover."

The scrolling text halting, Mahoney stared at the cryptic lines, rubbing his day-old bristle.

Dara hovered the cursor over each line, clicking at the keyboard, passing the flashing square down the list.

"That one!" Agent Quesnel tapped the screen with a shiny red nail. The flashing square stopped, then moved back up the list a couple of rows.

"Oooh. I like where you're going." Dara smiled, clicking several keyboard buttons simultaneously, highlighting a line of neon text. Clicking the "enter" button, she sat back in her chair. The results appeared with a synopsis flashing onto the screen.

"Bingo." Dara raised her arm, slapping Agent Quesnel's hand in a high five.

Mahoney scratched his head. "OK, Dara. Back it up for an old guy. I don't follow your computer witchcraft." Raising his hands and shaking his head, he gave Dara a helpless look.

"Bug. Don't give me that 'old guy' crap. And lay off yourself. We've been at this for hours. You just walked up."

Mahoney nodded. "OK. I won't argue with your wisdom. Bring me up to speed." Taking a swig of his dark roast, he pulled up a chair from the neighbouring cubicle.

"It's all in the magic of the beginnings of a worldwide computer network. You see, the concept is that computers all over the world will be connected. One computer will be able to access the information on all of the other computers, regardless of where they are located. Like the points in a gigantic spider's web, they will all be connected. But, it's in its infancy. Only certain institutions have access at this point. And tapping into all that potential data takes a little brain power and a lot of patience."

Agent Quesnel took a sip from the tattered department mug.

Dara scanned Mahoney's face. "To search for information, we can come up with keywords. Similar to the clues you follow to create paths in a case. For example, the message on the Eagle Woods body contained a couple of distinctive words. One of them was 'Dude.' We can simply type in a single keyword, but there could be many sources of information on the computer network that contains that word."

Mahoney nodded, sipping his dark roast.

"We can combine multiple keywords to narrow down the number of results a search comes up with, making those results more meaningful."

"Got it."

"In a similar fashion, we can add pieces to the search to include keywords from other clues. For example, the victim had on a red robe. We connect the different clues from each scene by turning them into multi-worded keyword searches."

Agent Quesnel smiled slyly. "She's a genius, you know." She tipped her mug at Dara, resting back into her seat.

Cheeks glowing rosy, Dara fiddled with the string of sparkly beads hanging from her glasses. "Oh no. What about you, Miss Math Wiz? Your understanding of philosophy logic combinations launched us forward. Not to mention the pulse you have on pop culture." She brushed Agent Quesnel's knee.

Mahoney grinned. *Two geeks. Bonding over math and computers. Who would have known?*

Agent Quesnel looked back at Mahoney. "A commercial spin on this computer network is starting to spring to life. We combined clothing, messages, hair, jewellery, and we topped it off with the rock scene spin. Sutton gave us some great direction. He talked to his daughter about current rock bands. Turns out she is quite the expert." Setting her tattered mug onto the desk, Agent Quesnel leaned toward the computer screen. "I think we've found the source of the messages and the inspiration for the outfits."

"What would that be?"

"You ever heard of MTV, Mahoney?" Agent Quesnel leaned back in her chair, crossing her arms.

"Negative."

"It's a TV station. Plays music videos 24/7. Not sure if they cover the blues, though." Agent Quesnel smirked.

Ignoring the jab at his ancient taste, a golden hue glowed from the badge lingering in Mahoney's mind, reducing the tarnish. *Maybe my gut was onto something here.* The melding of minds over computer searches may have diverted them down the right path.

"Fantastic work. Dara, can we view the videos with the team?"

"Yes. We can get copies at our local HMV store."

"I'll send Sutton and Hayes right away. Can you get us set up in the war room?"

"I'm on it."

A Trail of Rock Gods

Sutton and Hayes stopped in their tracks in the doorway to the stuffy little war room. A TV perched high on a stand had been wheeled to the front wall. Agent Quesnel bent over a VCR underneath the TV, working her hands over a mess of cables. Dara had settled into her usual seat, and Mahoney sat at the centre table, sipping from a chipped mug.

Agent Quesnel welcomed Sutton and Hayes. "Take a seat. We're about to commence on a review of all the messages the killer has been leaving us."

Sutton and Hayes quickly responded, taking seats along the long centre table next to Mahoney. Agent Quesnel clicked a button, bringing the TV to life. Dara slipped along the back wall, clicking the light switch off. Images flashed onto the small TV screen. A man approached them, coming to life from the tiny screen. Raising his arms, his shiny black cloak flowed around him. His pink lips began to move in slow, dramatic motions.

His voice reached out to them in slow, ariose streams. He sung of falling tears and broken ties. Drenched in drama, the voice rang throughout the stuffy little war room.

Sutton sat up, cocking a brow and taking a long swig of his Big Gulp. Hayes leaned forward, resting his elbows on his knees. Mahoney sunk back further into the cheap plastic of the chair. They all watched the mesmerizing scene unfold before them. The man in the flowing black cloak brought to life the gory scene plastered to the cream-coloured crime scene wall.

The insanity growing, the cloaked man's voice became raspy. The emotional monologue continued as he denied being a fool. His bandmates joined him in a chorus. Together, the glam group reached a climax.

The song came to an end. Agent Quesnel tapped the keyboard, halting the world emanating from the television set. The room went quiet. Dara crept along the back wall, switching the lights back on. The bright fluorescent light bathed the tiny space.

A smug smile crept across Agent Quesnel's face. "Your computer wiz was able to determine the source of each of the messages the killer has been leaving." Sitting back in her chair, she looked like a cat satisfied with his latest hunt.

Dara flung a rare comment from her back corner, "Well, actually, boys, Agent Quesnel here is somewhat of a math and computer wiz herself. I would say it was simply good teamwork."

Raising an eyebrow, Sutton inquired, "All the messages and outfits came from rock videos?"

"You got it. The music of the youth. I'm not your fool. Dude look like a fairy. I'm gonna watch D bleed. All three of these are slight modifications of lyrics from rock songs. The glam and hard rock bands of today." She said, "This explains *where* he is getting his messages from. It does not explain *why* he chose these messages. The lyrics probably resonate with him. He is using the words of his idols to express what he is feeling, his own suppressed emotions resulting from what is happening in his own life. The messages are likely directed at someone, the person causing him pain."

"Man, that is messed up." Hayes shook his head.

"Yes, it is." Agent Quesnel said, "We need to dig into this deeper. If we can find out what it is he is trying to accomplish through the script that he is playing out with each of his victims, then we may be able to narrow down who this guy is."

"OK. What do we know?" Mahoney said. "The lyrics are from rock songs. The clothing from each victim imitates the lead singers from these bands. Our guy is likely, what, in his early twenties? Maybe late teens…that seems to be stretching it."

Fuelling his path, Agent Quesnel said, "Typically, serial killers begin displaying concerning behaviour in their teens, but don't start their killing sprees until they are into their thirties. However, there have been cases in which the killing started earlier. Rissell, for example, committed his first murder when he was only eighteen. He was arrested for five murders before his nineteenth birthday." She paused, her voice losing a little volume.

Sutton shifted in his seat. "That's sick."

Mahoney took over, rubbing the bristle on his chin. "OK. So what's the demographic on the kids that are into this music and watch MTV? Are we talking early twenties? Late teens? Let's think back to the clientele at the rocker bar on the night of the show."

Agent Quesnel sat back in her chair, pondering the inquiry. "I would say 18 to 24. Almost everyone in that joint was a college kid. There were only a few older guys. Our victims would have been much more likely to respond to a kid their own age if approached."

Mahoney continued, "Let's go through each of these messages. The first one our guy left was 'I'm not your fool.'"

Agent Quesnel said, "He later adds in this 'D.' Maybe *your* refers to *D*."

"And the other lyrics in the song, the message says pain, hurt, with a tinge of anger," Sutton said. "Trust me, I know emotion. I have a teenage daughter."

Mahoney said, "The second message. He added the word fairy. Why?"

"The clothing was very feminine. The sheer, red robe. It could be this guy is being ridiculed for dressing, or wanting to dress, more feminine. Maybe whoever is making fun of him is calling him a fairy," Agent Quesnel fuelled the theory.

Mahoney said, "And that last message. 'I'm Gonna Watch D Bleed.' Even more personal. He's angry with D."

"I'm guessing 'D' is the person in his life causing him to experience all these emotions that he doesn't know what to do with," Agent Quesnel said. "Hurt, pain, humiliation, anger. A dangerous combination for someone who may be mentally ill, sexually fixated, and seeking release through torture and murder."

Hayes leaned over the centre table, meeting her gaze. "That's a deadly combination."

Sutton said, "Boss, we should watch the other videos. Dig into the messages and emotions behind them. Let's get a deeper profile on this guy. It might be our only lead."

Mahoney's shoulders relaxed. Sitting back against the hard-plastic chair back, he settled his hand around the fading coffee mug. "Agent Quesnel, could you play us that next video?"

Agent Quesnel tapped at the keyboard. Dara slipped along the back wall, clicking the room dark.

Bourbon and Silk

"You look like you've had a hell of a day, boss. The usual? Or something stiff?"

Mahoney thought for a moment. The bubbly ginger of his usual non-alcoholic ale just didn't seem appealing right now. He wanted to feel less. He wanted to be numb. *Screw it.*

"You know what, Simon? I think I'll have a bourbon. On the rocks."

"Good. It'll help you get some sleep, you know." Simon's words washed away the guilt riddling Mahoney's mind. The talent of the true bartender to make his guests feel better about their decisions.

Pouring a generous helping of brown liquid over clear ice, Simon slid a crystal glass across the bar. "Still on the same case?"

"Yeah."

"So, that scene by the ravine, where I saw you, it's part of this case?"

Mahoney took a sip of bourbon. The cold liquid slid down his raw throat. "It could be."

"You were looking rough when I ran into you. Feeling better?"

"Yes. Thanks. And thanks for helping."

"Of course, Boss. So, how many bodies now?"

Mahoney paused. His exhausted mind attempted to weed through what had been shared with the media. *They know there are three. We couldn't hold back with that body count. Sergeant was concerned with public safety.* "Three bodies."

Pursing his lips, Simon let out a long, low whistle. "Wow. That's crazy. Boss, you've been on the force a long time. Has something like this ever happened here?"

"Not of this calibre."

Simon's brow raised. Mahoney was used to this. People got really interested in murder, as long as they weren't involved and it didn't hit home. The more gruesome it was, the more interesting it became, as long as they were far enough removed. Simon was a problem solver. He liked to stretch the powerful muscle housed in his head. Mahoney threw him a bread crumb.

"We've expanded our strategies."

"Really?" Simon raised an eyebrow.

"Yeah. The murders seem intimate. Personal. We're looking at why he's doing this."

"So, you don't have any concrete evidence?"

"I wouldn't say that. We're just creating more paths to follow."

"But, sounds like you're stuck in the analysis phase of the investigation?"

Mahoney smirked. Trust Simon to retain every tidbit you threw his way.

"Good memory." Mahoney tipped his crystal glass toward Simon. Taking another swig, the rawness of his throat started to numb. "We brought in a criminal profiler."

Simon's left brow raised higher. A couple of guys walked in. Simon ignored them. "Profiler?"

"She analyzes the evidence from the perspective of the behaviour of the bad guy. It's a new field."

"Sounds scientific."

"Thing is, you still need evidence."

"And you have none."

Mahoney's mind swirled a little. His hands were a bit numb. "Not necessarily. Just adding on another layer to the investigation. In fact, seems our guy got a little lazy. He left something behind last time."

"Really?" Simon's eyes widened, his face sliding in close to Mahoney's. "What did he leave?"

Mahoney met Simon's gaze dead on. Mahoney's phone buzzed, snapping them both from their moment of intrigue. "Sorry, Simon. I've got to take this."

Simon retracted back to his bar space. "Of course, boss." He turned to address his new customers.

Mahoney pressed the "on" button on his phone, gruffly barking into it. "Mahoney here."

"Mahoney. It's Blackwood. The fibre lodged in the neck of the Eagle Woods boy has been processed."

"Hold on." Mahoney strode over to a quiet corner in the back of the pub. "Go ahead."

"It matches perfectly with the pattern of torn fibres in the scarf your boys fished out of that dumpster. And, get this, the piece of material found by that runner and her dog matches a second tear in the scarf."

Bingo. Mahoney inhaled deeply.

"Mahoney, you still there?"

"Blackwood. Have I ever told you that you're the best medical examiner I've ever worked with?."

"Ha. Flattery will get you nowhere."

"It's not flattery. It's the truth." His face flushed.

"Well...thanks."

Mahoney pressed the *off* button on his cell phone, its weight heavy in his hand as he made his way back to the bar. He shot back the last of the bourbon, letting it linger in his throat. Snapping a bill onto the bar, he slid from his seat and silently made his exit.

Masochist

Random thoughts raced through Seth's mind in a wild frenzy. His heart palpitated in a crazed pattern. He frantically rifled through the mountain of homeless cassettes that had accumulated on the small wooden table. A flash of relief lived for a mere instant as a title caught his eye. Snatching it up, he flung open the plastic. A crackle pierced his ears as a ragged crack ran its way up the front of the case. "Dammit."

He ripped the cassette from its broken plastic home. Cramming the tape into the open door of the boombox, he clasped it into place. A bead of sweat drizzled down the side of his face, launching itself off his chin, landing on the cassette. Snapping the door shut, he pushed his finger down hard onto the play button. The small spinners inside the musical contraption moved into motion, pulling the cassette wheels and guiding the thin strip of tape. Electric vibes spun through the air, tunnelling their way into his ears and pulsating through his body. Bowing his head, he closed his eyes. His body throbbed to the beat.

It wasn't enough. He needed more. It was only the rubber band, blocking his blood flow. Craving the sweet juice pumping through his veins, he needed the syringe.

Plucking a purple silk scarf from a hat rack hook, he held it between his pointer and thumb like a delicate flower. Fluttering the scarf through the air with elegance, he glided across the room.

Plunging his body into the soft purple velour of a small sofa, he sunk his head back into a fuzzy, hot-pink cushion. Gazing up at a dazzling disco ball, he watched it spinning from its hook, spattering little sparkly diamonds over the walls. His limbs melded into the mold his body had dug into the worn couch. Lifting his head just a tad, he slipped the scarf around the back of his neck. The silk slid against his skin, every nerve ending in his entire body seizing in anticipation. He slithered his hands along the luxurious material, stretching the two lengths out in front of him. In a smooth windmill motion, his arms crossed the two ends, making a full circle around the back of his neck. He repeated the flowing routine several times, his head held in a slight lift. Satisfied with his thorough wrapping job, he returned his head into the neon-pink pillow. Hanging his tongue out, he hissed a deep exhale. Tightening his grip, he pulled the two ends of the scarf in opposite directions. Wrenching his critical airway, he squeezed the life out of his own body.

Oxygen depleting from his lungs, sweat trickled down his face. Indigo snake-like lines protruded from his neck, weaving their way over his pale skin. His eyes bulging out of their sockets, his temples throbbing, a flush of blue washed over his face. Releasing his grip, the two ends of silk slipped from his fingertips. Dropping his hands hard against the purple velour, he gasped, sucking in deep breaths. Oxygen worked its way into his windpipe, finding his lungs. He let out a long sigh.

A rush of adrenaline hurled through his arteries. A shot of endorphins blasted his brain. In a flash, it was over. *That's it?* his internal voice shook. Head swirling, his heart relaunched into a mad race. He bolted to a sitting position as his mind demanded to understand why he didn't feel the release he longed for. The blood rushing back to his head, he closed his eyes on the spinning room.

"Why?" he cried out. "Why isn't this working? What did I do wrong? What's missing?"

Ticking off the items on his mental list, he searched his brain for the missing piece. *What wasn't right?*

Paranoia prickled his mind, twisting his thoughts till they morphed into wild images. He could see himself pacing back and forth between the concrete walls of his hideout, pulling his hair by the roots, unable to find relief from his crazed state.

His left leg twitching uncontrollably, he battled through the barrage of visions for a way out. Jumping from the couch, he launched himself across the room. Pawing at the loose cassettes with fury, his eyes darted from one title to the other. *The music! The music wasn't right.* His hands froze, eyes glued to the artwork symbolizing the potential of a heightened release. The gun, the rose, the scarf wrapping them together, as if they were items that had something in common.

That's it!

Yanking the cassette from the boom box, he shoved in the new selection. Depressing the play button so hard it threatened to stick forever, he watched the wheels turning again. A guttural riff grinding from the wired black speakers, his lids dropped. Willing every single particle of his physical mass to meld with the music, he swelled with desire. His journey now finding a proper path, his eyelids slid open. His gaze wandered around the room until it halted on a silver rectangular contraption. He stretched his legs out in a gallop across the room. Snatching up the shiny tool, he grabbed a black cardboard box. Sprinting to the couch, metal pieces clinking against each other inside the box, he plunked himself down.

More pain. More awakening.

Lifting the lid off the box, he fished through a jumble of metal pieces. He retrieved a long stud ending in a piercing point. Holding the stud up to the light, he admired his choice. Loading the stud into the piercing gun, he cocked the long silver lever and loaded the stud. He tore off his shirt and squeezed his right nipple hard. He pulled it away from his chest repeatedly until it grew red and inflamed, protruding straight out from his chest. He grabbed a rubber stop from the box. Sandwiching his nipple between the black rubber and the lever of the gun, he held his breath. Returning his attention to the output of the boom box, he waited. The vocals building in volume, reaching toward the bridge, he held his shiny weapon with patience. Right at the critical point, he joined in with his own wails.

As his lips formed the last syllable, he paired action with message, clamping down on the trigger. The metal lever shot out and the spiky point of the stud pierced through his nipple. The lever retracted back with a snap. Sharp pain rippled through him, stimulating every nerve ending. The pain was his heroin. Adrenaline rushed through his capillaries, like a liquid drug, diffusing in his bloodstream.

Like a ragdoll, his body slumped back against the purple velour. The weight of the gun suddenly amplified, his arm hung off the cushion. His silver tool slipped from his limp hand, hitting the ground with a clank. Chin touching his chest, lids dropping over his eyes, he succumbed to the haze invading him. His mental essence leaving his body, floating above himself, his hallucination took him to a lookout, examining his physical vessel.

Peace at last.

He smiled to himself.

Soiled Seedling

pril, 1977

Seth slammed his eyes shut. Clenching his teeth, his fists squeezed into tight little balls. It was as if he was smack in the middle of one of his recurring nightmares. The one where he was creeping down the creaky stairs to the dark basement, the forbidden place where he wasn't supposed to go. Peering into the darkness, he could feel a presence. Was it a ghost? Was it a monster? He didn't know, but he felt something. A chill took over him, running its way up his spine and tingling the tips of his fingers. Stretching his mouth open wide, he forced every bit of air into his lungs and launched a cry for help up his throat. Using every ounce of energy he possessed, he willed his vocal cords into action. All he wanted was to scream, for someone to hear him and save him. He could hear his screams in his mind, but only silent gasps of air escaped his mouth. Frozen in his spot on the creaky stairs, he stared into the darkness below, feeling the presence of the unknown monster.

Snapping out of his nightmare memory back to his present bone-chilling reality, he stared down at the shiny steel slab a mere inch from his face. He ground his molars against each other harder and harder until he swore they would crumble to dust. The binds confining his little wrists pulled at his skin. Beads of sweat dripped from his forehead, hitting the steel with tiny splashes. Hot tears sprung from his eyes. Mini waterfalls washed down his cheeks, mixing with the scarlet globs crusted on his torn skin. His stomach clenched. His heart pounded so fast he was afraid it would burst.

The shuffle of shoes on concrete prickled his ears as his monster approached him from behind. Pain sliced through his belly like a sharp knife. His little body tensed.

He felt himself spread apart. Something long and hard thrust into that one sacred hole that had only served as an exit for the waste his body didn't need. His skin ripped apart as the invasion probed further into him. Pain piercing every one of his nerve endings, fresh blood surfaced on his young, unblemished skin. As the crater ripped through his skin, a hollow crevice tore open inside of him, filling with emptiness. His young heart seizing, fresh tears trickled down his bloody cheeks to the corners of his mouth. Licking his lips, salt mixed with copper hit his tongue. His mind teetering on the brink of implosion as the act forced upon him was too much for his young brain to comprehend. He was just a seedling to the world.

His body quivering from head to toe, his shoulders fell hard against his cold steel bed. All of his limbs lay limp as his body succumbed. Gazing straight across the room at the grey cement wall, all thoughts disintegrated from his mind as his brain went numb. The hollowness grew within him.

Soulless Carcass

The radiant overhead light brought the glimmering golden pants to life. Each leg was precisely displayed, resting on the shiny steel table. Seth stroked the supple material, his hands lingering slowly up and down. He glanced over to the second pair of golden pants folded neatly beside the boom box. *Just in case these ones get tarnished.* He looked over to the far wall where his human doll hung, waiting to be clothed.

Seth's eyes moved along his model, examining the preparation he had performed. The glowing skin reflected how thoroughly he had scrubbed. All trickles of viscus red had been washed away. The arms stretched skyward, hanging the figure in a dramatic pose. The wrists were bound securely, confirming how meticulously he had tied the neat knots. The head drooped forward, chin resting on the bare chest, slick with sweat. The hair hung in long, luxurious waves, covering the face and stretching down the front of the body. Noticing the sandy-blond strands that he had brushed until they shone, Seth's mouth pulled in a wicked smirk. Delicately picking up the golden pants, he slithered his way across the room. It was time to begin preparations for his ritual.

Crouching down toward the concrete floor, Seth cautiously maneuvered the pants over the limply dangling legs. Stretching the pleather into place, he ran his fingers over the muscular contour. Starting at the waist, his fingers gently pulled the sinewy cording as he watched the glimmering gold close in over the rippling muscles. He scrupulously executed the delicate process of tightening until the criss-cross pattern wove its way down the entire leg in an impeccable pattern. After completing the process on both legs of his human doll, he stretched up and stepped back to examine his work.

Moving his eyes up the torso of the doll, he scrutinized his carefully carved message. The entire span of skin from nipples to navel was covered with meticulously cut letters. The symbols glistened with ruby droplets of sweat. After a long pause, he decided he was satisfied with his penmanship. He turned back to his preparation.

The translucent latex of his tightly gloved hand found its way through the lavish mane. He tenderly lifted the doll chin, long locks falling gracefully away from the smooth, white face. The doll face twitched slightly as the being inside started to waken. The effect of the powerful poisons injected into its veins was beginning to fade. The doll eyes opened sleepily, dilated pupils struggling to focus.

Finding the vacant stare of his playmate with his own, Seth hissed a raspy inquiry, "Will *you* be my physical vessel? Will you be the home for my soul?"

Locks slipped back in place over the doll face as Seth released his hold.

Fixating on the boom box perched on a rusty old table in the opposite corner of the room, Seth's legs twitched in anticipation. He quickly strode across the concrete floor. He scanned the rows of neatly lined and labelled cassette cases. Running his pointer finger along the top row, he halted suddenly, a satisfied sneer slithering across his face. Pulling the selected cassette from the plastic holder, he popped it into the open door of the tape player. The perfect accompaniment to the next step in entering his ultimate physical vessel, strong vocals, seething in emotion, blasted from the tiny speakers. Seth turned to his next task.

Snaking his way along the wall to the adjacent corner where a small, square table was securely set, he gazed intently at a tidy row of dark-purple and green glass bottles lining the back edge. Each bottle was labelled with an artistic deco, its contents identified by a beautifully handwritten name. Seth scanned the bottles, reaching for a very special concoction housed in deep-violet glass.

Cupping his gloved hands around the glass, he elevated the magic mix on its latex pedestal. Tilting his head back, he raised his gaze skywards.

The voice in the boom box was gaining momentum, simultaneously rising in volume and drama. Seth superimposed his own twisted version, intertwining his shrill voice with the wails of the rock god vibrating from the speakers.

The voices continued as one. Emotions building, the volume increased until the wails pierced every corner of the dark basement, approaching the climax, drawing out the grand moment.

His gloved fingers gripping dark-purple glass, he slithered his way over to his puppet. The doll head moved, a moan escaping from within. It was looking at him. Its glassy eyes flickering with cognition, its lips attempted to form a word. Seth placed the purple glass bottle gently upon a polished silver circular perch atop a tall pedestal. He reached up, pulling a soft silk scarf from around the doll's neck. The scarf slipped away, fully exposing the sickly purple-brown ligatures branding the moist skin. Folding the scarf into a neat square, he placed it gently beside the purple poison.

Seth reached for a dark-green vial, perched atop the pedestal with the growing collection of lethal items. Picking up the liquid concoction, he slowly unscrewed the lid. Pulling the cap from the bottle until just the tip of the dropper attached to it remained inside, he squeezed the rubber top. Transparent drops of death were sucked into the glass cylinder. Putting the bottle atop the stool, beside the neatly folded scarf, he walked straight up to his human doll. Grasping sandy strands, he wrenched the doll head back. The doll mouth opening, a whimper escaped. Seth squeezed the rubber and several droplets of clear liquid plunged through the air, landing silently on the pink sponge of their doll tongue destination.

Seth looked over his human doll in admiration. The perfect body with long, luxurious hair and rippling muscles. "You will be my physical vessel, my new home for my soul. My physical perfection and emotional freedom. You are my evolution in the pure form it was intended. Unscathed by suppression. My soul will reach its truest form."

Returning the green glass to the perch, he slipped his plastic fingers around the purple bottle. He held the dark vial toward the concrete ceiling, the liquid inside swirling.

He snapped his head skyward and howled, "Black Magic, do not fail me now! My time has come. The new home for my soul has arrived. The time for the ultimate transfer is near."

Slipping the glass lid from the purple vial, he poked a syringe into the bottle. Extracting the black fluid with care, he faced his doll.

In a demonic tone, he hissed, "It is time, my special doll, to come to life, once again."

Plunging the needle into the doll's arm, he pumped it with the oozing, black liquid.

"Now the time has come for the extraction of my soul."

Filling the syringe again, he pierced his own arm, shooting blackness into his veins. A swirl of dizziness hit him hard. The concrete walls whirling around him, he crumpled to the hard floor.

Losing control of all his senses, he declared his final plea with a desperate, raspy whisper, "Oh sweet poison, please take my soul."

He fell back, hitting the ground with a thud. Arms limp at his sides, his mind went black.

Carcass Climax

Mahoney trudged along, the thick mud threatening to devour his foot with each step. The rain pelted down hard, striking his face with ice-cold pellets.

"Medical shouldn't be leading this entourage. Behavioural clues should be the top priority." Yelling at Mahoney's back, Agent Quesnel pushed him toward his breaking point. "The last thing we need is Blackwood up there fucking something up. What does she know about entering a scene?"

Mahoney whipped around, facing her dead on. "Look, I don't know how things work down south. But up here, the body belongs to the medical examiner. The scene belongs to homicide."

Staring him down, Agent Quesnel refused to ease up. "You couldn't solve this case on your own. I'm here to save your ass."

Mahoney stared her straight in the eye, his nostrils flaring. "Nobody is saving anybody's ass here. We added you to our team. The word here is *team*."

The pitch in her voice reached a higher octave. "I'm only here because you came to us. I have bigger fish to fry back home."

Raising his voice a couple of notches, Mahoney challenged her, "Did I come to you? Yeah. Can your expertise help us with this case? Yeah. Can we afford friction between the good guys? Negative. I came to you to help beef up our manpower. To increase our chances of catching this guy. Now, you can either can it and help, or go home to your bigger fish."

He stood like a pillar, feet firmly planted in a muddy bath. His gaze bore into her.

Narrowing her eyelids, her mouth twisted into a convoluted frown.

"We need to get moving. This rain is washing away any chance of a trail," he barked hoarsely, his feet sinking deeper into the thick, black goo.

Indicating her agreement with a silent scowl, she tore her eyes from his and nodded toward Blackwood ahead.

Continuing their slow journey through the onslaught of the elements, the tension between them clung to the sheets of rain pouring over them. Slugging forward, one slow step at a time, they caught up to Blackwood as the group halted. Examining the scene, they all stared at the arduous trek before them.

Images flashed through Mahoney's mind, fogging his thoughts. The rain continued pouring down. He could see the gleam washing away from his golden badge, leaving it tarnished, destroying his track record. Pink boots sloshed through the muddy water, turning red with blood. Little ghost faces swirled through his mind, their bodies stacking themselves up until he could no longer count them. The pang in his stomach shot pain through his nerves. He could hear a muffled voice growing louder, breaking through his thoughts.

"Mahoney! You still with us?" Blackwood shouted at him through the sheets of rain.

"Yeah."

Blackwood stretched her long arm into the distant woods. "There."

"Bloody hell." Mahoney scanned the distance between them and the uniformed officer standing between the edge of the trees and the river. Remnants of a makeshift trail snaked along the water's edge. With every ticking second, the downpour devoured a piece of the path, turning it into a muddy mess.

He directed Blackwood. "I'll lead. You keep the techs with you." He shot a hard glance at Agent Quesnel. "We're all in this together. Can you keep up the rear?"

The scowl dissipating from her face, she shot Mahoney a sharp nod.

Raising his arms in a precarious balancing act, Mahoney slid his feet along the slippery, rocky ledge. In a close-knit line, they edged their way along the trail. The river rushed by them, crashing against the rocks. Approaching the uniformed officer, Mahoney stepped up into the trees. Turning, he extended a hand to assist each member of his team onto the high perch. Once they were all assembled, the officer filled them in.

"I've had the witness removed, given the weather conditions and his shaky state. The interview will continue back at the station. Good news is you've made it into the shelter of the trees. Bad news is, you still have some tricky climbing to do." Turning to face the woods, he pointed toward a short, steep, rocky path. "It's not far, but the rain has made it difficult. There's an enclosure just a few hundred metres in, through the trees. That's where it is."

"How washed down is it?" Mahoney inquired.

"Not too bad. It's in an enclosure." The uniform paused, wiping his brow with an arm. "You, uh, you should prepare yourselves. It's quite the scene."

Mahoney scanned the officer's tag. "Thank you, Officer Jackson."

Mahoney led the way over to the steep path. Looking down at his weatherproof hiking boots, he grinned. *Glad I brought these babies.* Lifting his lead foot, he stepped up onto the rocky incline. Sliding his boot until it found a grip, he tensed his leg muscles and launched himself up. He turned back toward the others. "Let's take our time here. We don't want anyone hurt."

He led the group uphill one cautious step at a time. At the top, facing a wall of thick firs, Mahoney searched for the way in. Ducking through the tree-lined entrance, prickly needles clung to his tweed coat. The other side of the tree wall opened up to a square-shaped hideaway. Stopping dead in his tracks, Blackwood bumped into him. They stood in silence.

Blackwood's voice was a mere whisper as she said, "Humdinger."

Two walls of dense woods closed them in from each side. A rocky cliff face provided the back wall of the hideaway. A slab of rock jutted out from the rocky cliff, a natural made roof. A body hung from the foundation. The arms reached high above the body. The wrists were secured to the rock roof with white ties drenched in dark red. The body's head hung forward. Lavish locks of sandy blond flowed over the front of the body, reaching down past the waist. Golden pleather clung to muscular legs, woven shut like two long corsets. The techies sprung into action with their cameras.

Mahoney thought out loud, "Geez. How the hell did he get the body all the way in here?"

Agent Quesnel said, "The scenes have progressed quickly. The killer's emotions are heightening."

"Look, the weather is against us. Let's take our time here. Process everything possible before anything is moved," Mahoney said.

Blackwood agreed, "Yes to that. The more we can process on the body here, the better. It's going to be near impossible to get it out of here untarnished."

Agent Quesnel, Blackwood, and Mahoney all exchanged a nod.

A gasp seized Mahoney's ears, his head snapped toward the hanging body. A chilling bolt shot through him.

Blackwood's face turned as pale as the corpse's. She stepped one booted foot onto a large boulder. She launched herself up, face to face with the body. Her latex-wrapped forefinger and thumb opening an eyelid, she illuminated the pupil with the lumens of her trusty Sunfire. She pressed two fingers into the neck, below the ligatures. Looking at Mahoney, her voice was barely audible as she whispered, "I can't be sure, but there might be a pulse." She removed the plastic sheath with a snap. Risking contamination, she pressed her bare fingers back into the neck and gasped.

She jumped from the boulder. "We need to get the body down. Now." Yelling over to the techies, she asked them to call for medical backup. Grabbing her backpack, she ripped open one of the zippers. Plunging her hand into the pocket, she retrieved a pocketknife. "Mahoney, grab the legs."

Mahoney and Agent Quesnel both jumped in response to the command, positioning themselves around the dangling legs.

Blackwood launched back onto the boulder. Teeth clenched, she sawed at the white ties furiously. Pieces of white fabric ripping away in random frays, one arm dropped against the body with a thud.

Blackwood leapt from the boulder. Bending down, she rolled the boulder toward the other side of the body.

Mahoney left his post to assist. As the second tie began to fray against the blade, Blackwood yelled out, "It's almost free."

Mahoney shouted back, "Can you get behind and support the back? We can try to lower him down to the ground."

Blackwood leaned at an angle off the boulder, stretching an arm around the back of the hanging body. "OK. Got it." The last fray of white tie giving way, the second arm dropped. Dropping her knife, Blackwood supported the body's back with both hands, stepping down from the boulder. "OK. I'm good," she confirmed.

Mahoney glanced from Blackwood to Agent Quesnel. "OK. Blackwood, lower the back toward the ground. Quesnel, keep a good grip on that leg."

Legs rising, back lowering, the body slid into Blackwood's arms. The three of them placed the body onto a bed of damp leaves. Blackwood snatched her backpack, zipped a pocket open, and retrieved a syringe in one smooth motion. She slapped at one of the motionless arms, popping the cap off the syringe. She plunged the needle into the pale skin. Blood shot into the clear tube.

"C'mon, breathe," she commanded the body.

Seconds into Blackwood's life-saving procedure, the victim took a raspy deep breath. Skin pulling in taut around the pale neck, blue veins popping.

Moving a wave of sandy blond, Blackwood peered at the pale face. "C'mon, stay with us."

An eyelid fluttered, both lids opening just a sliver. A weak moan escaped from the lips.

Blackwood found the face with her hand. "It's OK," her voice soothed. "Stay with us." Looking at Mahoney, she pleaded, "God, I hope the med team can make a speedy trek."

A gasp pierced the air. Blackwood snapped her gaze back to the victim's face. The body's eyes fluttering rapidly, another raspy breath escaped from the lips. Then stillness. The body lay silent, the eyes turning glassy, staring up at the darkening sky.

Blackwood tilted the victim's head back. With her hands stacked, she pumped the base of her palm hard into his chest, counting down. She pinched the victim's nose and breathed into his mouth.

The world blurred around Mahoney. Frozen, he watched Blackwood repeat the pumping and breathing routine over and over. Time didn't move.

"No," Blackwood cried. Pressing her index and middle finger into the body's neck, she shook her head. "Nothing. We lost him." Pressing her fingers hard into the cold skin of his neck, her eyes wide, she stared at the victim. "He's gone. I was too late."

Mahoney crouched down beside Blackwood, wrapping an arm around her back. "Look, you did all you could. You responded fast. You took charge."

She looked at him. Her purple almond eyes exuded anguish. "I know. It's just, I thought I could pull him back. I had a moment of hope."

"You did all you could."

She sat down, curling her knees into her chest. She rested her elbows on her knees and her forehead on her palms.

Mahoney sat down beside her and placed a hand on her shoulder.

After a few moments, she raised her head. "We need to get to work."

"He's gone. But you can still make a difference. Work your processing magic. The more you get for us, the better our chances of catching this guy. It's all you can do for this boy now."

She sighed. "I know." Stretching a fresh set of latex gloves over her hands, she turned her focus back onto the body. "I'll do as much as I can here. Might take a while. When the medical team arrives, we'll put them on hold until we're done here."

Mahoney scanned the group. "OK, everyone. You heard her. Let's get back to it. It's getting dark fast. We need to get moving." The techies sprung back into action, stretching the perimeter of their search, exposing dark crevices with the flash of their cameras.

Agent Quesnel slid up next to Mahoney, scanning the scene. "Mahoney. I see the processing of the body is in good hands." Her gaze met his, convincing him of her sincerity.

The wild ones always settle down, he told himself. *Just a matter of time.*

Continuing to meet his gaze, she said, "This guy, he's escalating. Look at this scene. The elaborateness is extreme. It looks like some sort of sacrifice."

That's it. Now we really get to harness her power. "Yeah. The body, hanging like it was, why?"

"His fantasy may be evolving, growing more extreme. He could be drawing out the torture, the execution of his routine. I think it's highly unlikely he would intentionally leave a live victim. It's too much of a deviation from his script. Besides, he's been keeping them long enough that they would have seen something."

"You think he was planning on returning?" Mahoney inquired.

"Yes."

"He might have left something then. We need a wide perimeter around this scene."

"Good idea, Mahoney. His emotions could be escalating with each failed attempt at recreating his fantasy. His perfect track record of leaving completely clean scenes is starting to tarnish. He left that fibre on the last one, then he purged his stash of precious scarves and blouses."

"You think he's getting more emotional? Starting to panic?"

"Definitely. But seriously, this scene is even more dramatic than the wild lion's mane stored away in the dark cave. He displayed this one more openly. Like he wants us to see it. He's showing off his work. He's proud of his accomplishment."

"What? He sees this as something to be proud of?"

"Yeah. These guys, they see it as their life's work. One guy I interviewed called it his vocation. To perfect his fantasy, he has to spend a chunky amount of time on this. Every little detail matters. It has to be perfect. Otherwise, it will be a failure, and he'll have to try again. With each unsuccessful attempt, his sense of failure could be rising. His self-loathing could be growing, and his rage could be getting out of control."

"It was out of control the first time he killed. This is crazy." Mahoney adjusted his derby. Rubbing the bristle on his chin, he stared at the body lying on the ground, under the careful scrutiny of Blackwood. "It would have taken a lot of work to get this body all the way in here. I'll talk to the techies, get them to scan all the way to the entrance. If his emotions are getting the best of him, maybe he slipped up again. Like you said, he did leave us that fibre and the scarf that it belonged to. He could have left us another tidbit."

"I think Dara could be a real a help again. She's got some crazy computer skills. She could extract some strong keywords from this scene, find out if this fits into the series of rock videos this guy was trying to recreate."

"I'll call her. Get her moving."

"Those golden pants must be a good item for her search criteria. And that vest. The hair definitely looks washed and brushed. I remember when my mom used to brush my hair till it shone. Wonder if this guy counts brush strokes."

"We need to see if there's another message."

"Mahoney." Blackwood's voice was icy cold. "C'mere. You need to see this."

Mahoney stepped toward the crouching Blackwood, Agent Quesnel on his heels. Looking down at the body, the two sides of the vest had been spread open, exposing moist white flesh. The entire upper body was covered in a sadistic version of calligraphy. Letters bordered in red streaks cut into the skin. A chill sprung into action, running slowly down Mahoney's spine, tingling the length of his arms all the way to the tips of his fingers. A pink book stormed into his mind, followed by a pale ghost face with blood-red lips. He forced it away. Clearing his throat, he read the prophetic words aloud.

"D you left Behind"

"I'M Buried In A Carcass"

"I'M Searching For MY Soul"

Failed Magic

Seth scurried along, maneuvering his feet through the tangled branches and wet leaves. The downpour had left a muddy mess. He was eager to get back to his doll.

I hope my doll is safe.

His mind raced. He figured the rock rooftop and forest enclosure would be enough to keep it from exposure. But he would feel a lot more at ease once he knew for sure that it was safe. Stepping his pace up a notch, his heart thudded against his chest. He swallowed hard, sweat wetting his skin.

It will be fine. Stop fretting.

This wasn't the time to worry himself sick.

Well now, I wouldn't have to worry if I had brought enough Black Magic with me, now would I?

Now, now, don't get so worked up. You couldn't have known that this doll would last so long.

I know. I just wish I had been prepared.

Stop it. Usually, the souls have slipped away after a single dose. This one hung on through multiple magic applications. It's a sign. You have finally found the one.

OK. I need to focus.

Concentrating hard on his footing, weaving through tangled roots and slippery stones, he looked up as he approached the opening. He froze, his muscles clenching down his back, turning to stone as his body seized to a halt.

"What is this?" he hissed into the chill air.

His doll hung right where he had left it. But it wasn't alone. The man with the strange, dark grey hat, the one he swore he had seen before, stood beside his doll. Several others were huddled together, intruding on his secret hideaway. Invading the home he had found for his sacred doll, his precious vessel.

Grabbing handfuls of long, dark hair close to his scalp, he pulled. Clenching his teeth, his skull vibrated. His blood brewed, scouring his veins.

"What IS this?" he hissed again.

Scuffing echoed from the forest behind him. Scanning his periphery, he darted up the steep, rocky incline to his left. Grunting as he hauled himself up, he clenched the broken branches, hanging on for dear life. Sweat dripped down his back. Reaching the top, he ducked low into the thick brush. Working his way along a ledge, he pulled large branches of pine apart, peering through. His arms stung with a series of fresh cuts.

Dammit. Frickin' branches.

He was tired of these intrusions. Why couldn't they just leave him in peace to carry out his plan? He looked again at the strange grey hat. The man was waving his arms, motioning to various areas of what had been his secret hideaway. A woman clothed in safari-like attire was listening to the man intently. Two other men in jackets with iridescent letters flashing against the last bits of the sun were hunting around the corners of the forest.

They better not move anything. Fuckers. Leave my doll alone. It belongs to me.

Suddenly, the intruders turned and stared at his doll. The safari woman launched herself onto a rock, touching *his* doll. The grey-hatted man and a shiny-booted woman grabbed the legs of *his doll*. The safari woman started cutting the ties that secured his doll on its hanger.

How dare you. Leave it alone.

Face glistening with a fresh coat of sweat, Seth widened his eyes and tried to control his spinning head. They were stealing his doll.

But this is the one.

This couldn't be happening. "Why?" he wailed, pulling strands of his long dark hair right from their roots.

He yanked his bag open. Fumbling inside until his fingers slipped around the smooth glass. The dark-purple vial resting in his palm, he slipped the cap off. Fixating his gaze into the purple vial, the black liquid mesmerized him. Time ticked away as his mind floated far from the disruption below. Blood pumping through his veins, his mind swirled. He snapped his gaze back to the unravelling scene below. The safari woman was crouched down beside his doll lying on the ground. The doll twitched.

There's still a chance.

Grabbing a syringe, he slipped it into the purple vial. Plunging the needle violently into his arm, he pierced his vein. The dark-green forest spun around him, blurring into one oversized paint stroke of green, brown and blue. Falling to his knees, he retched until his stomach burned and his throat tasted of acid. On his hands and knees, he crawled toward the forest edge, like a wounded animal.

The dark-purple vial slipped from his fingertips, landing on the soft forest ground, rolling toward the edge of the plateau. Seth watched it slowly gaining speed. The tiny glass bottle teetered precariously on the tip of the cliff. Struggling to move his hands, attempting to crawl toward the shiny purple, he crumpled to the ground. *No,* his mind yelled out. His mouth remained frozen. All he could do was watch in horror as the purple poison slipped over the edge, rolling with tremendous speed down the steep, rocky incline. Faster and faster, the vial spun straight toward the roof-covered enclave. Straight toward his doll.

What am I going to do? It was the one. This doll. The one I've been looking for all this time. The one that was meant to be my vessel.

Seth's mind plunged into overdrive. He sluggishly rolled his heavy body over. Lying on his back, he looked up at the blue sky turning black as night descended. The faint twinkling of a few stars sprinkled the dark horizon. The tall trees loomed over him.

Think, he yelled at himself. *What are you going to do?*

He needed his doll and his Black Magic. Without those two things, his future was hopeless. He would have to wait a while for the effects of his current dose to wear off. Then he could run home and get another vial. But by then who knew if they would have stolen his doll. They could be gone by the time he got back. He could try and sneak down the incline without being seen. If the vial hadn't made it all the way to the bottom, if it wasn't exposed, maybe he could find it. *Fuck.* Neither of these paths was in his original plan. *OK, OK. Get a hold of yourself.* Either way, he was going to have to wait to get control of his body again.

Get your mind straight.

Looking at the sky and the swaying trees, he attempted to clear his mind. He heard voices rising up from below. Rolling back over, his limbs were starting to gain movement. Crawling toward the ledge where his precious vial had taken a disastrous tumble, he peeked over. He could see the man with the distinctive grey hat again. And the shiny-booted woman. *Wait. Did that shiny boot woman talk to me at that show?* His stomach clenched. They had both emerged from the wall of trees between the bottom of the sharp incline upon which he perched, and the rock-roofed enclave where his doll hung.

Did they follow me?

He narrowed his eyes, trying to read their actions in the quickly descending darkness. Straining his eyes, his temples throbbing, he concentrated hard. Panic flushed through him. Eyes popping open wide, his stomach churned with a fresh wave of nausea. Looking at shiny-booted woman's plastic-gloved hand, he could swear she was holding a small, purple vial. His vial.

What the fuck! They want to steal my doll. Now they're taking my magic too.

He shook his head violently. Waving his hands vigorously, pins pricked his fingers, working their way up his arms. He continued shaking hard until the pins poked harder and the pain swelled. Moving onto his legs, he forced the feeling back into his feet, ankles, knees, and thighs. Standing up, he wobbled. Grabbing onto a tree trunk, he steadied himself.

Freakin' get it together, Seth. You need to get out of here.

Forcing himself to focus with everything he had, he stumbled across the plateau. Weaving his way through the tall trees, he stumbled along a dirt path, coming to an opening. The panic tearing through him dissipated as he emerged onto a street lined with houses. The feeling returning to his limbs, he picked up his pace, hobbling his way into the darkening night.

Carcass Chase

Mahoney's gut told him to turn around. There wasn't any noise to jolt him into action, just his instincts prompting him. Something small, purple and shiny was rolling, at an astonishing speed, toward them. The sky quickly turning from blue to black, it was difficult to distinguish precisely what the shiny purple object was. There was no doubt, however, that something was speeding toward him.

Blackwood was wholly consumed with processing the body. Agent Quesnel, taking Mahoney's cue, turned to see what had caught his attention. They both stared, in silence, watching the glinting object roll. It lost speed, churning its way to a stop, several metres from them.

Mahoney shot a look at Agent Quesnel. Shrugging his shoulders, he moved toward the unidentified object. Crouching down, he reached a tightly gloved hand toward the mystery item. "Looks like a glass bottle of some sort." Picking up the purple treasure with care, he stood up tall, turning to face her. He opened his hand, displaying the shiny glass vial like a special offering.

Inspecting the purple vial closely, Agent Quesnel proceeded to throw in her analysis. "Just as we expected. The killer is struggling to control his emotions. He is a hot mess of raging anger and panic. The perfect storm brewing within him, taking over his actions, turning his cool, calculated movements into accidental displays of sloppiness."

"This is an odd object to find in the woods. But how can you be so sure it's from him?" Mahoney continued to display the strange purple vial in one palm, rubbing the bristle on his chin with the other gloved hand. Turning toward the direction that the bottle had rolled, he looked up a sharp incline. *Bloody hell. I'm too old for this.*

"We follow your usual strategy. Follow the path that just opened up for us." Her eyes wandered up the steep incline.

Hiking up the sharp hill, their feet slipped on the mud-caked grass. Mahoney reminded himself again how amazing his new hiking shoes were. Looking over at Agent Quesnel, he couldn't grasp how she was trekking up this steep, slippery ascent with such grace and speed. And in her high-heeled platinum boots. *Geez. She's a mountain goat.*

Peeking over the edge of the climb, a plateau opened before them. A flat, lush, grassy opening, circled by thick forest. Mahoney peered down at the crime scene in processing. Blackwood was still perched over the body, deeply immersed in processing. The techies had moved to the very edges of the enclosure, examining the bordering trees.

Agent Quesnel broke into his reverie. "Perfect view from up here. Would be the ideal place to perch, if you were scouting it out to determine if it was safe to enter."

"You think he was up here…watching us?"

The words had barely left Mahoney's lips when a rustling noise snapped his attention to the far side of the open plateau.

The silhouette of a figure slipped into the tall trees.

Mahoney could have sworn he saw a long, black ponytail disappear behind boughs of pine.

Snapping into action, he yanked a plastic bag from his tweed coat pocket, wrapped it around the vial and slid it into his pocket. He ran toward the silhouette. Agent Quesnel on his heels, droplets of sweat popping up over his brow, his heart pounded in violent disagreement to the sprint.

Reaching the edge of the forest, Mahoney burst through the thick prickly branches. Little green needles spattering over the sleeves of his coat, he forced his way into the dense forest using his arms as a makeshift shield.

A rustling noise echoing from somewhere in front of him, he picked up the pace another notch. "I just heard something. Right in front of us."

Agent Quesnel remained right on his heels. He wondered if her heart was beating as hard his own.

C'mon, Bug, don't give out now. Forcing his mind away from the slice of pain shooting through his side, he wiped a tweed sleeve over the sweat sprouting across his forehead.

The thumping of his heart pulsating through his eardrums, he narrowed his eyes on the tiny slice of a trail winding its way through the clutter of tall, sturdy tree trunks.

A branch scratched across his cheek. A distant rustle lightly brushed his ears. His heart threatening to burst through his chest, sweat poured down the sides of his face stinging the fresh pine needle scratch.

Stumbling on a branch, the rough ground fast approaching his face, he grabbed onto a branch, the sharp needles prickling their way across his palm, ripping open the thin latex glove.

"You OK?" Agent Quesnel yelled, not losing momentum.

"Yeah. Good," Mahoney wheezed, gulping in breaths of air.

In a flash, he burst through the edge of the forest, halting on the side of a street.

Snapping his gaze to the right, then the left, his eyes darted in every direction. Head spinning, heart thudding, he scanned in desperation. "Where did he go?"

"I don't see him." Agent Quesnel slowly turned her head, like a great horned owl, scanning every square inch of the horizon.

"Where the *hell* did he go? I could have sworn I just heard a rustle."

"Let's split up. Unless he jumped a fence, he must have gone right or left. I'll take the right."

"I'll go left." Mahoney limped his way down the sidewalk, the erratic thudding against his chest slowly finding a steadier rhythm. Retrieving the handkerchief tucked into his coat pocket, he gave his forehead a good wipe. Dabbing at his moist face, his breathing normalized. The forest lined the sidewalk to his left. A road ran along the curb to his right. A line of fences closed in the other side of the roadway.

Where the hell could he have gone? Either he ran like a greyhound down this street, or he jumped like a gazelle over one of those fences. There's no other option. The further he chased, the more he could feel his prey slipping through his fingers. He wondered if this is what it felt like for the killer when he failed his hunt.

Date with a Dead Boy

Mahoney pushed hard on the heavy door, entering the morgue. The place was sparsely populated. Only Blackwood and her silent date.

"Mahoney, glad you're here," she greeted him, her eyes glued to the corpse, her plastic-gloved hands moving over the body with a shiny silver tool.

"Good to see you too." *As always.* The thought sprung into his mind before he could stop it. His heavy eyelids drooping, he sauntered his way over to the dead body lying on the shiny steel slab bathed in the bright light glowing from the overhead cylindrical bulb. "That was quite a night. You haven't had a break yet?"

"Nope. Not till my date with this dead boy is over. He needs me." She shook her head, stealing a glance at Mahoney. Dark shadows crept across the puffy skin underneath her bloodshot purple almond eyes.

"I should have brought you a coffee." An invisible wrench gave his heart a quick squeeze.

"Don't worry about it. No time for that." She turned back to her body and her scalpel.

I still should have brought her one. "Just thought I'd check in, before hitting the war room. Anything preliminary could help us here." *And to check on you. Damn, my thoughts are really running away with me today. Must be the exhaustion. Yeah. The exhaustion.*

"Well, I don't think I can tell you much that will surprise you at this point. Of course, we know the time of death." Her voice shaky, she paused.

"Blackwood. You know you did all you could. We were all there. We all saw it."

"I know." Remaining engrossed in her work, her eyes never left the body.

Mahoney changed the topic. "Is there anything you can tell me?"

"It's all the same as the other bodies. Hair, makeup, neck ligatures, messages. The same, but still no real clues. Even if he was interrupted, or panicked at all, he didn't slip up."

"He did drop the vial."

Blackwood moved her scalpel away from the body. "That's right. Speaking of which, the same blue-ringed octopus' toxic cocktail was found in the bloodstream. Along with other substances. The basic elements have been identified, but no match on a possible combination. It's perplexing. They have thousands of substances on record. Their database is quite impressive, actually."

"Oh, you mean for us folks up north, eh?" Throwing her a one-sided smile, he said, "But we have the vial."

A smile emerged over her tired face. "Yes, we do. It was empty. But, there may have been at least a partial print on it. I bet they're done lifting it."

Snapping off her gloves, she lifted the phone receiver off the cradle and rested it between her ear and her shoulder.

In a flash, Blackwood was off the phone. "It was only a partial print. And quite smudged. They're bringing it over now."

"I won't get too excited. A print takes time to process. A smudged partial probably won't get us far. But I bet that little purple vial will tell us something." *A little glass bottle. Slipped from his hands. Gotta be our guy. It could be the clue we've been waiting for. Let's mix a little Blackwood evidence with a bit of Quesnel behaviour.*

"Mahoney. Did you notice the label on the bottle?" Blackwood flipped open a folder, retrieving a photo. "Look at this. It's bizarre."

Mahoney looked hard at the photo. The label on the little glass bottle was golden-shaped like a scroll. In fancy, calligraphic lettering, the name read *Old World Apothecary*. "Geez. Do apothecaries still exist?"

"Yeah. I believe so. Some people still believe in old-world medicine." She smirked. "Like people who still wear corduroy and tweed herringbone."

"Oh yeah, very funny." His stomach fluttered, his face flushing with warmth. "Seriously, though, how many apothecaries can there be in this city?"

"Sounds like a good question for your computer wiz."

"It does. But if I get any leads, I'm gonna need a medical expert. Think you'd be up to a little road trip?"

"Hmmmm. With you? Why not. Sounds interesting. As long as I'm finished with my date here, I'm in."

A loud swoosh wafted through the room as the morgue door swung open. Blackwood turned, quickly moving toward the visitor. "Thank you very much." Taking a plastic bag from the short-haired, thick-spectacled man in a lab coat, she thrust it toward Mahoney. "Your vial, as requested."

"Blackwood, you have one hell of an influence on your colleagues."

"It's called good manners. Common sense, if you ask me."

"I've got to get back to HQ. I'll be in touch, about the apothecaries." Turning to leave, his heart plunged a couple of notches. *Sure hope Dara can find this place. Even if it just gives more time with Blackwood.*

"Take it easy, Mahoney." Her purple almond eyes followed him out of the room.

The Apothecary

Mahoney stepped from his orange Pony car onto the parking lot pavement. A clicking noise coming from the passenger side of the vehicle, he saw Blackwood fumbling with the door handle. Opening the back door, behind the driver's seat, he reached for his derby.

"Hold on. I'll let you out. That handle is a little sticky."

He moved swiftly to the other side of the car. With a quick snap of the door handle, he opened the creaky door. Blackwood emerged, her full height still surprising to him.

"Mahoney. You might consider trading in this old clunker for something a little…newer." She smirked at him.

Slamming the door shut, he shook his head. "What? It's not always about new and shiny, you know. Some things are more important."

She laughed out loud. "More important than getting locked *inside* your rust machine, or stranded when your clunker dies?"

They crossed the parking lot, approaching the sign in calligraphic-style black lettering. The words *Old World Apothecary* staring them down, almost like a warning.

"Yikes. Now tell me that isn't creepy." Blackwood looked up at the sign.

The sign led to a wooden door, the silver paint flaking off in chips. A decal was pasted to the top of the door, a black bottle with puffs of potion escaping from the top. Mahoney turned the shiny golden doorknob, pushing the wooden door open.

They stepped through the door, into a small, dark space. Several rooms wove through the space, like a miniature maze. Tall shelves lined every wall. Any available space between the shelves was packed with ornate metal tables, all presenting strange treasures.

"This place gives me the creeps," Blackwood's voice pierced the quiet.

"What? After all the scenes you've worked on, *this* place bothers you?"

"Look at this." Blackwood pointed to a tall silver pedestal with a circular top. Perched on top, like a fancy meal being presented on a silver platter, was a small metal skull. Red rubies adorned the base of the skull, its dark sunken eyes glaring at them. On either side of the skull, tall silver candle holders, covered in long drips of black wax, held brightly burning, long, dark candles. Behind the pedestal, a red velour tapestry was draped, golden slivers of thread weaving an ornate pattern through the velour.

"Wow. This is nuts," she exclaimed.

"Oh yeah, what about this wall over here." He walked across the room.

Along the wall was a shelf housing an extensive collection of glass bottles. Each was ordained with a handwritten label. Glass bottles of dark purples and greens, some clear, some crystal, all containing mystery liquids.

A crackling noise emanated from the back of the store. A doorway covered with long strands of beads parted as a tall, thin man with long black hair emerged. Gliding toward them, as if floating through the air, his pale hands in a prayer position, his long, thin fingers drumming together at his fingertips, he looked at them with a piercing stare.

"Can I help you?" His deep voice reverberated through the silent space. He continued gliding across the room, floating over to the counter, then behind. Leaning his hands on the golden countertop, his long, pale skeleton fingers spread out on top.

Mahoney cleared his throat. "I'm Detective Mahoney. This is my colleague, Terra Blackwood. We are trying to determine where someone would get their hands on this item." Retrieving a photograph from his coat pocket, he slid the picture of the dark-purple vial across the golden countertop toward the long-haired man.

Bony fingers grazed the photograph. The man's deep voice vibrated eerily through the silent room. "Oh yes. Isn't that a special item?" The man looked up from the photo, his sinister smile creeping across his face.

"It certainly is unusual," Mahoney confirmed. "I noticed a shelf of dark-coloured glass bottles along that wall over there. Do you recognize the bottle in this photo? Do you sell the same bottle?"

"Hmmmm. Well, yes, I do carry a rather unusual line of concoctions," the man crooned. Looking back at the photo, he opened a drawer, pulling out a long cylindrical, golden object. Turning the glass end, he pressed it up to his right eyeball. Shutting his left eye, the man lowered his face toward the photo. Inspecting it closer with his antique looking glass, he lifted has gaze again. "I see the vial you are looking for does have my handwritten label on it. Along with my emblem." He plucked a card perched atop a holder on the countertop and slid it toward them.

Mahoney picked up the card, examining the small emblem: a black bottle, wisps circling the top animating the look of the potion escaping. The words *Old World Apothecary* were written across the top in antique-style letters. It was just like the one on the front door that led them into this strange world.

"So the vial in the picture, it was purchased here, then?" Mahoney said.

Forming a teepee with his long fingers, the dark-haired man crooned his confirmation, "Yes, sir, it certainly appears so."

Blackwood chimed in, "Sir, would you be able to tell us anything about the substance in the bottle?"

"I just might be able to do that, yes. You see, the vials are colour coded. Thus, the shade of the glass indicates the liquid contents within." The syllables of his words drew out in long strands. His accent was unusual, as if it indicated a time period more than a geographical location. It was like listening to Count Dracula drawling away.

Mahoney half expected to hear the man burst out in an evil laugh. "The bottle in the photo is a deep-purple colour. What would that mean?"

"That, my friend, is an extraordinary bottle. I don't sell many of those. The contents are said to be capable of invoking Black Magic."

What the hell is this? This case only gets more whacked the deeper we delve. Geez. Mahoney attempted to layer logic onto the completely absurd situation. "Black Magic? Can you explain that?"

"Well, sir, Black Magic cannot be explained by the rules of this world. It is, you see, something that creates the reality within the individual mind. It will morph reality into whatever shape its invoker desires."

For fuck's sake. This isn't getting us anywhere. What the hell is this maniac talking about? Mahoney shot a look at Blackwood. She attempted to pursue her own line of logic. "Are the contents liquid?"

"Hmmm. Yes."

"What colour would they be?"

"Well, now, this one, it's very special. The contents are an unusual black."

"Black?"

"Hmmmmm. Yes." The man's smirk grew sinister. His finger tips drummed together in their teepee stance. "Like I said, Black Magic. But it only works if the invoker believes."

"Do you know the chemical makeup of this black liquid?"

"I do. I mix all my elixirs myself. I am the apothecary."

"Could you provide us with the details?"

"Well, I could. But, I like to keep my products on a low profile."

Mahoney pulled a paper from his pocket, unfolded it, and slid it over the counter.

The dark haired man stared at the paper. "I see. Well then, let me slip into my lab. I will be back momentarily." Floating across the room, slipping through the beaded curtain, beads clinking behind him.

Mahoney looked at Blackwood. "What the hell is this?" He whispered in a raspy voice.

"I told you this place creeped me out. My gut talks to me too, you know." She whispered back. "If we can get a chemical breakdown, we may finally be able to get a match on what we found in the bloodstream of our boys."

"Yeah."

Mahoney's eyes moved around the room, jolting from one strange object to another. His eyes landed on a shelf of books, moving from one label to the next. *Witchcraft 101, The Art of Black Magic, Magical Transformation. Geez. This is some weird shit.*

Beads clinking, the man returned to the counter in a swift float across the room. "Here you go." He slid a thick, silver piece of paper toward them.

Blackwood picked up the heavy paper, scanning the page. Mahoney peaked across her arm. The silver page was covered with the same calligraphic black lettering that seemed to be a common theme around this place. "This is a complete list of what composes the liquid in the purple bottle?"

"Precisely."

"Do you combine your own elements?"

"I do."

She scanned the page, then looked straight at him.

"It's all up here." He tapped his head with a skeleton finger. "It's all up here."

Mahoney inquired, "Would you have a record of who has purchased this particular item from you?"

"My clients prefer discretion."

"This is a murder investigation. College boys. I already showed you the warrant. Interference with a homicide investigation can impact your business." Mahoney stared into the man's dark eyes.

The man swallowed. "Fine. I do not accept cash. It's caused me certain, well, troubles in the past. I only accept credit card payments. I would have credit card imprints." He opened a drawer and shuffled through it. Pulling out a box, he plunked it onto the counter and sifted through a series of thin papers. "Ah, here. The purple vial that you are seeking, there have been three purchases this year." He placed three credit card imprints on the counter.

Mahoney flipped through the papers, looking at the names. Flipping open his notebook to a fresh page, he jotted them down. "I need a copy of these records."

The man sighed. "Fine." He snatched up the papers and walked over to a photocopier in the corner of the room.

The copier hummed to life. The man returned with three sheets of white paper.

"One more thing. What do you do on Saturday nights?" Mahoney stared at the man.

The man poised his elbows on the countertop and rested his chin on his steepled fingers. "I'm here until ten. Some of my more eclectic customers tend to drop by. Then I head over to Venom."

"Venom?"

"Yeah. It's a small joint. Quiet. They serve red wine."

"You go there every Saturday?"

"Yes." The man narrowed his eyes.

"Would anyone have seen you there?"

"Yes. They know me."

"Thank you." Mahoney slid a card across the golden countertop toward the skeleton hand. "Thank you for your time. If you think of anything further, we would appreciate it if you could contact us."

The man eyeballed the card with suspicion.

Mahoney turned, Blackwood glued to his heal. In a flash, they slipped through the silver door back into the land of the sane.

As they walked away from the door, Blackwood grabbed his arm. Clutching the silver paper, she looked at him intently. "These aren't simple chemicals. These are complex combinations. They'll have to be broken down into simple elements to confirm, but my suspicion is that they don't do a thing. Just placebos."

"Let's get you back to the lab, then."

They bolted for the orange rust machine.

Hunting

Seth picked up the small shot glass between his pointer finger and thumb. He lifted it to his lips and whipped his head back. The potent liquid stung his throat. A slight burn tingled the back of his tongue. He set the tiny glass back on the counter.

"Another round, sweetie?" Sasha asked.

"Sure." He leaned back against the bar and scanned the crowd. It was starting to get busy. They show was due to start in a half hour. If the band came on in time. Clusters of college kids were pressed together in clumps near the stage. Big hair and tight pleather reigned this evening.

"Here ya go, hon."

He snapped his attention back to the bar. "Thanks." He slid a bill across the counter.

Another quick shot slid down his throat. He grabbed the tall glass of Night Train and made his way to the back of the room. Lounging close to a high table, he examined the inventory.

Wrong night for what you need.

Shut-up. This is the right place. I always get what I need here.

I've been telling you to spread out your hunting grounds.

I told you to shut-up. I like it here. I feel calm.

His mind went silent. He took a deep breath and a long swig of strong wine.

Alright. Let's find a doll.

Taking his time, he inspected every patron mingling, sitting, drinking, talking and standing. One by one, he dissected each college kid with his eyes. He stared them up and down, from his corner perch, analyzing their hair, skin, posture, and clothing. He skipped over the old guys. Their skin was too wrinkled and sun damaged. Clanks and clatters rung out from the stage as drums, guitars and microphones were set up. He was running out of time. Once the show started, it would be hard to keep track of his target. If he found one.

He took a slow sip of his drink and focused hard.

There you are.

He glued his gaze to a young college kid. Probably a freshman. Smooth, white skin, long, dark hair, feathered down his back, and simple jeans and button up shirt.

Yes. Clean. Fresh. Ready for transformation.

The freshman was lingering up at the bar, alone, sipping a beer. Seth had seen him before. Multiple times. He was hoping that he'd see him here tonight. Things were falling into place.

He took a deep breath and shot back the rest of his wine. Up to bar he went, sliding in next to the freshman.

"Can I buy you a round?" He asked the freshman.

"Oh, uh…" The freshman looked at his almost empty glass. "Sure, why not?"

"Sasha. Can I get another round, and round for my friend here?"

"Coming right up." She smiled.

Don't look like such a loser.

Shut-up.

Don't blow this.

Shut-up.

"You, uh, like live music?" He asked the freshman.

"Yeah."

"Me too. But none of my friends will come."

"Oh, yeah. I understand. I'm new here, so don't really know anyone yet."

"Well, now you know me. I'm Seth."

"Ted."

"Here you go." Sasha slid two tall glasses toward them.

"Thanks." Seth slid a bill across the counter. He turned to face the stage. "Have you seen this band before?"

Ted turned his back to the bar and looked at the stage. "No. Heard they were good." He sipped at his dwindling beer and leaned against the bar.

"Yeah. They are." Seth slid his hand into his jeans pocket. He pulled out a tiny plastic bottle. Ted stared at the stage, nursing the last bit of his beer. Seth leaned harder against the bar, twisting his arm behind him. He stole a glance over his shoulder, perched the plastic bottle over the beer glass and squeezed. Drops plunged from the plastic tip into the fizzing beer and vanished. Seth snapped his gaze back to the stage and stuffed the plastic bottle back into his pocket.

He looked at Ted. "Time for another." He turned and picked up the two fresh drinks. He handed the beer to Ted.

"Oh, thanks." Ted placed his empty glass on the bar and took the fresh beer from Seth.

The lights dimmed. Voices rumbled through the room. The crowd grew restless.

"Show time." Seth said.

"Cool." Ted responded.

Puzzle Piece

It was late when Mahoney walked through the front doors of the homicide unit. Darkness had descended upon the quiet streets of the city. He had made it all the way home. He had even started his bedtime routine. But something had grabbed his gut, and just wouldn't let go. Taking long strides, he covered the ground between the main entrance and the war room with expediency. Clicking on the bright fluorescent lights, he scanned the tables of evidence lining the perimeter of the room.

OK, you're here, I know it. I just need to find you.

Scratching the bristle on his chin with his calloused hand, his brain strained to place the pieces of the puzzle into a configuration that would click together. Something just didn't quite fit. But his gut told him that what he needed was here. He just needed to see it. His eyes rescanned over the pieces of evidence that had been laid out carefully, spanning several long tables along the cream-coloured crime scene wall. Each scene was re-enacted with a glam outfit meticulously laid out just as it had been found on the body.

A flowing red robe of soft silk, paired with a dangling, sparkling earring. The attire of a glam queen, ready for a night onstage. A dark, shiny cloak, tassels stringing themselves from the sleeves, paired with skin-tight pleather. Accessorized by the haunting arctic-ocean pendant. The one that hadn't left Mahoney's mind since the moment he first saw it, lying against the pasty skin of a young, dead boy. A rough jacket spattered in buckles and binds, equipped to suppress a man plagued with insanity. Paired with black-leather pants that had tightly encapsulated the dead legs. Glimmering golden pants accessorized with a woven vest. Each costume uniquely created. Each mimicking the lead singer of a rock band.

What does this all mean? Mahoney quizzed himself harshly, penetrating deep into the crevices of his brain, searching for some hint to show itself. Even a tiny thread hanging, just enough to start pulling on, would be something. Something to lead him from this stagnant, stale, dead end of a place that he was cornered into.

He looked at the brand-new eagle-winged cloak, hung on display. *I bought that stupid thing thinking it would tell us something. Matched the one on the Frog Lake boy perfectly.* He shuffled over to the bagged red fibre. *Damn fibre matched the scarf tossed in the garbage by Mr. Black Ponytail. But nearly every woman's clothing store sells silk scarves.* He stared at the purple vial. *Even with credit card records from the apothecary we were sent down a path to nowhere. Two names checked out. And one dud. Who the hell is Dave Sabo?*

Walking over to the whiteboard, he picked up a bright-red marker. Finding a free white space amidst the dense clutter of colourful notes, he drew an upside-down triangle. In the top left corner, he wrote the single word EVIDENCE. He labelled the top right-hand corner as BEHAVIOUR. He paused, stepping back, addressing an absent audience. "Blackwood doesn't deviate from evidence. It's all about data and information. Quesnel has an intent focus on behaviour. She examines the evidence from the perspective of what our guy would *do*, how he would *behave*."

He stepped back up to the triangle, completing the triage with the word TRAIL on the bottom point. He continued lecturing the vacant room, saying, "Homicide always builds a trail on evidence. My team creates a path based on clues, leading us to the answer. In this case, there is a severe lack of evidence." Pausing, he stared at the triangle, red marker in one hand, scruffy bristle in the other.

"We've tried merging evidence and behaviour. We still don't have a concrete lead." Clicking the lid onto the pen, the wheels of his mind gained momentum.

Walking over to the long tables covered in a masquerade of rebuilt scenes, he stopped at the very beginning of the story. He made his way slowly along the first long table, meticulously scanning every bagged and tagged item, disassembling and rebuilding the puzzle over and over. Intently inspecting every clue, he attempted to turn it into the missing piece. He stopped at each reconstructed scene, mentally reliving it out in the wild. Matching each record of the analogy in his mind to the corresponding items sprawled out before him. He attempted to build a full story, retracing the steps of the hunter, one by one.

When he reached the straitjacket, encased in clear plastic, he stopped dead in his tracks.

This has got to be the single strangest piece of evidence I have ever seen. Scanning the cloak, the robe, and the golden pants, his mind continued to drive forward. *And the only piece of clothing that could lead to a name.*

His eyes leaping further along the table, they landed on the dark-purple vial encased in its own plastic home. Something pulled at his gut. Taking a seat, he perched his elbows on his knees, leaned forward, and rubbed small circles into his temples with his middle and pointer fingers. He stared at the purple vial, scanning the list of names his mind had memorized from the credit card imprints in the *Old World Apothecary. Another dead end.*

The jacket. The only item that might give us real names. The clock is ticking. We don't have time to rifle through every box of files before this guy strikes again.

Mahoney plunged his hand into his coat pocket, finding the smooth, polished quartz. His gut swelled with a rush of warmth. He bolted out of his chair. Walking over to his scribed triangle, he once again equipped his hand with the red marker. Beside the word *evidence,* he noted *straitjacket.*

That damn purple vial. Blackwood said the list of ingredients were placebos. No effect on the physical body. Black Magic. In the mind of the beholder.

He stared at the vial, the dark-purple hue glaring back at him. Returning to his triangle, beside the word *behaviour,* he wrote *Black Magic.*

Why were we even able to obtain this vial? Every scene was organized beyond belief. He never left a trace. The only reason that we have this purple prize is his behaviour. He came back to finish his script. We were there. He panicked, and he lost the vial.

Taking a moment to give his tired mind a chance to absorb the direction his train of thought was going, he grabbed for a chair. Turning it backward, he straddled the plastic seat, leaning into the back. Resting his chin on his arms, he stared hard at the bright-red triangle.

Something jolted in his head. His hand reached into the inside pocket of his tweed coat. The small pink stone was smooth against his hand. Pulling out the rose quartz, he held it in his palm, inspecting it.

He keeps slipping through our fingers. At the dive joint. In the parking lot after his clothing purge. When he dropped the vial. He's been slipping under the radar for a long time.

He stared at the pink stone. *His murders are intimate. He's emotional. Obsessive. Crazy?*

Mahoney sprung to standing, slipping the quartz back inside his coat. Grabbing the buckled jacket, safely stowed in a clear plastic home, he made his way to the door in no more than three long strides. The click of the door echoed into the empty hallway behind him. In a flurry of speed, he rushed toward his desk, plastic bag in one hand, cell phone in the other. Rapidly pushing buttons on his phone, his leg twitched. "C'mon, pick up." He impatiently willed a response on the receiving end.

"Dr. Crighton," the Doctor's crisp voice rang through the phone.

"It's Mahoney. Detective Mahoney. I'm sorry to disturb you so late." Urgency riddled his voice.

"Not a problem at all, detective. Looks like we're both burning the candle at both ends."

"The database search you ran for us on that jacket serial number? What would be the age range of the patient records?"

"Those would have been for patients eighteen and older."

"Can you re-run this search, on *juvenile* records?"

"Well now, access to those records is more restricted. However, I trust you will deliver the appropriate warrant."

"I'm on it. I'll be over to pay you a visit in about half an hour. And I have a blue-ringed octopus toxin to layer onto your search."

Home of Crazy

M ahoney strode across the parking lot, through spans of darkness interrupted by splashes of bright light. A shadowy figure lurked at the front entrance of the medical institution. *Must be Crighton.* Quickening his pace, bright lights surrounding the front entrance bathed away the shadows.

"Dr. Crighton."

"Detective Mahoney."

Mahoney followed the doctor through the doors and down the white hallways. Focusing on Dr. Crighton's shiny black shoes, he forced his stare ahead. The building was quiet, except for the occasional whimper seeping through one of the heavy steel doors, or the creak of a wheel as an attendant slipped by with a table of supplies.

His heart pounded against his chest. His back was slick with sweat. His shoulders relaxed at the transition from the sterile hallways to the cheery back office.

Dr. Crighton turned the key in the lock of his office door.

"Please, have a seat."

Mahoney sank into a plush, leather chair.

"Detective. I found your jacket." Dr. Crighton sat behind his desk, hands folded.

Mahoney slid a slip of paper across the desk. Dr. Crighton opened it, took a quick scan, then turned to his computer. A couple of clicks on the keyboard and he turned the screen toward Mahoney.

"I searched the juvenile records of all our patients for the last ten years. As I mentioned, that's as far back as the database goes. I found a match on the serial number for the jacket you found."

Mahoney clenched his teeth and blinked hard at the bright print on the black screen.

Patient Record
Name: Seth Henderson
Sex: Male
Age: 12
Admission Date: June 22, 1976
Release Date: April 13, 1977

"This is the last reference in our files of that serial number. It doesn't appear again in either the juvenile or adult records."

"It went missing from your institution."

"Yes, it appears so. How someone was able to get a straitjacket out of here is beyond my comprehension."

"Did he have any family? Did they visit?"

"Yes." Dr. Crighton turned back to his computer. "It appears that his mother was the one who had him institutionalized and then later argued for his discharge. Do you think she had something to do with the jacket?"

"A 13-year-old kid. He needed someone to come get him when he was discharged. Would he have had any items, clothing perhaps, that he would have taken with him?"

"Yes. Patients are allowed clothing and personal items. They are usually inspected. Whatever was approved upon arrival they would take when they left."

"So, his mom would have picked him up?"

"According to our records, yes."

"And the jacket, could it have been in his room?"

"I suppose that's possible too. We have records of what equipment was used on what patients. But the life of the item isn't tracked. Not here in the digital files."

"The mom, she would have brought a suitcase or bag, packed the clothes. Could have stowed the jacket. We know the last known patient to have been in contact with that jacket was this Seth. I need to find this kid. Guess he'd be, what, twenty-two now?" Mahoney scanned his notepad. "One more thing, doctor. Would you have a record of medications administered to the patient?"

"I believe so. Let me take a look." Dr. Crighton turned back to his computer. "Yes, here. The list of medications administered to Seth."

Mahoney searched down the list of complicated names. "This kid was pumped up."

"Unfortunately so. I read through the notes from his doctors. It seems he had extreme episodes. They had to give him medication to calm him down. Some of these substances are rarely used on someone so young, but the alternative was to let him harm himself. It looks as though they trialled several different medications. It's a tricky balance to calm without subduing the patient too much."

Mahoney jolted. His eyes glued to a single word in bright-green letters on the black screen.

Strata-octin.

"That's it." He pointed to the chemical name on the screen. "We've been on quite a hunt for that one. It was found in all our victims. We think the killer was using it to paralyze the victims, but allow them to feel all the pain he inflicted."

Dr. Crighton's eyes widened.

"Point is, we've been trying to find out where he got this strange toxic combination from. We scoured the few medical institutions and rehab facilities that came up in our searches. Nothing but dead ends."

"Until now."

"Until now. If this Seth somehow got away with a stolen straitjacket, perhaps he slipped a vial or two of this medication in his pocket. Or had help from Mom."

Dr. Crighton folded his hands and placed them on the desk. He looked squarely at Mahoney. "This is a twisted path you are on."

"Tell me about it. Doctor, can I get a copy of that record?"

"By your paperwork, yes. It'll take me a moment to print this out."

Mahoney pulled his cell phone from his belt and punched in the numbers. "Dara. I need a search on a name, right away."

TORTURE

DUNGEON

Torture Dungeon

A profusion of tactical personnel slipped through the dark night in silence. Decked out to the nines in dark camouflage and a plethora of weapons, they looked ready for war. Strategically making their way toward the old battered house, they moved as a single unit. Communicating with hand signals and head nods, the unit stealthily crawled across the rotting grass. Movement ceased when the weather-beaten house, barely holding itself together on rusty hinges, was completely surrounded. All windows were covered, and each doorway had its own watchman.

Detective Mahoney watched the scene unfolding before him, falling in line behind the smooth operation. The weight of his tactical vest heavy against his chest, his limbs tingled as he awaited the launch of the assault on his target.

I hope he's alone. Unaware of the assault outside his door.

Obsessively tightening the velcro enclosures over each pocket spattered across his vest, he double checked his gun, cuffs, and extra ammunition, ensuring they were securely intact and readily accessible.

Pink boots and blonde curls flashed through his mind. Shoving them aside, his gut seized.

This is our guy. I went over the evidence a million times.

As sure as he was, as strong as the pangs of instinct throbbing from his gut were, a flush of worry flooded over him. He gave his head a firm mental shake, trying to convince himself that he hadn't launched an over-the-top tactical take-over of a peaceful little residence in a run-down neighbourhood for no good reason.

Light glowed from the small windows. The entire operation was waiting for launch.

Four men stood facing the door, guns pointed, helmets tightly strapped to their heads. A golden badge drifted through Mahoney's mind. Dark rust crept its way across the shiny, polished metal, threatening to devour every last glint. The seconds ticked away, the rust crept across the badge, a pink boot trudged through the clutter building in his brain.

The tactical leader, moving his radio toward his lips, made eye contact with Mahoney. Mahoney nodded.

The radio crackled to life. The tactical leader barked a single order.

An echo of shouts shot through the air in acknowledgement.

Old wood crinkled, disintegrating into clouds of sawdust, as both front and back doors were busted from their hinges.

Tinkling rang through the entire house as glass shattered into a million tiny pieces. The hollers of the tactical team throbbed through Mahoney's ears, the mass of sounds merging into a single loud mess.

Before he could take a single breath or blink an eye, every corner of the main floor of the small dwelling was invaded. Repositioned as strategically as they were during the approach, the entire tactical team stood still.

Mahoney scanned the frozen scene.

A woman sat in a battered chair, curlers in her hair, a filthy nightgown falling over her frumpy form.

He addressed her directly. "Ma'am, please do not move. Is this the residence of Seth Henderson?"

The woman scowled at him, muttering her response, "Yeah. My good-for-nothing son still sponges off me. If he's home, he'd be down in that trash hole of a basement he calls a hideaway."

Mahoney was positioned inside the front entrance opening onto the main floor. He visually located two sets of stairs, one across the room, and one on the wall he was hovering against, to his right.

He probed his unwilling participant, "Ma'am. Is there anyone else, other than you and possibly your son, currently in this house?"

"No," she confirmed, her voice drowned in annoyance.

"The door directly behind you, does that lead to the basement?"

"Yeah." She shot him a glare.

Mahoney nodded at the tactical leader. Several orders were barked. Several operatives moved up the stairs, to Mahoney's right, while several others descended the stairs across the room.

"Sutton, Hayes, join me. Let's go into the basement." Mahoney crossed the room, slipping in behind the operatives.

Sutton and Hayes on his heels, they moved in a huddle, slowly stepping down each stair like one big crawling animal. Gifted with a series of gruesome scenes left by the killer, Mahoney's team had been through a grisly journey. Yet, they were still unprepared for what appeared before their eyes.

Reaching the bottom of the staircase, Mahoney halted in line with the operatives.

Music blasted from a boom box perched on an old wooden table in the far right-hand corner across from the bottom of the staircase. Drums hammered through the speakers, accompanied by deep reverberations of electric extremes, and topped with a wailing voice. Posters plastered the walls, surrounding them in a collage of leather-clad, wild-haired, prettily painted rock gods, staring at them with savage eyes. Small lamps were scattered around the room, dimly lighting the dark dungeon in a soft glow. An operation-room-style table was perched in the middle of the room, directly under the only bright light in the dark cave.

The hunter's young, fresh prey lay helplessly on the shiny steel slab.

The young boy's wrists and ankles were slashed, ripe blood seeping out of the deep cuts. He wasn't tied down, his body appeared invisibly taped to the table beneath him.

His badly battered face was contorted in an expression of sheer terror. His long hair was wild and tangled with blood. His eyes were wet with bloody tears.

As the hunter's hand struck the side of the boy's cheek, a scream pierced through the boombox ruckus, sending a chill down Mahoney's spine.

Completely consumed with his torturous task, the hunter was oblivious to the invasion. He stroked a red silk scarf between his hands, slithering closer to his prey. Sliding the silk behind the young prey's neck, he began an intricate wrapping procedure. He added his own chorus to the noise blasting from the small black speakers, mixing his own wails with those echoing through the room.

Mahoney's head spinning, beads of sweat sprung across his forehead. The pink boot shoved its way back into his mind. A second boot joining it, the pair stomped through his head. A bright-red glob slid its way down the shiny pink rubber. A little ghost face formed, staring through his mind, weaving through the clutter of images. Shrugging it off, he worked his way quietly to the front of the operation to confront the wild man. It was time for the hunter to become the prey. This case had just reached the end of its life.

"Seth Henderson. You are surrounded. Put your hands in the air. Step away, slowly, from the boy." Forcing his words over the rock chorus, a chill washed through Mahoney.

The hunter froze, his hands idling on the scarf. Slowly raising his arms, he pointed his fingers toward the overhead light and bent his elbows in a cactus form. The scarf slipped from his fingers, drifting in several spirals before silently landing on the concrete floor. Taking one small step backward, away from the steel slab, he fell still and silent.

"Sutton, take care of that racket," Mahoney barked.

Sutton swiftly moved across the room. Pressing the plastic button marked *off*, the chaos was silenced with a loud click.

Mahoney continued to direct his prey. "Seth. Turn around. Slowly. Keep your hands raised, where I can see them."

The hunter slowly began his revealing spin. His long hair, neatly tied in a ponytail at the nape of his neck, began to disappear. His pale face, glistening with sweat, exposed itself one familiar feature at a time.

A flash of his routine at the end of a long day appeared in Mahoney's mind. He watched a replay of all the times a friendly face had greeted him as a bubbly ginger-ale was poured, and a hot cheesy pizza was ordered, *pronto*. He looked directly into the eyes that had belonged to a trusted friend. Those same eyes that now stared at him deceptively in an evil glare, fully revealing who he was. What he was.

The single ghost face suddenly split into dozens of pale little faces, swirling through Mahoney's mind. He was sitting at the high-legged chair at the bar of the Stepping Stone Pub. A cheery face looked him in the eyes, asking him if he wanted his usual. A thousand similar images flashed through his mind, taking over every corner of his brain, shoving out every other memory.

Hey, boss. How ya doing', boss? Long day, boss? You want your usual, boss? Simon's voice rang through his mind. Simon's gaze stared him down. Simon's long, black hair tied perfectly in a neat ponytail. Simon's baby blue eyes looking into his own, inquiring about his current case, probing him for information on the apparent serial killer taking over their lovely little city.

Cheerful, trustworthy Simon. His happy smile turning into a sick, sadistic, evil grin. Simon, the friendly neighbourhood bartender and local confidante, in an instant turned into the sick hunter that Mahoney had been tracking.

Mahoney wiped his forehead vigorously with his sleeve, mopping up the sweat pouring down his face. Shaking his head hard and fast, he struggled to regain control of his thoughts. *How could it be? This guy's name is Seth.*

Mahoney took a few long strides toward the man that was both friend and prey. He looked directly into the hunter's eyes, locking his gaze for a long moment. The stranger known as Seth stared back at him with a sinister smirk.

Mahoney's gruff voice broke the silence. "Turn around. Put your arms behind your back. Slowly."

Seth turned as Mahoney secured his wrists, pulling them behind his back. A click and a zipping sound erupted as Mahoney cuffed his prey. Mahoney gravely declared the purpose of the confinement. "Seth Henderson, you are under arrest for the murders of..." Mahoney's voice continued on autopilot as his mind struggled to grasp the new reality forced into it. Handing Seth over to two operatives, Mahoney confirmed the next direction. "Secure him. Take him in. Get the medics down here pronto."

The operatives moved to the stairs, sandwiching Seth between them. Seth stepped a black booted foot onto a wooden stair. Mahoney stared at the shiny, black boot. *Doc Marten.*

Mahoney turned toward the steel slab. He walked up to the badly battered and beaten boy. Quickly assessing the damage while simultaneously providing words of consolation.

"You're going to be OK. We have him. He can't hurt you now."

Tears sprung from the young boy's eyes. His lips trembled, mucus seeped from his nose, mixing with trickling salt water and oozing blood into one thick mess.

Mahoney looked him directly in the eyes. He offered up a soothing voice, saying, "Listen. The medical team will be here right away. They will clean you up, check you over, and have you out of here in a flash."

The young boy's arm jerked as he tried to move it. He looked at Mahoney with pleading eyes. He sputtered out a few words, his voice shaking, his lips continuing to tremble. "P-p-p-lease. I…I c-c-can't move. Don't. Go."

Mahoney didn't move. He secured his gaze onto the boy's eyes. His shoulders relaxed, and he cleared his throat. "I'm not going anywhere." Pink boots and blonde curls found their way back into his mind. He tried to push them out, but they wouldn't budge. Little ghost faces began to materialize, strengthening the image. He shuddered, not wanting to hear what they had to say. One little ghost face opened her tiny blood-red mouth. Her lavender eyes pierced Mahoney's mind, her small hand reaching for his heart. *Thank you, Bug. You saved them. All of them. All the ones that were to come will now be safe.* Warmth rushed through his heart, into his limbs, engulfing his stomach. The little mouth moved again. *Thank you, Bug.* In a flash, every boot, every blonde curl, every little ghost face vanished. His mind was clear.

He looked back down at the young boy, and he smiled.

Portfolio

P unching the buttons on his phone, Mahoney turned from the steel slab, now surrounded by medical personnel. "Dara. It's Mahoney. I need you to run a name for me. Actually, a pair of names. Seth Henderson and Simon Frederick. Find out anything at all you can about who these two are, and how they are linked or related."

Shoving his phone back into the holster, he returned to his team.

Sutton muttered his thoughts to the group. "That psycho wasn't going to quit. Good thing we showed up when we did."

Clicking on the stairs snatching his attention, Mahoney saw Agent Quesnel descending into the basement. "We might get lucky here, boys," she chimed. "He was in the middle of his next sacrifice. The scene will shed light on his ritual. Perhaps it will confirm everything we suspect so far and take us to a new level of understanding of his script. He didn't have time to clean up. Let's beef up our evidence."

Hayes looked at her wildly. "More important, the kid was still alive. And we got the sick fucker."

"I agree." Agent Quesnel calmly returned his gaze. "But the more we can learn here, the more we can get into his mind. We've got him, but there's work to do to build a solid case. What happens next could entirely hinge on what we find down here."

"Boss. It's like an operating room," Sutton, scanning the room, observed.

"This is where he conducts his ritual on his victims," Agent Quesnel concluded.

Mahoney continued to scan the room. The corner of the room to his right was adorned with an ornate silver pedestal. Upon the stand, a purple vial was perched. From the ceiling, two hooks protruded, upon each a length of rope was twisted into a circular noose. Strings of sinew stained in black-red stripping away from the ropes poked wildly into the air.

Agent Quesnel said, "Mahoney. Check out the ropes hanging from the ceiling. He could have hung them from their wrists, like the one that was still alive."

Not ready for a full conversation, Mahoney continued to visually process the scene. The far back wall was plastered in a series of posters. Working his eyes from left to right, Mahoney scanned each, his mind flashing back to Frog Lake Park, Eagle Woods, Clear Creek Ravine and Gleaming Reservoir.

The first poster featured a man in tight chaps, sides of his legs exposed, a red, silky robe weaving over his arms, down his back. The man's mouth was stretched wide over a silky-scarf-endowed microphone.

The next poster featured a man wearing a shimmering black cloak, his arms spread wide into the air, staring back at him. The cloaked man's mouth was poised dramatically like he was trying to share a crucial secret.

The third poster revealed a man with a barbaric white chest, a wild orange tiger mane, and tight black-pleather pants clinging to his muscular contour. The orange-maned man stared at him with crazed eyes, boring their way into Mahoney's soul. The man's mouth stretched over the bulb of a microphone, threatening to devour it, and anything standing in his way.

The fourth poster presented a man with long, luxurious waves of golden hair and tight golden pants clinging to his muscular legs. The man's eyes emitted a look of sadness and desperation. The poster collage ended there. A table stretched the length of the wall. Below the first free space on the wall, a rolled-up poster lay.

"Holy shit. Will you check this out?" Hayes approached the poster collection. "It's just like the murder scenes."

Mahoney, snapping on a second skin over his hands, walked toward the unopened poster. Picking it up, he slowly unrolled it, revealing another long-haired, tightly clothed man. Long, raven-black hair flowed over the man's shoulders. He wore a black-leather jacket, the sleeves drowning in a plethora of silver studs. Black-leather pants, studs running along each side, encased his legs. His black-gloved hands were stretched open, his fingers piercing the red background. His eyes and lips were thickly lined in black. His mouth was pulled into a sneer. Across the top of the poster, in dark-purple lettering, the single word was stretched: POISON.

Agent Quesnel slid up behind Mahoney. "Looks like this is a collection of his work. His portfolio. Mahoney, looks like you've uncovered his final fantasy."

Mahoney scanned the wall again. His eyes lingering over the posters, they wandered over to the wall on the left of the room. Another series of posters crawled their way across the grey concrete. *Were there others?* Goosebumps tickling their way up his arms, Mahoney put the poster down on the table. Directly to his right was a neatly folded, black-leather jacket, spattered in silver studs. In the right corner, a set of shelves housed a meticulously organized series of cassette tapes.

The boom box Sutton had quieted during their confrontation with the hunter was settled next to the tapes. Mahoney walked over to the sound system, peering into the plastic door. A cassette tape had been inserted. Clicking the play button, Mahoney stepped back, curiosity taking over him. From the wire-mesh black speakers, a violent riff filled the air. A raspy voice threw itself across the room, singing of a woman's poisonous love.

Mahoney clicked the player to a stop. The tiny wheels halted; the voice vanished. Turning, he took another scan of the room. The side of the room furthest from the wooden staircase was decked out like a living room. A small purple couch sat atop a lime-green throw rug. The sofa was cluttered with hot-pink pillows. Little diamonds spattered their way across the couch, the concrete floor, and the surrounding walls. Mahoney tilted his head upwards, his eyes settling on a slowly spinning disco ball.

What the hell is all this? It's like a secret hideaway. Where he could bring his victims. Execute his ritual. It's a torture dungeon. A glamorous torture dungeon.

"Boss. This is weird," Hayes broke through his thoughts.

"You got that right. It's like he set this place up to hide away, but also to bring his victims. To torture them down here in peace."

Agent Quesnel probed, "The glam flair to this place reflects what he wanted to be, how he saw himself. The posters represent his collection, his *portfolio.*"

Sutton inquired, "You mean like a portfolio of his work?"

"Yes. He was proud of all the effort he put into this. It was his life's work."

Mahoney walked up to the steel slab. A new image flashed into his mind. A young boy in a shiny black cloak, his body battered and bloody. Another young boy joined him, dancing around in a flowing red robe. His neck brutally branded, his face ghastly pale. A third boy followed with a wild tiger's mane framing his face. Screaming wildly, his eyes crazed, blood oozing from the cuts across his forehead, the word BLEED jumping from his head into Mahoney's. A fourth boy with glimmering golden pants stared with glassy eyes, gasping for breath, his face turning blue. Mahoney's mind whirled, he grew lightheaded, his gloved hands reached for the purple couch.

"Mahoney, you OK?" Agent Quesnel's voice shot him back to reality. He stared at a hot-pink pillow.

Shaking his head, he turned back toward the steel slab.

"We need to scour this place. Upon scanning, it doesn't look like anything we don't know. It just puts together all the pieces we already found. We know what he did. This is where he did it. Let's take advantage of this. The more evidence, the better."

"Sound good, boss," Sutton confirmed.

Hayes wandered over to the pink-and-purple relaxation corner. Shuffling through the collection of cassettes, Sutton stationed himself by the poster portfolio. Agent Quesnel drifted over to the bloodied ropes, inspecting the silver pedestal.

Where the hell to start. This place is cluttered with potential clues. Think, Bug, think. A new ghost face popped into his mind. The smooth white face of a young boy, his eyes lined in black, his lips painted pink. Closing his eyes, heat surged through Mahoney's gut. He didn't back down from the new little ghost face. He stared it straight in the eyes. *Where would you start?* he asked the young boy. Mahoney's body turning, he took a few steps. He opened his eyes. He was facing the steel bed. Scanning the slab from left to right, then top to bottom, his eyes halted on what appeared to a be built-in drawer, close to the concrete floor. Sliding the drawer open, his heart palpitated, his eyes widened. Reaching a hand into the drawer, he grasped a small brown teddy bear. Its glassy black eyes stared back at him. *What the hell is a child's toy doing in here?*

He looked back into the drawer, scanning its scarce contents. A pair of metal scissors, a round of rope, and a small leather-bound book. Lifting the book from the drawer, he carefully untied the leather tie holding it shut. He gently opened the hardcover. Elaborately scrolled black-inked words covered the yellowing paper. His eyes scanned the first page.

Journal

of

Seth

Henderson

Turning the page, his eyes found the first entry.

Date: April 3, 1975

I wish he would just kill me.

Search for Simon

Mahoney swept through the glass doors. *Back at good ol' HQ.* A tremor shot through his core. The place was familiar, but the interview he was about to conduct was not. Passing by the introductory room, where a suspect was dropped to settle in until the interviewing process would begin, Mahoney shot a glance through the window. Seth sat in isolation, hands folded in front of him, resting on the table. Free from cuffs, giving a false sense of freedom. Caged in by four walls of glass, he wasn't going anywhere. After Mahoney introduced him to good ol' HQ, the next stop would be the elevator of doom.

Dropping his derby onto his desk, Mahoney hung his coat on the back of his chair. Without losing momentum, he swung over to Dara's desk.

"Dara. How's the name search?"

"Bug. Glad to see you made it back in one piece." Sliding her thick black-rimmed glasses down her nose, she let them slip from her fingertips. Dangling on the shiny beaded string around her neck, the glasses landed softly against her blue suit jacket. Scanning him up and down, she nodded her approval.

"All in one piece." He placed a hand on her shoulder.

She snapped back to business. "I got your search done, all right."

"Great. Thanks for the speedy work."

"Of course." Her smile lasted a split second before fading away. Worry wrinkled her forehead. "Are you sure you're ready for this?"

"Hit me."

"Bug. It turns out that Seth Henderson is one and the same with Simon Frederick. Actually, his birth name is Seth Simon Henderson. Some of his legal identification is under Seth, other items are under Simon."

His face flushing, Mahoney forced back the turmoil churning in his stomach, unsettling what little tidbits of food might still be living in there. He couldn't even remember the last time he had eaten. Forcing his mind back to the task at hand, he manually wrenched his brain around the fact that his friendly neighbourhood bartender, who had been serving him up late-night dinners after long days, was, in fact, the sadistic killer he had been hunting. *Cunning little fucker.* Pressing back the rage rising within, he looked at the black screen blinking the bright-green truth.

"Good work. Really appreciate it." Leaning a hand on her desk, he stared again at the screen. Even though he had looked Seth in the eyes, he still couldn't believe it. Standing up tall, he moved his mind and body into action. "Got to review what we found at the scene with the boys. Then get onto the interview. Thanks again, Dara. Stand-up, speedy job on this whole case. We'll continue to need you until everything is closed out. Lots of data. Lots of files. We need your organizational skills on this one."

"My job isn't done till the last file is signed and sealed." Touching his arm, her eyes washed with concern. "Bug, you sure you're OK? You look pale."

He stood up. "Seth. Our killer. He's also a bartender who goes by the name of Simon. He serves at the pub near my place." He paused. "Simon's been serving me most nights, for years now."

Dara gasped. "Bug. There's no way you could've known."

Meeting her eyes, he responded, "I know."

"Do you?"

"Yeah. I know. Just, give me some time to wrap my head around this one." His hand dug into his pants pocket, his fingers sliding across the polished rose quartz.

"All right. I don't mean to pry. I…I just want to be sure you're OK. You're awfully hard on yourself." Dara had been around a long time, seen him through a lot of cases. She never pried. Unless it was necessary.

"Thanks. I gotta go. Guys are waiting." He turned away and headed to the war room.

Journal

Bursting through the war room door, Mahoney scanned his team. Sutton and Hayes were eagerly perched at the front of the room. Agent Quesnel was in her usual sly spot at the back. Dara followed him, finding her quiet corner.

"OK, boys, girls, let's get going. Quick brief before we get the interviewing started." Mahoney made his way to the front of the room in a few solid strides. "We've gathered a lot from the scene. Sutton, Hayes, I'm going to count on you to go through this with Agent Quesnel meticulously. Make sure Dara gets an accurate account of everything we found, and the status of each item. Nothing leaves this room until it's properly listed and accounted for. We have our guy. We still have a lot of work to do before we reach closure."

Sutton sipped his Big Gulp. "Got it, boss."

Hayes scribbled furiously into his notebook. Agent Quesnel leaned against the back wall, arms crossed.

Reaching for his non-existent coffee, Mahoney sighed loudly. *Guess I'll just have to wait.* Continuing forward, he turned to the cream-coloured crime scene wall. "Might help to create a picture of the last scene our guy was planning to create."

Agent Quesnel nodded from her back corner.

"I think a strong piece of evidence will be the journal I found under the steel bed." Mahoney walked over to the series of boxes laid out on the long centre table.

Scanning the labels on the sides of the boxes, he halted. Sliding the top off a box, he retrieved the leather-bound book wrapped in a plastic cover. Snapping latex over his hands, he pulled open the plastic bag. Picking the book up carefully, he flipped through the pages.

Returning to his place at the head of the room, he proceeded with a grim reading from a horrific tale. "This journal, it appears to belong to Seth. According to the dates, he's been keeping this journal for a very long time. You should see some of the entries from his childhood. It seems like he's been the victim of torturous routines very similar to the ones that he has been playing out with his own victims. His later entries…well…listen to this one. It was written the day that our Frog Lake boy disappeared. He starts it out with 'Dear Doris,' like he's writing a letter to his mother. It's this part in the middle, listen to this…" Clearing his throat, Mahoney looked down at the yellowing page.

"I'm not stupid. I'm not a fucking fool. I'm not YOUR fool. You think you can lock me away like some wild animal. You know what happens to a caged animal, Doris? It turns crazy. Its mind reaches into psychotic realms. Its anger swells within it until revenge is screaming to escape."

Mahoney paused, looking at his small audience. "He keeps going back to this, like a chorus almost, saying he's not her fool. Listen to this ending."

Looking back down at the yellowing paper, Mahoney slid his finger down the page until he found his spot.

"I'm not a fool. You're the fool. You're MY fucking fool."

"I have my way out. You can't stop it. My essence will flourish. My true being will come alive. My soul will transform into its ultimate form. I will be immortalized. You will have no control. Your words will vanish into thin air. You will be powerless against me."

"I will find my vessel, my way out. I will live again. I will morph into who I truly am."

Sutton lowered his Big Gulp. "Wow. Messed up."

"Yeah, this guy is sick. His brain is wired wrong," Hayes said.

Closing the book, Mahoney walked over to the long centre table. He slid the plastic bag back over the book.

Agent Quesnel walked over to the long table, leaning over, resting her hands on the tabletop. "You boys are right. This guy is sick. He likely has a severe mental illness. We can leave the full assessment to the professionals. What we do know is that he appears to believe that he is both Seth and Simon."

Mahoney looked at the ground, his teeth clenched. "Yeah."

Agent Quesnel redirected the discussion. "We can get something from these journal entries. If you listen to the words, he's describing his fantasy, in detail. He's also expressing his rage against his mother. It sounds like she was the main source of his turmoil. It also sounds like this has been going on for a long time. If it started when he was a young child, his corrupt wiring, as you pointed out, could be long-lived and deeply rooted."

Mahoney slid the latex off his hands. "We need to go through that whole journal. Dissect the entries. We have no idea how long his acts have been going on. How many other victims he had, whether they ended up dead or not. Our purpose is two-fold. To see if there were others. And to strengthen our case. I'm counting on all of you."

Mahoney scanned the room, assessing his team. "It's going to be a long night, gang. Get your coffee, grab a bite and settle in. I'm off to meet our hunter." He started walking toward the door.

"Wait," Agent Quesnel called after him.

Mahoney spun to face her.

"You're not dealing with your typical interview here. You may have two people in one."

He swallowed the rage burning in his throat. "Yeah. I know."

"You arrested him as Seth. Go in as if he is Seth and Seth only. See what happens. He could be completely wrapped into one personality, or you might see both."

"Got it." He swung the door open with force and stepped through. His face flushed with heat, he stopped and looked at the floor. His forearm was tight. He looked down at his hand, balled into a fist. *C'mon, find your cool.* He looked across the clutter of cubicles, out the window into the dark night. A couple of stars twinkled. His shoulders relaxed and his mind whirled to a halt. Turning, he made his way swiftly down the hall toward the caged hunter.

Meet Seth

Taking a sip from the chipped bright-blue mug, Mahoney looked down at the weak coffee. *OK, Bug, time to meet Seth-Simon.* Turning from his desk, he made his way down the small hallway toward the glass cage holding his interviewee. He'd been through the introductory interview a million times. The room was bright, cheerful, on the main floor, intended to provide a welcoming introduction to homicide headquarters.

Sliding his card over the control, the door clicked open. Turning the knob, his heart beat hard against his chest. Pausing, he took a deep breath, willing the pumping to stop. Swinging the door open, he smiled broadly, closing the door behind him.

"Seth Henderson. I'm Detective Mahoney."

Seth-Simon looked up from his seat on the opposite side of a small table. Strands of dark hair escaping the elastic at the nape of his neck sprung wildly around his face. Squinting his eyes, he raised an eyebrow. Looking back down at the table, he remained silent.

Sitting down across from Seth-Simon, Mahoney placed his mug onto the table. He proceeded to prod his interviewee. "Seth, do you know why you are here?"

Seth-Simon shot a glare across the table. "I don't know you. I don't know what you want from me." Lowering his gaze down to the floor, he snapped his mouth shut in silence.

"OK. How about we step this back a bit. Can you tell me your full name?"

"Seth Henderson."

"Do you know your middle name?"

"I don't have a middle name."

"OK, thank you. Do you know where you are?"

"This is a police station. They told me I was at some sort of homicide department."

"Yes, thank you. Do you know why you are here?"

"Yeah."

Relief washing over him, Mahoney relaxed his shoulders. Taking another swig of coffee, he calmed his stomach and his nerves. "That's good. Can you tell me why you are here?"

"Yes. I was having a quiet afternoon in my music-listening room. Some people raided my mother's house, where I stay sometimes. I had popped over to visit her. I like to check on her. She's getting a little older, and I worry about her sometimes. So I stopped in. Thought I'd listen to a tune or two while I was there. So I went down to my listening room. She never got rid of it when I moved out." Pausing, Seth-Simon looked at Mahoney's coffee mug. "Say, I don't suppose I could get something to drink?"

Mahoney said, "Of course. But first, could you tell me who these people were that raided your mother's house?"

"Oh, I'm not sure. But it probably has something to do with my mom's ex-boyfriend. He was a horrible man, you know. People came looking for him from time to time. They were probably there for him. Somehow I got mixed up in this. Probably because I was in his basement. I mean, it was his basement, until he moved out. Then I took it over."

Mahoney's mind buzzing, he closed the loop on his promise. "OK. Thank you, Seth. What do you want to drink?"

"Something cold. Maybe a ginger-ale. You probably like ginger-ale, don't you?" Seth-Simon smirked fiendishly.

Mahoney froze. Washing all emotion from his face, he kept the conversation going. "Well now, I guess from time to time I do, yes. I'll be right back with your cold drink." Lifting his mug from the table, he turned and left the glass-walled room. Locking the door with a click behind him, he sauntered down the hallway. *Why would he ask me if I liked ginger-ale? He responded to Seth. Is Simon underneath there? What the hell is he doing? Playing me?*

Mahoney stared at the vending machine window. Scanning the rows, he found the bright-green can labelled *Schweppes*. Fishing for the spare changing floating in his pocket, he inserted the coins and clicked the required combination of numbers. The machine whirred to life, the ginger-ale loomed toward him, then clunked its way to the plastic opening at the bottom of the machine. Retrieving the cold can, Mahoney turned back to the glass-walled room.

Scanning his card at the door, the lock clicked open, and he re-entered the room. Seth-Simon looked at him. Sliding the cold can across the table, he sat back down.

"Thank you," Seth-Simon calmly spoke. Pulling the silver tab, pressing it into the can, a hiss escaping, Seth-Simon continued to look his way.

"You're welcome. You helped me out, I delivered the promised drink." Mahoney paused, watching Seth-Simon take a sip from the green can. "Now, Seth, you said that the people raiding your house were looking for your mom's boyfriend?"

"*Ex*-boyfriend. He was not a good man. I was happy to see him leave."

"You think they were after your mom's ex-boyfriend. So, there wouldn't be any reason for them to be looking for you?"

"Not that I am aware of, no."

"Was there anything in your music-listening room that they might have had an interest in?"

Seth-Simon rolled his eyes skyward as if searching his brain for an inventory on the items in his torture dungeon. "I doubt it. I just store my rock tapes down there, and I've got a cozy little area to listen to them." Taking another sip of bubbly pop, Seth-Simon continued to look his way, expressionless.

"And you say you don't know what your middle name is?"

"I don't have one. My mother didn't give me one."

"I see. And, has anyone ever called you Simon?"

"Simon? No. I have a friend named Simon. Do you know him?"

"I don't know. When is the last time you saw your friend Simon?"

Seth-Simon snorted. "I don't keep track of when he shows up. I think I saw him last week sometime at the bar I go to when I want to chill."

"Do you know Simon's last name?"

"No."

"Do you know where he lives?"

"No. Listen, man, I don't know anything about him. I just see him at the bar sometimes. We talk. About music. That's all." Seth-Simon pulled the elastic from his hair with snap. He ran his fingers through his long, dark locks, his mouth clenched in a thin line.

"All right. Let's get back to your mom's house. You were there, listening to music. Do you remember anything else at all about what you were doing when the policemen came in?"

Seth-Simon glared straight at Mahoney, his shoulders shaking, his teeth chattering. "No. I told you. Nothing!" Spit flew as he hissed the last word.

Mahoney placed both palms on the table and leaned in toward Seth-Simon. "All right, Seth. I am going to give you a few minutes to enjoy your cold beverage. I will be back. We are going to continue talking. You should think more about your mom's basement. It's going to be a long night. I wouldn't want to be stuck in here with nothing to drink."

Mahoney turned, slipped through the door, clicking it to a locked position before heading back down the hallway. *What the hell is going on here? So, he is Seth. There is no Simon. He says his name isn't Simon. He's fucking playing with me.* His fist pumped hard several times. *Is this some kind of sick game? How can he have no memory of torturing a boy in his mom's basement?* Walking briskly down the hallway, he headed for the war room. *Agent Quesnel, I need a dose of your behavioural hocus pocus. Now.*

Multiple Diagnoses

"**I** say fry the fucker. He chose to take lives. Lives of innocent people." Hayes' nostrils flaring, sweat drizzled down his burning forehead.

Sutton stood up. "Hey, tone it down, Hayes. I agree, he doesn't deserve to live. The bodies he left behind, they don't get a second chance. Neither do their families. But let's keep things in check here."

Little wrinkles crawled across Blackwood's face. Her booted feet thudding across the thinly carpeted floor, she waved her hand across the crime scene collage. "You don't have the death penalty in Canada, so it's not an option here. I do agree it takes a cruel man to leave a trail of carnage like this. But, for sake of argument, you guys, you're talking about playing God here. What right do we have to take his life? Doesn't that put us on the same plane as him?"

Hayes stood. "We're not sick psychos. We have respect for human life."

Blackwood's face relaxed, the tiny wrinkles vanishing back into her forehead. "Then respect his right to life. He's human too." She pleaded with her eyes.

"He lost his rights when he broke the law." Spit flying from his mouth, Haye's temples throbbed.

Sutton glared at Hayes, then turned to Blackwood. "Say he lives. What do you suggest we do with him?"

"Rehabilitation," Blackwood said. "Caging in a person like him indefinitely only heightens the situation. His mind is sick. He needs professional help. It's the most constructive path for society as a whole."

Sutton sat down hard. Removing the lid from his Big Gulp, he took a long, loud slurp.

Hayes continued his line of questioning. "A guy like that can't be rehabilitated. How do you even test something like that? Just release him onto more innocent people?"

Agent Quesnel, leaning against the wall at the back of the small room, shiny boots gleaming under the fluorescent lighting, clicked her tongue. "Most of society doesn't want to deal with guys like this. They want them dead. They turn their cheek and ignore the fact that they are choosing murder. They don't care how hefty the price tag is either. Society simply wants these guys gone. Poof, like magic, into thin air. But the fact is, execution is a lengthy and expensive process. And it leaves its own cruel path behind. Someone has to flip the switch."

Sutton sipped away at his sweet pop, eyebrow cocked, forehead wrinkled.

Hayes sat down and propped his feet up on the long table. "OK. What's your solution, Agent?"

"Behavioural models suggest that someone like our hunter cannot be rehabilitated," Agent Quesnel said. "According to social learning models, the behaviour he learned during critical stages of his development is, well, already fucked up. He was never habituated acceptably to society. Thus, there is nothing to re-habituate him to."

Blackwood crossed her arms, leaning against the wall, next to the crime scene collage.

Agent Quesnel slid her hands into the pockets of her slick black pants, walking across the room with slow, intentional steps. "Habilitation. It's a concept of teaching this human how to be. Giving him a set of behaviours acceptable to society. The cost of habituation is far less taxing, and the chance of reoffending is lower than both rehabilitation and long sentencing."

Mahoney snapped a file folder onto the long table running down the centre of the war room. "We can debate all day. But, our options are limited, and not by our choosing. Sutton, Hayes, you know we don't have the death penalty here. That option is taken off the table, even if you did want it. And I don't believe you do. He's going to be locked up, but likely not where you want him."

His team fell silent. Picking up the folder again, he waved it at the photos of the dead boys. "Multiple psychiatrists, each with different preliminary assessments. We have to wait for the full diagnosis. How the hell can the same man have opposing assessments? From professionals?" The hot air stifling him, he pulled at his collar. *Geez. How many days have we been cooped up in here? Even when it's over, it's not over.*

All eyes were on him. Hayes shifted in his seat. Sutton leaned forward in his chair, resting his elbows on his knees, running his hands through his hair. Dara, perched in the back corner, as usual, poised perfectly in her crisp blue suit. Agent Quesnel stood, arms crossed, expressionless. Blackwood took a seat in one of the cheap, plastic chairs, resting a booted foot on her knee.

Flipping the folder open, Mahoney pulled out several pages stapled together. Taking a long swig from his Styrofoam cup, he placed the cold coffee on the centre table. *I'm really getting sick of Styrofoam.* A flash of his sunny blue mug, sitting lonely on a shelf in the cupboard of his apartment kitchen, snuck through his mind.

Standing tall, he shoved the image away. Scanning the paper, he delivered the information to his team. "One doctor said Seth has multiple personality disorder. He is literally two people. Apparently can't control it. I guess we've all seen Seth. And as I've disclosed, I've had many encounters with Simon." He clenched his fist. "So, this one may not be a stretch."

Lowering his Big Gulp, Sutton pondered, "How can you tell if he really is two people? Couldn't he be making this all up?"

"Yeah. Couldn't he be using this so-called second personality to pretend he doesn't know anything about the murders? 'Oh, the other person inside of me must have done it, I don't know what you're talking about.'" Hayes waved his hands around his head dramatically.

Agent Quesnel said, "It's possible. Mahoney, what did the other assessments indicate?"

Looking back at the paper, Mahoney said, "There are two opposing views. One that he is a sociopath, and the other that he is a narcissist."

"Are those really opposing? Aren't they both egocentric points of view on the world?" Sutton twisted to face Agent Quesnel.

"Yes, they are. A narcissist is primarily concerned with his or her own world. To the point where he or she will hoard conversations, interrupt others and behave in an entitled manner. But, they can also charm. They are able to be persuasive and charismatic to get what they want. A sociopath also uses people, but he or she makes it clear they don't care about others. A narcissist isn't good at hiding his or her egocentric view of the entire planet. Both lack empathy and have a weak sense of right and wrong."

Sutton pitched in his two cents. "So, our guy, Seth, or Simon, or whoever the fuck he is, he sounds like a mix of both. He didn't try and attract attention. But he had the Simon side to him. Our friendly neighbourhood bartender. The one everyone liked, confided in."

Mahoney looked at the ground, his fist tightened into a ball.

Agent Quesnel continued her explanation, saying, "Yes. Simon was charming, but from what we know, he didn't focus on himself." She glanced at Mahoney. "I'll take it one step further. It seems to me like Seth and Simon had different characteristics. You have this Simon who is friendly, likeable, intelligent. Then you have Seth who was emotional, dramatic, sadistic. It could be the hints of organization we saw were coming from Simon. The drama and brutality of the sense came from Seth. There may be a touch psychopathic narcissism blending the two. He pretends to be interested in people to manipulate them.

And, well, he's in love with an idealized image of himself which he has projected to replace his wounded reality."

Sutton snapped his Big Gulp against the centre table. "But, if he is able to mimic emotions, be who he wants, pretend in front of others, couldn't he just be faking all of this? How would anyone, even a professional, know if he's actually mentally ill or not?"

Agent Quesnel crossed her arms. "It is possible. I have seen cases where a complete rehabilitation was declared by a professional. After being released, the patient committed a series of murders. But, our Seth-Simon, well we've seen how emotional his Seth side is. And it shone through in his murders. I think his raw outbursts are authentic."

Beads of sweat popped through the skin on Mahoney's forehead. His stomach churned. He took a big gulp of cold coffee, washing down the rising bile. Clearing his throat, he redirected the discussion. "There was one more diagnosis. Seems one of the doctors thinks there isn't a difference between Seth or Simon. He is the same person. This doctor claims that social learning disorder is the primary reason for the way that our Seth-Simon is. What the hell does that mean?" He looked at Agent Quesnel.

Striding across the room, Agent Quesnel approached the front. Facing the group, she calmly proceeded with a concise description. "Social learning disorder is a theory that the set of societal rules that an adolescent takes on as normal is corrupted at an early age. This usually occurs in the early teen years, or even earlier. In some extreme cases, the disruption goes on for a significant period of their childhood. The set of rules that their mind should see as normal are non-existent in the neural network. They were never implanted. Rather, a set of corrupted rules are set in the child's brain as normal."

"Can you translate that for us a bit?" Sutton took a sip of Big Gulp.

"How about an example?" Hayes asked.

"Sure, boys. One solid example would be when the role of the mother is seen as sexual. The mother replaces the girlfriend or wife. This happens when a mother places herself in an unnaturally strong role in her son's life."

"What? That is messed up." Sutton furrowed his brow. "That's just not right."

"I think in our case, with our Seth-Simon, his set of rules is quite complex. He views people as inanimate objects. He used them for his own purpose, to bring to life the reality that he saw as necessary. The way he talked about his victims, they were only objects to him. They weren't real beings. He learned this somewhere. We have insight into the torture he was put under. He was locked away, potentially for a good portion of his teenage years. Living in isolation, having little interaction with other human beings, and being used for whatever purpose his mom saw fit. This is what he learned during the years that his mind was forming ideas, rule sets, of how to interact in the world."

Mahoney summarized, "So, our Seth-Simon could have two personalities. On the other hand, he could have learned a messed-up set of rules that he plays along to in society. Or he could be sociopathic, narcissistic, or a psychopath. Or a combination of these. Bottom line is, we have no way of knowing for sure. But, he clearly displays symptoms of being messed up some way or another."

"You're right. Unfortunately, with the typical serial killer, our research has indicated that they cannot be accurately diagnosed at all. Most likely because they can take on the symptoms they choose, to lead the professionals into the diagnosis they want to be labelled with. The doctors, they are nothing more to them than another toy. The assessment, it's just another game." Agent Quesnel crossed her arms.

"So we can never truly know with certainty what is wrong with our Seth-Simon?" Sutton plunked his empty Big Gulp cup onto the centre table, teetering his chair back on its legs.

Agent Quesnel replied, "There's no guarantee that we will ever really know. But, the glaring quality about our Seth-Simon is how emotionally driven he is. I think at the root of him is the multiple personality disorder. I think he has created Simon to survive. To hold a job. To plan his hunting schedule. To enable him to survive. But his true core is Seth. In the end, he was driven by his hurt, his anger, the abuse he was put through. He wanted to become someone else. His mind is so contorted, he believed he actually could. And now, Simon has vanished. I think we are seeing him for what he truly is. I would argue that there is a layer here representing what he was taught. But I think he's really Seth as we see him."

Hayes, face flushing, shifted in his seat. His tone grew angry. "But we won't one-hundred-percent know that there really is anything wrong with freakin' Seth-Simon?"

Agent Quesnel shifted from one platinum boot heal to the other. "Well, boys, there are no guarantees. But I honestly, one hundred percent, believe that there is something wrong with his brain. Whether it be psychological or a fissure in his brain, he does not respond to situations the way most of the human population does. He is sick."

Sutton said, "That's undeniable. So where does this leave us, boss?"

Mahoney provided the unsettling resolution. "There's nothing we can do about how the multiple diagnoses are taken into consideration. He may end up behind bars. Or, he may end up in a mental institution until deemed rehabilitated."

Hayes said, "So he may end up on the streets just as sick as he is now."

"It is a possibility," Mahoney said. "Team, let's focus on what we *can* do. Let's comb through everything we have as carefully as possible and present a real tight case. We just have to give it our all."

Scanning his team members, Mahoney took in the worry and disappointment flooding from their faces. *Wish I could promise you more, boys.*

Sleeping Quarters

Mahoney snatched up the folder lying on top of all the others piled on his desk. He swiftly made his way down the bright corridor, and firmly pressed the elevator button. The *elevator of doom,* as his guys called it. Only the darkest of the criminal filth were transported on this elevator, down into the basement.

He watched the elevator doors closing, the buttons lighting up in sequence, transporting him down into the depths of the *dungeon.* Another term created by his guys, referring to the dimly lit holding cells, a second world, lingering right beneath the clean, brightly lit office space lined with desks and large windows. Mahoney couldn't resist a slight chuckle. *The guys here love to nickname things.*

Clenching his stomach, Mahoney swallowed hard. The elevators doors slid open. The dimly lit corridor loomed before him. Walking down the hallway, his black shoes clicked along the yellowing linoleum floor. Taking the first left, he scanned the line of holding cells. Halting at the second door on the right, a green light signalled its occupancy. Mahoney swiped his card. The lock clicked. He swung the door open abruptly.

The tiny, windowless room ebbed the same dim light as the tight hallways leading to it. Other than a stainless-steel toilet and a rusty old table set with two chairs, the room was empty.

Looking at the single occupant of the room, sitting in silence, head bowed, Mahoney wondered who he would get. The chair legs screeching against the floor as Mahoney pulled it out from the table, he snapped the folder down onto the tabletop. Greasy, tangled, long black strands of hair slid away from the man's face as he slowly lifted his head. Mahoney sat down in the chair and folded his hands together, resting them on the table.

Leaning in toward the man's face, he shot an emotionless greeting across the table. "Are you aware of why you are here?"

"Where's my doll?" the man hissed.

Mahoney's mind clicked into place. *Aaaah. So, I've got Seth, then. Means I'm talking to a crazy man.* Switching gears, he tried again.

"Seth, is it?"

Seth stared back at him coldly. "Yes. Where is my doll? I saw you steal it."

"Your doll." *OK fine, let's play his game. Maybe it'll get me into his deranged mind.*

"My doll. You stole it from its hiding place, near Gleaming Reservoir."

"Do you mean the one wearing the gold pants?"

"Yeeessss," Seth hissed again, spit flying from his mouth.

"This doll, it was important to you?"

Seth's bloodshot eyes glared at him. "It was my vessel. I'm not supposed to be here."

"Your vessel?"

"My physical vessel. It was a perfect specimen. It was *the one*. I was supposed to be reborn, my soul transferred into this perfect physical vessel."

This is fucked up. Go with it, Bug. Keep him talking. "I see. You say this was *the one*? Were there others?"

Droplets trickled down Seth's face. His cheeks growing red, he swallowed.

"Would you like some water, Seth? If you can tell me about the others, I can get you a glass of water."

"Don't you already know about the others? Didn't you steal them too? I saw you at the ravine. I saw you take that one away."

"Yes, I was there, Seth. I guess I do know about that one. It was wearing a rather special jacket."

Seth jolted upright. A vacant stare washed over his face.

Keep him talking. Come back to the jacket. Mahoney probed, "Were there other ones?"

"I've had plenty of dolls. It took me a while to find the one I really wanted."

"I see. So these dolls are very special to you. Do you dress them up?"

A sinister smile crept across Seth's lips. Sitting back in his chair, he challenged Mahoney, saying, "Oh, I'm sure you'd like to know. But you need to keep your promise first."

"Of course. Water. I'll be right back." Stepping through the door, the electronic lock clicked. Returning with a plastic cup of fresh water, he slid it across the table toward Seth.

Taking a few sips, Seth continued the story of his dolls. "I had other dolls. Three of them disappeared. The others are safe though."

A chill ran up Mahoney's spine. "The three that disappeared, where did you keep them?"

"I made nice hiding spots for them. I gave one of them a special gift. An arctic ocean."

"Really? That was nice. What type of gift?"

"A treasure. A symbol of rebirth."

The pendant. "Where was the nice hiding spot for that one?"

"You know." Seth's eyes narrowed. "I bet you were the one that took it."

"I'm not sure. Was that the one in Frog Lake Park?"

Seth nodded.

"Seth, I know where that one was taken. If you tell me about the others that were taken, maybe I can tell you where they are."

Seth's shoulders quivered. "Just like you got me the water, and the ginger-ale."

"Yes."

"I told you I was at the ravine. There was one in a nice little cave. You know about that one?"

"Yes. You said three went missing. Where was the third one?"

Seth closed his eyes and placed his trembling hands on the table. His eyelids creeped open. "A pretty place with trees near the water."

"In a park?"

"Yes."

"What park?"

Seth sat silent.

"Seth. If you want to know where the dolls are, I need to know which ones you are looking for."

Seth swallowed. "Eagle Woods."

"OK."

"You know about that one?" Seth leaned toward him.

"Yes. Seth, I want to ask you about the one in the cave at the ravine. It was wearing a jacket. A straitjacket."

A blank slate swiped over Seth's face. He stared past Mahoney. His shoulders shook and tears trickled from his vacant eyes.

"Seth. What can you tell me about that jacket?"

"They made me wear it."

"Who?"

Seth's lower lip quivered. Silence swelled in the small room.

"Seth, the other dolls, the ones that didn't go missing. Can you tell me where they are?"

Seth sat back in his chair, a glazed look in his eyes.

"Seth, these dolls, they're important to you. Maybe I can get them for you."

Seth bowed his head. "My mind. It's fuzzy." His shoulder convulsed. His head lolled from side to side. "Leave me alone."

For fuck's sake, Mahoney thought to himself. His face was an emotionless mask. He could keep a completely blank slate for as long as it took. In this scenario, he was a mecca of time and patience. *You had him talking. Don't ruin it.*

"Would you like to rest for a while?"

Running his fingers through his hair, close to his scalp, Seth weakly replied, "Yes. So tired."

"OK. Put your hands behind your back," Mahoney instructed calmly.

Seth moved his limp arms behind his back. Mahoney approached, cuffing one of Seth's wrists. Grabbing Seth's other wrist, Mahoney joined it to the first, clicking the cuff shut.

"Stand up." Mahoney's voice remained calm as he guided Seth to standing.

Seth's head remained bowed. Mahoney guided him down the dimly lit corridor, to the end, and steered him left. Jerking the cuffs lightly as an indication to halt, Mahoney swiped his card and briskly opened a heavy door. Pushing Seth through, the door slamming behind them, Mahoney almost let out a smirk of his own as he eyeballed the sleeping quarters that he, the host, would provide to his guest. A single, small mattress leaned against the wall. Smeared in strange colours tinged with brown and red, yellow stuffing escaping through a spattering of holes, this makeshift bed had seen better days. Mahoney nudged the bottom corner with his foot, dislodging the mattress from its resting place. Sickly odours permeated the stale air as the low-class bed plummeted toward the filthy floor, landing with a puff of dust.

"Sweet dreams," Mahoney muttered as he re-entered the holding cell hallway. The door shut with a loud click. On the other side of the doorway, Seth let out a sinister laugh.

Doll Collection

Mahoney snapped the leather-bound book onto the steel table and stared into Seth's eyes.

"Seth. I brought you water. I let you rest. It's time to talk."

Seth leaned forward, staring at the book. Greasy locks of dark hair fell limply around his face, sticking to his cheeks.

Mahoney flipped open the top cover of the book and pointed at the writing. "This journal is yours. Right?"

Seth stared at the writing.

"Right?" Mahoney slapped the table.

Seth sat up, slowly moving his eyes to meet Mahoney's. "Yes."

"We talked about the dolls you lost. Now I need to know…"

"Where are they?"

"They are safe. They are in storage," Mahoney said.

"Storage? When can I see them? Who has touched them?"

"Don't worry. They will be well taken care of. If you want to know more, you need to talk to me about the others."

"The others," Seth repeated in a monotone.

"In your journal you've described over two dozen of these dolls. Four of them fit the descriptions of the dolls that we found. Where are the others?"

He stared into Seth's bloodshot eyes.

"You'll just take them too."

"Do you want to know more about your lost dolls or not?"

"It doesn't matter. It's too late. The souls are lost. The one. It's gone." Seth rested his head on the table. His shoulders slumped. Whimpering mixed with sniffling flowed from across the table.

What the hell is this? Mahoney sighed. "Seth. Your dolls aren't lost."

Seth's muffled response was barely audible. "Doesn't mater. Souls. Gone."

Mahoney pursed his mouth. *Dammit.* "Seth. If you help me, I can help you."

"No one can help me."

Final Fantasy

"**I** can't justify a search of every city park. How are we going to find these other bodies?" Mahoney sat down hard in a chair and slapped his palms onto the long centre table.

Agent Quesnel leaned back against the wall, arms crossed. "We may never find all the bodies. Our quickest way to finding out where any of them are, if there are actually more, is to keep talking to Seth."

"He's unreachable. His mind isn't right. He's in some other world."

"He's deep into the fantasy that he's created. Look, I know it's frustrating. But talking to someone with a mind twisted like his is, well, it takes patience. And perseverance. If I've learned anything from interviewing sick, distorted minds, it's that a deep dive into such a psyche takes multiple interviews, over time. You need to let him tell his story, when and how he wants to."

Mahoney grunted. "The more I played his game, talked how he talks, the more he told me. But then he just shut down. When I talked about the straitjacket."

"Hmmm. I bet that jacket brings up some bad memories for him. He would have had to have help stealing it. Maybe he wasn't involved at all. Maybe his mom stole it. He said 'they made me wear it'?"

"Yeah."

"Maybe Doris and her ex-boyfriend were in on this together."

Mahoney sat up straight, cocking his brow. "They could have taken it. Made Seth wear it."

"Precisely. I've been talking to the professionals who assessed Seth. Looks like he'll be locked up, but not in prison. Probably a mental institute. High security. This could be to your benefit."

"My benefit? How."

"He'll be treated. They'll dig into his mind. You'll have access to his doctors. And to him."

"Visit him?" Mahoney shook his head. "Maybe you should talk to him."

"You've already got a rapport going with him. Interrupting that could be detrimental. This won't be a friendly visit. You've got him talking. I know it's slow. But he's talking to you. He's telling you his story. You keep visiting him, keep him talking. Get him to describe everything about his fantasy. Act like you care. He might eventually tell you about the other victims. He won't be able to resist talking about his dolls to someone who will listen."

This could work. "You dig into the mind."

"Exactly. In Seth's case, we have two streams to his journey. His own torturous childhood. And his final fantasy. The journals directly indicate the type of emotional, physical, and potentially even sexual abuse that he endured. There is a high possibility that Doris and this ex-boyfriend were the ones that abused him. A lot of what was done to him is showing in how he treats his own victims."

Mahoney flipped through the pages of the journal. "There's some grisly stuff in here. If this is a reflection of his reality, then he's a broken being."

"It explains why he does what he does. The other part of it is the final fantasy. The outfits mimicking rock stars and the messages mirroring their lyrics. The purple vial with placebo chemicals that have no effect on the physical body, yet he has some delusional idea that the liquid is black magic that will transfer his soul into the being he truly wants to be. The being represented by these human victims that he has completely objectified."

"Now that was an elegant way of summing up everything Seth has been spouting."

"You use this. Use his final fantasy. Goad him on to tell it in his own words. Eat up every bit. Then he might open up. You might just find the rest of the victims. Or at least be able to provide some closure to their families."

"Yeah. If they want it. Sometimes they just don't want to know."

"But you do."

Mahoney closed the leather book, resting a palm on top. He looked at Agent Quesnel, still leaning against the wall. He scanned the line of photos above her head, reliving the scenes he had been a part of. "Yeah. I do."

Lost Soul

Seth squeezed his legs in tighter toward his chest. His t-shirt stuck to his back, wet with sweat. A blazing fire rushed through his cheeks as he pulled the wool blanket tighter around his back and across his chest. Cold and hot clashed through his body in a rage. A shiver ran through him.

He rested his forehead against his knees. Dark strands of hair clung to his forehead and his face.

Fuckers. Locking me in here. This is worse than Doris' makeshift crazy room. Dammit. Let me out. Let me out. LET ME OUT.

His voice screamed inside his head as his mind spun round and round. He choked back a surge of bile, feeling the acid burn down his throat.

He pulled the blanket as tight as he could around him, imagining the straitjacket, longing for Doris to tighten the buckles.

His pants were wet and warm against his groin. The smell of vinegar stung his nose. He shifted his sitting position on the floor, leaning harder against the wall.

A click as the lock released. Light pierced his eyes as the steel window slid open.

"Seth. It's dinner time."

The attendant slid the tray over the silver slab, through the window in the top of the door. Her eyes peered through the small slit. "Don't you want to eat? You look pale. Oh my, and you smell like you need a good cleaning. I'll come back and take you for a shower."

He stared in silence.

"Do you want the light on?"

"No."

"All right. I'll be back in a bit."

A click of steel locking into place.

He glared at the tray of food.

Fuck them. Putting me in here. They still have my dolls. They want me to tell them where the others are. He stretched his lips into a devilish smile. *I'll never tell them. When I get out of here, I'll get them. Take them away. Save their souls. And find the one. The one.*

Bourbon

A clink shattered the silence as ice cubes hit crystal. Detective Mahoney grabbed a bottle of Makers Mark and screwed off the cap. As he poured the brown liquid into the glass, sweetness permeated his nose. He unbuttoned his shirt down to his chest. He picked up the glass and walked over to the barren room. With a clank he set the glass onto the cluttered coffee table, staring at the unopened bills. He plunked down onto the well worn, tattered couch. *Just like me. Old. Worn.*

He raised the crystal glass toward his lips, closed his eyes, and savored a long sip. The cold, sweet fluid lingered over his tongue then stung the back of his throat. He took another, longer sip, placed the glass back on the table, and leaned back against the couch. With one hand, he massaged circles into each of his temples with his thumb and forefinger.

He pictured Pegs, talking to him as he left HQ only an hour ago. She had told him there was no way he could have known that Simon was Seth. That he had done all he could. That he had worked non-stop since this case started. That he had caught the killer. He could see her smiling as she told him to take some time off. His shoulders sunk deeper into the soft couch as the sound of her voice rang through his ears. He opened his eyes and looked around the empty room. Coldness slithered through his insides.

Four bodies. Almost five. In a matter of weeks. A short time for such a body count. He had hoped he would never see something like this again. The little ghost faces had vanished from his mind. No more blood red lips talked to him. They were satisfied. But was he?

What will they do with Seth? He'd probably end up attending therapy and journaling about his feelings.

What about the bodies? The victims they hadn't found? As winter subsided and more people came out of hibernation to play in the parks, would more innocent children be traumatized by grisly discoveries?

Slipping his hand into his jacket pocket, he pulled out the small, polished pink stone and set it beside the crystal glass. What was it the gem store woman had said? *Self care. Warm hug. Ease the guilt you are carrying.*

A collage of faces floated through his mind. Pegs. Dara. Sutton. Hayes. Quesnel. Blackwood. They had all given him a similar speech, every one of them finishing off by telling him that he caught the killer. *I caught the killer.* Even by the book Hayes acknowledged the new methods and how they might not be such hocus pocus after all.

He looked at the stone. *I caught the killer.* He picked up the glass, rested his feet onto of a pile of flyers, and sank back against the couch. *Now, what would I do with some time off?* He finished the drink in one long swallow and closed his eyes. He dreamed of salty waves crashing against a sandy beach and his daughter giggling as she ran along the shore.

THE

PREDECESSOR

The Mummy

Mahoney scratched the bristle on his chin. Whipping out his notepad and flipping it open in one smooth shot, he retrieved his pen from his tweed pocket. Scanning the fitted black pants and long red jacket of the officer who had greeted him, his eyes landed on the shiny, wide black belt completing the uniform. *The horsemen. It's been a while since I've dealt with these guys. Since they called me, perhaps it will be different this time.*

Attempting to keep his tone calm, he launched his line of questioning. "Officer Williams, exactly how many people have been on this scene? I'll need names and ranks."

Officer Williams, the colour drained from his face, sweat beading on his forehead, blinked at Mahoney. "Uh, yes, of course." Clearing his throat, he wiped his forehead with a crisp, white handkerchief. "Let me see now. My team arrived first. Only three of us have been in there. Myself, and two of my officers, Roberts and Rudson. We talked to the couple who, uh, found the body. They're really young. About 18 or 19, probably. They were out here on the beach by then. We proceeded into the cove. Following the instructions they gave us, it was straightforward to find the, uh, grave. It's at the very back of the cave."

Officer Williams' eyes glazed over. Mahoney prodded him, saying, "Tell me what you saw in there."

"Right. Well, we found what seems to be a, uh, coffin. Buried in the sand. Like I said, at the back of the cave. We dug out the sand around the top, enough to get it open and take a look inside. I have no idea how long it's been in there.

The body, it's, well, it's all wrapped up, like a mummy. Those kids, they ventured far back. Must have been looking for some privacy, I guess. You know, at that age." Williams' face revealed a slight smirk.

Mahoney poked harder. "The body. Anything else you can tell me?"

The paleness returned to Williams' face. "No. We didn't touch it. We re-closed the lid. I'm guessing it was buried way back in there where no one would find it. We've had higher tides this spring than usual. That water could have worn away some of the sand, exposing the box. There's something shocking about it. The way it's laid out. And some of the items around it. You've got to see it for yourself."

"We'll do a thorough scan of the area and determine how to process the body."

"This, uh, it isn't what we normally see out here. Only dead bodies we get are usually accidents. Hikers getting hurt or lost. Usual cause of death is dehydration. In some cases an animal gets them. That can be a bit grisly. But nothing like this. That's why we called you. I've seen the articles on the serial case your team has just wrapped up. I can't get a hold on it, but something told me this was similar."

"Blackwood, you ready?" Mahoney looked over toward her jeep. She was rummaging in the back, dressed in her green safari gear, just like the day they met.

"Ready to go." Shooting him a wide smile, she walked toward him.

"OK, Officer Williams. We're ready." Mahoney goaded the horseman into action.

Following the shiny black belt, Mahoney's hiking shoes sunk into the sand. *Never go anywhere without these trusted babies anymore.* His coat flapped in the breeze. *Well, at least the boots, anyways. I'm not abandoning my derby or coat for safari gear. I'm not in Africa and I'm not on a safari.*

The three of them trekked across the beach in a line. Shiny black belt, followed by derby and tweed, with safari gear in tow. A black-and-grey cave of rock bordered the far end of the beach. White waves crashed wildly against the jagged rock, white-blue spraying in all directions. Seagulls screamed, zig-zagging a frantic flight pattern. Greyish-white thin cotton strings stretched out between clusters of puffy clouds. The sun made spontaneous and brief appearances before quickly retreating to its hiding spot behind the white puffs. The wind picking up, Mahoney tightened his coat around him. Closing in on the rocky enclave, the wet sand was hard against his steps. A thunderous crash bounced off the rock, fresh spray splattering across his face. Fastening the buttons on his coat, he pushed the top of his derby, securing it onto his head.

"Be careful, these rocks are slippery," Officer Williams yelled back at them.

A series of smooth rocks poking out of the clear water formed a pathway around the side of the rock cave, toward the crashing waves. Gingerly placing a foot onto the first rock, Mahoney followed the horseman over the stepping-stone bridge.

The horseman paused at the last step. "We need to time this to avoid getting drowned."

The surf building into the next wave, the white-capped blue charging at them, a loud crash vibrated through their ears as the wave hit the cave.

"Now! Hurry," the horseman yelled. As the horseman's shiny black belt disappeared into the cave, Mahoney jumped in behind.

Mahoney followed the red-coated horseman into the opening of the cave. Blackwood remained tight on his heels, never missing a step or a beat. The mouth of the cave wrapping around them, the greyness of the day turned black as Mahoney peered into the cave. Squinting his eyes, he searched far into the black hole, looking for the back of the cave. Eyes adjusting, he made out the outline of the cave, curling over him, reaching over to the other side about three feet away.

"You said it's at the back of the cave?" Mahoney asked the horseman.

"Yes. At the very back. The kids went way in there. Again, I guess they were, uh, looking for privacy. Or digging around. Kids get curious."

Walking the length of the cave, Mahoney's eyes narrowed, seeking out the target of his hunt. His feet stopping dead in their tracks, a tingle crept across his neck, trickling down his spine one vertebrae at a time. *Horseman wasn't exaggerating. This is creepy.*

The sand was wet, dark brown and hard packed. It looked like it had been clawed away in chunks, crumbling around the top of a rectangular, steel box. The lid was closed. Mahoney ventured up to the box. Slowly, he lifted the lid, letting it hang on its hinges over the back of the box. Blackwood clicked her Sunfire 6 to life. *Can always count on Blackwood to bring light to a situation.*

The lumens shone into the darkness of the box, bringing the contents to life. Mahoney stared, his mouth opening slightly, beads of sweat sprouting across his forehead. Lying flat, the framework of what once had been a living being was wrapped in yellowing lengths of white material. *Just like the horseman said. A mummy.* An image of a young boy shot through Mahoney's mind, the boy's fingers digging into wet sand, grasping desperately, pulling his hands, his arms, his body, away from the horrific torture that was ripping him apart. Shaking his head, Mahoney focused again on the wet sand floor.

Blackwood looked him in the eye. "Mahoney. If we unwrap this here, we risk exposure. We'll need to move it, in the box."

"Seems like since I met you, my murder scenes have gotten really weird." He shot her a smirk.

She smiled back, her purple almond eyes piercing through his. His heart fluttered. *Bug, focus. This is a bad idea. You won't mix murder with love.*

"I'll make sure the techies get their photos when they arrive. I'll scan what I can and arrange transport."

Mahoney nodded.

Another flash of the young boy forced its way into his mind. The boy's body ripping apart into pieces, his flesh tearing, blood pouring out, drenching the hard-packed sand floor. The boy's mouth stretching wide open, screams escaping, vibrating through the air, calling through the quiet darkness for help. But no one could hear him, here in this dark solitary cave. Shaking his head again, he scolded himself. *C'mon, Bug, focus. Stop imagining things and look for clues. Search the cave. Work with Blackwood.*

Moving away from the coffin, he wondered what this all meant. He wondered what their involvement would be. *Should we even be venturing out of our jurisdiction?*

Blackwood proceeded with a meticulous scan of every tiny bit of Mr. Bones. The techies scurried through the cave opening. In a flash, they were creating a picture collage of the mummy. Mahoney stood up, rubbing the bristle on his chin. His gut kicking into to full gear, he took a long, slow scan of the dark enclosure. "Hey, Blackwood. Can I borrow that Sunfire of yours?"

"I've got a spare you can use. Top pocket." With a quick nod at her pack, she continued her work.

Zipping open the pocket, he pulled out the compact flashlight and flicked it on. Darkness dissolving around him, the bright light illuminated his surroundings. Slowly stepping his way across the compact sand, he searched along the crevice at the back of the cave. His eyes taking tiny movements, he scanned along the line of wet sand meeting rugged rock. He froze. The tingling in his neck surged. Guiding the lumens toward the rock wall, he searched for something shiny that had caught his eye. His mind buzzed as his neurons shot a rush of signals back and forth. His brain connected with a striking image on that sunny day in Frog Lake Park. His eyes widening, he shook his head. *Am I hallucinating?* his brain implored. Crouching, he moved closer into the concave shape of the rock wall. Moving the light into the dark edge, his eyes locked on an object. An oval-shaped pendant, the colour of an arctic ocean, hypnotized him. An ice wave sliced his gut.

Fishing in his pocket, he retrieved a pair of latex gloves. Pulling the casing over his hands, he snapped each one into place. Reaching toward the arctic-ocean oval, he dislodged it from the crack. Pulling it away from the rock wall, a long silver chain snaked across the compact sand, pulling wet granules along.

"Blackwood. Come here," his weak voice cracked out. He pulled the top of the chain from the wet sand with his pointer and thumb. Hanging the top of the silver chain from his pointer finger, the arctic oval swung back and forth, mesmerizing him.

Blackwood crawled in behind him. "Wow. Now that's a humdinger."

ACKNOWLEDGEMENTS

Writing this book was a journey, and one that would not have taken the path it did without the knowledge, experience and support of many people. Thank you to every single one of you who helped me and encouraged me along the way.

Dave Sweet – Thank you for teaching me the principles and strategies of homicide investigations, helping me to conduct a fictional investigation, and for taking on many roles in supporting my book throughout the entire project.

Axel Howerton – My mentor and the first author I stalked. Thank you for encouraging me not to give up but to keep on growing, and for showing me that writing is an art and that my art needed a piece of me in it.

Sarah L Johnson – My kindred spirit and evil BFF. Thank you for always being there to share honest advice, a warm hug, a glass of wine, and your passion for reading and writing. Thank you for teaching me that writing is individual and unique. Thank you for helping me to find a piece of myself that I was longing for. And for being a kick ass cover model. You *rocked* those golden pants!

Konn Lavery – Thank you for being an inspiration, setting a shining example of commitment and hard work, and showing writers and artists how to infuse their work with passion and sense of self. Thank you for all the advice along the way.

Taija Morgan – My co-partner in scaring people out of the coffee shop as we casually discuss murder over a warm latte. You knew I would finish my book the minute we met. You opened my eyes to all the delicious evil seeping through my story and the beauty of my characters, no matter how evil and dark they are. Thank you for pushing me, and for endless hours of brainstorming and input.

Liz Grotkowski – Thank you for welcoming a totally green grasshopper into your fold, for encouraging me every step of the way, and for teaching me the critical concept of 'what if' in a story.

Philip Vernon – Thank you for handing me the key to unlock my story telling ability. Thank you for answering my millions of questions without hesitation and with sincere, Philip style enthusiasm.

Steve Peake – Thank you for teaching me crime scene techniques, for sharing phrases that naturally transferred onto the page, coming out of the mouths of my characters, and for sharing many of your stories.

Sylvia Nunweiler, Cami Schulte, Bri Helgin, Dianna Martin, Dwayne Clayden, Valerie King, and Dave Sweet – Thank you for finding the time to read a rough version of this book and for providing insightful feedback. Your honest reactions to my story thrilled me. Your input was critical in helping me to improve the shape of the story and the quality of the writing.

Chris Aune – Thank you for embracing a weird and wacky photo shoot, turning it into a journey back to the 1980s and sharing your amazing talent.

Josh Pantalleresco., Konn Lavery, and James Hiner – Thank you for providing honest reactions and for helping to shape the cover into an effective display.

Valerie King – Thank you for believing in my ability to write a dark, serial killer novel, and for supporting me along the way with words of encouragement and warm hugs.

Author Bio

Julie Hiner spent endless hours during her childhood lost in the pages of books. She could tune out anything and immerse herself in the worlds of fictional characters for an entire day. The only thing that took precedence over a book was her Walkman. To this day, Julie is a hardcore 80s rocker at heart. In high school, her favorite classes were science, math and English. During this time, her love for writing surged.

After securing a solid education in computer science at the University of Calgary, Julie spent over a decade working on large scale network systems. On a break between contracts, Julie followed her longing to finish a book she had been writing in bits and pieces. After finishing her non-fictional book portraying her personal story of facing fear and anxiety on a bicycle in the European mountains, she did some deep soul searching. This is when she decided to write a novel.

For a long time, Julie has been fascinated with the complexity of the dark mind of the serial killer and obsessed with trying to understand how murder can occur. Finding inspiration at a talk given by a local homicide detective, Julie surged down her new path to writing a dark, serial killer novel. She continues to write, focused on dark crime and horror. Her favorite parts of her new found writing process are the detailed research, creating an in-depth character and digging deep into his, her or its mind, and unleashing her inner artist on photos to create the cover and marketing material.